# 299 Days VI: The 17ᵗʰ Irregulars

## by

## Glen Tate

*Book Six in the ten book 299 Days series.*

**Prepper**Press

*Dystopian Fiction & Survival Nonfiction*

www.PrepperPress.com

# 299 Days VI: The 17th Irregulars

ISBN 978-0615828503

Copyright © 2013 by Glen Tate

All rights reserved.

Printed in the United States of America.

Prepper Press Trade Paperback Edition: June 2013

Prepper Press is a division of Kennebec Publishing, LLC

- To Stewart Rhodes, the real-life founder of Oath Keepers, who has inspired and organized the real Special Forces Ted, Rich Gentry, Dan Morgan - and Grant Matson.

This ten-book series follows Grant Matson and others as they navigate through a partial collapse of society. Set in Washington State, this series depicts the conflicting worlds of preppers, those who don't understand them, and those who fear and resent them.

*The 17th Irregulars* is the sixth book in the *299 Days* series, where, in some ways, post-Collapse life at Pierce Point resembles the everyday normalcy that Grant and others still hoped would return. The community is organized and humming along smoothly, the young guys on the Team are partnering off with local "Team Chicks," and Grant's daughter has found a boyfriend. For most, the new reality has been accepted and a calm, self-sustaining groove is setting in.

For others, though, life is far from normal. Special Forces Ted returns with an offer that cannot be refused. In the blink of an eye, Grant Matson has another title he can add to father-of-the-year and prepper-in-chief: Lieutenant Grant Matson, Commander of the 17th Irregulars. Grant and the Team are whisked away to Marion Farm, where they will train civilians and be trained to become a special squad in a Special Forces guerrilla group. The slower, simple life at Pierce Point is about to disappear to make way for a community that is well-trained and battle-ready, posed to fight the Loyalist opposition. This cannot happen fast enough, though. Gangs are growing steadily and the government is becoming a bigger threat to freedom and the nation. Violence is turning into an everyday occurrence outside of Pierce Point and it is only a matter of time before the peaceful community will need to protect itself from external dangers. Grant feels the weight on his shoulders as he now needs to protect not just his family, but the entire community, and possibly, all of Washington State.

For more about this series, free chapters, and to be notified about future releases, please visit **www.299days.com**.

# Books from the 299 Days series published to date:

Book One – *299 Days: The Preparation*

Book Two – *299 Days: The Collapse*

Book Three – *299 Days: The Community*

Book Four – *299 Days: The Stronghold*

Book Five – *299 Days: The Visitors*

Book Six – *299 Days: The 17th Irregulars*

Book Seven – *299 Days: The Change of Seasons*

Book Eight – *299 Days: The War*

## About the Author:

Glen Tate has a front row seat to the corruption in government and writes the *299 Days* series from his first-hand observations of why a collapse is coming and predictions on how it will unfold. Much like the main character in the series, Grant Matson, the author grew up in a rural and remote part of Washington State. He is now a forty-something resident of Olympia, Washington, and is a very active prepper. "Glen" keeps his real identity a secret so he won't lose his job because, in his line of work, being a prepper and questioning the motives of the government is not appreciated.

# Chapter 168

## *"Hit 'Em Hard"*

### (July 4)

The helicopter engine started up with its distinctive high-pitch whine. Slowly, the blades began turning, adding a second distinctive sound. There is no sound like that in the world, thought Tom Kirkland. He got excited every time he heard it. His blood pumped. He loved that sound, which made him feel fully alive when he heard it.

He'd heard that sound plenty of times. He was a Special Forces soldier in the First Special Forces Group at Ft. Lewis. Most of his fellow Green Berets joined the Patriots. Not Tom, though. He had a job to do and he was only able to do that job by not joining the Patriots. It was complicated, but it was just the way it was.

"We have a credible report of a teabagger position outside of Olympia," Joe Brown, the military intelligence, or MI, officer told Tom. "It should be a cake walk. No anti-aircraft defenses, of course," the MI officer said to Tom and rolled his eyes. "Just some dumb ass hillbillies. A cake walk."

Tom nodded. He was in charge of the TOC, the Tactical Operations Center, at Camp Murray. It was a military base and seat of the legitimate government of Washington State. He managed the raids that went out. He couldn't go out on them because of his left hand, which was severely burned a few weeks before the Collapse and was put on medical leave from his unit.

Tom heard the sound of helicopters warming up several times a day at Camp Murray. Intelligence reports were now streaming in about so-called Patriot positions throughout Washington State. Well, western Washington State, Tom corrected himself, the half of the state with Seattle and most of the population.

The Patriots were becoming bolder – and effective, Tom had to admit. When the Collapse first happened in May, the Patriots weren't much of a factor, and they especially weren't a threat. May had been the month of chaos; neither side could organize much of anything.

In June, the mayhem of the situation calmed down quite a bit for civilians. They were getting fed under the hastily created FCard system. It seemed as if everyone – the government, the Patriots, and

1

especially the population – was settling into a new and very different routine. Not that people were adapting easily, just that they were adapting.

Political killings became part of that new routine that developed in June. The assassinations started on the very first day of that month. It wasn't full-scale military action; it was a string of assassinations with rifles, pistols, even knives, and an occasional small bomb. The number of assassinations was actually small – a dozen or so state legislators, some mid-level federal officials, and about a hundred local elected officials, like county commissioners and city mayors. Despite these seemingly small numbers, the assassinations still shocked everyone. Political killings were not something that had ever been part of the American landscape. It was both frightening and hard to wrap their heads around. In the beginning, the media ran huge stories on the first few assassinations, but as they continued and became more common, the media quit covering them. Why continue to scare the population and contribute to additional anxiety and chaos?

Tom got the daily briefings at the TOC during the month of June. Because of that, he knew that the Patriots were popping up everywhere and it was way beyond a law enforcement issue where individual assassins could be caught and the problem would stop. This was a much larger, and well organized, problem for the legitimate authorities.

Knowing a war was inevitable, both sides tried to organize militarily during the month of June. While a war might not have seemed inevitable to the general population, Tom and the Loyalist military planners knew what was coming. Their intelligence reports showed the formation of hundreds of small and large Patriot regular and irregular units. Most of the military had defected and now they were getting ready to finish off what was left of the old government.

During the wave of political killings, at Camp Murray there was a tremendous sense of urgency to plan a military solution to stop the Patriots because the assassinations really hit home for the officials there. Tom found that the military planning was very difficult. He was accustomed to having high-tech assets like aircraft, communications, satellite intelligence, the ability to listen in on cell phones and read emails, and an almost unlimited supply of special operations personnel to strike anywhere at any time. That was no longer the case. Almost all the high-tech gadgets Tom formerly had at his disposal were inoperable, needing parts and personnel that were no longer around.

By the beginning of July, the rudimentary military planning on both sides was done and the skirmishes started. They were small at first. Both sides were probing each other. The battles started getting bigger and more sophisticated. But they were still low-tech, basically small infantry units with light weapons and some explosives fighting it out.

The Patriots were doing this primarily with regular military units that had defected. While the exact figures were classified, Tom knew from chatter at the TOC that about eighty-five percent of the active duty military forces in Washington State were no longer reporting for duty. Of this figure, over half were AWOL. They just packed up and left. They weren't getting paid after the government officially ran out of money on May Day. Before the checks stopped coming altogether, the preceding budget cuts meant that pay was delayed and there was absolutely no money for training or even fuel to get from one end of the base to the other. They were shut down, stuck in their barracks or, if they lived off-base, told to just not come to work.

Nearly half of the military who took off joined the Patriots. Whole units packed up, often with most of their unit's weapons and gear, and just walked out. They left the heavy equipment behind because it took too much fuel to move it. And, besides, with how broken down things were, who really needed a tank? They required constant maintenance and complex parts that no one had.

Some of the AWOL military units formed gangs and went into business for themselves, but this was the exception. No one talked much about them; the legitimate authorities didn't want to publicize that military units defected and the Patriots didn't want to highlight that some of the defectors were basically criminal gangs.

Tom was not happy with the quality of his troops. The legitimate authorities had mostly support troops – cooks, administrative, and equipment technicians – and National Guardsmen hastily trained up into combat units. Pretty shitty ones, Tom had to admit; nothing like the active duty combat units in the past, but combat units nonetheless. They were mostly the people who did what they were told and stuck around base while everyone else was leaving. They weren't really fighters; they were government employees doing their jobs.

In late June, the legitimate authorities flexed their muscles and used what remained of their operable helicopters and took out a few Patriot units. The Patriots hit back hard.

Today they were going to mount a big coordinated raid on the Tacoma TDF and freed several hundred political prisoners. The

Patriots did this with some very good special operations soldiers, mostly Rangers from Ft. Lewis. They also brazenly drove civilian vehicles full of regular forces and irregulars right into the heart of Tacoma, slicing through the woefully weak roadblocks and quickly shooting up the pathetic Freedom Corps guards. They fought their way out of town after they got the prisoners into city buses they'd stolen. It was impressive. Tom knew which side had motivated troops and it wasn't his.

"I got a load of contractors," Tom said to Brown over the increasing noise of the helicopter. There were almost no elite troops who were still working for the legitimate authorities; most were on the Patriot side or contracting for private parties who needed security. So the legitimate authorities had to rely on contractors who were well paid and didn't ask any questions.

"They're ready to go out," Tom said to Brown, having to shout now that the helicopter blades were turning faster. "Give me the coordinates and I'll get it started." The MI officer nodded and handed Tom a scrap of paper with some numbers on it. Tom walked it over to the communications officer in the TOC and wrote down the numbers for her.

"I'm supposed to have that," she said, referring to the original scrap of paper.

"Archives," Tom said. "I gotta archive this stuff. Didn't you get that briefing?" She shook her head, assuming he was right; he was her boss, after all. She was trained to follow instructions without questioning them.

Tom walked out of the main room of the TOC and put the scrap of paper in his pocket. He turned around and almost bumped into his boss, Major Saunders.

"I heard the bird," Maj. Saunders said with great excitement, like a child, "Is there an op?"

Tom hated Saunders. He was such a pencil pusher. He tried to be "tactic-cool" by using words like "op" when he had never even been on a real operation. Filling out forms – and political butt kissing – was all the action Saunders had ever seen.

"Yes, sir," Tom said, "Some teabagger camp outside of Olympia. The boys are going out to take them down."

"Hit 'em hard," Saunders said and punched his fist into the air.

"Yes, sir," Tom said, wondering how he could stand to be in the same room as this idiot.

Suddenly the helicopter blades started to slow down. It was powering down.

"What's that?" Saunders asked.

"I'll find out," Tom said. He knew exactly what it was. The same thing it always was.

Tom ran out to the helicopter as the helicopter crew chief was running in toward Tom.

"What's wrong?" Tom yelled.

"Low hydraulic pressure in the main power unit," he said, pissed. "I have no auxiliary unit. This is the second time this week this has happened. I need a new unit. Now. Or this thing won't fly." There were no more power units on base and it would be a joke to order them.

Tom turned and made a hand signal to the TOC signifying that the mission was being cancelled. He ran back to the TOC and saw the contractors.

"Aborted," he said to them. They didn't care. They had no desire to go on a mission. They got paid the same whether they went out on raids or sat on base. They walked away without saying a word.

Tom knew what was next. Saunders came up to him. "Well, it lifted off, didn't it?" he said to Tom.

"Yes, sir," Tom said, lying. Of course. Everything was bullshit here. Everything.

"Too bad we had to turn back," Saunders said. Tom hated it when this desk jockey used the word "we" to refer to the men who actually fought.

"Yes, sir," Tom said, and added, just for fun, "Too bad we couldn't go out and hit them hard." We. Ha.

"You'll make a report," Saunders said anxiously to Tom.

"Yes, sir," Tom said. A report meant that Tom would write down that a "counter-terrorist mission was initiated but had to return due to a helicopter malfunction." This meant it would count as a mission for Saunders' statistics. Then Saunders could tell his boss about the mission that went out, and their bosses could tell their bosses that it went out. Except it didn't. Everyone's statistics would look good, which was much more important than actually fighting the Patriots.

Before he wrote the report, Tom grabbed one of the outdated search and rescue radios, the kind used by pilots to radio in their positions if they were downed, and went outside to get some fresh air. Those old radios ran on a set of frequencies that weren't used much anymore because there were so few air missions going out that no one really monitored them.

      Once he was outside and away from anyone, he pulled out the scrap of paper and called in the coordinates.

# Chapter 169

## *Pretty Good ... Considering*

### (July 5)

Tammy Colson was running late for work. She hit the snooze bar on the alarm clock, which was always dangerous, and now she was seven minutes late. She had her morning routine down to the last minute.

Tammy, who was a typical American woman in her late forties, was getting dressed and checked the clock again. Dang. She was definitely going to be late, which she hated.. She always had. She paused and chuckled to herself. No one was on time anymore. Being exactly on time was what people did before the Collapse. Now, everyone pretty much showed up when they showed up. Life had slowed immensely.

OK, I'm late, she thought. Deal with it. She laughed at herself. Years and years of habit, like being perfectly punctual, were hard to break. She wanted to work on breaking her habit, so instead of her usual routine of rushing out of the house without eating, and then being hungry all day until lunch, Tammy made herself breakfast. Oatmeal. Her neighbors out here, the Matsons, had plenty of it and had given a five-pound bag to her family. Plain oatmeal was nothing special, but the Matsons gave them a bunch of hot cocoa mix, too, which Tammy put into the oatmeal. Now she had sweetened chocolate oatmeal. It was really good. She felt relaxed. She was going to be late to work, and it wasn't going to stress her out.

Tammy got into her car and headed to work at the local power company. She was the only driver on the roads in Pierce Point. She was the only person (at least that she knew of) in Pierce Point who got free gas, so she still drove places.

There was a deal of sorts. The government needed the people, like her, who could run the electrical system to be at work so they made sure key workers at utilities had gas for their cars. They looked the other way when those key workers sold the small amounts of the extra gas they received. It was considered a "retention bonus" to keep key people. The last thing the government wanted was for the utilities to be cut off to people they were trying to keep happy and calm...and compliant.

Having gas wasn't the only concern that utility workers had. They also had to get to work safely. Luckily for Tammy, the power company was only five miles from the Pierce Point gate. Tammy, a country girl through and through, carried a 1911 in a shoulder holster, making it much easier to access when driving than it would be if it were in a belt holster. Mark, her husband, had initially wanted to ride with her, but then realized he had to stay at her office all day because he couldn't drive back and forth. The extra gas was only for an employee to get to work and get home; the extra trip for someone dropping an employee off and picking him or her up was not allowed. They were lucky to have gas at all, and there was no reason to push it with extra trips.

Mark and Tammy talked about it and decided the risk of Tammy driving a short distance alone, well-armed, was worth it because Mark could be back at Pierce Point all day to do all the things he needed to do there.

Oh crap, Tammy thought, as she was leisurely driving to work. She remembered that there was a reason she had been keeping her commitment to being on time lately. Given the dangers of getting to work, the power company had a system where an alarm went off if an employee was late, alerting them to a possible ambush on the roads.

Tammy was now a solid twenty minutes late. They were probably out looking for her. She got on her cell phone and called in to let them know that she was fine, but running a little late. She decided that her habit about being on time was more important than being a free spirit and being late. She was just wired to be on time.

Tammy was technically the billing supervisor, but they weren't sending out bills anymore, but the company found plenty of other work for her to do. She had been at the power company for over thirty years and knew how just about everything worked. She had evolved into the company manager's right hand person, and could problem solve just about anything, which was good since the company had plenty of problems that needed solving.

When the Collapse started, they had the blackouts to deal with. The Feds shut down the grids when the hackers figured out how to overload the system with surges of power. The hackers, who everyone thought were the Chinese even though the news kept saying they were teabaggers, disabled the computer routing switches regulating the levels of electricity in the lines. With the flow switches off, it was very easy for too much to flow and blow up a line along with all the transformers on that line. Because the switches were sometimes off due to the hacking, the Feds shut the system down for about two days until they got control over the computers. Then they lost control a few days later from more hacking—from Russia this time—and shut things down again. This happened a few more times, but the Feds were getting a better handle on things. Now blackouts were less common.

A new problem quickly emerged. Running a power company required lots of machines, which required lots of replacement parts that need to be delivered by trucks, which required diesel and safe roads. The same just-in-time inventory fiasco that the rest of the U.S. was facing also hit the power company. They ran out of parts in two days. They had to shut the power off to a third of the county while they waited for a $35 part to arrive. When the highways were jammed and the diesel was gone, it took three days to get the part. It was the company manager's friend who lived in Seattle who braved the roads during the initial chaos and got the part there.

The distribution system improved slowly, although it was still horrible. The government threw almost all their military and law enforcement resources at the task of taking control of the highways. With troops and police forcibly occupying onramps and off ramps, and overpasses, the government prevented civilians from travelling, sometimes violently. Only government-approved shipments such as fuel, spare parts, and military supplies, got through. Similarly, the government took over all the gas stations and refineries. After a while, they were getting enough fuel out to take care of the greatly reduced levels of travel. Tammy estimated that there was only about five percent of the normal traffic, and most of that was semi and other trucks and military vehicles. Individuals like her, driving cars, were almost unheard of. More and more people were staying at home waiting for food to arrive at a store and then walking there to get it. They spent most of their day trying to stay safe and trading rumors about who had supplies for sale.

"Mornin' Tammy," Dan Morgan said. He was at the gate, as usual. "A little late this morning," he said to her. He was so on top of everything. Dan was doing a fantastic job of running the guards.

The rest of the drive to work Tammy thought about how lucky they were. All the amazingly talented people they had out there. All those guards who were well-armed and so organized. Other than the differing guns and clothes, they looked like a military unit. There was also that fabulous Team who took down the animals in the meth house.

9

Pierce Point had Rich, who made everyone feel so safe. And there was Grant who really got people feeling like they were going to make it. Then there was Lisa. A doctor! They actually had a doctor out there. Pierce Point had a clinic and even a newspaper and a church. Life was semi-normal for Pierce Point. It was different but it could have been a lot worse. Tammy felt like they had the things they needed out there, like security and food, but none of the unnecessary things that had previously piled up in their lives, like running all over town to buy this year's outdoor furniture, only to throw it in a landfill after a summer or two. Getting new outdoor furniture had been on her to-do list right before May Day. She had actually been stressed out over which lawn furniture to buy for the coming BBQ season. She now realized just how insignificant a thing that was to worry about. Her perspective felt like it had shifted dramatically. Being safe, having food, the lights being on, and having her family safe with her was what mattered. That's what matters, she said to herself. Although, in a weird way, she wanted her "normal" life back, like the mad dash for this year's patio furniture. She didn't really want the patio furniture; she just wanted the "normal" of the patio furniture.

As she kept driving the few miles to work, as fast as she wanted because there were no cars on the road, Tammy thought about her family. Mark was hunting and fishing, which he loved to do. He had been happier than she'd seen him in quite some time. Little Missy was having a ball with Manda and Cole Matson. It was good for her to have some friends and a teenage girl to look up to.

But Tammy's biggest joy was her son, Paul. He had come out of his shell. He had been so depressed before the Collapse. That custody fight was so hard on him and he had gained all that weight. Before the Collapse, he spent all his time laying around the house and complaining about everything.

But not now; he built that metal gate for the entrance. She thought about it every day that she went through the gate on her way to work. He got to put his metal fabrication skills to use and was proud of what he'd done.

But, the best thing for Paul was that he was on the beach patrol. He was putting his knowledge of the currents and tides of the inlet to great use. They were out there preventing people from coming ashore and doing God knows what to Pierce Point. Paul was so busy that she didn't see him much anymore. But, when she did see him, she noticed how much weight he'd lost, how tan he was, and how he smiled all the time. He was confident now.

10

Things were pretty good, considering. She pulled into work and got ready for a day of problem solving. She had a feeling she would be doing a lot of that today.

# Chapter 170

## *Grandma Did a Bad Thing*

### (July 5)

As she pulled into work, Tammy noticed two things. First, the clock in her car said she was late. Second, there was a new vehicle in the parking lot. It was a State Parks Department truck, which was odd. The nearest state park was a few miles away, but had been closed for over a year because of the budget cuts.

Tammy parked in her usual spot and got out, hurrying because she was late. Bill Stadler, the company manager came out and motioned for her to come over to him.

Bill was in his sixties, had glasses, and wore short-sleeved buttoned shirts during warm weather. He had a pocket protector and something not too many electrical engineers had: a way with people. He was one of the kindest people Tammy had ever met.

Bill looked nervous when he saw Tammy. He motioned for her to keep her voice down.

Tammy whispered, "Sorry, I'm late Bill. I hit the snooze..."

"Shhhh," Bill said. That was unlike him to interrupt. This must be important.

He pointed at the state pickup truck. "The FC are here," he said, referring to the Freedom Corps.

Oh crap. This wasn't good. Their little power company had been left alone throughout the Collapse. Tammy had wondered how long they could continue to do things without any government interference. Not much longer, it appeared.

"What do they want?" She asked in a whisper.

"To take over," Bill said. For the first time in the twenty or so years Tammy had known Bill, he looked pissed. He was defending his people and his beloved power company from those outsiders.

Bill explained that a man from the FC had come an hour earlier and told him that the government was going to take control of the power company. It was part of a plan, the FC man said, to "focus resources." Bill interpreted that to mean cutting off power to areas of the county, or maybe the whole county.

Bill was not a political person. He was an electrical engineer by training and had taken a lot of management courses to become the manager of a little power company. He was very smart. Since before the Collapse, he could see where things were headed and wondered when the government would try to use utilities as a weapon. He kept telling himself that wouldn't happen in America, although it was easy for the imagination to conjure up.

But, Bill was an engineer and realized how vital the electricity flowing through his company was to the wellbeing of the county. It was absolutely critical. Nothing could make people want to leave the rural areas more than cutting off the utilities. He figured the government knew this, too.

Bill kept coming back to the idea that, at some point, the government might try to take over the utility. They had taken over the highways and fueling stations. Hell, they had taken over everything else, hadn't they?

Bill was like most Americans: an Undecided who was just trying to get by, but the more he saw of how the government was treating people—especially how they let the gangs run wild and how corrupt things were—the more he felt himself leaning toward the Patriots. He was an engineer, not a fighter, he kept telling himself. He was not a hero. But he kept returning to the idea that he had some control over a vital asset: electricity in his little county. He could not talk himself out of the logical conclusion that, at some point, his control over that asset might put him in conflict with the government. He really didn't want to do that, but he loved this county and its people. He wouldn't let them suffer like that.

"Tammy, you know what would happen if they take over," Bill said, trusting Tammy like a sister. Bill never talked to her about politics, but had picked up on several signs that she was either a full-on Patriot or Patriot sympathizer. Bill was now risking jail or worse by talking this way, but he had to trust Tammy for his plan to work.

"Are you sure they want to take over?" Tammy asked Bill. She was hoping the FC was out just to give another one of those talks about keeping alert for terrorists: Ron Paul bumper stickers, Don't Tread on Me flags, etc.

"Yes," Bill said. "They told me. It's part of some new program. He said some National Guard troops would be coming out later this afternoon along with a team of officials who would oversee the shut offs." Bill looked terrified when he said "shut offs." Those words scared him.

"Does he think we'll just do that?" Tammy asked.

Bill nodded. "I told him we were all loyal. I told him we were committed to the recovery efforts." Bill pointed to the FC sign in the parking lot that said "We support the Recovery."

Bill continued, but lowered his voice now to a faint whisper and pointed to the FC man walking into the power company office. "He seems kind of stupid. He's from Olympia where I think everyone just does what they're told." Bill looked at Tammy in the eyes and said, "We're different out here."

Tammy interpreted that as some kind of code, like Bill wanted to do something drastic to prevent the FC from taking over. "What do you mean?" she asked.

Bill looked Tammy in the eyes again and said, "I mean we can't let this happen."

"How?" Tammy whispered.

Bill just stared at her, then he looked at the pistol in her shoulder holster and then he looked over at the FC man. Bill nodded slowly.

Oh, God. Kill him? Was this really happening?

Was there a choice? They couldn't let the government shut off the power. But...were they supposed to murder someone and then have all the cops come out?

"You're not suggesting..." Tammy whispered.

Bill slowly nodded.

Tammy thought about it. Things had been going too well. It was impossible to get through the Collapse and war, or whatever it was, without being directly involved in it. Was she going to let those corrupt bastards permanently destroy her county? Hell no. She had long ago told herself that she would die to protect her children. Well, this was her chance.

"How? How will we do this?" she whispered.

Bill looked around again to make sure no one was listening. "Here's an idea," he said in that faint whisper.

Tammy listened as Bill outlined idea for getting rid of the FC man. It was a good plan.

"Do I have to be part of it?" she asked, knowing the answer.

"Yes," Bill said. "Can you think of another way?" Bill was a little hurt that Tammy, who he trusted so much, was trying to get out of this.

Tammy thought and thought. Her mind was racing. How to do this differently? How to do this without hurting anyone? She came up blank.

She paused. She was about to make the most important decision of her life.

"OK. I'm in," she said, very quietly. She wasn't proud of this, but also didn't feel like she had much of a choice.

The next hour or so was the longest wait in her life. She knew what was going to happen and had to play along like she didn't. She was trying so hard to act normal.

They were in the conference room with the FC man. He was a typical looking white-collar guy in his mid-forties. He had a pistol on his belt. He looked tired and never introduced himself to Tammy. He was kind of a dick and talked down to them a little.

It was pretty obvious he was not leveling with them. He would say that the shut-off would be temporary, but then said that trucks would come to take county residents to Olympia where the power would be more reliable. Why truck people out of the county if the shut-offs were just temporary? They had been living with intermittent power outage for weeks. Why, all of a sudden, did that mean depopulating the county? The story the FC man was telling was so laughable that it was insulting. Did he think they were stupid?

Yes, he did. And it showed.

Tammy and Bill and two of the younger electrical repairmen were in a conference room getting a "briefing" from the FC man. Bill motioned and the two repairmen left. Then, a few minutes later, Bill said to the FC man, "Tammy can take you out to the switching shed to show you where the master switch is."

Bill pointed at Tammy. That was her cue. Her hands started to shake and she felt dizzy. It took a few seconds for her to regain her composure. She took several deep breaths. She had a job to do. Her family, and the whole county, was counting on them to prevent the shut-off.

Finally, she was calm. In fact, after the initial shakes, she amazed herself at how calm she was. It was only because so many people were counting on her.

"Sure, come on," Tammy said. "The shed is just down the road. Can we take your truck?" she asked the FC man.

"Whatever," he said like Tammy was wasting his time.

Tammy chuckled to herself; who would really think the master switch for turning off the power to a whole county would be in a shed a mile from the main building? This FC guy was either really stupid or just a robot doing what he was told.

Tammy left the room and Bill didn't even look at her. He

wasn't going to give her a look that might tip off the FC man.

Tammy took the FC man out of the building and they got into his truck

"Which way?" he asked, a little curtly, like she should have been giving him better directions.

She pointed out of the parking lot and down the road, and he began following her direction.

"How far?" he asked impatiently.

"Oh, about half a mile," Tammy said. "Then we turn off on Dearborn Road. Take a left on it." Her heart was pounding. She was trying her best to be calm, but she was afraid she wasn't pulling it off. It only took a minute to get to Dearborn Road. He turned left.

"How far now?" he asked.

"Just around this corner," she said.

They turned the corner and there was a pickup truck in the road. It looked like they had broken down.

"Oh, great. Some hillbillies," the FC man said. Tammy looked at his pistol. This wouldn't be easy, but it had to be done.

He honked the horn and stopped the truck. He yelled at the men in the pickup, "Hey, move!"

The men got out of their truck. They looked familiar. They were the repairmen, but were wearing different shirts and now had sunglasses. The FC man obviously didn't recognize them from the conference room.

Tammy opened the door and sprinted out of the way. She ran as fast as she could. Away, away, away from there she kept thinking as she ran. She wanted to be as far away as possible because of the...

Boom! Boom! Boom! Boom!

Because of the loud gun shots. Tammy hoped those were the repairmen's guns going off and not an FC pistol.

Tammy got ahold of herself. She realized that she was a coward running away like that.

Missy. Tammy thought about her sweet, innocent little granddaughter Missy, who would grow up in a destroyed country if the power were shut off. She might not even live, because of what these bastards had done. Tammy stopped and turned around. She ran back toward the gun fire, suddenly wanting to be a part of this. She wanted to do something to change the horrible situation. She wanted to do her part. She ran up and saw the two repairmen with shotguns leveled at the FC truck. She saw a person in the truck slumped over. As she got closer, she saw some big holes punched in the driver's side door of the truck. They had used rifled slugs, which had punched through the truck door, like a nail through a soda can. There was blood all over the inside of the windows of the truck. It looked like the FC man exploded.

Tammy saw the blood. She wished she hadn't looked at it. She started to feel sick. They had killed a human being. Her mind started racing: she didn't know for sure that the FC man was a bad person. Maybe he wasn't there to shut off the power. Maybe he didn't have to die. Maybe he had kids like she did. Maybe they didn't have to kill him. It was so final. If this were a mistake, she could never undo it.

"Let's go," one of the repairmen yelled.

The other repairman came over and they both ran to the FC truck. One of the repairmen ran back to their truck and got a can of spray paint. He sprayed a big red star on the FC truck and wrote "Red Brigade" on it.

The first repairman came over to Tammy and said to her, "OK, remember. The truck was stopped by two men. They had ski masks on. They made you get out and then they shot him. OK? We're going to take off now. You just wander back to the office." He didn't even say good bye or look at her. They just got in their truck and they took off.

Tammy wanted to get out of there. She didn't want to look at the FC truck again, or especially the bloody dead man in there. It was too disturbing. She realized she'd have this scene in her mind for years to come; likely the rest of her life. This "do-your-part-for-the-movement" thing was all fine and good, until you were looking at a dead man blown to pieces and you helped to do it. Tammy knew she'd have nightmares, but it had to be done. She would have worse nightmares if the power had been turned off.

Missy. This is for Missy; for her future. That's what this is for, Tammy kept saying to herself as she ran back toward the office.

She got winded after running a while, so she started walking down the road. Walking? No, that wouldn't be believable. She had to run. If she had really just been ambushed, but managed to escape and really wanted to summon help, she would run back to the office. She would sprint. She started to run. It was hard to keep running, but she had to make this convincing.

She only got a few hundred yards until she had to stop. She started walking again. Then she'd jog a little and walk some more. Pretty soon she was at the office. She started yelling when she got in the parking lot.

"They attacked us!" she screamed. "They shot him! They shot him!" Bill came running out, acting very surprised. He was surrounded

17

by other employees who looked confused and scared.

She told the story to the crowd of her co-workers huddling around her at the entrance to the power company. The same simple story she'd been rehearsing on the way back to the office. She didn't tell the part about the red star. She wouldn't have known that because she just got out of the truck and ran. She heard the shots and kept running toward the office. That was the story. Everything was a blur.

"Someone call the police!" Bill yelled. That scared Tammy. She didn't want anyone actually investigating this. Too bad; she was in it too far now.

"Send someone out to go see if he's still alive!" Bill yelled. "And be careful. They still might be in the area." Two trucks left the parking lot and headed out toward Dearborn Road.

About twenty minutes later, which seemed like twenty days, the two trucks came back to the office. "Terrorists!" one of drivers said. He described the red star and "Red Brigade" on the truck. He wasn't in on the plan, so he really believed it.

"Tell the police we have terrorists here!" Bill yelled. "Everyone, back in the office! They might be coming back for us!" He was so convincing.

Employees started running back into the office. People were running out to their trucks and grabbing rifles and shotguns to take with them into the office.

Everyone was hovering around Tammy. They were offering water, asking her what the terrorists looked like, and what kind of truck they had. What was the license plate? She couldn't remember. "It all happened so fast," she kept saying. Which was true.

Before the Collapse, the police would have been on the scene in a matter of minutes. Now, however, they probably wouldn't even make it out there. A killing on the side of the road? Take a number. But, the call came in that "terrorists" had attacked. That got the attention of the police.

Lt. Bennington was the first to arrive. Terrorists? Oh wow. This was getting serious. He wanted to find them. He interviewed Tammy. She kept telling the same story. She said she needed to go home. Bennington said she wouldn't be safe there. The terrorists might try to get her at her home. She needed to stay at the offices for a while. She'd be safe there. She knew that, if her story had been true, they would be right about that, so she had to play along.

Someone sent for Mark and he came, appearing very worried for her. She couldn't tell him what had really happened. That was

18

going to be extremely difficult for her. She knew she'd eventually cave; she couldn't keep something like that from him. The day seemed to go on forever, until that evening when an agent of some kind came from Olympia. He wanted to know all about the terrorists. Tammy kept telling the same story. She was hoping she was telling it consistently. She didn't want to slip up. She would get out of telling details by saying she needed a break and that it was too traumatic. She had already told the other police. Could she just have a break?

That night around dark, Bill came into the conference room where Tammy was and closed the door.

"You won't believe this," he said with a smile. A smile? What was there to smile about?

Tammy just stared at him. She was drained. Emotionally and mentally drained. She'd never had a day like this before.

"The Feds say that the FC man, who was named Arthur Durman, was acting on his own!" Bill said. "Can you believe it?"

"Huh?" Tammy asked. She did not see that coming.

"Yeah!" Bill said as he clapped his hands. "They say Durman was not authorized to come out here. They say the idea that they would turn off the power was crazy. They told me that the President would be going on TV tomorrow for his daily update to tell the country that rumors of the Feds cutting off power to rural and Southern areas was 'terrorist' propaganda."

That didn't make any sense to Tammy or Bill. A few days later, Patriot ham radio operators were getting the word out about the Utility Treaty. Then it made sense why the Feds claimed the FC man was acting on his own.

Tammy kept thinking about the Durman, the FC man. If only he would have just waited one day.

Oh well, Tammy later told herself. Durman had no business trying to cut off electricity to tens of thousands of people. He volunteered for that FC job. He got to wear a little helmet and drive a government truck. He had a job, and his FCards had lots of credits. Durman knew exactly what he was doing and he started to do it, anyway.

That night, around midnight, they let Tammy go. Mark took her home, and they didn't talk at all. Tammy was all talked out. Mark's presence and the silence comforted her.

Everyone had heard about this at the Pierce Point gate. They were quick to ask her how she was doing and told her that no strangers would get into Pierce Point. They were on the lookout for the Red

Brigade. Tammy felt bad fooling them, too, but it had to be done. It was for their own good. If the government showed up with a tank and said they wanted to arrest Tammy, the guards would have to fight, and die, or turn her over. By lying, she was allowing them to avoid that.

Mark and Tammy came down Over Road. They were almost home. Gideon came out of the guard shack with his AK pointed in the general direction of the truck. He was making sure no one came through who might be after Tammy.

"Glad to see that you're home safe and sound," Gideon said. "Have a good night. You're safe here, ma'am."

Tammy started to cry. She was safe there. Thank God. But the real crying came when she walked into the house.

"Grandma!" Missy yelled. "You're home!"

Tammy grabbed her granddaughter and hugged her so hard she thought she would snap the little girl in half.

Tammy cried and cried.

"Are you OK, Grandma?" Missy asked.

Tammy looked at Missy and said, "Oh, yeah, Grandma is OK."

Tammy paused and thought, Grandma did a bad thing.

# Chapter 171

## *Utility Treaty*

### (July 5-13)

Indeed, Forks, Washington had been one of about one hundred remote little towns to be the first test of Operation Cracker Corral. "Cracker" was a pejorative term for white trash. "Corral" was, of course, a cowboy term meaning to force animals from one area to another.

The idea was to force people in rural Patriot areas to move to suburban and urban Loyalist areas, which would concentrate resources in Loyalist areas and break the Patriots still left in Patriot-held areas. To accomplish this, the goal of Operation Cracker Corral was to deprive Patriot areas—primarily rural areas, the South, and mountain West states—of much-needed electricity. The people staying in the Patriot areas would be broken and powerless. Good. That was the plan.

The government was smart enough not to do this all at once. Suddenly shutting off power to half the country would cause an uprising and flood the Loyalist areas with too many hungry mouths at once, so the government decided to slowly shut off the power, beginning with the most isolated areas first. It would not seem odd to people in the shut-off areas because there had been so many periodic outages since May Day. Those people would not suddenly jump on their ham radios and tell the rest of the country what was happening. People in the shut-off areas would take a while to realize it. Slowly, they would either move to Loyalist areas, where they were easier to control, or they would…die.

Of course, the government planners who came up with this didn't dwell on the part about dying. They actually thought they were doing people a favor. All the government services were in the cities. People should want to be there. Government was fabulous and helped people. The people just needed a nudge to get them to the places where they could take advantage of all the wonderful things government was doing for them.

Cracker Corral was not a new idea. For centuries, governments had been using shut-offs of vital supplies to control populations and win civil wars. Back in ancient times, it had been shutting off irrigation water. Then, in the modern era, it had been shutting off electricity. Dictators knew how powerful this tool was.

Electricity was an even more potent weapon in the United States. People were so dependent on artificial things, like electricity, that a shut off was essentially a death sentence. Soon after a shut off, food would go bad and gas pumps wouldn't work. Then people would figure out they needed to move to the cities.

For decades, the government had studied the effects of an electromagnetic pulse, or "EMP," where a small nuclear device is detonated high in the atmosphere sending a pulse of electromagnetic energy—basically static electricity—downward on a large area, like North America. The pulse fries all electrical wiring and circuitry, instantly destroying all the electrical devices on the ground. Car and truck starters, gas station pumps, computers, refrigerators, hospital equipment, communications equipment. Everything would be permanently destroyed because the wiring is basically soldered together by the EMP pulse. They can't be repaired. It takes a brand new electrical device, but they can't be manufactured because everything necessary to make them—manufacturing plants, trucks to transport them—have also been destroyed. It would take a century to recover. That is not an exaggeration: one hundred years. Following an EMP, a majority of the population would die from starvation, lack of medications, communicable diseases, gang violence, and eventually, war.

The government knew how absolutely dependent American society was on electricity. They ran the scenarios. They knew American society could only last about two weeks without electricity before the areas without it would be totally broken and submissive.

Their plan was to totally break the Patriot areas, which was easier than a military invasion and occupation. Besides, the FUSA did not have the military resources for a fair fight.

Operation Cracker Corral was brilliant, but too brilliant. Because it was basically a genocide plan, it was inevitable that one of the thousand or so people planning it would be reluctant to kill several million of their fellow citizens. However, the government was so desperate when they hatched their plan that they got sloppy as they hurried to come up with a solution. They got sloppy by getting too many people involved.

It was a quiet nerd, Andrew Berkowitz, who saved millions of lives. He was a stereotypical short, thin PhD mathematician who wore big glasses.

Andrew was an analyst for one of the many government think tanks. He had been brought in on a contract with the Department of Homeland Security to work on the plan to shut off electricity. How ironic it was that the people planning how to murder millions of people in the American homeland worked for the Department of Homeland Security.

Andrew's background was thoroughly checked out. They determined that he was safe. He had no outside interests; all he did was work, so he wasn't political. He didn't drink, do drugs, or chase women (or men), so he wouldn't be compromised that way. He was Jewish so the assumption was made that he wouldn't be one of the Bible-thumping right-wing Patriots. He would probably be afraid of what the redneck Patriots would do if they got power: set up an evangelical Christian theocracy. That's what the Loyalists kept telling themselves. By breaking the Patriots in Operation Cracker Corral, the Loyalists thought they were preventing a bigoted Christian theocracy. Surely, a Jew would want to help with that effort. Therefore, Andrew could be trusted with some of the most sensitive secrets the FUSA had.

At first, Andrew was just doing his job. With all the other government workers out of a job, he was glad to have the work. He really didn't care what he was working on; he was working. He began his work by reading the top secret project overview memorandum for something called Operation Cracker Corral.

The moment Andrew saw the project overview he knew exactly what it was: genocide. His grandfather had lived through one of those and it wouldn't happen again, no matter what religion the victims were. Not if Andrew could do anything about it.

And he could. Rod Evans, a neighbor in his DC suburb, seemed like one of those Patriot people. Before the Collapse, Andrew noticed that Rod occasionally wore one of those "Don't Tread on Me" t-shirts. Rod had a younger brother who was a math geek, so he felt for Andrew and knew how hard it to be social when you're so brilliant in one concentrated part of your brain. He went out of his way to be friendly to him.

Andrew didn't know why, but he was definitely drawn to Rod. After a long sleepless night of worrying about Cracker Corral and wondering if he could trust Rod, Andrew went over to Rod's house the next morning.

"Um, Rod," Andrew whispered while looking down at the ground, "can you get a hold of the Patriots?"

"No," Rod said, "Of course not. I don't know any of those people." This wasn't true, but Rod was going to play it safe since he had no idea if Andrew was working for the Freedom Corps.

Then Rod thought about it. He knew that mathematicians' brains, like Andrew's and Rod's brother's, were almost always stuck in logical, concrete thought, and were nearly incapable of making things up. This generally made them terrible liars. Ron's gut just told him Andrew was trustworthy.

"Well," Rod said, "maybe."

Andrew felt a surge of confidence. He couldn't explain it, but he knew with absolute certainty that he was doing the right thing. He kept thinking of those pictures of his grandfather as a little boy in a concentration camp.

Andrew whispered, "I have an important document — a very, very important document — that I need you to get to them."

Rod nodded. He could sense that Andrew was not exaggerating and that this was extremely important.

"I'll have it in a few days," Andrew said and then abruptly walked out of Rod's house. Andrew wasn't rude; he was just socially awkward.

Andrew had to go through a lot to print out the memo and smuggle it out of his office. It was easier to get through the security system by printing it out rather than making an electronic copy. Besides, Andrew wanted to print it on official Homeland Security letterhead because he knew the Patriots analyzing it would be able to tell it was real DHS paper. Andrew needed the Patriots to understand that this memo was real, not some sick joke.

Two days later, after the daunting feat of stealing the memo, Andrew put it in an envelope and gave it to Rod.

"This is sealed," Andrew said to Rod. "Don't open it. They need to know it's authentic." Andrew included in the envelope his official Homeland Security ID badge, an item that would let the Patriots know he was legitimate.

Rod nodded and took it the Patriots that he knew, who were some low-level guys. He hoped it got to the right people.

It sure did. Within a few days, the memo was in the hands of the top Patriot intelligence people. They verified the contents of the memo with their moles in the FUSA intelligence community.

The Patriots quickly came up with a plan and contacted the top Oath Keeper generals in the FUSA military.

There weren't as many Oath Keeper generals as there were

lower level officers and enlistees because only politically loyal people were promoted to general and admiral. However, there were still a few officers who were so good at their jobs that they had to be promoted, even if they were not "political." Most of them didn't care about politics at all, but they saw what was going on and could not be a part of it. They were Oath Keepers because of the gravity of the situation, not because they wanted to be.

A handful of Oath Keeper generals were not doing this out of a sense of necessity. They were actively trying to infiltrate the military to have the maximum impact they could, in order to save the country. They stayed in the military because they knew they could do more for the Patriots where they were: on the inside, and at the top. Andrew's memo was the perfect example of why they needed to be where they were. Their plan capitalized on the fact they were generals in charge of powerful military assets.

The generals came up with what became known as the "Utility Treaty," and then they met with the FUSA Loyalist leadership and offered them a deal. If the Loyalists did not go through with Cracker Corral, then the generals would not defect to the Patriots. If the Loyalists took the deal, the huge military assets the Patriot generals and admirals commanded—divisions, air wings, and aircraft carrier battle groups—would "sit out" during the Collapse. They would not join the Patriots, but they would not join the Loyalists, either. They would just sit it out, which was very popular with the generals' troops.

Besides humanitarian motives, the generals also knew that cutting off utilities to rural areas and the Southern states would mean massive civil unrest; even more than there already was. They knew that they, and their troops, would be called on to go put down the revolts and be drawn into an unwinnable insurgency in the American heartland. They didn't want to kill thousands of Americans, or be killed themselves. Sitting it out seemed like a much better option for everyone involved, except the douche bag Loyalist politicians, but who cared.

The Loyalists' first reaction was to call for the court martial of the generals and admirals. They even briefly detained them until they realized that they could avert a full-scale civil war simply by not going through with Cracker Corral. At this point, the regular military, or what was left of it, was largely leaning toward the Patriot side, and the Loyalists were terrified of even more regular units going over to the Patriots. Besides, many Loyalists were opposed to Cracker Corral, themselves. It went too far. It would kill too many Americans.

The Loyalist leadership agreed to cancel Cracker Corral. That whole process—from Andrew Berkowitz discovering the plan, getting the memo to the Patriots, the generals' meeting with the Loyalist leadership, and the Loyalists' decision to cancel the operation—lasted eight days. Those were the eight days that Forks, and about a hundred other towns, were without electricity.

# Chapter 172

## *Born In This World as It All Falls Apart*

### (July 6)

Manda Matson got up a little early. It was 6:00 a.m. and the sun was up. It was yet another beautiful sunny summer day.

Manda was very careful not to wake her brother. They slept in the same bed in the upstairs loft of her family's cabin at Pierce Point. In the next bed over, were her grandma and grandpa. Grandpa snored, but Manda was getting used to it.

It was so quiet. The loft had a huge window looking out onto the water. There were giant trees on each side of the cabin blocking any view to the sides. In the absolute silence of an early morning, Manda just stared out the window at the water. Some birds were flying around and the harbor seals were out. She loved the harbor seals. They were so cute.

After a while, Manda needed some noise. She grabbed her iPod, one of her most prized possessions. Thank goodness it still worked, she thought. She could keep the battery charged because they still had electricity. She couldn't go onto the internet and get new songs because her dad said the police were looking for him and he didn't want to be tracked. Luckily, she had her huge library of songs and videos on there. With all the changes in her life in the past few weeks, at least she had her songs and videos. Listening to them made her feel like things were normal.

She had her iPod on shuffle so songs came up at random. The first one was "Young" by Hollywood Undead. The first lines were:

We are young.
We have heart.
Born in this world as it all falls apart.
We wave this flag of hatred.
But you're the ones who made it.
Watch the beauty of our lives.
Passing right before our eyes.

It was like that song was talking directly to her. She was born in this world as it all falls apart. She was sixteen. This was supposed to be a magic time in her life. It wasn't.

Manda remembered when she was in the third grade. Her best friend, Emmy, had a big sister in high school, Ashley. Emmy and Manda worshipped Ashley. They wanted to be a high schooler, like her. Ashley told Emmy and Manda how cool it was to be in high school. You got to drive your own car to school. You could pretty much pick the classes you wanted. You could pick out what you wanted to eat for lunch. There were football games on Friday nights. Best of all, was the prom where you got to dress up in a beautiful dress, get your hair and nails done, and go have a nice dinner with a cute boy. Then, after high school, you got to go to college where you got to live on your own, there were tons of cute boys, and the football games were on TV and everything. Manda and Emmy couldn't wait to be high schoolers and then go to college.

Well, fast forward eight years. Manda was in high school now, but it was closed. It was too dangerous to go there. The teachers stopped coming to school weeks ago when the school district ran out of money to pay them. Now, according to someone who had heard it on the news, Olympia High School had become a Freedom Corps training facility or something.

There were no more proms. There never would be. Not now, while people were too worried about having enough to eat and everyone carried guns because of all the criminals. Manda and Emmy had always talked about how they wanted their prom dresses to be. They would draw pictures of them. Manda still had some of those drawings at her Olympia house, which had been destroyed by the government people who hated her dad.

Trying not to wake anyone, she looked around the loft for a piece of paper and a pen. She wanted to draw a picture of her prom dress, just like when she was in third grade.

She couldn't find any paper. Of course not. Nothing ever worked out, like having paper around. Then she started to cry, quietly so she wouldn't wake up her brother and grandparents. She realized that she would never have a prom dress. Her dreams would never come true. Her teen years had been taken. This stupid Collapse had taken everything away from her. All she had wanted was a prom. Was that asking so much? Why couldn't she have things that everyone else got before the Collapse? Why did this have to happen when she was in high school? Why couldn't it wait until she got to be a normal teenager,

28

at least for a little bit? Why couldn't people just get along and quit fighting each other? Why couldn't things get back to normal? And why didn't anyone care about her prom? All they ever talked about was food and guards and medicine. No one cared about proms.

"Play the cards you're dealt," her dad always said. She stood up straight. She would deal with this. She wouldn't let a prom get her down. She thought about all she had out here. Her family was together. There were a few days when she didn't think that would happen. She remembered when her dad left and her mom said he was gone forever. Manda thought her dad was dead, or would be dead soon. She knew he would fight the government people and that they had more guns than he had. She even made up a funeral for him in her imagination. That was her way of saying goodbye to him. She imagined who would come to it and what they would say about him. She realized what a good life he had led and how he was just trying to protect them.

She remembered when Pow came to the door of their suburban home and said they should come with the armed men and go out to the cabin, where her dad was alive. In an instant, she was so happy. It was like she had a second chance to have a great dad. She realized how lucky she was.

She also knew that most of her friends were trapped back in Olympia. Almost all of their parents were government workers, so they probably wanted to be in Olympia. Manda hoped they were OK and that Emmy and Ashley were doing fine. At least Ashley got to go a prom and college. She was lucky.

Manda heard someone stirring downstairs. It was probably her dad; he always got up early. She was awake and hadn't gotten to talk to him lately because he'd been so busy, so she quietly went downstairs without waking her brother or grandparents.

Her dad was in the kitchen, starting to make pancakes. She realized that some things never change, when, for a moment, she thought she was back before the Collapse, when they first got the cabin and she would come out with her dad. Back then, she would sleep in the loft and come downstairs and see her dad making pancakes. Just like the good old days, she thought. There was comfort in that.

"Hey, Dad, how's it goin'?" she asked.

Grant smiled when he saw her. He had been missing her and Cole so much.

"Mornin', dear," He said. "How's my best daughter?"

"Great," she said. "How's my best dad?" The "best daughter" and "best dad" lines they used were an inside joke. Grant would say that when Manda was little, and then one day, when Manda was in the second grade, she said, "Wait. 'Your best daughter?' I'm your only daughter." Then she turned it on Grant by calling him her "best dad," to which he would reply, "Wait. I'm your only dad." Even that exchange of lines from an inside joke felt so comforting. So normal, during such an abnormal time.

"Oh, I'm fine," Grant said. "Would my daughter like some delicious pancakes?"

"Of course," she said and then paused. "Hey, Dad, do you remember Ashley?"

"Yeah, sure. Why?" Grant asked. He hoped Ashley hadn't been killed.

"Remember how me and Emmy wanted to go to a prom like she did?" Manda asked.

Grant could instantly tell what was bothering Manda. He felt terrible that his little girl couldn't have a prom. She deserved it. She'd been talking about it for years. She had even drawn elaborate pictures of how she wanted her dress to look.

"Yeah, I remember. Why?" he asked, as if he didn't know the answer.

"Well, I wish…" she trailed off., "Do you think we could have a prom out here?"

That was what he was hoping she wouldn't ask. It would be impossible to have a prom out there for quite some time.

"Of course we can have a prom," he said, realizing that his daughter needed the hope of a prom to help her get through this. He was going to do all he could to get his girl a prom. He had no idea how this would be possible, but he was going to do it.

She started squealing with delight. She started talking to him about her dress so fast that he couldn't understand her. Besides, he had no idea what she was talking about: colors, fabric, sewing.

As she went on and on with a huge smile on her face, he realized that he needed to reel in her expectations.

"Of course, it won't be for a while," he said. Her squealing stopped. She was silent and then she started to sniffle.

"How long?" she asked, sniffling more now.

"Not long," he said, lying. "Maybe a couple of months. Maybe in the fall." He realized he needed to channel her energy into something positive to take her mind off of the disappointment of a delay – and possible never-occurring – prom.

"Between you, your mom, and grandma, I'm sure you'll come

up with something awesome for a dress," Grant said. He thought that others, probably including Mary Anne Morrell, would help find some fabric.

"Gotta play the cards you're dealt," she said, forcing a smile. Then she broke into a genuine smile. She realized that this prom would be more "real" than the old pre-Collapse ones. Before the Collapse, people just bought dresses, wore them once, and then threw them out. But out here, they would make a special dress just for her. She would keep it forever. This might even be better than the prom she had envisioned.

Manda hugged her dad. She was so glad he was here and that they were together.

Lisa came out of the bedroom and into the kitchen to see Manda and Grant hugging.

"What you guys talkin' about?" Lisa asked.

"Nothin'," Manda said. "Just hugging my best dad."

# Chapter 173

## *Kellie Is in Love*

### (July 6)

"I'm in love, dude," Wes said to Grant one morning as the Team was getting into Mark's truck to go out to the Richardson house for training. Just as Wes said that, a beautiful girl in her early twenties came out of the yellow cabin.

She had light brown hair and was in perfect shape, something Grant could tell from her shorts and tank top. He tried not to pay too much attention to her because she was half his age, but damn, she looked fabulous. She came running up to Wes and hugged him.

"When are you done with work?" she asked Wes, practically making out with him as she spoke. "I'll be waiting for you," she said extremely seductively. Grant knew what Wes had in store for him after work; hours and hours of it. He was a lucky bastard.

"I'm done around dinner time," Wes said. "We'll be back as soon as we can," he said, trying to be semi-business like with Grant around. Wes realized that he hadn't yet introduced his girlfriend.

"Grant, this is Kellie," Wes said. She snapped out of her love trance and broke off from her hug of Wes. She turned to Grant and tried to act polite, even though she was a little annoyed that someone was distracting Wes from her.

Grant put out his hand and said, "Pleased to meet you Kellie. I'm Grant. I live over here," he said pointing to his nearby cabin. "I work with Wes."

Kellie saw Grant's pistol belt and his military-contractor looking clothes. Like the Team, Grant was wearing 5.11 pants and had a Raven Concealment holster, which set him apart from the local guards, who usually wore hunting clothes. She realized this Grant guy must be one of the Team, although she hadn't seen him around and he was older than the other guys. He must be a boss or something. She vaguely remembered one of the Team saying something about a "Grant" guy being a judge and on the Team, or something. She figured she better be nice to him so Wes didn't get in trouble at work. She needed Wes to be home where she could… do more of what they had done all night.

"Nice to meet you, Grant," she said. She paused a moment to be polite and then went back to hugging Wes. She just wanted to hold him. She didn't want him to leave because she was afraid he'd get in a gun fight and not come back. She kept telling herself not to fall for some military guy, or whatever it was the Team did out there, but she couldn't resist. Wes was so cute and he was new.

Kellie recalled how she met Wes a few weeks ago. She had grown up at Pierce Point with the local boys. She'd dated some and done the usual dumb teenage stuff with them. She had a steady boyfriend, Ethan Meecham, for about a year, but he was so small-time, just a Pierce Point boy. She had decided to break up with him before the Collapse started, but she didn't have the nerve to do it. When Ethan went off to guard duty at the gate, Kellie was relieved. He'd be busy with that and not have any time for her.

Then she saw them; a pickup load of cute guys. New guys she hadn't seen before, and they came with guns. Way cooler guns than the hunting guns everyone else had. The guys in the truck had military looking clothes; not camouflage or uniforms. They looked like they were professionals, but not soldiers... like guys in all those movies she'd seen. She was amazed at how calm and confident they looked as they drove by. Luckily, they were driving slowly so she could get a good look at them. One of them smiled at her. He was so cute. She fell in love with one look.

Kellie thought it was great that the guys in the truck were riding around and looking for bad guys, who they would shoot if they had to. They weren't afraid of anything.

Kellie was drawn to that. She had some bad guys in her life she wanted people to go get. She wanted to be protected, and these were the type of men who would do that. She felt so safe just seeing them. It was a peaceful and exhilarating feeling. Nothing could hurt her when they were around.

It was a momentary feeling, though, because they drove by and then they were gone. She had to meet them, just had to. She would do anything to meet them, especially the cute one who smiled at her.

She was in her yard when they drove by. Once they were gone, she panicked. How could she meet them? Were they gone for good? She was terrified she'd never see them again.

Kellie found her mom, Sheila, hoping that she would know who they were. She frantically described what she'd seen and asked her mom who they were.

"The Team," her mom said. "Some guys from Olympia who are

out here doing police things. Nice guys. I met them at the Grange a few nights ago. Were you scared by the guns?" her mom asked. Sheila still thought of Kellie as her "little girl."

"No, I wasn't scared," Kellie said. She remembered that her mom still thought she was dating Ethan so she stopped herself from saying that she wanted to meet the cute one, the smiley one.

"I just wanted to make sure people with guns were OK to be here," Kellie said.

"Oh, they're OK to be here," Sheila said. "We're lucky to have them. They apparently trained together before all of this, like a SWAT thing or something. I'm not really sure," her mom said.

"The Grange?" Kellie asked. "Are they at the Grange?"

"Yeah," Sheila said, "for the meetings at 7:00. They eat there, too," Shelia said, starting to figure out why Kellie was so interested in meeting them. She saw this as an opportunity to get her daughter out of the house and do something productive.

"You could volunteer to help serve meals at the Grange. It wouldn't kill you," Sheila said.

"Great idea, mom," Kellie said. It had been about ten years since Sheila had heard her daughter say that.

"Great idea?" Sheila said, in complete shock at what her often unruly daughter had just said. "I love hearing that." They hugged. Her little Kellie, the one who listened to mom, was back. Maybe these boys on the Team were actually going to be a good thing for Kellie, Shelia thought.

"I'll go up to the Grange now and volunteer," Kellie said, impulsively grabbing her car keys.

"Whoa," Sheila said. "Gas. There's no gas to just drive around. Remember? You need to walk. It's only about a mile."

"Sure," Kellie said. "Sounds good, Mom." It was another shocking statement from the rebel child.

"I gotta change," Kellie said. Kellie got in her sexiest shorts and tight fitting tank top and put on some makeup.

Kellie came out and Sheila said, "You look fabulous. You'll be the most beautiful kitchen helper there." Kellie realized she was being obvious about her true intentions with the kitchen helping, but loved that her mom was in on it. Kellie hugged her mom. She hadn't done that in a couple of years.

Kellie started walking, which was something she hadn't done in so long. She was accustomed to driving anywhere and everywhere.

Before the Collapse, Kellie had a job in Frederickson at a local supermarket, Martin's. Her job sucked, but she was one of the few her age who had one during the horrible economy. Being beautiful might have had something to do with that; customers liked having a pretty girl around. She'd been working there part-time in high school and then, after she graduated two years ago, she went full time.

Her mom wanted her to go college, but Kellie didn't see any point to it. There were no jobs and the economy was terrible. She didn't feel like going to college only to graduate with tens of thousands of dollars of loan debt and no job prospects. .

Now, the economy was virtually non-existent. She quit going to her job in Frederickson when gas hit $12 a gallon and there was way too much crime in town. When it became obvious that life as they had known it was essentially over, Kellie started worrying about her future. Would she just sit at home and eat that awful deer meat, which is all they had? She couldn't drive anywhere and be with her friends. Her little brother was so annoying. She needed a life.

Then the truck went by and that boy smiled at her. That's what she needed; a new and wonderful life could be hers if she could only get that boy. And he was so cute and new and exciting. It would be perfect. Everything would be perfect.

Kellie walked up to the Grange and received a warm welcome from the ladies in the kitchen. They were happy to have a new volunteer and put her straight to work.

It was dinner time and people started coming in for dinner. Kellie saw a big Asian guy with a gun wearing those contractor-looking clothes. She realized that the Team must be there, and her heart stopped when they walked in. She looked quickly to see if he — the boy who smiled at her — was with them. Sure enough, there he was. He looked great all sweaty and dirty with all those guns and all that gear.

She decided to be forward. He probably was getting lots of offers from other girls, so she needed to snag this guy.

Kellie walked right up to him and said, in her sexiest voice, "Is there anything you'd like?" and winked. That was pretty obvious.

The other guys laughed and teased Wes, but he was just silent, staring at this beautiful woman who obviously liked him. Wes was a proper Southern gentleman. Courtship was a subtle dance where he was from. But, then again, a gorgeous woman was coming on to him. There was no harm in that. Subtle wasn't all it was cracked up to be.

"Hi," is all Wes could manage. The guys laughed at him for that, too. "I'm Wes," he managed to add.

Wes stuck out his hand. She shook it with a soft and gentle

shake and kept staring him in the eye with her most seductive look, which was intoxicatingly powerful. No guy could resist it.

"I'm Kellie and I just wanted to meet you," she said. Their handshake was still going; they were basically holding hands now. They were just staring at each other.

The guys quit laughing at Wes. They realized that this was a very serious moment for him and this hot girl. They were happy for him. Wes had apparently snagged a great girl and they didn't want to ruin that. They were silent for a few seconds, waiting for Wes to say something.

"You asked what I'd like," Wes finally said. "I'd like you to join me for dinner, ma'am," he said in his Southern accent. There. He'd put some subtle courting back into this encounter.

Kellie smiled a huge smile. She started to hug him, but caught herself. It was too early for that. She needed to let this play out a little more, even though she wanted to hug him. A lot.

The Southern gentleman in Wes took over. "I will be serving you tonight, ma'am," he said, in what could be a reference to dinner...or whatever else might happen later that night. He left to wash up and then went into the kitchen to get a plate of food for Kellie. The guys moved around so Kellie had a seat next to Wes, of course.

At dinner, Wes and Kellie had the most amazing conversation. They talked about everything. Wes found out that Kellie lived with her mom and younger brother. Her dad had left them a few years ago, which was a good thing since he regularly hit Kellie and her mom. They were still worried that he would come back, although they heard he was in jail. They also knew that the jails had been emptied.

Wes sensed that this was one of the reasons Kellie was so attracted to him. She wanted a man to protect her from any bad people who might come, like her dad. This bothered Wes. He didn't like the sexist idea that a woman needed a man for protection. He had been raised that men and women were equal. Well, they are, he thought. But why deny that this woman is looking for something if he had it? Kellie wanting to feel safe was not a terrible thing. Everyone wanted to feel safe. Wes desired it, too. He wanted to be with the Team since he was so much safer with them around.

Wes realized that he, too, was attracted to her for a sense of safety and protection. It wasn't safety and protection from bad people, though. It was a sense of safety and protection that he could provide for someone. He could help Kellie by making her safe. He could help her. He could make her life spectacular. He wanted to do that. He wanted to be the best boyfriend ever, or maybe the best husband, if life provided him that opportunity.

Whoa. It was way too early to be thinking about that, he said to himself. Then he took it all in. The conversation, how fabulous she looked, how he had been put in this place at this time with her. He just knew this was it. He'd met the woman he'd be with for the rest of his life.

One by one, the rest of the Team finished dinner and were taking their plates into the kitchen. They were talking with the Grange ladies and others while all the other diners were finishing their meals. But not Wes and Kellie. They just sat there, talking and laughing, until their butts got numb on the picnic table benches in the Grange.

"Hey, Wes, you comin'?" Ryan asked, which startled Wes back to reality.

"Oh. Yeah," Wes said. "Wait. Goin' where?"

"Back to the ranch," Bobby said, referring to the yellow cabin.

Wes looked back at Kellie. He didn't want to leave her, but Kellie didn't want to be the only girl out at the cabin, either. She wanted to be the most popular girl at Pierce Point by inviting her friends to meet these guys.

"I have some friends who would like to meet the other guys," she said with another wink.

"Female friends, I'm hoping," Wes said with a smile.

Kellie nodded slowly and said, "Some girls you guys will like to meet."

"Well, I wouldn't want to disappoint your friends," Wes said. Could this be going any better?

"Why don't you tell my colleagues about your friends?"

"Can I bring some of my friends over to meet you guys back at the ranch?" Kellie asked the Team.

Ryan blurted out, "Are they hot like you?"

Everyone laughed, including Kellie.

"I think you'll be happy to meet them," she said, using body language that suggested they were as hot as she was.

"We'll be back in about an hour to pick you and your friends up," Pow said with a giant smile.

"OK," Kellie said and hugged Wes for the first time. He felt so strong when she hugged him. He returned the hug, warmly and softly, but strongly. She felt amazing to him, so soft and so outrageously sexy.

"Let's go," Ryan said. The Team started walking out and Wes made an effort to break off the hug with Kellie and walk out to show the Team that he wasn't smitten. He actually pulled it off, which surprised him. He was being deceptive because he was, indeed, smitten.

"See you in a while," Wes said to Kellie, who just stared at him with puppy love eyes.

After the Team left the Grange, Kellie got her phone out and started texting the girls. She was glad that texting was working then; sometimes texts wouldn't work for a day or two.

In about twenty minutes, Kellie's friends started showing up. She made sure there was one girl for each guy. The guys came back earlier than the one hour estimate and took them back to the yellow cabin, but as soon as they got to the yellow cabin, they had to go out on some mission or something and said the girls had to go back. Luckily, about two hours later, the guys returned and picked them up, bringing them to the cabin, yet again.

The next events of the day were pretty predictable. Wes had a private room in the cabin. After about two minutes of small talk, he and Kellie tore each other's clothes off. What followed was amazing. Kellie had never been loved like that. Ethan was nothing compared to Wes.

# Chapter 174

## *Team Chicks*

### (July 6)

The girls were throwing off the Team's focus. Actually, the Team had no focus on their jobs; the girls quickly became all they thought about and did. Two or three days after meeting them, the Team stopped patrolling. They spent most of their time hanging out at the yellow cabin and having sex. Tons and tons of amazing sex.

After the first night, each guy had a girlfriend. Everyone was getting along so well. The girlfriends, who became known as the "Team Chicks," had all been friends since grade school. They loved being a Team Chick. It gave them status in the community. They had the best guys, who were new to the community and weren't the same old Pierce Point guys that the girls had grown up with. To be a Team chick, a girl had to be hot; really hot, and have game. The Team could get any girl they wanted out there.

Grant was busy doing his civil affairs work. He was organizing things and being the judge. He wasn't out with the Team so he didn't notice that they were pretty much hanging out in the yellow cabin, or the "Love Shack," as they started calling it.

Chip noticed, though. He was busy guarding the Grange during the day and kept track of what was going on there. He saw the Team and the Team Chicks come in for brunch. Brunch? Was this a survival situation or a party?

When Chip went home to the Morrells, he went by the Love Shack and saw what was going on. The Team wasn't patrolling; they were just getting laid.

Chip talked to Grant about it.

"Crap," Grant said. "They are bringing their girlfriends to the Grange to eat? Only people working for the community get meals. This is bullshit." Grant knew he had a discipline and political problem on his hands. The other residents would be jealous that the Team Chicks got meals without working for the community. The guys on the Team were his friends and he was happy that they had girlfriends, but this had to stop.

Grant and Chip went to the Love Shack in the late afternoon

and asked the girls to leave for a while. They had "operations" to discuss with the Team.

The guys on the Team were not happy about this.

"What operations?" Ryan said with an edge to his voice.

"That's my point," Grant said. "There have been no operations for a few days while you guys have been getting' your groove on. Guys, I'm all for a little R&R for you. It's well deserved." The Team was stunned that Grant was basically lecturing at them.

"But, c'mon, guys," Grant continued, now with a near-yelling tone. "Letting your girlfriends eat at the Grange? When food is scarce and we've worked hard to get the community to buy into a system where only those who work get fed. You guys go and do this? The rumors are flying that the 'Team Chicks' are earning their meals in the Love Shack."

That got the guys pissed off, which was good. It was the reaction Grant intended, and was why he made up the part about the rumor, although it was probably true.

"No more Grange meals for your girlfriends," Chip said. "Does everyone understand?"

They nodded. It made sense. They had been working so hard and everything in life had changed. It felt so great to be able to take their girlfriends out for brunch. They had been escaping from all the horrible things going on, but escaping too much. They'd forgotten about reality.

"You guys know what happens if these ladies get in the way of your ability to do your job?" Grant said. He was using his dad voice.

Silence.

"Off the Team. That's what," Grant said. "Will that suck for Pierce Point? That some very talented and well equipped fighters aren't patrolling and ready to help? Oh, yeah, it'll suck for Pierce Point. But can we have an elite group who doesn't have to follow the rules? Hell, no. Guys, we're on political thin ice out here. All it takes is that douchebag Snelling to make some speech at a Grange meeting and all of a sudden these people turn on us. Trust me, I know politics." They knew Grant spoke with authority on this topic.

"This is a survival situation, gentlemen," Chip said in a calmer tone, appearing as the voice of reason. "We have to get through it. We can have some fun." Chip had a huge stash of condoms—that he was hoping to use himself—and had given them to the Team. "I *am* the one getting you rubbers so don't think I'm against you having fun." Good point.

"But what the hell good is a girlfriend," Grant asked, "if we get kicked out of here or there's nothing to eat because everyone is squabbling and jealous?" He didn't think the girlfriend situation was as dire as he was making it out to be, but he and Chip wanted to keep control over the Team. Small, elite groups tend to do things their own way and not listen to authority. Grant and Chip wanted the Team to be an asset to Pierce Point, not be perceived as out of control.

"OK, but how do our girlfriends eat?" Scotty asked.

"They need to work at the Grange or do some other work for the community," Grant said. "Or bring their own food over. Hell, they can help garden or go get oysters. They need to follow the rules so no one says Team Chicks are above everyone else. We're done for out here if that happens. Life is pretty good for us here. We can't blow it."

The guys started nodding. This made sense. They were realizing they had gotten a little out of control over the past few days.

Grant could tell they were coming around. Now was the time to soften the "dad voice."

"Guys," Grant said, "you can spend evenings and nights with them. That's cool. But all day? Every day? Nope. You guys have work to do. Door-bustin' gun fightin' work to do. Cool shit. It is what you guys were made to do."

That was motivating them; they started nodding even more.

"OK," Pow said. He was the leader. It was about time he agreed. "We'll get back to work and the girls don't eat at the Grange unless they're following the rules. Sounds fair."

"Cool," Grant said. "Now, speaking of getting back to work, I will be coming out with you guys tomorrow morning to the Richardson house to practice taking down a building."

"You're comin'?" Pow asked.

"Sure, I'm in," Grant said. He had missed the Team and door bustin'. He had done plenty of office work the past few days and needed a break. He needed to re-bond with the Team, especially because they would be a big part of Ted's fighters. Grant would be part of that so he needed to be as close as possible to the Team. Grant had established himself as the organizational guy at the Grange, so he could take a little time and do some fun stuff for a while if he wanted to.

"Chip?" Pow asked. "You in?"

"I think I can get someone to cover for me at the Grange tomorrow," Chip said. "I can only take so much standin' around. I'm old, but I can help with the training a little. Besides, I'm hopin' one of

41

the Team Chicks' moms sees me and wants to hook up," he said with a laugh.

"Grandmas," Pow corrected him. Everyone laughed.

The Team—the whole Team—was back together. It felt great.

# Chapter 175

## *Armed Serenity*

### (July 7)

The Richardson house was the ideal training location for the Team. It was abandoned and isolated enough that there wouldn't be anyone watching them. The Team had been trying to get a training day in since after the raid on the tweaker house. There had been a million projects for the Team to do at Pierce Point after the raid like training the gate guards and patrolling. Finally, they had a day when they could all go out and train. This required Grant to participate; he was part of the Team and could be called out with them to take down another house. He had to participate in the training.

The next morning, Grant got ready for work and didn't tell Lisa what he was going to be doing. He didn't want to start the day with an argument. Like a coward, he waited until she was in the bathroom and then got his kit and AR and left. It was better to be a coward than to have to spend the entire day worrying about her being mad. He didn't need to be distracted as he practiced house clearing.

Grant walked out of the cabin into the sunshine and went a few yards down the road toward the yellow cabin. He saw the rest of the Team coming out and heading over to Mark's black Silverado, which was parked and idling. They piled into the truck, each taking their familiar places in the bed of the truck.

The Team looked at Grant, expecting him to say the phrase he always said as they got into the truck. Grant paused for dramatic effect. Then he smiled and proudly said, "This never gets old."

They all smiled. Then it was Pow's turn to say his usual phrase.

"Beats the shit out of selling insurance," Pow said, right on cue, to another round of big smiles and fist bumps.

This felt good. No, it felt absolutely fantastic. Armed serenity; riding in the back of the truck out to train to save people. They were the sheepdogs for some very nice sheep, and were up against some very bad wolves.

The Team rolled into the Grange for breakfast, without their girlfriends in tow. People noticed that. Grant and Chip were with the Team in full kit. People noticed that, too. They were all eating together like the old days.

Lisa was coming to work at the clinic early and saw Grant at the Grange. She put two and two together.

"You going to be here today?" she asked, referring to the Grange.

"Nope. Training day with the Team," Grant said, expecting a fight.

"Oh. Cool. Be safe," she said and smiled. She hugged him.

She knew Grant was going to do this, anyway. She had been surprised at how easily he had just quit working with the Team and started doing office work. She knew he wanted to be out there with them. It was harmless. They were just training today, not getting in any actual gun fights.

Lisa was trying very hard to be understanding of all the new things that were happening. She realized that she had been a little too hardcore on the whole "just be a lawyer and have an office job out here" thing. She had increasingly been admitting to herself that Grant was right about the need to prepare. She also admitted to herself that he had done a good job of getting them out of Olympia and was running things very smoothly out here. She was blessed to have a husband like him. She didn't want to admit it to him, though; that would give him a big head.

"Will do, dear," Grant said, signaling by the use of the word "dear" that he appreciated her coolness on the topic.

Wow. This was just like the old days. Grant got to go out shooting with the guys and his wife was cool with it. Oh, wait, he told himself. In the old days, she was "cool with it" only because she never knew what he was doing. This was even better. She was fine with it while even knowing what he was doing.

Grant had to admit that Lisa was working hard at getting over normalcy bias. She still wasn't fully over it; not at all. She was still hesitant about many aspects of life out at Pierce Point. She never seemed comfortable with the situation out here. She wasn't complaining, but it was obvious she wasn't glad to be out here. But it was equally obvious that she was trying hard to accept what was happening.

Grant thought about it for a few minutes. He had to give credit where credit was due. Lisa was adapting to the new conditions of life much better than he thought she would. He remembered back to when she was crying in their Olympia house and screaming at him not to leave. That seemed like a different Lisa. Thank God. He didn't want to tell her how much better she was being. That would just give her a big head.

After a big breakfast of biscuits and gravy with delicious fresh strawberries on the side — the first berries of the season — the Team was ready to get to work. They headed out to the Richardson house. It felt so good to Grant to be out riding with the guys. It was a beautiful sunny day.

When they got to the Richardson house, Rich and Dan were there. Kyle Lemond, the new dog handler, was also there with the dogs. The "Crew" was there, too.

The Crew consisted of five new guys who worked on securing the perimeter when the Team went into the building. They had tactical shotguns and AKs, and one even had a vest with magazines. All of them had pistols, of course.

The Crew's job was to make sure no one escaped from the building that was being raided. This role had been the missing piece during the tweaker raid. The occupants of that house could have escaped once the Team flushed them out because there were only enough Team members to go in.

Dan solved this problem by recruiting the five best guards. It was a promotion for them and the possibility of being on the Crew motivated his other guards to work hard. Being on the Crew was a status symbol.

The Crew was made up mostly of guys in their thirties. No teenage boys. Dan wanted mature men for this job. The Crew couldn't get caught up in the excitement and shoot just anyone running toward them, like innocent civilians being rescued by the Team. They had to have judgment. They couldn't be rookies who wanted to show the world how tough they were. They needed to be quiet professionals and also needed to have the temperament to detain people who might end up being good guys.

The Crew's job wasn't just to grab people who were running out from a building and cuff them with zip ties. They were also in charge of making sure that no new bad guys came to the building trying to help their buddies inside. In a big fight, there was a very real possibility that the Crew would be shooting.

Chip led the Crew, which made sense. Chip was a member of the Team, but wanted to sit out the heavy stuff. Chip had the full confidence of the Team and knew them. He could tell the Crew what the Team would be doing since he knew exactly what they would do.

A final, but very important, piece of the Crew was Kyle

Lemond, who ran the dogs. He was in his thirties with black hair and a scar on his chin, but he didn't look like a criminal. He looked more like a logger. He was a quiet guy who had worked in a motorcycle shop before the Collapse.

The dogs Kyle handled could be used to secure the premises or to go into the house ahead of the Team. The dogs were the Team's secret weapon.

Grant had a unique role during the training. He would be a member of the Team, but would be a "floater," an optional add-in guy. He would not be a core member of the Team since there was a good possibility he would be doing office things at any given moment the Team could be called up.

Rich was in charge of the house-clearing training. Ryan assisted because he had done a lot of urban warfare training in the Marine Corps. His knowledge and experience was better than Rich's somewhat dated law enforcement training. Rich and Ryan went through the process in slow motion, talking out each step. Everyone made suggestions to Rich's basic plan of how to clear the house and secure the premises. They came up with a better system of communications. They already had been using basic terms like "moving!" that they practiced at the range before the Collapse. Now they expanded on them and came up with a command for everything they would likely run into. It was good to have Grant as the "floater." When he was taken out of the mix, simulating when he would be away in the Grange and couldn't' get on scene with the others, this forced the Team to change up who had various roles like lead entry. This meant each permanent member of the Team had to cross-train. They learned each role better by actually doing it, over and over again, all day.

After a few hours, each man on the Team knew exactly what every other member of the Team was doing at any given moment, and would be doing next. It was like on a basketball team when a player knows who will be where and exactly when. They were truly operating as a team instead of individuals.

It was hard work. They had to stay mentally alert for hours. It was mentally tiring, as well as physically. By the end of the day, they were a pretty good integrated team. The Crew was working out just fine. Kyle and the dogs were working well, too.

That day of training took the Team to the next level. They would need several more days of training to be semi-decent under stressful conditions. Grant heard that in the stress of combat, a person is only able to do 50% of what they are trained to do. So, they needed to train up to a level of double what they wanted to accomplish in real life.

"Whaddya say we call it a day?" Rich finally said. He could see the guys were starting to make mistakes because they were so tired and hungry. Rich didn't want the training to reinforce the mistakes. They had done an amazing job all day, and he wanted to end the day on a high note.

When they broke for the day, Grant noticed the Team and the Crew talking and laughing. They were getting along just fine, which was not a guaranteed thing. At the beginning of the day, there had been a little tension between the two groups.

Having an elite group and a "junior varsity" can often lead to conflict. The elite group might act like dicks. Not the Team. They appreciated having the Crew back them up. They knew the Crew was risking their lives to make the Team safer. And they knew the Crew was the best of the guards, which was a pretty high level.

A big flatbed truck with wood side boards came by a few minutes after Rich called it a day. The Team, Crew, Rich, and Dan got in. The dogs went into the cab. All together, they rolled down the road. The closer they got to the Grange, the more people saw them. People took note that the Team was expanding to add plenty of local men. This was a relief to some who had worried the Team—who were outsiders—might turn into a gang.

The Team integrating with the local men of the Crew was a clear sign that things were progressing in a good way. Pierce Point was getting a fighting unit together. Grant was glad to see the people witnessing this development. He expected they would be called upon to support a bigger fighting unit in the coming months. He wanted Pierce Point residents to feel pride and see that they could turn some good ole' boys into real fighters with a little training and equipment. And some help from Special Forces Ted.

When they pulled into the Grange, there was an awkward moment when the Team and Crew needed to pick a table. Grant solved that problem.

"We eat together, gentlemen," Grant said, motioning for the Crew to join the Team. They all sat down and recounted the day's events and joked. Dinner came and the men wolfed it down. Salmon and biscuits. No butter, but they were too hungry to care. Desert was heavenly: tons of ripe strawberries and whipped cream. Real cream, from real cows, whipped up with some sugar in it.

They were full and happy. They had done some great work and

everyone in the group could see that they would be doing lots more great work together. They had an amazing unit. They felt they could do anything together.

It was almost 7:00 p.m., and people were arriving at the Grange for the nightly meeting. The Team sat with the Crew, and listened to the nights' meeting, while their taste buds were still remembering the strawberries and biscuits filling up their stomachs.

# Chapter 176

## *Walk-Ons*

### (July 7)

The meeting started with Rich calling on Al VanDorn, and Kate Henley, who helped keep track of the coming and goings of non-residents into Pierce Point. Kate was in her fifties, smart and quiet. Part of her job was to verify if a person was really a Pierce Point resident who hadn't been able to get there until then, and was showing up for the first time since the Collapse. That was pretty easy.

The harder part of her job was handling requests from strangers coming to the gate who wanted to live in Pierce Point. Kate and Al would interview the stranger and see if he or she had some skills or equipment that could be contributed or, if they were leeches instead. They would make a recommendation to the community and the residents would vote on it at a Grange meeting. So far, there hadn't been any votes on letting people in because no one worth considering for admission had come to the gate. There were plenty of strangers who had come to the gate, but they were clearly not worth even asking the residents about; most seemed like drifters and petty criminals.

"We're seeing something new now," Al said. "A spike in strangers coming to the gate who might be decent candidates for admission," Al said. It had been over two months since the Collapse and the flow of decent people at the gate was just now spiking? Grant wondered. Then he realized what had taken people so long to start coming out to the country to try to find a place. The long walk, for one. The roadblocks, for another. He assumed that as long as there was enough in the stores to survive and the FCards were flowing, people wouldn't come. But now they were.

Maybe the government increasingly wasn't able to get enough in the stores, Grant thought. Maybe the crime was getting too awful. Maybe the government was starting to take away FCards from "trouble makers." That would make sense. He had a hunch that many of the people out in the country who were trying to find a place to go were political troublemakers, which meant Patriots. They were very likely Grant's kind of people. People who could become fighters. People with no other way to eat and nothing left to lose.

He felt a little guilty about taking advantage of hungry people, but he had to think about the survival of his community, and he wanted skilled people for Special Forces Ted's unit that was forming up. Besides, if these people had their FCards taken away by the Loyalists, Grant was doing them a favor by feeding them, and likely getting some fighters in return. Everyone was better off, except the government, which was fine with him.

"Most of the recent ones seem like decent people," Al said. "We're interviewing them and we will have some recommendations for you tomorrow."

"What do you do with them before you let them in?" someone asked.

"We let them camp across the road from the entrance," Al answered. "We give them water."

"Are they being checked for diseases?" another person asked.

"If we think they're worth consideration for admittance then we will have the medical people look at them," Al said.

Grant didn't say it out loud, because he didn't want to alarm people, but checking for diseases would become even more important as the weather got colder and diseases would become rampant when malnutrition started to weaken people's immune systems.

"Why are we even thinking about letting people in?" someone asked. That started a long, and important, discussion.

"Because it's our Christian duty," a man said, and quoted some verse of the Bible.

"Not everyone here is a Christian," Grant said. "Not everyone is motivated by that," he added. Grant could speak with authority on that because, while he was a Christian, he was not exactly advocating the opening of the gate to let every poor soul in. A topic as critical as the standards for admitting new people to Pierce Point needed to be broadly agreed upon; it couldn't be limited to either Christians or non-Christians.

"Forget the Christian part," a woman said, "we need to take in anyone we can. It's the right thing to do."

"Anyone?" another woman asked. "They can just come in here and eat our food? I don't think so."

"Yeah," a man added. "I work fourteen hours a day in my garden and hunting. I'm just supposed to hand some stranger my food because he managed to walk to the gate? Are you kidding me?"

"Maybe we just give some drug addicts all the food in the semi," another woman said sarcastically. "Why in the world would we do that?"

"Are you going to turn away a starving child?" the first woman asked.

It was silent for a moment as people thought about this. While it was quiet, Grant thought about how he wanted to agree with those who wanted to help everyone. As a Christian, he wanted to take in everyone; he honestly did. He even wanted Loyalists to live, as long as they weren't in a position to do bad things. People would be judged for what they did – or didn't do – to help others during this terrible time, but it wouldn't be by a human like Grant. He knew he was obligated to help everyone he could.

Could. Grant was supposed to help everyone he could. Well, what did that mean? He was limited to what he was able do as a practical matter. His ability to help people was severely limited.

Grant had the deep and unshakable feeling that he was being tested by the outside thought. He was being tested throughout the Collapse to see how he reacted. If, say, a semi load of food were put in his lap, would he share it or sell it? Would he squander it by handing it out, or would he lead the community to only use the food when they needed it most? It was that kind of test. Will the example Grant set inspire others to do good things? That was a test, too. Grant felt arrogant for thinking he was part of some cosmic test, but he just knew he was being tested.

The scarcity and limited options were a test, Grant came to realize. These conditions were intentional. He didn't understand why, but he accepted that things were unfolding according to a plan. A big plan; the biggest plan.

Grant knew that it wasn't possible to help everyone who needed it. Not in this sinful, fallen world. Many of the people needing help—like the grasshoppers—were wholly or partially to blame for their predicament. They could have prepared. The signs were there when twenty-five pounds of beans were $13 before the Collapse. They could have said no to "free" stuff from the government.

Blaming people for their predicaments, Grant realized, wasn't universally true. What about the little kids who were hungry, sick, had been beaten, or lost their parents? What had they done to deserve this? He didn't have an answer for that, which troubled him.

*You will need some of the strangers coming to you.*

Grant felt his arms break out in goose bumps while sitting there at the Grange meeting. He had that amazingly calm feeling he experienced before when he realized *who* the outside thought was and

51

what it meant. Grant knew that he couldn't lose with what he was doing. He had help; he had the biggest help possible. Grant just soaked in the calm he was feeling. It was like nothing in this world.

He snapped back into the world of the here and now. It was time to get to work. Grant could see that food was the main issue, which was no surprise. That was a way to solve this problem, he thought. He decided to put his idea out to everyone for consideration.

"What if any person coming in had to be sponsored by a current resident?" Grant asked. "So if you want a person to come in, you have to feed him or her. The community is off the hook for them."

Most people seemed to like the idea. In the discussion that followed, several people made the point that if a person were sponsored, and wouldn't be a burden on the community, then there was no harm in letting them in. It would also prevent people from letting in too many people, because each sponsoring person had to provide for the new person.

"It prevents people being generous with other people's money," a man said. "We've seen too much of that in the past," he added.

"OK," the Bible-quoting man said, "but what about if no one can sponsor a person for whatever reason?"

"Skills," Grant said. "If that person has skills we need, we could take them even if no one sponsors them. Their skill might be so valuable that we decide to feed them in exchange for the community getting their skill."

"Like what?" some asked. "What kind of skills?"

"What if there is a person who knows how to run water systems?" Grant asked. "I'd love to have him or her out here in case anything happens to our well system and pump, that kind of thing."

Most people seemed to like this idea, too.

Grant's mind then switched to the topic of getting Special Forces Ted as many skilled people as possible. First dibs would go to Pierce Point, but there might be some skilled people, particular former military and law enforcement people, who could be a big asset to Ted.

Grant made a quick mental note to get to know Al. When walk-ons came, maybe Al could be in on the "Ted project" as the Team was calling it. Al could help divert walk-ons to the Ted project's compound.

That would be hard to pull off. Lots of guards would see the new arrivals come, but then they would not be seen again for a while. Grant would have to think about how to do this. The first step was to get to know Al and be able to trust him.

When the debate wound down, Al said, "By the way, speaking of valuable skills, a resident returned today. He's Randy Greene, and he's had a cabin out here for years. He's a podiatrist. You know, a foot doctor."

The crowd murmured. As an actual resident, as opposed to a stranger, they had to let the foot doctor in. Besides, the residents liked the idea of more medical people, even if their feet didn't hurt. Al continued, "Dr. Greene brought a truck load of gear with him, too. Now, he's a resident so we let him in, but that's the kind of thing I think Grant is talking about. So if Dr. Greene wasn't a resident, but a stranger, we'd be considering letting in a person with medical skills and, as a bonus, a bunch of gear. He'd probably be the perfect type of person to welcome to Pierce Point, just for example."

Grant was glad to hear Randy Greene, or "Doctor Greene," as he insisted on being called, was back. Doctor Greene's cabin was about six cabins down the beach from Grant's. Grant had met him when he first got his cabin. Greene was a big hunter and fisherman, so that truck load of gear Al referred to was probably full of lots of good stuff. While a podiatrist had limited medical skills, they were medical skills, nonetheless.

For the next part of the meeting, Lisa gave a report. Grant hadn't seen her all day. She was really warming up to her role as the community doctor and described how people were still dying from a lack of medication. Some people, like Mrs. Roth, died quickly from this. Others, who were less dependent on their medications, were dying more slowly. Now that America was over two months into the Collapse, many of these less-dependent people were starting to die.

Lisa named four people who had died in the past few days, all from a lack of medications. She also mentioned that a teenage girl who cut her hand while filleting fish had a bad infection. They had some antibiotics for the girl, but couldn't use too much on just one person. Finally, she described some of the lingering problems from people not having their mental illness medications. The very medicine-dependent had gone insane early on, but now the less-dependent were, too. Two people were detained and would be up for a mental ward commitment trial tomorrow.

Grant knew that he wouldn't be training with the Team tomorrow, at least, not until the commitment trials were done. The commitment trials were a top priority. Two people were being detained, perhaps for no reason, although if Lisa thought they needed to be committed, they almost certainly did. Another reason for Grant to miss training with the Team tomorrow was that he should probably get to know Al better. He could do that tomorrow along with the commitment trials. Training with the Team would have to wait. Grant had plenty of things to do at the Grange. He needed to accept that he wasn't a twenty-something year old gun fighter. He had different skills and a different job.

At the end of the meeting, Ken Dolphson handed out the latest edition of the *Pierce Point Patriot*. The only stories in it were the obituaries. Grant would need to go to the funerals on Sunday after church. He hated doing that. It was so depressing, but he had a leadership role out there and needed to be at community events, like funerals.

The meeting broke up. Tired on their feet after a long day, the Team shuffled toward Mark's black Silverado with the extended cab and Marine Corps bumper sticker that was outside waiting for them. Lisa got into the front cab. The Morrells got in the rear cab. The Team, including Grant, piled into the back of the truck.

The guys were tired so they didn't say much. They were excited because it was nighttime, which was girlfriend time, although they were tired. Grant quietly wondered how much more activity they could take. Oh well. It was a good problem to have.

In the back of the truck with the largely silent guys, he had a chance to reflect on the day. It had been good and bad, like so many things out here. Good in the sense that they had an amazing crew of fighters and some great equipment and training. Lots of "coincidences" that made them much better off than almost everyone. That was good.

But, the day showed the bad things, too. People dying and going crazy just because they lacked simple medications. Life threatening infections that would be no big deal when there were plenty of antibiotics. And refugees with nowhere to go who were forced to camp out while some people decided if they can come in. Grant could only imagine what it was like in places that weren't as organized as Pierce Point, like Frederickson, Olympia, and Seattle. Let alone Chicago, New York, and LA.

"Collapses suck," Grant said. He had anticipated the Collapse and had been frustrated when it was so long in coming, but he didn't enjoy it now that it had come.

# Chapter 177

## The "Ted Project"

### (July 8)

Grant and Lisa slept soundly until the sun came into their room. When they woke, they didn't even remember getting into bed the night before after the Grange meeting. Given the angles of the windows, the sun didn't come into the window until mid-morning this time of year. Grant noticed this and realized it must be late, like 8:00 a.m. or something crazy like that.

It was 8:16 a.m., to be exact. He knew Lisa needed to get up to go to the clinic so he woke her up by hugging her softly. She slowly woke up to him holding her, which she had always loved, but now it felt even better, more significant. She had often taken these quiet moments in bed for granted, but not anymore.

Grant, being a typical guy with typical appetites, was getting a little charged up from the hug, which wasn't his intention. He just wanted to wake her up and let her know how much he loved her. His lower brain functions took over and then he wanted to take the hug farther.

That wasn't going to happen. Grant didn't want to blow the cool points he was getting for a no-strings-attached hug. Besides, he could hear the kids were up, and so were her parents. Not exactly a good ambiance. He decided to fight the urge and just kissed her on the forehead.

"Good morning, dear," Grant said. "Your husband loves you."

Lisa had a big smile on her face. That smile of hers meant everything to him. It was what he lived for. Grant forced himself to get out of bed before he tried to take the hug further and then went out to say good morning to the kids and Drew and Eileen. He hadn't seen them in quite some time.

They were starting up some pancakes, of course. Grant had purchased over 100 pounds of pancake mix before the Collapse. It seemed crazy at the time; not anymore. The Morrells and Colsons (except Tammy) were coming over. Gideon would also be there as he ended his night guard shift by coming over to Grant's cabin and having breakfast with everyone.

Gideon could eat at the Grange, but it was usually hard to get a ride up there and back in time to let him sleep during the day. Besides, it took him hours to get out of the Grange because everyone came up to him and thanked him for the semi-truck of food. He didn't mind their kind words; it was just that after a night of guard duty, making small talk with people was the last thing he wanted to do.

Chip came over for breakfast, too. He was just stopping in to say good morning before he and the Team went to the Grange. Mark would take the Team, Drew, Grant, and Lisa up to the Grange where they would eat breakfast. They usually tried to be up there around 8:00 a.m. and they were running a little behind this morning.

"You still got gas?" Grant asked Mark, to which Chip laughed at the unintended double meaning.

"Yep," Mark said. "I actually don't drive much; just taking you guys around in the morning and getting you at night. Once in a while, I go out hunting. Tammy keeps my tank full with gas from work."

"How is she doing?" Eileen asked. "That horrible attack she suffered through. Have they caught the people who did that?"

Mark, who had not been told what really happened, said, "Nope. They must have taken off. There's been nothing like that around the power company. They all travel now in pairs and are well armed. Tammy insists on driving herself to work alone. I tried to talk her out of it, but she just thinks she's OK. She seems very confident it won't happen again."

They all talked about what they would be doing that day. John and Mark would be setting some crab pots when the tide got right, which was in about an hour, and then they would go deer hunting until dinner. Mary Anne and Eileen would be working in the garden and making some strawberry jam with the ripening berries. Manda and Cole would play with all the neighborhood kids. Lisa would be at the clinic all day. Chip was running the day shift of the Grange guards. He was done overseeing the Crew; they were on their own now and were integrating very nicely with the Team. Drew was keeping track of people's contributions to the community and overseeing the meal cards. He was also compiling a secret Patriot/Loyalist list for Grant.

As they got into the truck, Grant said his predictable "This never gets old." There was that armed serenity feeling again; riding in the back of the truck, AR on a sling, with his guys.

"Beats the shit out of selling insurance," Pow added, just as predictably. That always reminded them how lucky they were to be out here doing what they were doing. It was a good mental framework to begin a day of hard, potentially dangerous, work. During the ride up to the Grange, the Team talked about their girlfriends. Time dedicated to discussing tactical preparations was non-existent. Instead, they meticulously planned who would have the rooms with a door that closed and when they would rotate. That consumed their planning energies. Grant and Chip looked at each and both sighed and smiled. They'd been young once, too.

Mark dropped them off at the Grange and took off. They all went in and started to eat a breakfast of biscuits, deer meat, and fresh raspberries. Lots of other people from the community were there, engaged in several conversations about a variety of topics.

Grant saw Rich and Dan talking and went up to them.

"Good mornin'," Dan greeted him. "I'm surprised your guys can walk after what they've been doing the past few nights," he said with a smile. Word travels fast.

"Hey, guys," Grant said, disregarding that comment about the Team Chicks and getting down to critical business, "I need to talk to both of you about something pretty important. Don't worry, it's good news." Grant wanted to put a positive spin on the topic of the Ted project. He was always amazed at how much more receptive people were when someone prefaced the topic with "this is good news."

"This is something," Grant continued, "that we need to concentrate on and I'll need your planning help. It's top secret so we can't talk about it just anywhere. You guys got some time?"

"Sure," Rich said, wondering what Grant was talking about. "How about now? We can go outside."

Grant would have preferred to talk to Rich and Dan over some whiskey, but he couldn't wait until later that night for the conversation. He didn't want them to hear about it from someone else, like the Chief, Paul, Gideon, or Chip, all of whom knew about Special Forces Ted.

Grant nodded and walked outside, with Rich and Dan following him. They went outside, toward a corner of the gravel parking lot that was out of everyone's earshot. It was becoming obvious that this was going to be an important discussion.

When Rich and Dan got to the corner of the lot, Grant looked them right in the eye and grinned his biggest grin. "Well," he said, "we have some help coming." He paused and said, "Quite a bit, actually."

Rich and Dan both had an inkling of what kind of help was coming, as well as the dangers that came with it.

"What sort of help?" Dan asked.

"Special Forces," Grant said, still grinning. "Patriot Special

Forces will be training up a unit out here." Grant nodded his head as if to say, "See, I told you that would be cool."

Rich and Dan weren't smiling. To them, this wasn't good at all.

"What?" Rich said loudly. "What the hell do we need Special Forces for out here?"

"Yeah," Dan said, "we're not trying to be some military unit. We're trying to protect our people so they can survive this." He was pissed. "I've seen enough combat," he said, "I'm not looking for any more fights. I want to protect my people and get through this. Wars aren't good survival plans."

Grant was surprised that Dan didn't realize how awesome it was to have Special Forces Ted out here. But, if Dan's focus was surviving, then Grant would tailor his arguments to address that concern.

"Guys, winter is coming," Grant said. "We can't just sit around trying to survive. We need to do what it takes to reverse this whole situation. To fix things."

"By drawing attention to our little area?" Rich asked. Dan was nodding.

"These guys train covertly," Grant said. "You know how SF operates. We'll have a secret place out here. We'll come up with a cover. Besides, I know the lead SF guy, Ted. I've been friends with him for years. He trained the Team. That's why they're so good. We'll get lots of trainers and equipment. They're based...nearby," Grant said, not wanting to give away their location in Boston Harbor. He trusted Rich and Dan with his life, but saw no need to tell people more information than they needed to know.

Rich and Dan were still silent, thinking about the whole situation. The fact that the SF unit was led by this Ted guy that they'd heard about from the Team's stories, and the fact that Grant had known Ted for years, was something to ponder. This meant this wasn't some harebrained scheme with some Patriot stranger.

Grant sensed this was the time to present his best argument.

"You guys are Oath Keepers," he said, looking them in the eyes. "You get why this is necessary. You've seen this coming for years. Don't deny it. You knew that eventually it would come to this. This is our moment, gentlemen. We've been called on to do what's necessary, just like the Founding Fathers' generation. It's our turn. It's a huge honor to be given this opportunity. A huge honor." Grant kept staring them in the eyes, waiting for that to sink in.

Rich and Dan were still silent. They were thinking. Something

58

like this couldn't just be agreed upon on the fly. This was serious stuff, with many implications. And it was a game changer for Pierce Point. This would mean the Limas would be gunning for Pierce Point if the existence of the Patriot unit was discovered, as it probably would be. That meant fighting regular Lima forces, which could easily overpower the gate guards. It also meant dozens or even hundreds of well-armed strangers in their midst. Rich and Dan had heard the stories about defecting military units turning into gangs. And now Grant wanted to invite them into Pierce Point?

Dan was the first to speak. "Grant, I hate war. I've been in it. I've seen horrible things. People's heads blown off. Legs blown off. Ever seen a guy who gets blinded and comes running at you, screaming that he can't see? Ever talk to his wife?"

Grant was silent.

"A rocket attack on the Bagram Airfield," Dan said, staring out into the surrounding area. "Explosions everywhere. Shrapnel everywhere. You ever seen what shrapnel does to human beings?"

More silence. Grant was unqualified to disagree.

"You know," Dan said, "that the other side will have rockets, mortars—God I hate mortars—and probably air cover. You know what a 500 pound aerial bomb does to a few dozen of your closest friends? Or your neighbors? Kids and all. Or what a helicopter gun ship can do? That shit ain't fair. It ain't the rifles and pistols we use out here, where you basically know who you're killing. The shit they'll have is indiscriminate and lethal. And maiming."

Dan straightened up his posture, as if to deliver something he didn't want to say.

"With all due respect, Grant," he said, looking Grant straight in the eyes, "you have no idea what you're getting into."

For the first time out here, Grant was scared and wondered what he had gotten himself into. He worried that he'd made a wrong decision, a huge miscalculation.

Rich finally spoke, interrupting Grant's worrying mind.

"What can the Patriots do for us if we provide sanctuary, fighters, and a training facility?" Rich asked. He was thinking of this as a business transaction; not a greedy transaction, but a prudent one.

"Protection," Grant said quickly. He had thought of the answer to this question in advance of asking them for their blessing. "A shit load of extremely well trained and well-armed troops. It beats the crap out of anything around here. The Blue Ribbon Boys against Special Forces? Please." He sighed.

"Intelligence," Grant added. "That's another thing we'll get. We'll know way in advance of what's coming into our area and across the state. We'll be days ahead of the curve of other communities. That alone could save all of us."

"Oh," Grant said with a big smile. "Supplies. Food for the fighters and equipment. We'll be in the Patriot system. The support system. If we need resources from the wider area, we'll have them."

Grant had no idea if that was true. Sometimes a leader has to do or say those sorts of things on a whim, and then has to figure out how to make the promises come true. Grant figured this was a safe promise and that Pierce Point would get supplies from being the Patriot system. Probably. Hopefully.

"It's the beach I'm worried about," Rich said, switching the topic and keeping the conversation going, which was a good sign.

"And the skies," Dan said. "Air cover is a bitch. Grant, you need to quit thinking about this as a small-arms, police-type situation. What you're suggesting is a full-on military situation. Bombs. Rockets, helicopters. Massive civilian deaths. Maybe even your own family."

That stung. Grant realized he had never thought of any of this affecting his family. He had been thinking of himself: any impact on his family would be from him being gone for a while. In fact, Grant had only thought about the impact on his family as being that his wife would be pissed at him. Not that a bomb would demolish his cabin and those around it. Or level the Grange and everyone in it. Grant was terrified. He had not considered what a real military fight was all about.

*You will win. Faith.*

Grant got goose bumps. Actual bumps on his arms followed by that unexplainable calm feeling. Was it really the outside thought or was Grant just trying to comfort himself? There was no way to explain the calm. It was not a human thing. Grant relaxed and became confident again.

"We will win," Grant said, not really sure what he was going to say next. The words were just flowing like he had no control over what was coming out of his mouth.

"Look at how weak the government is," Grant said so persuasively that he surprised himself. "We're finishing them off. They can't mount offensive operations. Maybe in Seattle or DC or wherever, but not out here in the sticks. They don't give a shit about Frederickson, let alone Pierce Point. They've left this territory to hacks, like Winters. He's just a corrupt politician running some rackets, with a couple dozen Blue Ribbon Boys who are not exactly top-notch fighters. Rich, you saw them."

Rich nodded slightly.

"If the government was so strong," Grant said, once again wondering what would come out of his mouth next, "why haven't they attacked us yet? If they had any strength, they should have stormed in here and looked for that semi of food. You know what that thing is worth?"

Grant pointed in the direction of the gate, which was a few miles away. "What did they do to go get their extremely valuable semi-truck full of food? They sent two cops and Rich bribed them with a bottle of booze. That's all they got. Two cops who can be easily bribed. That's what we are supposed to be afraid of?"

Grant looked at Dan and, wanting to puff up his ego a bit, asked, "Why didn't the authorities come into Pierce Point, Dan? Your guards and those dogs. Did you see the look on Bennington's face when he saw the dogs? We have a unique position here, guys. We have an extremely defensible position. And assets. Dogs, guards, snipers, beach patrol. We're not some typical subdivision of unarmed and scared suburbanites—those are the only people the government has the strength to push around."

Grant shook his head. "That ain't us, gentlemen. We have a functioning system out here. We're feeding our people; they're standing in lines for sacks of flour back in town. It's a natural fit for us to work with these SF guys and get things back."

Returning to a time of decency was his best argument, so Grant pressed it.

"You like things the way they are?" He asked Dan and Rich. "You like having to guard your community full time? How long can we keep that up? A year? A decade? Are you kidding me? You know, and I know, that in a few months or a year, tops, the super gangs will be roaming." He said, referencing when separate gangs united and started massive raping, pillaging, and killing sprees. "They'll come out here," Grant said. "You know what that means."

Dan and Rich started to acknowledge to themselves that the current situation could not last. Something long term needed to be done. If the Loyalists won, they would roll into places that had food and resources and pick the place clean. Places just like Pierce Point. Or maybe the super gangs would get there before the Loyalists did. Pierce Point had no choice.

"I'm an Oath Keeper," Dan said after a long pause. "I will

honor my oath. And that means doing whatever I can to stop what's happening and fix things." Dan dreaded saying that, because he knew exactly how painful that would be. He'd seen it at Bagram.

"Me, too," Rich said. "I don't want to do this. But what are the options? You and the Team will just leave to join the Patriots. Then we're screwed."

Grant had never even thought about leaving Pierce Point in order to join up with Ted. He would never leave his family and friends, but if Rich thought Grant was threatening to leave with the Team, and that would be a reason for Rich to agree to let Ted come in, then Grant would roll with it.

"I have no intention of leaving," Grant said, which was true, "but I can't control my guys, who definitely want to join up with Ted. They already have." Grant let that sink in.

He decided to switch from mildly threatening Dan and Rich to focusing on the positive aspects of them getting behind the Ted project. "We're in a much stronger position," Grant said, "with a bunch of well-trained, well-equipped, well-led fighters who are tapped into a much larger network than our little community."

He looked Rich and Dan in the eye again and said, "In the situation we're in out here, more is better. More fighters, more guns, more supplies. We will get that with the Patriots. Or, by doing nothing, we will get slow attrition and eventual death."

Rich and Dan just stared at Grant. They were thinking.

Then Rich started nodding slightly.

"Ask yourselves this," Grant said, suddenly thinking of a great argument. "Which would Winters and the gangs rather see: Pierce Point having a big and well-trained fighting unit or just guarding the gate and beach with volunteers?"

That sealed the deal. Rich and Dan both were nodding solidly now.

"OK," Rich said, "I agree that we should explore a relationship with this Ted guy and the Patriots."

Rich turned to Dan and said, "Dan, what you think?"

"I don't want to do it," Dan said, shaking his head.

Grant's heart sank.

Dan looked at Grant and said, "However, I can see how we might be better off. But I have some questions. Like, about air cover and what kind of assets the Loyalists can throw at us. I also want to know how many other places will be like Pierce Point. Are we the only place training fighters or are we one of a hundred in this part of the state? That would have a huge impact on the odds of some F-15s flying overhead or some helicopters coming to call."

Dan pointed his finger at Grant and said, "I'm serious, Grant. I want answers before I'm OK with this. If I am ever OK with this. I want a military plan presented to me. A detailed and professional military plan."

Then Dan's demeanor softened up and he said, "I'm open to hearing the facts, but they need to be facts and not hopes."

Grant couldn't ask for more than that.

"Sure," Grant said. "I'll arrange for Ted to talk to you guys. He just pops by whenever." Actually, Sap left a radio with Scotty so they could get a hold of them, but Rich and Dan didn't need to know that. Grant felt bad keeping secrets from his friends, even little ones like the radio.

"Hey, Grant," Dan said, realizing he'd been a little too negative about this Special Forces thing, "I'm not on you about this. I am grateful that you know people like this Ted guy. I'm glad you're doing all you can to change things. I just have some experiences that mean I question all this war talk. It ain't all fun and games. I used to think so. If I get satisfactory answers, I'm all in. I'm a Patriot. I just don't want to get my people killed for no reason."

"Fair enough," Grant said. "No offense taken, Dan. I want guys like you who know more about this topic to help us make the best decisions."

"Well, time to go to work," Rich said, switching gears. The meeting was over abruptly. They walked silently back into the Grange as if they had just had a discussion about…treason. They had. At least treason to the former government.

Grant went to Linda, the dispatcher, and asked her to get Scotty on the radio. He knew the Grange radio was not secure, so he chose his words carefully. He didn't want to give too many details, even in code speak, but he wanted Scotty to be able to tell Ted and Sap that there was a valid reason to come out. Grant realized that they should have come up with some code words for many situations like this one.

After a few minutes, Scotty came on the radio. "What's up, man?" he asked in the disciplined military protocol the Team was known for. Yet another sign that they weren't taking themselves too seriously or being mall ninjas, Grant thought.

"Ted project, dude." Grant said. "Get them out here tonight for cocktails after dinner. It's a dog and pony show for Fred 1 and Badger 9." No one had used those cheesy code names they came up with in so long that Grant had trouble remembering Rich's and Dan's handles. He wasn't sure he got the numbers right, but "Fred" and "Badger" were close enough to tell Scotty that the meeting guests of Rich and Dan were important enough for Ted and Sap to come see.

"RT," Scotty said, which was their term for "roger that." It was an acronym they came up with before the Collapse when they would text each other about when a shooting session would be. Besides, Grant felt stupid saying "Roger that" when they weren't really military or law enforcement. He also thought "RT" might throw off anyone who could be listening.

"Let me know tonight at dinner that you've made the arrangements," Grant said.

"RT," Scotty said again.

Grant handed the radio back to Linda who had absolutely no idea what he had just been talking about.

# Chapter 178

## *Sandy and Walter*

### (July 8)

Grant finished the morning with two commitment trials. He empanelled a jury and heard Rory, one of the nurses, describe how two people went off their mental meds and needed to be committed.

Rory was becoming the mental health nurse, even though he wasn't trained in that before the Collapse.

The first person to be committed was Sandy McPherson. It was absolutely heartbreaking. She was in her mid-thirties with blonde hair and was the mother of two great little kids. She originally lived in Seattle. After her first child, Eli, was born, she developed very severe postpartum depression. It got worse after the second child, Josh. She essentially couldn't function and her husband left her. It was just her — a severely depressed single woman — with two kids.

She was determined to do the very best for her little Eli and Josh, no matter how hard it was. She came out to Pierce Point and got a job at her cousin's store in Frederickson. She got on various medications and, after some trial and error, found trazodone (Desyrel) to work well and she was able to function normally. She was very proud of how hard she worked to make everything OK, especially for her kids. No one knew she had depression.

Then the Collapse hit. She only had a few days of Desyrel left. She zoomed into the Frederickson pharmacy on the first day and tried to get a refill. They didn't have any and the next day, the pharmacy closed. All the other pharmacies in the area closed then, too. At the last pharmacy she tried, she saw the sign on the door that said "Out of Business." She cried in her car in the parking lot for over an hour. She cried until her face hurt. The drive back home was the scariest time of her life. She knew she would have to try to live without Desyrel.

The stress of knowing the medication was running out and all the stress of the Collapse was too much. Two days after the Desyrel ran out, she hit a new low. All she thought about was killing herself and, on occasion, killing little Eli, age four, and Josh, age two. They were the most adorable little boys; blond hair and smiling all the time. They were so huggable and loveable, which is what drove her to think about killing them. They were so precious and innocent. She didn't want them to live through the hell that was all around her, and she was convinced that the hell of the Collapse would never go away. Never ever. Things would never get better because she would never have her Desyrel back.

She kept dwelling on the idea that she was being the best mom in the world by taking the kids out of this horrible place. She had fantasies of Eli and Josh thanking her for taking them away. She had a little gas left in her car and decided to run the engine in the closed garage and they would all go to sleep, forever.

She was trying hard to fight against the part of her that desperately wanted to do that. In a moment of panic, she stumbled over to a neighbor's house and told them what she was thinking and begged for help. She was so ashamed about her thoughts of running the car in the garage, but she knew that she had to go to the neighbors and get help. Her motherly instinct to protect her young was still stronger than the depression.

As Grant listened to the evidence in the case, he became furious at the Collapse. As horrible as the past system was with all its corruption, at least the government had managed to make sure there was Desyrel at the Frederickson pharmacy for Sandy. Now there wasn't any. The Collapse did this. Well, the government giving everything away in exchange for votes and people thinking they could live like kings on other's labor, was what caused the Collapse. But still. It felt like the Collapse was to blame for what was happening to Sandy.

He hated the Loyalists even more right then. They had built up a system that was bound to fail and it was hurting people like Sandy. And Eli and Josh. Loyalist officials in Olympia, Seattle, and certainly Washington, D.C. had all the medication they needed. Pierce Point could go to hell as far as they cared. Sandy could go to hell; she was already there. The Loyalists would never know about her, or Eli or Josh. Sandy and her kids were a problem for the hillbilly teabaggers to solve.

Challenge accepted, Grant thought. We'll do the very best we can.

The neighbors had locked Sandy in a room in their house, which was what Sandy had asked them to do. Pleaded, actually. The neighbors went over and got the kids, called more neighbors and decided to take Sandy to the Pierce Point clinic so see if there was anything they could do for her. Lisa and Rory checked her out and quickly realized that there was nothing medically they could do without some more Desyrel. Sandy asked that she be put somewhere where she wouldn't hurt the kids. She was relieved, in some small way that her secret was out. Hiding this had been more of a weight than she realized.

This was a very easy case. The jury took about five minutes to come to a decision. Sandy needed to be confined; she was asking them to do it. She wouldn't be in the mental house because there were raving lunatics there and Sandy didn't need that. She would stay with the neighbors. Eli and Josh would stay with some volunteers—a nice couple whose kids and grandkids were trapped in Tacoma—and would get to see their mom as often as possible. Pastor Pete was organizing visiting parties to make sure Sandy had many visitors. She would have people around—many of them people she hadn't known before the Collapse—to keep her spirits up. They would remind her that she was not alone and that the community was doing all it could to help her, because she mattered. And that she was a great mom for saving Eli and Josh.

The community, Grant thought. Yes, the community was taking care of Sandy and Eli and Josh. Was this the socialism that Grant hated? Not at all. People helping people wasn't socialism; it was merely a reflection of a healthy society. People privately helping other people, without coercion, was a humanitarian society. The government forcibly taking money from people, wasting it on their politically connected buddies, and giving people the scraps from the spending, like Desyrel, was socialism. Grant had to admit that a constant supply of Desyrel would help, and at some level the former government did manage to make that happen, but Pierce Point would do a pretty good job of helping Sandy. Eli and Josh were young enough that they might not remember when they stayed with the nice people.

Sandy showed her appreciation by doing all the work she could for the community. She came up with a brilliant idea: the battery bank. She organized a drive where people took out all the batteries from things they no longer used, like the remote control for the TV, and sent them to the Grange. Sandy sorted them and put them in tubs. She put sheets of cloth between rows so the contacts didn't touch and drain them. People who were working for the community and needed batteries could come in and get them. Plus, the battery bank gave Sandy a chance to talk to people and feel like she had a job.

The second commitment trial, for an old man named Walter Winces, was not a sad story. No one really knew much about Walter; he was a bit of a hermit. One day, Walter's neighbor's dogs started barking, like they always did. Walter told them to shut up. He came over with a rifle and said he was going to shoot the dogs if they didn't quiet down.

He wouldn't stop screaming at them. The neighbors got their own guns out and Walter ran away. Then he went, with his rifle, to the other neighbors' houses in his area and started screaming. He started smashing their mailboxes with his rifle. A neighbor used his CB to call the Grange, but before the Grange could get anyone there, Walter dropped to the ground and started crying. A brave neighbor girl ran up and kicked his rifle out of the way and another girl grabbed it. Walter was in a fetal position wailing.

Rich came and handcuffed him, and then went into Walter's house and found all the pictures of what appeared to be his wife on the kitchen table. She had died five years earlier. Walter wasn't drunk and wasn't on any medications. After he calmed down, which took over an hour, Walter told Rich that just couldn't stand living like this anymore. The barking dogs sent him over the edge. Walter said he was sorry, but didn't want to live anymore. When Rich asked if he thought he'd do it again, Walter said, "Yes." Rory came out to Walter's house and could not point to any apparent medical condition. It appeared that Walter had just decided he wanted to die and was going out kicking. He was a mean old bastard; pathetic but mean.

The jury, hearing all this evidence, decided to put Walter in the mental ward, at least for a while. He would get weekly evaluations by Rory and then Rory would report back. Walter didn't seem to care. Whether he was locked up in the mental ward or stuck in his house with all those pictures of his late wife, he was just waiting to die either way. Walter later apologized to his neighbors, and then asked them to kill him.

Grant wondered whether Walter going nuts was from the Collapse. Maybe, maybe not. The stress of the Collapse was overwhelming. It felt like the world was ending. Some people could adapt to that mentality, that type of living. Some couldn't and the stress impacted them in different ways.

Maybe, Grant thought, it just seemed like there were more people going crazy like Walter. That was probably part of it. In peacetime, the police, courts, and social workers just took care of the Walters of society. Most average people woke up the next day and had no idea that a man was screaming at his neighbors, except the people paid to deal with it. Now the whole community dealt with it, like the jurors sitting there listening to this.

It was lunch time. Grant ate lunch with the jurors since their cases were over and it would now be proper to interact socially with them. He loved meeting all these new people and learning how things were going with them, what they were eating, how things were being shared, and, in some cases, who wasn't sharing. He gained an enormous amount of intelligence about the operations of the community from those informal visits.

Besides, Grant had to admit, he was an elected judge and had to take every opportunity to meet people voting for him.

It was time for Grant to talk to Al the immigrations guy.

# Chapter 179

## *Undecideds*

### (July 8)

Grant hitched a ride down to the gate. There was usually a vehicle ferrying people every few hours between the Grange and the gate ferrying replacement guards and bringing them food.

Grant had originally planned on telling Al all about the Ted project because he assumed Rich and Dan would be on board by then, but they were still thinking about it. So, until they were on board, Grant couldn't tell Al because that would be a little presumptuous. This delay was probably a blessing in disguise because Grant needed to get to know Al before he could trust him with life-and-death information, like the Ted project.

When Grant arrived, he was glad about what he saw. Ever since the false alarm attack on the gate, the guards were even more organized and disciplined. They looked like a real army, except for the lack of uniforms and standardized weapons. But other than that, they looked like a formidable force. They weren't the average Bubba guards; Dan had whipped these good ole' boys and country girls into a very professional force.

While Grant was unloading the food on the truck he had ridden in on, Dan came up to him.

"To what can we attribute your visit, your Honor?" Dan asked Grant. He knew Grant was working on his goal of getting the Ted project going and that Dan was not yet on board. He was a little pissed that Grant was down there; probably trying to poach Dan's best guards for the Ted project.

"I'd like to talk to Al," Grant said, "about how things are going with people coming in and out of the community. Find out what's going on here on the ground."

Al heard his name and came over.

"Judge Matson," Al said as he extended his hand to shake Grant's. Al, like just about everyone else, had lost a little weight in the past few weeks. He was tan, too, which was new. When Grant first met him, it looked like Al's sixty or so year-old balding self hadn't been outdoors too much in the past few decades.

"Oh, please, Al. 'Grant' is fine," Grant said.

"OK, Grant," Al said. "What can I do for you? This isn't about all the hitchhikers I killed, is it?" He said with a smile. Grant liked to see a sense of humor.

"Well, yeah, it is. You're coming with me," Grant said with a smile, too. "No, I just want to find out what you're doing down here. How everything is going for you. What kind of people are coming to the gate."

"Sure," Al said, a little flattered that the "big wigs" wanted to see what he was doing out there. He had been doing this for several weeks and no one had shown any interest in it. Now he felt important. Al motioned for Grant to follow him into the fire station and the little table Al used as his desk.

"Well, most of the time I'm just a backup guard," Al said, pointing over toward his shotgun which was against the wall of the fire station near his desk. He had a revolver on his belt, too. Al, who wasn't in great shape, wouldn't be a frontline guard in a firefight, but he could sure help.

"Dan tells me what I can do to help," Al said. "That's usually making sure everyone eats, knowing who is on which shift, helping unload things, keeping an eye on the guards to make sure they're not too tired or getting heat exhaustion. That kind of thing."

Grant nodded. This guard force was a very well-oiled machine.

"There are two kinds of people coming to the gate: residents and strangers." Al said.

"Wait," Grant said in a panic. "Residents are coming and going?" Rich had said only approved people would go into town on the FCard runs; approved people who would maintain the story about the "fifty Marines."

"Oh, no," Al said. "There are the town run people. They're the guys Rich and Dan have to go into town with the FCards. They bring back food. Dan said that only certain people go into town; the well-armed ones. Apparently, it's really dangerous in Frederickson and along the road to and from."

Grant was relieved. The town runs were made by the same people. Thank goodness.

"So," Grant asked, "if residents aren't coming and going into town, why are residents showing up at the gate?"

"They have been trapped in a city like the foot doctor," Al explained. "They're making their way here, which can take a very long time with all the roadblocks. Almost all the residents who are showing up now are cabin people. They have a place out here and didn't get out of the cities when it was easier to do. Gas is so hard to get that some people had to save up gas until they had a full tank, which can take a while with what gas is going for in the cities. But eventually they are getting here. And they're damned glad to be here."

Hearing this reminded Grant how fortunate it was that his family came out when they did. He couldn't imagine them trying to get out there now. He thought of what a gang's road block might demand of his wife or even — God forbid — daughter to get through.

"Some of the people coming to the gate are residents or their approved guests," Al continued to explain. "I tried to get a list of all residents, but one doesn't exist, so I try to figure out who knows who. Who I can get a hold of to verify that a person is a resident." Al pointed over to Heidi, the communications person. "It really helps having her. She can call into the Grange and connect us with someone who can verify if a person lives out here. Sometimes it takes a few hours to get a person verified, and they usually get mad having to wait. But, it's my job to make sure some criminals don't walk right in. Why have all these guards and this gate if dirt bags can just walk in?"

Grant nodded.

"Residents are pretty easy to verify," Al continued, "even if it takes a while. The harder ones are the residents' guests."

"Isn't there a list people provided of their approved guests?" Grant asked, remembering that this was discussed at a Grange meeting.

"Yeah, there's a list," Al said. "But sometimes relatives or friends who aren't on the list try to show up. They remember someone had a cabin out here and they come hoping their uncle or friend or whatever will let them stay. That means we need to reach the resident and ask them if it's OK to let the person in. The resident almost always says 'yes' when they are put on the spot like that."

"That's when the Immigrations Committee kicks in?" Grant asked.

"Yep," Al said. "If a resident says they will sponsor a new person, we take it to the Immigrations Committee, which is pretty much me and Kate Henley. We get the information about what resources the resident has to support the new person. We take that information to the Grange and they vote on whether to let the person in. They approve people when there is proof the resident can take care of them."

"We also report to the Grange if people show up with food and

72

guns," Al said. "Oh, and if someone looks like they might have health issues, I get one of the medical people to look at them."

"So most people coming in don't get a medical screening?" Grant asked.

"Nope," Al said, "they don't. I think that needs to change, especially if the rumors are true."

Grant got scared. "What rumors?"

"There is supposedly some flu or something going around," Al said. "Mostly on the East Coast. The rumor is that it's bioterrorism, but we hear so many wild rumors, I have no idea if that's true."

"At the next Grange meeting," Grant said, "I will support medical screenings for all new people coming here." Grant, by saying "I will support," sounded like a politician. He caught himself sounding that way, but didn't care. It was important to do whatever it took to prevent a disease from infiltrating Pierce Point. Grant needed to do what he could to make sure it didn't happen, even if that made him a "politician."

"So far, there haven't been any 'neck tattoos,'" Al said, referring to the Grange discussion a few weeks ago about a resident's approved guest who looked like a criminal and whether to exclude them even if a resident wanted them in.

"What about strangers?" Grant asked.

"Like I said at the Grange," Al answered, "we've seen a spike lately. Today, for example, we've had four. Three were kids. Well, college kids. The fourth was a homeless-looking guy. We turned them away. We let them fill their water bottles in the creek and told them to move along."

Al paused and looked out at the gate. "The strangers that come by are telling us that there are people walking on the roads with their things. We should be seeing many more coming here."

Al started getting a little choked up. "I hate turning people away, especially the little kids. I get nervous every time Heidi says someone is coming—how does she know in advance? It's like there's an observation post out there."

Grant knew that Sniper Mike was calling in approaching people to Heidi, but Grant didn't want that getting out, so he changed the subject.

"Do you work twenty-four hours?" Grant asked.

"No, I try to go home at night," Al said. "We just hold onto people who come overnight and I sort them out in the morning. Since deciding who to let in is so important, and I'm the only guy who really knows who to let in, Dan thought it made sense for me to be the only one making that decision."

Grant was surprised there weren't more strangers trying to come in. He had always thought of a collapse resulting in roving bands of homeless people, but he hadn't appreciated how different a partial collapse was. The government's ability to supply some level of food to the cities and to keep the utilities on was apparently slowing that down. Grant assumed this meant there was probably more food in the cities than people could find out wandering around. Good.

"I'm former Border Patrol," Al said. "Kinda comes in handy now."

"When were you in?" Grant asked.

"Just three years, back in the eighties," Al said. "I was in south Texas. The job sucked. I got out and went into construction. Did that for twenty some odd years."

Grant asked Al about his life story. Where he grew up, whether he had any kids. Al told him that he had been married and divorced, had three kids, and four grandkids. Leading up to the Collapse, Al had lived on various government programs, like unemployment, earned income tax credits, mortgage assistance, and food stamps. He was just like about half of Americans before the Collapse. Al, who was a baby boomer, was expecting a comfy retirement with Social Security and free medical care. It no longer appeared that this was a reasonable expectation. To supplement the government programs he was barely living on, Al worked side jobs for cash before the Collapse. Under the table, of course. He was a very typical American. His story was the story of how the American dream died. And why it died.

Grant wanted to know even more about Al than that life story told him, so he popped the question.

"Not that it matters," Grant asked, "but may I ask what your politics are?" Grant realized this might be a sensitive question, but he needed to know if he could trust Al with knowledge of the Ted project.

Al shrugged. "They all suck."

Fair enough. Both parties contributed to the Collapse, one at a moderate pace and the other at warp speed. Still, Grant needed to know more about Al.

"So, what do you think will happen in the long term?" Grant asked.

Al shrugged again. "Dunno. Things will suck for a long time. America blew it. We had it all and pissed it away."

Al was a tough nut to crack. Grant decided to try it from

74

another angle; a more direct angle.

"You think the Patriots or Loyalists will win?" Grant asked Al.

"Depends," Al said. "Are the American people worth a shit anymore? If people want freedom back, the Patriots will win. Assuming they hold onto the key military units, like I hear they are, then the Patriots have a chance. But, if the people," Al pointed out toward Frederickson and Olympia, "just want 'free' food, then the Loyalists win." He shrugged again.

Al was not giving Grant any indication which side he was on. Maybe he wasn't on a "side."

Grant realized Al was like the majority of people at Pierce Point: an Undecided. They probably wanted the Patriots to win. They were not a fan of the Loyalists, but were not willing to commit to the Patriots, either. They would wait and see who was going to win, and hope it wasn't the Loyalists. Grant needed to plant some seeds of political thought in Al, even if Al was still a solid Undecided.

"What do you think would happen to us if the Loyalists somehow won?" Grant asked. He threw in the "somehow won" to indicate confidence in the Patriots.

Al shrugged again. "Not much would change. We would still have to wait in line for flour and potatoes. Gas would still be scarce, or for sale by the gangs. Crime would be out of control. Small business would be impossible. It would be a lot like things are now, but maybe a little better because we'd be used to it by then."

Al had a good grasp of the situation. One didn't need to be politically minded to understand the political effects of things. A person could be like Al and just know that things would suck if the current people stayed in charge. That was about all the politics someone needed to know. Luckily, most Americans had Al's common sense. But, like Al, they were just shrugging and trying to get through another day. They didn't have any grand plans about fixing the problem.

"So, Al," Grant asked, "what happens if the Patriots win?"

"Well," Al said, "that will take a war, for one thing. That will suck. People will get killed, including lots of Patriots, like you," Al said with a smile.

Al thought some more and said, "The food will stop flowing, at least from the government, and at least for a while until the Patriots can get things back on track, if they can. That's an open question. How do you fix this place?"

"Long term, what happens if the Patriots win and fix the

place?" Grant asked. He was giving it one more try.

"We get America back," Al said. "My grandkids have a chance to live in a free and prosperous country, like I did." Then Al smiled slightly and nodded slowly. Bingo, Grant thought.

"Yeah," Al said. "We get America back." Grant decided to try to get a commitment from Al.

"Isn't that worth fighting for? For your grandkids?" Grant asked.

Al thought for a moment. "Yeah, I guess. But it depends on whether I'm fighting on the side that can win. If not, I'm just getting myself killed, for no reason."

"What would you need to know about the Patriots to know that they are going to win?" Grant asked.

"I'd need to see some victories," Al said. "I'd need to see the Loyalists crumbling. I think the Loyalists are big talkers and have lots of stuff on paper, but once those Freedom Corps dicks and corrupt cops and scared nineteen-year old soldiers who are in the National Guard just for the free college actually start getting shot at, I wonder if they'll run. That's what I need to see: Loyalists crumbling." Al thought some more.

"Oh, and one other thing that I would need to know," Al said. "And that's whether the Patriots can run things better. I don't want the new guys to suck as bad as the old guys—or maybe suck worse. I hate politicians and I need to know—I need to see with my own eyes—that the Patriots are getting things done and taking care of people."

Grant couldn't resist. "You mean like feeding people, schools, a library, postal service, guards, beach patrol, police, court system…"

"… and a newspaper," Al said with a smile, obviously onto Grant's mild bragging. "Yep," Al said, "what you guys are getting done out here tells me that it can be done, but I'd need to see things squared away in the whole country like they are here."

Grant nodded. He realized that Al was like the majority of Americans. They basically wanted the Patriots to win, understood that it wouldn't be easy, and would wait to throw in their support until they saw the Loyalists crumbling and that the Patriot way got things done. Speeches wouldn't persuade them. Winning, feeding people, and acting fairly would. This is why it was so important for the Patriots to lead by example, to do things right, and to not abuse people.

*Resist revenge. That's why you're here.*

That was one of the most powerful messages yet.

That's it! Grant thought. He was out here not only to help get

Pierce Point through the Collapse, but to try to prevent Patriot atrocities against Loyalists.

*Yes. I will help.*

There was that indescribably calm and confident feeling. Grant couldn't lose. He had help.

"Al, I might need your assistance, secretly. You OK with that?" Grant asked, suddenly surging with confidence.

"Depends," Al said. Predictably.

# Chapter 180

## *Dealt a Historic Hand of Responsibility*

### (July 8)

After talking to Al, Grant spent the rest of the afternoon with the guards. He wanted to know exactly how things were going there. How their spirits were, how organized they were, how well they were armed, how their communications systems worked. He was very impressed. Dan was an amazing leader.

Around 5:00 p.m., a truck came down from the Grange with dinners. Grant helped serve the food and then helped pack up some supplies that needed to go back to the Grange. He hopped a ride back there.

When Grant got to the Grange, he saw Drew, pulled him aside and asked, "Can you get me the home address for Al VanDorn?"

"Sure," Drew said as he looked at the plat map. He told Grant the address and Grant looked at the map and sketched out a crude map of the surrounding area on a napkin. Drew didn't even ask why Grant might want Al's address.

A few minutes later, the Team rolled into the Grange. They'd been training all day at the Richardson House and were tired and hungry, like the day before. After letting them settle in, Grant grabbed Scotty.

"Call made," Scotty whispered. "Guests coming tonight at dark."

"Does the Chief know?" Grant asked.

"Way ahead of you," Scotty said with a smile.

"You know, man," Grant said, "the girls can't be over tonight when the guests are there."

"Oh, I know," Scotty whispered. "And it sucks. But I'll do it for my country," he said with another smile. "Besides, I'm tired. Two days of this training. We'll be up late tonight with the visitors. I need some sleep tonight."

"Ha!" Grant said. "Feel my pain. The pain of an old guy. You never thought you'd turn down lovin' just to sleep, did you?"

"Never," Scotty said. "Now I know how much it sucks to be one of you old dudes." In two weeks, Scotty would turn twenty-three.

Grant started to eat dinner with the Team and the Crew. Scotty was telling them that they needed some sleep tonight and that the girls needed to take a night off. Everyone agreed, except Wes.

"C'mon, guys," Wes protested, "just because you're tired pieces of shit doesn't mean I have to suffer."

Then Scotty mouthed "Ted" to Wes.

"Oh, never mind," Wes said. "I could use a night off."

Scotty saw one of the girls serving food in the kitchen. "I'll break the news to them," he said as he got up to talk to her.

While Scotty was having his conversation, Grant saw Lisa getting dinner. "Excuse me, gentlemen," Grant said. "I'm going to eat dinner with my girlfriend." Grant joined her, as she was sitting down with the other medical people.

"May I join you?" Grant asked Lisa.

"I guess so," she said with a slight smile. He could tell she was tired.

He asked her about her day, which consisted of a lot of work for the medical team. They were hampered by a lack of medical supplies and the lack of transportation. They couldn't go out to see people, except in emergencies when it was worth the gas. People had to get patients to them in the clinic, which was hard to do. They had to find a ride or walk. Everyone was realizing how much they had taken transportation for granted before the Collapse.

The Grange meeting was very short, and Rich came into the Grange at the last minute and announced that he had no updates. He asked if anyone had anything that needed discussing. No one raised their hands. "Good night," he said. People started leaving.

Grant talked to some people for a while, while Mark waited around to take everyone back to Over Road. Drew and Lisa got into the extended cab of Mark's truck and the Team, including Grant and Chip, got into the bed for the familiar ride home. There wasn't much chatter on the ride back, as people were tired.

They pulled onto Over Road and there was Gideon on guard with his borrowed AK-74. He waved them through, but was looking at each person in the truck to make sure everything was OK. He was an outstanding guard. They were so lucky to have him out there.

Everyone slowly piled into their cabins. The Team was dragging their gear a little bit. Grant really looked forward to seeing Cole and Manda. He missed them. He didn't know if he would ever adjust to this new schedule that didn't allow him as much time with his kids as he'd had before the Collapse. He had worked his tail off before the Collapse, but it seemed like he was working even more now, even though he didn't have a traditional "job." Now, surviving was his "job."

When Grant and Lisa opened the door, the kids came running up to them, like they did when they were little. It was heartwarming. Grant and Lisa asked them about what they did that day. They told stories. Ellen described how well Cole was talking recently. They spent the next two hours...being a family. Grant was even home early enough to tuck Cole in.

"Thank you for tucking me, Dad," Cole said with a great big smile. Grant melted.

"You know, Cole, that I want to tuck you every night," Grant said. "But sometimes I have to work during tucking time."

"I know, Dad. You're keeping us safe," Cole said.

Grant melted again. He started to tear up. Cole might not be able to talk well, but he knew what was going on.

For those two hours of family time, Grant wasn't thinking about war, supplies, politics, or medical care. It totally vanished from his mind. It was like he was a different person. Grant was about to say he was like his old self, but he realized that wouldn't be exactly accurate. He was like his old self in the sense that during family time he wasn't a judge and organizing a guerilla band, but his old self didn't appreciate his family as much as his new self. His old self cared more about his career; his new self-appreciated his family. Those two hours with the family were the best of both worlds: his old self having the time to hang out with the family, and his new self-appreciating it.

After tucking in Cole, Grant went downstairs. It was dusk and would be dark in about a half hour. He wanted to see if Lisa was available for...the perfect end to the day. He was too late. She was asleep. Dang. Oh well. She needed the sleep.

Grant sat down on the couch in the living room and, for the first time all day, enjoyed silence. He had been talking to people or listening to them since the early morning. He just soaked in the silence until someone knocked at the door. He unholstered his pistol out of habit, but didn't point it at the door or put his finger on the trigger; he was fairly sure whoever was at the door was OK because they would have to get past Gideon first. And assassins didn't usually knock.

Grant got up and, as he was walking toward the door, asked, "Who is it?"

"Chip, man," Chip said. "You're needed. No crisis or anything. Just a meeting."

Oh crap. Back to work. Grant really wanted to go to sleep with his family. For the first time out there at Pierce Point, Grant really wanted everyone to go away. He was feeling tired of the nonstop everything.

As Grant was walking toward the door to leave the cabin, he realized he needed to quit whining about having to go to work. He was about to meet with Ted and Sap and try to convince Rich and Dan to approve the use of Pierce Point as a guerilla training area. This was important stuff.

Grant suddenly felt guilty. He had been playing with his family like a devoted family man while he was hiding from them that he was going to meet with a rebel Special Forces official to plot the overthrow of what was left of the government. He was voluntarily joining a war that he could theoretically sit out. He was risking his life and putting the lives of everyone at Pierce Point in danger, and doing it behind their backs. What kind of father and husband does that? And then acts like nothing is happening?

I do, Grant thought. I'm the kind of father and husband who has been dealt a historic hand of responsibility, and who will play the hand to the best of his ability. As Grant approached the door, he realized that he was repeating in his head the previous struggle to decide whether to join Special Forces Ted's unit. He had already decided. He didn't need this loop running in his head. It wasn't helping him do what he needed to do.

When Grant opened the door, there was no one there. He looked outside and saw Chip walking over to the yellow cabin.

"C'mon, man," Chip said impatiently. He was nervous about the meeting and wanted it to go well. Chip knew what was at stake.

"It's not dark yet," Grant said in a loud whisper so he wouldn't wake Cole, who was upstairs in the loft. It was dusk, but not dark.

"Rich and Dan are here for a pre-meeting with us," Chip said.

OK, that was worth getting him for, Grant thought. He walked over to the yellow cabin. On the way over, Gideon nodded at him as he continued to scan for threats. Grant walked into the cabin to see the Team, Rich, and Dan.

"Thanks for coming, gentlemen," Grant said.

"No problem," Rich said. "This is kinda important." Dan nodded. Rich and Dan seemed more relaxed and open to this proposal than they had been when Grant first sprung it on them earlier that morning.

Grant realized that he called this meeting so he needed to get it started. "Well, everyone knows why we're here. Rich and Dan don't know Ted like we do," Grant said, gesturing toward the Team. "And Rich and Dan haven't had the benefit of already hearing from Ted and Sap like we have."

"Sap?" Dan asked.

"Oh yeah. He's Ted's buck sergeant," Grant said.

"Here's our bottom line," Dan said, looking over at Rich. They had obviously met before hand and had worked out the terms they would ask for. "We don't want any attention coming to Pierce Point because of this. We don't want our happy little community to be a military target of the Loyalists. As I told you, Grant, I've seen full-scale military weaponry used on fixed targets and I've seen what it does to human beings. We have no defenses against rockets, mortars, artillery, helicopters, or, God forbid, air strikes. The Loyalists have this hardware and would use it in a second against a guerilla facility. Then they would probably make sure they got all the guerillas by destroying everything in Pierce Point — civilians and all. That's how it works in the real world."

Grant didn't appreciate that "real world" comment. He thought he was doing a pretty good job of navigating through the "real world" of a collapsed America, but Dan's opinion was important and Dan deserved respect.

"Understood," Grant said. "I don't want that to happen either. Obviously, this plan will only work if we have some assurances that Pierce Point won't be bombed. That's what our guests will talk about," Grant said, hoping they had some answers to Dan's very valid concerns.

"Our other bottom line," Rich said, "is that we don't want our guards or you guys poached by the SF guys. We need to keep some defensive capabilities here."

"Another valid point," Grant said. "And it is something Ted can address." Hopefully, Grant thought. Grant knew that the Team was joining Ted's unit, but he would let that fact come out later in the conversation.

"While we're waiting for Ted," Grant said to Rich and Dan, "we should fill you in on how we know him and why we trust him." The Team spent the next half hour talking about how they met Ted, how he helped train them at the range, and how devoted Ted had been to Oath Keepers since the beginning. They told Rich and Dan about the briefing they had from Ted on the Free Washington State Guard's

Special Operations Command there in Boston Harbor. Rich and Dan seemed impressed. They had not heard how weak the Loyalists were. The idea of having a semi-open Patriot Special Operations Command so close to Olympia was intriguing to Rich and Dan. It meant the Loyalists were far weaker than they had thought. If the report about Boston Harbor was true, which was a big IF in their minds, they could more easily see how they could win this thing. They trusted Grant, but expected descriptions of things to be slanted in favor of the Patriots.

"No offense to your friend Ted," Rich said, "but I'm gonna need to see this with my own eyes. I'm not betting several hundred lives at Pierce Point, including mine, on your friend telling you something."

"No offense taken," Grant said, even though he was a little offended. Not really offended, but disappointed that Rich and Dan didn't just accept his judgment. Grant and the Team had signed on with Ted's unit without verifying the Boston Harbor situation. Was Rich saying that they were stupid for signing up without verifying things?

Rich was right, Grant realized. Trust but verify. Especially when your life, your family's lives, and the lives of several hundred neighbors are on the line.

Scotty's radio crackled. It was the Chief. "Guests arrived."

Dan looked at the radio and asked, "The Chief knows about this?"

"Yep. They come by boat," Bobby said.

"Who else knows about Ted?" Rich asked. He was getting concerned.

"Don't worry," Grant said, even though he was a little worried, too. "Only the people who have to know so they can make beach landings and meet with us. That means the Chief, Paul, and Gideon, and the people in this room. I haven't even told my wife. I'll wait until the last minute before I destroy my marriage," Grant said very flatly. He wanted everyone to know how committed he was to this.

"I'll go down and bring them up," Ryan said, grabbing his AR.

"I'll join you," said Bobby. He was tired, but meeting your Special Forces liaison on the beach wasn't something you got to do every day. The young guys on the Team were a little more star-struck by Ted and Sap than the old guys were. The "Ted project" was a young sheepdog's dream.

While they were waiting for their guests, the men in the yellow cabin talked about little things at the Grange. Chip talked about how his Grange guards were working out and Grant told Dan how impressed he was with what he saw of the gate guards that day.

Finally, the guests arrived. Ted and Sap had on full kit. They each had an M16A4 with an M203 grenade launcher. They had plenty of grenades on their kit. Sap had a very sophisticated radio with a computer keyboard on it. They were wearing uniforms that said "Free Wash. State Guard" on the name strip that had formerly said "U.S. Army." They looked very professional. Grant was sure this would impress Rich and Dan. Ted and Sap wanted them to know that they were real military operatives and they had ample supplies of the good military-grade hardware. They weren't bubba guards. The grenade launchers successfully made that impression.

More important than the military trinkets, Ted and Sap were politically well prepared. Ted walked right up to Rich and Dan and shook their hands. Sap did, too.

When Ted shook Dan's hand, he said, "Master Sergeant Morgan. Nice to meet you. I understand your Air Force Security Forces background has been pretty helpful out here. I heard that the cop who came out here was terrified of your dogs at the gate. Good." Dan did not expect Ted to know his background. He was pleasantly surprised that they had done their homework.

"You must be Rich," Ted said, as he turned to Rich and shook his hand. "Very nice job out here organizing things. I have heard great things about you and appreciate you taking the time to meet with us."

Yes, Ted was sucking up. But, just as he'd been trained, he was showing respect to the leaders of the local fighters and he was showing them that Special Forces needed them.

Ted introduced Sap. When he shook Rich's hand, Sap said, "Former Sheriff's Deputy and current Oath Keeper, if our intelligence is correct." Rich nodded. He was a bit impressed.

Sap had double and triple checked that their intelligence on Rich was correct. He wanted Rich to know that they had intelligence on things like this and that their intel was correct. By mentioning Oath Keepers, he was subtly reminding Rich that even a stranger like Sap knew that Rich was an Oath Keeper, so lots of Loyalists probably did, too. Sap was reminding Rich that Rich had chosen sides long ago and the Loyalists knew which side Rich was on. "No way to sit this one out" was the message Sap was conveying.

These Special Forces guys were "smarter than the average bear," as Yogi Bear used to say. Back at Boston Harbor earlier that day, Ted and Sap had spent over an hour learning all they could about Rich and Dan and planning out how to persuade them. Political planning was as much, or more, of their job as military planning.

Rich and Dan were already impressed with the two of them. Rich and Dan had talked on the way over that maybe the Team had just agreed with an old shooting buddy, like Ted to go do some heroic, and stupid, military stuff. Dan had even suggested to Rich that maybe the Team was "playing Army" and was about to get everyone in Pierce Point killed as a result.

Rich and Dan were no longer having those thoughts after meeting Ted and Sap. Maybe the Patriots actually had functioning Special Forces units and Pierce Point would be one of them. It didn't seem so crazy, anymore.

Rich and Dan kept telling themselves that, while Ted and Sap were impressive, this didn't mean the Patriots had a chance of winning. Rich and Dan wanted to know more about exactly how the Patriots thought they could win.

It's hard to wrap your head around the idea that anyone can beat the U.S. military. Well, it was now the Former USA, the "FUSA" as everyone called it. For their entire lives, Rich and Dan had thought, rightly so, that the U.S. military was invincible, so the big question was whether Rich and Dan were being asked to fight the U.S. military or the FUSA military. There was a big difference; a life-and-death difference.

Ted pulled a document out of his kit. "Lt. Col. Hammond, commander of the Free Washington Special Operations Command, sends this," he said, handing the letter to Rich.

Rich and Dan read it. It was on the letterhead of the "Free Washington State Guard" and looked very official. In the letter, Lt. Col. Hammond said that he was very hopeful that Pierce Point would help in the fight to finish off the corrupt and failed government. The letter recited some of Rich's and Dan's background, especially their Oath Keeper background. Both Rich and Dan realized that if a letter like this got in the hands of the Loyalists, they would be executed. Exactly. That was one of the reasons Lt. Col. Hammond put it in the letter. "You've already picked sides gentlemen" was once again the message.

In the letter, Lt. Col. Hammond promised Pierce Point training by Special Forces personnel like Ted and Sap, weapons, food for the fighters, communications equipment, medical supplies, and intelligence.

The letter ended: "We promise you a future. The status quo is not sustainable. You know it. We need a long-term solution. That means the people who did this to us need to go. Pierce Point has been blessed with certain amazing attributes. It is time to use them for a worthy cause: getting America back. Your children and grandchildren, and people for a hundred years, will look back at what choice you made."

Rich and Dan were impressed. They were getting the royal treatment, but two guys with cool gear and a nice letter on official-looking letterhead was not something that you bet your life on. Rich and Dan needed answers to some hard questions.

"Thank you," Rich said to Ted after he was done reading the letter. "Thank Lt. Col. Hammond for the time he put into this. But we have a few questions."

"Certainly," Ted said. He knew what the questions would be.

# Chapter 181

## "It's 'Go' Time, Gentlemen"

### (July 8)

The first question was the biggest one.

"How do we protect Pierce Point from being attacked by air, artillery, mortars, etc.?" Dan asked.

Sap smiled because he had a good answer. "The Loyalists pretty much don't have any," he said.

"What do you mean?" Dan asked, a little indignant. "The U.S. military has plenty of that."

"True," Ted said. "But the FUSA military doesn't." Ted then described, at length, how most military units had either defected to the Patriots or had been ordered to sit out the fight by their Patriot-leaning commanders. After the explanation, Ted handed Dan a thumb drive.

"After we leave, put this in your computer," Ted said. "It's a series of videos showing commanders of various units who have come over to our side. They describe how their units are either fighting for us or won't be fighting for the Loyalists. There are dozens of videos of troops describing how everyone in their units went AWOL. You'll love the submarine guy who said that only three of his shipmates were left. Hard to spark off sea-launched cruise missiles or nukes with only three guys."

Sap said, "There are too many videos for us to be making this up. They have their equipment in the background. The sub guy? How could we have 'borrowed' his sub for that video if this wasn't legit? You'll see when you watch it."

Ted could see that Dan was not entirely persuaded. "Dan," Ted asked, "what does it take to launch a mortar attack on a place like Pierce Point?"

"Mortars," Dan said, "A crew, logistics to get the mortars within striking range, and safe passage to get close enough to strike," Dan said.

"Right," Ted said. "The Loyalists have very few mortars. With all the AWOLs, they have very few crews. Virtually no units left entirely intact. They might cobble together new units from the stragglers left behind, like the three submarine guys. It's hard to round up a handful here, a handful there, and make up a functioning military unit when it comes to using gear like mortars. It takes training to use them. You can't assemble a pick-up team of random guys and instantly turn them into a mortar crew."

"Logistics," Sap added, "are the weakest link in the FUSA's chain. How do they get the mortars here? They have to have fuel and trucks. Let's say they do. It takes them forever to get from Ft. Lewis to here. You would have plenty of warning that a column of military vehicles was coming. We have people everywhere who tell us everything."

"Safe passage," Ted said, "is a huge problem for a FUSA mortar crew. This cobbled-together mortar crew would get shot coming down the road, and if it came close to Pierce Point," Ted said with a wink to Dan, "I'm guessing you might have a well-trained sniper before they got to the gate." Dan had to smile at that. Chip must have told Ted about Sniper Mike. These guys did their homework, and that was reassuring.

Sap continued where Ted left off. "The gangs would want to have those mortars. So, assuming all the other stuff—trained crew, logistics—could happen, the mortar crew needs to have a heavy escort, which means using a bunch more units, which are hard to come by now. Oh, and it means using more fuel for the escorts, which is also scarce now."

Bobby raised his hand. "What about tanks?"

"Same thing as mortars," Ted said, "but worse, for the Loyalists. All the supply and logistical problems from a few hundred pounds of mortar are multiplied several fold for a few tons of tank. They burn ungodly amounts of fuel, and they're too heavy to just drive down most civilian roads. The main road from Frederickson might hold up - maybe. But, the road into Pierce Point? No way. And that bridge at the gate I've heard about? There is no way that holds a tank."

"But, a tank doesn't need a road," Bobby said. "It could just go on roadless, rough terrain."

"True," Ted said, "but, the terrain around here means that the only way to get anywhere is often right where the road is, like the road from Frederickson to here. It hugs the shore, and therefore is the only way in and out, which means that road needs to be used. This then means the Loyalists would need to repair the road the tank chewed up. They need that road for other things like moving trucks of troops or semis of food."

"Bridges," Sap said. "Most of the civilian bridges from Olympia to here cannot hold a tank. There is no way to drive one, even if you are OK with destroying the road in the process. No way."

Bobby had seen tanks used in Iraq on TV and assumed they must have been good at urban fighting or they wouldn't have been used there. Besides, he wanted to see if he knew more about the military than two Green Berets. The result was predictable.

"Well, if tanks suck so bad at urban warfare," Bobby said, "why are they used? Like in Iraq."

"Because of combat engineers," Ted said. "In a fight like Iraq, the Army had combat engineers to either make a bridge capable of handling tanks or they could repair civilian bridges damaged by tanks. The Loyalists have no combat engineers. Sure, maybe a couple of units, but they can't go around repairing all the bridges and roads necessary to move tanks now."

"Besides," Sap continued. "There are almost no tanks at Ft. Lewis and the Washington National Guard's tanks are all in Yakima at the firing range there, courtesy of a Patriot officer who is 'sitting it out.' Even if the Loyalists had tanks all fueled up in Olympia and the bridges weren't a problem, there is still the enormous problem of the crews. Most of the regular Army is AWOL. The National Guard? Forget it. They can't put together any tank crews and don't have any tanks handy. No combat engineers. No fuel. No go."

"OK," Rich said, "but you have to admit that if the Washington National Guard or a regular Army unit wants to pound Pierce Point, they could do it. Maybe not with tanks, but with lots of other stuff that kills us dead. I mean, you admit that, right?"

"Yes," Sap said. "But that assumes there is only one Pierce Point for them to concentrate on."

"What do you mean?" Grant said, wondering what the point was. This idea of more than one Pierce Point was news to him.

"The Limas," Sap said, "could rally and mount up to come here if this was the only place they had to worry about. But there are lots of Pierce Points they have to worry about. Lots," Sap said with a big smile.

"Like how many?" Dan asked.

"Sorry, Dan, can't say," Ted replied.

"OK," Dan said, "Ballpark it."

Ted thought. He seemed to be counting up things in his head. He paused. "Well, let me put it this way. There were 120 guys in our old unit, right Sap?"

Sap nodded.

"Almost 100 of them are with us now, so if it takes two of us to work with a group of local fighters...do the math. Let me put it this way: all my former colleagues are busy right now."

Fifty Pierce Points? Wow. That made quite a difference. The Limas couldn't destroy fifty of them. Maybe one here and one there, but not all fifty.

"Plus, we have significant regular forces," Ted said. "We have whole aviation units that came over. We have more helicopters than they do. Now, I admit, fuel and parts are a problem for our birds — but it's a problem for theirs, too."

"Have you heard any helicopters flying since the Collapse?" Sap asked. "Nope. With all these 'relief efforts' of the National Guard and FEMA, you'd expect lots of helos, right? But you haven't heard any. A lack of fuel and parts will do that."

"The FUSA forces were so amazingly dependent on technology," Ted said. "If just ten or fifteen percent of the technicians are gone, it is virtually impossible for all the guidance systems, communications, and just-in-time supply systems to work. Way more than ten or fifteen percent of them are AWOL. The AWOL rate in some units is over ninety percent."

Rich asked, "So, neither side has all the whiz-bang gadgetry of laser guided bombs and things like that?"

"It's worse than that," Sap said. "Not just laser guided bombs. Even the lower tech things have been hobbled for both sides. Take artillery, for example. That's a threat you mentioned, Dan. All the supply problems we've mentioned apply to artillery. Artillery shells are being stolen and used for IEDs. They're worth a fortune to Patriots, gangs, paras, you name it. But even if an artillery unit has shells, they need intel to know where to shoot them and they need communications. Just about all the intel people are gone. In fact, most of them came over to us and we have incredible knowledge about the Limas and civilian Loyalists, but I'll stick with the artillery example for now."

Sap went on, "The comms systems aren't maintained, so it's very hard to tell an artillery crew where to go. You can't really text artillery coordinates. Speaking of the coordinates, the computers the artillery pieces use need to be maintained and they aren't right now. Not just anyone knows how to use the system even if it's working. It's a mess."

"Exactly," Ted said. "So, while we don't have many operational artillery or aviation units — the threats you mentioned Dan — neither do the Limas," Ted said. "And that's worse for them. They're the ones who don't have the support of the population. They're the ones who are supposedly in control. They need to pound rebels to show everyone who is boss. When they can't do that, people notice and realize the old government really isn't in control of anything, except the gangs. We don't need to pound the Limas. We just need to survive and wait for them to collapse further, and then we waltz in and pick up the pieces. We feed the civilians and restore government services," Ted said looking right at Grant.

It was silent for a while.

"This is a lot to take in," Dan finally said. "Don't be offended, but when people come to me and say 'Let's take on the U.S. military,' I am a little skeptical."

"The FUSA military," Ted politely corrected him. "Take on the FUSA military — that's what we're proposing." He paused. "There is no more United States of America."

It was silent in the room again. Everyone there had experienced that thought in one way or another. But to have a soldier — a Green Beret — say "there is no more United States of America" was earth shattering. The statement kept echoing in their heads.

Ted and Sap went on to describe how the Southern states, including the Mountain West, had either formally seceded or just quit cooperating with the federal government. Denver was a Loyalist holdout. Most of the Loyalists from the surrounding states flocked there. In the Northeast, Midwest, south Florida, and West Coast, the Feds controlled the cities and suburbs. The rural areas were on their own. Gangs and paras were running wild. Not Mad Max end-of-the-world wild, just doing what they wanted. State Guards were springing up everywhere, replacing state National Guards. It was a collapse. A slow, quietly crashing, partial collapse. "Sap mentioned that we have great intel," Ted said. He looked at Sap and said, "Go ahead and tell these guys about Cracker Corral."

Sap described how Patriot intelligence learned of the Loyalist plan to cut rural areas off from utilities and how the Utility Treaty solved that problem. That example showed Rich and Dan not only that the Patriots had good intelligence, but also how weak the Loyalists were and how military units just sitting out the fight had an enormous impact. It wasn't a dramatic civil war with two opposing armies. It was chaos and weakness.

"And the side that is better organized and motivated will win," Ted said. "And that's us. Look at this area," he said motioning over in the direction of Frederickson. "There's us and then you've got Winters' corrupt little gangs and those pathetic Blue Ribbon Boys. Are you kidding me? But it shows that this isn't a fight of laser guided bombs versus laser guided bombs. It's these," Ted said pointing to his rifle. "Low-tech, baby."

Then Ted pointed to everyone in the room, "And, more importantly, it's people. Who is more motivated? You guys who want your country back and your families to be safe, or Winters who wants a cut of the gas sales? Which side is going to crumble? Which side is going to see this through to the end?"

"I know which side will win," Sap said. "It won't even be close. Why do you think I'm here? I could have gone AWOL and gone back to Wisconsin. I knew all this was happening months before it did. But I know the Patriots will win and I'm going to be a part of it."

Sap pointed at Rich and Dan and said, "You guys are Oath Keepers. Time to keep that oath. It's 'go' time, gentlemen."

# Chapter 182

## *Local Control*

### (July 8)

Rich and Dan had come into this meeting with low expectations of the Patriot forces, but they hadn't known the pathetic condition of the Loyalists. The news Ted and Sap had, especially the Utility Treaty, was powerful. It got Rich and Dan to start thinking it was possible to take on the FUSA.

In particular, Rich and Dan started to realize that they were better off with professionals, like Ted and Sap, than just holding out on their own. They had always thought of Pierce Point as the whole world. In their minds, there wasn't much outside of the gate, but now they realized they were just a little village in a bigger region of western Washington State. They needed the whole region to be stabilized and restored before their little village could get back to normal, let alone thrive. For things to get better, the whole region needed to get better. Maybe the whole state and country, but that may never happen. However, the few counties around them needed to be functioning or Pierce Point would never make it. Even people who only cared about their own little communities quickly realized that they needed stability outside of their communities.

Now that Rich and Dan were starting to understand the low-tech nature of this situation, having a Special Forces unit out at Pierce Point was an asset, not a liability. They now thought they were lucky to have pros, like Ted and Sap, who could help them. There wasn't a high-tech and all-powerful enemy that would crush them for having a Special Forces unit out there. They were fortunate to be part of the Patriot supply system, to get grenade launchers like Ted and Sap had, for example. By being in the Patriots system, Pierce Point could have a team of trained and well-equipped fighters, not amateurs like the Blue Ribbon Boys on the other side. Much like the Team was a gift for them, Rich and Dan were starting to think of Ted and Sap as a gift, as well.

Dan looked over at Grant who was slowly nodding like he was reading Dan's mind. He realized that Dan was officially willing to consider letting Ted and Sap come out to Pierce Point and train, and Rich was, too. But they still had some items left to hammer out.

"OK, if we were to let you come out here," Rich said, "we have some questions."

Ted and Sap knew they had persuaded them on the big picture and now it was down to details. "Sure, ask away," Ted said.

"We don't want our guards and constables, like the Team, to be poached," Rich said. Dan was nodding.

"We need to continue to protect ourselves from external and internal threats," Dan added.

"Of course," Sap said. "And speaking purely selfishly, we want Pierce Point to be very secure. We'll be here, too." He smiled.

"We won't poach anyone," Ted said. "We will bring in fighters. Many will be former military."

"Whoa," Dan said. "How many former military?" he asked. He was afraid that a big gang of well-trained military were coming in and could easily take over Pierce Point.

Ted knew why Dan was concerned; they dealt with this in Special Forces training and planning. Local leaders were often afraid of letting in a strong outside unit, but the truth was on Ted's side. He wouldn't be bringing in too many seasoned troops because he didn't have too many of them.

Ted answered Dan: "I dunno. Maybe a quarter of the unit will be military. We would like a 100-man irregular unit out here, so that's maybe twenty five. Probably fifty, at the most. They won't all be infantry types. We have lots and lots of non-combat military joining us. Navy and Air Force technicians, that kind of thing. They no longer have any technology to work on, so we can use them as irregulars. While they're technically military guys, most of them never had any combat training so, in many ways, they start off with less training than you guys, but we train them like we train locals wanting to join us."

That was semi reassuring to Dan. "Who is in command of the unit?" Dan asked.

"One of you guys," Ted said. This, too, was a topic Special Forces often dealt with when recruiting local fighters. Local leaders wanted to know that they were still in control of their people, which was perfectly understandable.

Ted continued, "Whoever the unit elects. He will get a commission as an officer in the Free Washington State Guard. Sap and I, as NCOs, are under your person's command."

Grant knew exactly what Dan's concern was and had a solution.

"Hey, Dan," Grant said, "you know how we talked at one of the first Grange meetings about the checks and balances out here of the guards and the Team being a check on each other becoming too powerful? Well, the guards and Team will be a check on the irregular unit."

"Which is another reason we want most of the guards to remain here," Sap said. Everyone noticed that Sap was now saying "most of" the guards, not all of them, would remain.

"You deserve the assurance," Sap said, "That you're protected against external and internal threats." This was going almost according to the script of how Special Forces trained for solving the political problems of working with local leaders.

"Yeah, but hasn't the Team already joined the irregular unit?" Rich asked.

"Yes, we have," Grant said. The rest of the guys were nodding.

"So you've already poached our best guys," Rich said to Ted.

"Kinda," Ted said with a smile. "But it's not like I own them. If I want to take over Pierce Point, they'll shoot me. There are just two of us. The Team can off us easily. There's your assurance you're still in control." Everyone knew that there were two of them now, but the plan was to have up to a hundred trained irregulars out there, so the gate guards and the Team as a check on irregular unit was a pretty bad argument.

"Besides," Sap said, "If Ted and I wanted to take over someplace, we have a lot of choices. We would have gone AWOL and started a gang. We wouldn't try to take over a place with guards like yours and guys like this," he said gesturing to the Team. "I'm here instead of home in Wisconsin. I'm making quite a sacrifice. I'm doing it because I want my country back. I want to train here, but then move on to fight elsewhere. Get this damned war over with and return home to a fixed Wisconsin. Pierce Point is a step in that direction, an important step, but just a step in the bigger picture."

Rich and Dan thought about it for a while. Ted and Sap could take over Pierce Point if they wanted to. Instead, they were there asking to work *with* Pierce Point. Once again, Rich and Dan were thinking of Ted and Sap as a gift.

"OK, but you only get as many of my guards as I say, and that's not too many," Dan said. "I decide."

"Roger that," Ted said.

"I want the Team, and now the support team, the 'Crew,' to remain on call for me here," Rich said. This was a big concession from

Rich; he only wanted the Team and Crew on call for Pierce Point. He had started off this meeting by saying Ted couldn't have the Team at all. "I will start having more crime here and other uses for a SWAT team. The Team and Crew can train with you guys, but are on call for me. Understand?"

"Affirmative," Ted said. "When I say that Pierce Point needs to be secure, I mean it."

Rich and Dan weren't sure that their people wouldn't get poached, but all they could do was lay down the rules and hope Ted and Sap would follow them.

"How are you going to train a hundred fighters in secret?" Rich asked.

"A very fair question," Ted said. "Before I answer that, I want to remind everyone that these kinds of issues — locals retaining control over their people, training in secret — are exactly what Special Forces does. My people have done this for decades all over the world. We've come up with some methods of making this work and spend a lot of time sharing what we have learned with each other, because if it doesn't work, we die. You guys will benefit from what we've learned."

"The precise answer to your question," Ted continued, "depends on the facilities we have here and whether the people out here are down with the program. If we have secluded facilities and the local population supports us, we can keep this secret."

"Hey, wait," Rich interrupted. "I almost forgot something."

"What?" Sap asked.

"The Marines," Rich said. That got everyone's attention.

"I told the cops in town," Rich continued, "that we had about fifty Marines and some ex-military contractors living out here. I told them that so they wouldn't try to mess with us. When we go into town to get FCard food, we keep up the appearance of having the Marines. I have some military-looking guards go into town and make vague references to the 'Corps' around the Blue Ribbon Boys. I'm sure that rumor has gotten out by now."

"So," Rich went on, "we say to our residents, if they notice a secret group of people living out here, that they are the Marines and ex-contractors. We can tell our people that we're just keeping up the appearance of having the Marines."

Chip wasn't so sure the fifty Marines thing would work. He said, "There will be some people here who see the irregulars, who are all strangers, and will ask, 'I thought the fifty Marines were made up.' We need a second explanation."

"I got it," Grant said and clapped his hand. "How about we tell the residents that we are training a few people out here? As undercover cops to go fight corruption and the gangs, and that they are some special government police force."

It sounded hokey, really hokey. There was no real government, and what little government existed was corrupt and working with the gangs. And no one would think Grant would be working the government.

"Well," Chip said, "I'm not sure anyone would believe the undercover cops story, but all we need is a counter rumor to throw out there. Just to get people saying, 'No, I heard it was a special undercover police force. Maybe the FBI.' As long as the rumor isn't 'Some Special Forces guys are training guerillas,' then that's good enough."

Marines and contractors, Grant thought.

"Hey," Grant said enthusiastically. "I've got an idea."

# Chapter 183

## *The Rental Team*

### (July 8)

"What about a 'rental team'?" Grant said.

"A 'rental team,'" He repeated, letting that sink in. "We'll say that we, the Team, are training up a second team." People looked puzzled.

Grant smiled and continued. "Pierce Point will rent out the second team to a neighboring community in exchange for food and gas. They'll be a rental team."

Grant looked at Ted and grinned. "This will explain all the increasingly large food and other supplies the Patriots will be sending out here, right?"

Ted chuckled. Already, Grant was leveraging Ted for more supplies. That was what a good leader does for his men, and Ted respected that.

"Here's what we'll tell need-to-know people in Pierce Point," Grant said. "The rental team will be working to guard some neighboring community's crops and livestock, stored food, and their people, of course. We have to keep the training secret, we'll tell people, because the community hiring the rental team doesn't want people to know they have food worthy of guarding. Also, the Loyalists might get uptight about a second group of well-armed men out here. And we can say that we are keeping the 'rental team' secret because we don't want the gangs in Frederickson or anywhere else to know we got guys with valuable guns out here. Whaddya think?"

Ted had been smiling as Grant first started describing the idea. Maybe it wasn't so bad to have a lawyer out there. He never thought he'd say that. But then again, lawyers were trained in deception. Ted's ex-wife's lawyer was a good example of that.

"Fabulous idea," Ted said before anyone else could.

"Very nice," Sap said. He was kicking himself that he hadn't thought of it.

Ted, wanting to give Rich the respect he deserved as the de facto leader out at Pierce Point, said to him, "Sound good to you, Rich?"

Rich nodded and said with a grin, "It'll work just fine. It covers all the bases: a reason for the secrecy, an explanation for why strangers are here, and an incentive for Pierce Point to have them out here and to keep quiet about it. I love it."

"Oh yeah," Rich said. Not wanting to leave Dan out, he said, "Whaddya think, Dan?"

"Works for me," Dan answered. Dan was understating himself. It more than worked for him; he thought it was brilliant.

"OK, then, we have a cover story for Pierce Point's guerilla unit," Ted said. "By the way, I'm going to bring that cover story back to HQ and suggest we use it elsewhere. I'd like you to come with me, Grant, and meet some people."

Grant felt a rush of enthusiasm and pride. Ted wants *me* to come to HQ?

"Hell, yes," Grant blurted out, just like the excited little boy he was at that moment.

Ted smiled and said, "That way you can correct me if I start to take credit for this idea." Of course, Ted really wanted to get Grant out to Boston Harbor, have all the brass tell Grant how wonderful he was, and then have Grant commit to the unique mission they were planning to ask Grant to undertake.

"I'll keep you honest," Grant said. He knew he was being wooed to get him even more firmly committed, and to get Pierce Point's support. He didn't care. He wanted to do it. He knew this was part of the plan for what he was supposed to do. He was getting that weird feeling again where he could see the pathway of what the future held. Not all the details, just the basic pathway. He knew he was supposed to do this.

With the cover story taken care of, they moved onto the next big topic.

"What kind of facilities have you got out here that we could use?" Sap asked. A long discussion ensued between Rich and Dan about some of the local properties. They settled on the Marion Farm. Grant laughed out loud when he heard the name. He thought of Francis Marion, the "Swamp Fox" in the Revolutionary War who led rebels against the British and hoped to replicate that.

The Marion Farm was a recently abandoned farm in one of the most remote parts of Pierce Point. It was near the very end of Peterson Inlet so there was a beach landing about a quarter mile from the property. The farm had been foreclosed on about two years earlier, but Ken Dolphson, the realtor, told Rich that he was still trying to sell it and that it still had electrical and water service. The utility companies weren't even trying to shut off service anymore, which was a blessing. All the livestock and crops were gone, but the farmhouse and a big barn remained. There was a large machine shop and several outbuildings. It didn't look very pretty after two years of abandonment, but that was actually good. No one would think anyone would be living there.

The Marion Farm had one little road in and out. There were not many houses on that road. The people in the houses along the road would be key; they had to be trustworthy.

"Would this place work?" Rich asked Ted after he had described it.

"Probably," Ted said. "We'll need to see it, of course, but it's a good start."

"How are we gonna feed a hundred fighters?" Chip asked.

"This is why it's nice to be in the Patriot supply system," Sap said with a smile. "We steal it. Lots of it. We have quite a few 'requisition teams' out hitting Loyalist semis. Trust me, you'll eat well."

"So this place is near a beach landing?" Ted asked. "That's how we could get supplies there. And then move them along the quarter-mile, did you say, road to the compound?" Ted was thinking. This might work, depending on what the place looked like. He at least had a solid proposal to take back to headquarters. They had done a tremendous amount of work so far tonight. They got the Pierce Point leaders on board and might have a facility.

Ted looked at his watch. He wanted to start acting on the plans before Rich and Dan had time to rethink their decision to participate.

"Hey," Ted said, "you guys mind if Sap and I go out and get a quick tour of the Marion place? We have a boat here. I want to see how the beach landing is and how far it is to the place. We won't be able to see much of the place in the dark, but it's better than nothing. I mean, we're already out here. We might as well make the most of it."

The guys were tired. But they all said, "Sure."

Dan said, "Rich, you can take them. I'm tired. And I've learned what I needed here tonight." Ted and Sap were hanging on Dan's every word to make sure he was on board.

Dan looked at Ted and Sap and said, "I'm OK with you guys coming out here with the conditions I set out: no poaching and keep it totally secret." He said this knowing that there was no way Ted and Sap could abide by these terms, but he wanted them to succeed out there. He was glad they showed up and would make Pierce Point even better than it was.

"How many spots you got in the boat?" Scotty asked. The Team had been virtually silent for about two hours, which was unusual. Everyone on the Team wanted to hang out with the Green Berets.

"Four," Sap said. "So, with Rich showing us the place, we can have one passenger."

"Paul," Grant said. "He's your most valuable passenger. He knows the tides out here. Knowing whether you can use the beach landing will be critical. Paul will help with that."

Ted had met Paul now twice when he came ashore and didn't want even one more person to know about the Marion place than was necessary.

"Could we keep Paul at the landing so he doesn't see the place?" Ted asked.

"Sure," Grant said. "It is a good idea, but he'll figure it out."

Rich got up to leave with Ted and Sap. "Well, I think we're done here this evening, gentlemen," Rich said, like he had been on board with this idea the whole time.

It was past Grant's bed time. He would have fallen asleep if it wasn't for the extremely important topics being discussed. He said goodnight to everyone and made sure to thank Ted and Sap for coming out. He left the yellow cabin and headed home, waving at Gideon as he passed his post.

Grant was a liar. He had to tell his family that nothing was going on. He had to lie. Lives literally depended on it. He thought about how Lisa would react when it was time for him to ship out with the guerilla unit and she found out that he had been lying to her for months. His marriage would be over. "Never go off to a war that you don't have to," he heard his Grandpa saying. But Grant had to…didn't he?

He spent the next few minutes in his bedroom with a sleeping Lisa as he tried to get undressed quietly so he wouldn't wake her. He was also silently debating with himself about whether he really needed to do this Ted project thing. His brain was back in the loop of debating whether he should join up and fight a war.

Grant fell asleep as soon as his head hit the pillow. That was his body's way of telling him that he had made the right decision.

# Chapter 184

## F$

### (July 9)

"Light 'em up, boys," Joe Tantori said with a huge grin as he handed cigars to his guys, the fifty plus Marines and the two dozen military contractors and former law enforcement personnel he had working for him. Cigarettes, and especially cigars, were extremely hard to come by these days. The cigars seemed like incredible luxuries. Joe was handing them out and making sure they had lighters. He was in heaven.

Joe acquired the cigars from the bank deal he had just put together. As he was distributing the cigars, he thought back on the deal he had just made an hour before.

Before the deal, Joe had been making money in a pretty much honest — but unconventional — way. During the Revolutionary War period, America had "privateers" who were essentially a private, for-profit navy. Privateers would intercept and capture enemy naval cargo and independent pirates and keep most of what they got. They would give a portion (usually) to the Patriot government or military units.

They were on the Patriots' side and were taking out Loyalist naval equipment; they just kept some of the money. It was a way for the cash-strapped Patriots to have a naval force they otherwise couldn't afford, and a way to keep groups of well trained and equipped sailors with something positive to do instead of being pirates or joining the Loyalists. George Washington used privateers masterfully during the Revolutionary War. They were a huge asset. Joe knew they could prove to be so again during the Collapse.

Joe's Marines, military contractors, and ex-law enforcement officers were a very well-equipped privateer force. He had two fast military interception boats he used for the military training he once did as a contractor. He had plenty of diesel in his underground tank, and he had over seventy men who were very well trained and extremely well-armed. They had to have something to do, and Joe had to feed them. The answer was obvious.

The waters off of Joe's compound were teeming with targets. The Loyalists were using the waters of Puget Sound to supply their fortress of Seattle. Most of the Loyalist ships were well protected, but many little ships, most of which were not well protected, took the "shortcut" to Seattle which took them right by Joe's area. In addition to the Loyalist supply vessels, there were plenty of pirates setting out to steal whatever they could.

Pirates? That sounded farfetched to Joe before the Collapse. Men with eye patches who talked funny and had parrots on their shoulders? The fake Hollywood pirates had been replaced with real ones. Modern day pirates were essentially gangs in boats. They stole, killed, and raped all they could. The pirates were vicious, as bad as any of the gangs – biker, Mexican, black, Asian, skinhead – that sprang up everywhere. They were also as brutal as some of the satanic cults that were terrorizing a few parts of the country.

The highways on land were the government's main security concern when it came to moving goods, but a tremendous amount of goods before the Collapse had been transported by sea, at least in coastal areas like Seattle. The Loyalists didn't have the resources to protect all the maritime freight, even the fraction of freight moving after the Collapse. The freight was protected by Loyalist naval units and they were very good, but most were essentially mercenaries. Their true loyalty was always in question. The government nearly stopped trying to protect all the maritime freight, concentrating on only the most important shipments that went to key places, like Seattle, and using their Loyalist naval assets to do that. The government didn't even try to protect against pirates. It was very low on their priority list.

The Patriot military forces made contact with Joe, who was an Oath Keeper and it was likely he would be receptive to the Patriot's request of him.

One day, a visitor, Lt. Cmdr. Travis Dibble, came ashore to Joe's facility. He was a young guy, in his late twenties, which was very young to be a lieutenant commander, essentially the equivalent of a major. But Joe realized why a young guy like Dibble was a lieutenant commander: he had a military academy ring on. The writing was too small to see, but it was probably Annapolis.

Lt. Cmdr. Dibble had a letter from the General of the Washington State Guard. The letter conferred "privateer" status on Joe and made him immune from any prosecution by the Patriots, provided he maintained "good behavior" during his work for the Patriots. Lt. Cmdr. Dibble explained that Joe and his men could keep whatever they needed from the supplies they recovered, but would be expected to give the remainder to the Patriots. It would be on the honor system. A

Patriot vessel would appear periodically to take back supplies Joe's men "liberated."

Dibble was very clear: if Joe's crew acted like pirates, they would be treated like pirates. Dibble knew of Joe's Oath Keeper background and said he did not expect there to be any problems.

"Besides," Dibble said holding up a GPS unit, "If you guys start freelancing as pirates, we can let the Limas know where you're at." He read off to Joe the exact latitude and longitude. "It would take about an hour," Dibble said, "for the Lima airstrike or helicopter assault to annihilate this place." That was an effective deterrent to becoming pirates.

Joe used the privateer letter to do some good things for the Patriots. They started small. They didn't have a lot of diesel, so they didn't patrol outside of the immediate area of the compound. They boarded about a dozen ships that came near their area. Most ships were carrying people who were getting out of the cities. Three were smugglers. They weren't hardened pirates. One boat was full of drugs and alcohol. Joe kept the alcohol, but dumped the drugs. Two other vessels were full of ammo, food, fuel, and medicine. They kept all of it; they needed the supplies. They captured the two smugglers who were not dangerous and turned them into laborers at the compound. The smugglers were grateful for their fate.

One vessel caused them problems. It was operated by a small band of pirates who were definitely very bad guys and were a drugged out gang on the water, which significantly degraded their combat effectiveness.

The pirates fired on one of Joe's patrol boat at a very long range, which was a very big mistake. Joe's boat radioed to the second boat and the chase was on. It lasted about 20 minutes. Joe's boats got within range and let loose with the M240s that the Marines brought with them. They had to be careful not to sink the pirate boat because they wanted the loot. They disabled the boat, got closer, and had the Marines take the pirates out with rifle fire. Man, those Marines could shoot accurately, even on bobbing water.

They recovered a huge treasure of gold and silver. The vessel also held guns, most of which were high-end antiques and obviously stolen. They recovered some ammo, alcohol, and food. Joe kept half the gold and silver and planned to buy more diesel with it. It was reimbursement for the expenses he had made while doing the patrols, especially the diesel fuel. He gave the alcohol to his men, of course.

Joe put aside the other half of the gold and silver, and all the antique guns, for the Patriot vessel to retrieve. The Patriots were very happy to have the gold and silver. Revolutions cost money; lots of money.

Joe was a little disappointed at the privateering. He thought he would make more money at it than he was, though it wasn't like he was doing it for profit. He was doing it to pay his expenses. The fuel he used to patrol was very valuable. He would go out on the water and fight all the Patriots wanted as long as they would get him the diesel.

Joe had plenty to feed his guys. They still bartered in town with people for security, which was his main source of income. They grew some of their own food and gathered lots of seafood. They weren't doing without, but Joe knew that he had some very valuable guys working for him who had options in the marketplace. He had to do something to keep his guys paid and happy.

Then he got a call from his old friend in town, Bruce Cohutt. Bruce was in his fifties with silver hair and was very distinguished looking. He had come from Georgia and still had a Southern drawl. Bruce was originally a financial adviser but came to Washington State to take over his father-in-law's boat parts shop. They made custom boat parts for yachts, which was one of the only manufacturing businesses left in the county.

Bruce had always liked Joe. He wasn't like the Yankee wimps up there. Bruce loved to shoot and Joe had invited him out to the compound a few years ago. They had something else in common: the county was trying to shut both of them down. They wanted to shut down Joe because he had a shooting range that bothered a county commissioner living a mile away, and they were out to get Bruce because he employed people who didn't work for the government. It really seemed like the county wanted to control all economic activity. They came after Bruce's boat shop with "environmental" concerns, even though Bruce complied with, or exceeded, all regulations.

"Joe, can you come into town for a meeting?" Bruce asked on the phone.

"What for, Bruce?" Joe asked.

"A business proposition," Bruce said. "You'll see. I won't be wastin' your time."

"Sure," Joe said and they made arrangements for the time.

"Where will we meet?" Joe asked.

"At the bank," Bruce answered. "The old one." All the other bank branches in town were for large corporate banks. The old one was a historic building that had been built in 1890.

"Why there?" Joe asked.

Bruce chuckled. "You'll see."

Joe went to the meeting with a small group of four guards. There wasn't too much crime in town, but Joe still travelled with security. While no one outside of his compound knew it or could know about it, Joe was a Patriot privateer. Although his role as a Patriot privateer was highly confidential, he couldn't be too safe, so it was best to take some guys in case there were any Loyalist bounty hunters out and about.

Besides, Joe was in the security business. He needed to show people he traveled with plenty of security. He had a PSD, or personal security detail, of four of the military contractors from the Dirty Dozen. Led by Andy "Booger" Borger, the former Ranger, the PSD looked like they were protecting a Congressman when they moved around. It was the perfect image Joe wanted to convey. He didn't need to feel important, but he needed everyone to see that Joe's guys were the ones they came to for security services. That's how he made a living.

Joe and his PSD met Bruce at the bank, who was there with his favorite rifle, a wood-gripped FAL.

Bruce introduced everyone and they sat down. "We're thinking about starting a bank," Bruce said.

Joe instantly knew why he was there.

"We need a bank in this town," Bruce continued. "It's hard to do business without one. Businesses will need loans at some point, and even if you're not a business, it's hard to live without a safe place to put money. What if some gang sweeps through here, like they did over in Port Angeles? People are keeping everything to themselves. We need a big ole' safe deposit box," Bruce said, motioning to the historic bank. "Here it is."

"Bank" and "banker" had slowly become dirty words over the past few months. People hated them—and for good reason. The old banks had been closed since May Day. The government had taken everyone's deposits and retirement accounts, and the banks were very happy to help in the largest theft in the history of the world. Tens of trillions of dollars.

"But people need banks, at least the kind we want to start," Bruce said. He went on to explain that the new bank would not be like the old kind that got electronic credits from the Federal Reserve and then loaned the money out and got interest back, with everything being paper or electronic. No, the new banks springing up would be like the old kind of banks: a place where value could be stored and honest loans could be made. The community would be in charge of the bank instead of some corporation in New York. Most importantly, the banks would be where money was backed up by something real, not the "full faith and credit of the United States of America," an entity which pretty much didn't exist anymore.

The new banks, called "free banks" because they would operate in the free areas of the country, would be like the ones 100 years ago. They were totally private enterprise ventures; no government involvement. Each bank issued its own bank notes, which resembled dollars and were hard to counterfeit. They were like certificates of deposit. They created their own currency, which became known as "Free dollars," or "F$."

For example, a person might deposit F$10,000 worth of gold or ammunition with the bank and receive F$10,000 worth of bank notes. The depositor essentially sold the bank the goods and took bank notes in exchange. Any person with the bank notes could walk into that bank and redeem them for gold or ammunition, or anything else worth that amount that the bank had.

These bank notes could be traded like paper dollars – with one huge exception: the bank notes were backed up with actual value. Real, valuable things like gold, silver, and hard-to-get commodities, like fuel. The bank wouldn't issue more notes than it had assets to back up the notes; if it did, the value of the notes would plummet and no one would use them. And the people in town would probably kill them.

Bank notes would be redeemable on the spot, not some electronic credits on a computer that said the person had some dollar amount and then the bank put that amount worth electronic credits onto the account of that person. No, free bank notes could be redeemed for real things.

Barter could only go so far. A person could only trade items with someone who wanted the items they had. This was a huge limitation. If the buyer and seller didn't need the exact same thing, then no trade could happen. People in Joe's area needed a currency. They needed a way to buy and sell things.

Lots of little trades were currently being done by barter. Actually, new mini forms of currency were being used. Silver coins and ammunition were common currencies. There was an incredible demand for .22 ammo, since it was small and (before the Collapse) cheap so it could be used as change. If a round of 9mm was worth $20 in FUSA, or Former USA, money, a round of .22 might be worth $1 in FUSA money. Therefore, .22 could be used to make change and to trade things with smaller values.

Obviously, FUSA dollars were worthless. Worse yet, no one even had access to their FUSA dollars because the government had taken them all away by closing the banks. FCards, or "Freedom Cards," were kind of a currency, but they were still based on electronic credits in a computer and were controlled by the government. The government could shut down a person's FCard account in a few keyboard clicks. More importantly, there wasn't always food or other items in the stores to buy with the FCards. The people in Joe's area needed a new currency.

But, if the run up to the Collapse had taught people anything, it was that a fake currency based on electronic credits and promises to repay were worthless. It led to inflation—horrible inflation because the dollars weren't backed by anything since the Federal Reserve created the dollars out of thin air. Savings held in FUSA dollars were eaten up by inflation, which meant the savings were basically taken by the government. A local currency could solve the problem.

The free bank note would only work in the areas where the notes were recognized, which was a limitation that would have to be solved later, on the larger scale. But at least the free areas, which were the rural areas at that point, would have local currencies.

There was one "disadvantage" to a free bank that was also actually an advantage. With a free bank, a person couldn't "instantly qualify" for a $10,000 credit card and go spend the electronic credits on a computer ledger on vacations, expensive clothes, or whatever. Instead, with a free bank, someone needed to have $10,000 worth of value to deposit and then he or she got a note worth that amount. The old bank's $10,000 credit card—backed up by nothing, easily spent on stupid stuff, and putting the card holder in debt for years and years— was hardly an advantage to the consumer. It was a huge advantage for the old bank and the merchants who took the fake money to sell useless things. The last thing America needed was more of the fake money, overspending, and debt that marched the country right into the Collapse.

Free banks would solve that problem by making money scarcer. That's right: less money could be a good thing. It's possible to have too much money in circulation, which can lead to $10,000 pre-approved credit cards. It also led, Joe remembered, to $100 trillion in unfunded liabilities by the federal government and runaway inflation.

Bruce continued, "People depositing things of value need to get them to our bank. And our bank needs to guard them once they got there. If a depositor has ten ounces of silver to deposit, he needs to physically get it to the bank and we need it to stay here." Bruce paused and then said, "Joe, that's where you come in."

Joe smiled. "As you might have heard," he said, "I happen to have a few armored cars. Could that be something of service to your bank?" Of course, Joe knew the answer.

Bruce smiled back. "Well, yes, now that you mention it." He gave Joe a big Southern grin that spoke volumes.

"Might you need some guards for the bank?" Joe asked with another smile.

"Hmm. I guess so." Bruce chuckled and went on to explain that they could hire local guys to hold rifles and guard the place, but they needed training for them. And, more importantly, they needed outside guards who could guard the local guards.

"How can you trust me to not rip you off?" Joe asked.

"We've known you for years here," Bruce said. "Besides, if you wanted to rip us off, you could do it now."

"And," another banker said, "Everyone in town knows that you and your guys are the only security in town. If we try to set up a bank without you, it's pretty obvious that you could ride in and take all the deposits. Having 'security by Joe' is what people need to see so they'll have some confidence in the security of their deposits."

"OK, you guys trust me," Joe said to them, "but how do the rest of the people in town trust me not to take their stuff?"

"Same reasons we have to trust you," Bruce said. "Hey, people need to trust us. If they don't, then they don't have a secure way to get their deposits to us and they don't have our bank notes to use. If they don't want to use our services, that's fine. They're on their own. They can try to buy a piece of land or a factory with ammunition if they want. Good luck with that."

"Yeah," another banker said, "we have a profit motive in making sure people trust the bank. We'll do lots of things to increase people's trust, like let people come and see our assets. So they don't think it's some myth like all the gold bars in Ft. Knox." That was a reference to the FUSA's claim that there was enough gold under guard at Ft. Knox to back up the dollars in circulation, which was a complete fantasy. At the beginning of the Collapse, it was revealed that there was no gold there.

"This will be a community bank," one of the other bankers said. "It will be by us and for us. It's local. We'll only prosper if our customers do. It's that simple."

"Trust?" the first banker said. "Sure, we're asking people to trust that we won't take off with all the gold and silver, but people had to trust that those old FUSA dollars were worth something, which was a much bigger leap of faith. A piece of paper is 'worth' whatever amount was printed on it. Really? We all saw what happened when people figured out they couldn't trust those dollars. I think we're asking people to trust us much less than that."

Joe nodded. He wanted to be part of this, to help people in his area by having a bank. He also wanted to make some money. He could have started stealing and running protection rackets long ago. Everyone in town knew that. He was a good man who used the incredible power he had very sparingly and only for good.

"OK," Joe asked, "so how does the bank make any money?" He knew the answer, but asked anyway.

"Well, eventually by loaning money," Bruce said. "But that's a ways off."

"What?" Joe asked. Banks made money by loaning it. How come they weren't going to do that right away?

"We won't loan money like the old banks," the first banker said. "They did 'fractional reserve banking.' That's where they only had to have a tiny fraction of their deposits on hand and could loan huge multiples of their deposits. So, if an old bank got a deposit of $10,000, they would loan out a million. This is why the old banks couldn't come close to paying every depositor. Remember the long lines right before May Day when word got out that the banks would be closed in a few days? Those banks never had anything close to the amount of cash that they owed depositors. We'll be different. We have to be or no one will deposit with us."

"We will have the money on hand to cover the notes we issue. Period," a third banker said. "We might loan a small percentage of our money eventually, but we'll never get into that fractional reserve banking nonsense like they used to."

"Joe," Bruce said, "loaning money won't be the main way we'll make money. Instead, we'll basically be a safe deposit box. We'll charge a fee for safely keeping the deposits. I think people will gladly pay to have their valuables safely locked up instead of worrying about gangs coming to their homes or business to steal...or worse. They'll pay quite a lot, actually. People are paying you for security contractors now. Looking at this as a business person, what good is having stuff when it might get taken? People will pay something to have their things safe."

Bruce continued. "Then, when the rebuilding starts, there will be a huge demand for credit. There will be so many businesses starting up. People will pay fairly high interest for a loan. We'll loan part of our assets—but only part, like maybe a quarter, max. We'll only loan to people we know can pay us back, like a solid business starting up in town. We'll earn interest on the loans. We'll pay people a little interest on their deposits and we'll keep the difference between the interest we charge on loans and the interest we pay on deposits. Plus, we'll still make money for the safe deposit boxes."

"But let's be honest," another banker said. "We're doing this because we want to have some security and economic growth in our town. If we make any money, it won't be for years from now." All the bankers would deposit their own wealth into the bank and use that as seed money for the bank's expenses. It was an investment for them.

This plan to start an honest bank made sense. Joe realized he had quite a business opportunity here. "So," he asked, "you would pay my company from the safe deposit charges now and maybe interest later?"

"Yep," one of them said. "Directly from the safe deposits, as in you physically keep a portion of whatever items a person gives the bank as the safe deposit fee." They started to talk about what percentage Joe's company would keep. That discussion lasted several minutes, and ended with Joe keeping 50% of the safe deposit fees for the first year because the bank's major expense, at this early point, was for security. It would take many of Joe's guys and equipment to secure the bank. It would be a fortress.

Joe was beaming inside. All of his hard work and preparations had put him in a position to essentially be a 50% partner in a bank without investing a dime, just giving his guys some work. Before the Collapse, he had worked so hard at a traditional business, only to have the government shut him down. Now, no government could shut him down, and he didn't have to pay any taxes. He would have never thought people could do quite well after a society collapses, and that they could do it honestly, without having to rob and kill for it. But it made sense: in every human situation, some people do well and others don't. Most of the population was doing horribly. It was inevitable that some people, the prepared and smart people, would actually prosper from the Collapse.

He extended his hand to Bruce. "Deal," Joe said. That was how business was done now; a group of local people who knew each other, a handshake. In so many ways, the Collapse was like pressing a giant reset button to the way America originally was, and to the way the country became so prosperous before it went insane.

One of the bankers came up to Joe with three cigar boxes. "Hey, Joe, I know you like cigars. Consider them a signing bonus."

Joe smiled. "I got about seventy guys who would love a cigar. It's a pleasure doing business with you, ladies and gentlemen." That's how Joe Tantori got into the banking business.

# Chapter 185

## *Commissioner Winters*

### (July 9)

Ed Winters couldn't sleep. Again. He was sleeping in a bed in a spare conference room in the courthouse. This is weird, he kept thinking. He couldn't get past the oddness of a bed in a conference room. Or sleeping at his office. It just wasn't right.

He felt like he was in a jail, but he was glad to be there, given the alternative, which was getting killed "outside the wire," the area outside the fortified courthouse. Outside the wire is where all those pathetic animals—the townspeople—lived.

Winters tossed and turned some more. It was no use. It was 3:45 a.m. and he wasn't going to get any sleep, which was amazing because he was so tired. He got up and walked down the hall to his office. It was just so weird getting up from bed and already being in his office. It made time blur together. There was no "work day" and "home." It was just one big, run-together blur of working.

County Commissioner Ed Winters was in his early sixties and had a full head of silver hair. He was short and thin and looked like a CEO. He was a typical politician-looking guy.

Winters was the boss of Frederickson. The undisputed boss. He liked that part. It made him smile every time he thought it because he had come out on top, just like he knew he would from the day he moved to this piss-ant town.

He arrived in the early 1970s when he was fresh out of college. He had a job in the office of the local wood products plant and rose up the ladder quickly. He was active in civic affairs until the plant closed in 1989, when the spotted owl going on the endangered species list shut down logging in western Washington. By that time, he was the assistant manager out there and "Mr. Frederickson," serving on every board and charity. He was the Grand Marshal of the Timber Days Parade for so long that people had forgotten who else had ever done that.

With the plant closing and Winters being "Mr. Frederickson," it was only natural that he would run for office. He ran unopposed for mayor of Frederickson in 1990.

As mayor, when the spotted owl crisis hit, Winters got to dole out all the state and federal money for the closed plant. All the worker retraining money, all the displaced worker grants; all that money. Gobs and gobs of it just showed up from Washington DC and Olympia.

It was largely up to Winters to decide who got the money and who didn't. He settled a lot of old scores that way. He had a very long memory. One minor comment that could be taken either as a joke or an insult ten or twenty years before was all it took for Winters to use his "discretion" to steer favors away from one person and toward another. He loved it. It was like there was a giant scoreboard in his head. The scoreboard showed who acknowledged that he was the boss and who crossed him.

Winters did a magnificent job of handing out the state and federal cash during the rough times of the early 90s. He easily won a spot on the county commission, which consisted of the three elected officials who ran the county. Now, with more territory, his reach was wider than just Frederickson. There were more permits that needed his approval, which came at a price. Not cash in brown paper bags. He was more sophisticated than that. Getting a subdivision or commercial building approved by him, or getting a county contract, or getting a cousin out of jail meant that you owed Ed Winters for the rest of your life. And he would call in the favor. At a minimum, if Winters helped someone then they would vote for whomever Winters said. They would donate to causes he told them to, most of which weren't really charities but hired Winters and his friends as "consultants." Winters might ask someone to invest in one of his real estate ventures. And they did.

Winters spent the next twenty plus years building up an empire. Nothing happened in Frederickson or the county without him. Nothing. He viewed Frederickson as his town. He owned it. The people living there were like the little plastic human figures in a toy train set. The "townspeople" as he derisively called them. They were little people playing a part, and he ran the show. He loved that.

In the early 2000s, a threat to his empire emerged: Mexicans. They started to move in, and they didn't understand how things worked. They actually ran independent little businesses, without cutting him in. What were they thinking? This was giving others in town the idea that it was possible to do things without him. That had to stop.

Winters started a campaign to shut down "unlicensed businesses." The townspeople, who were not keen on these new brown-skinned people who talked funny, were happy to rally behind their leader...and make the town "safe" by having only licensed businesses. New ordinances were passed, imposing fines and even jail time for the heinous crime of operating a little grocery or used tire business without several licenses and approvals. The city attorney — a pathetic bootlicker who did whatever Winters said — started suing the Mexican businesses for licensing violations. The Mexicans thought they had left this kind of thing in Mexico, but quickly concluded they needed to play ball. Just like in Mexico.

Soon the Mexicans came to Winters asking for relief. He told them how his "charities" and investment opportunities worked. He also told them how to register to vote. Washington State had a very strong "Motor Voter" law that allowed anyone applying for a driver's license to register to vote. No proof of citizenship was required. Hell, no identification of any kind was required. Anyone could vote – several times in each election, for whomever they were told.

Washington State went to an all vote-by-mail system instead of requiring people to physically go to the polls. This was to save voters the "extreme inconvenience" of going to a school or church every few years and taking ten minutes to vote in person. Of course, the politicians had a bigger reason to impose vote-by-mail. The county would mail a ballot to each name appearing on the voter registration list. It was not uncommon for one household to get two or more ballots per "person" because signing up with at least two names was encouraged. Multiple voter registrations was "how we do it" in Frederickson, the Mexicans were told.

All this voter fraud was actually considered humanitarian and enlightened. Winters even got a grant from the state election office to register "underserved" voters in his county. The easier they made it for anyone to vote (several times), the more they were doing to encourage minority voting. And voting was always good; politicians would ask, "You're not against voting, are you?"

To "help minorities," Winters ran a Mexican on the city council to show everyone how "diverse" Frederickson was. Everyone — white and Mexican — thanked Winters for his "leadership" on bringing the two communities together. Of course, the Mexican city council member did whatever Winters said. He got more and more Mexicans elected, and they stayed elected as long as they did exactly what they were told. All the while, everyone lauded Winters for fighting "racism" by bossing around brown-skinned people and taking advantage of them. He laughed at that.

115

Now that he was firmly in control of everything, Winters was glad to have the Mexicans in town. He was very happy to have all the new Mexican "customers" for his much-needed services, like permit approvals. He was happy to have all those votes — not just for him, but for other candidates. He could make deals with state legislators and even the area's U.S. Congressman to deliver votes in exchange for grants and government programs, that Winters got to administer. It was beautiful.

The stupid townspeople, Winters marveled, never said anything. They never demanded clean government. They never questioned what he was doing. They did what they were told. They wanted free stuff. They had been convinced their whole lives, starting in elementary school, that the solution to a problem was more government. They were so used to corruption that they just assumed that was how it was. One time, when a new editor for the newspaper came in and started asking questions, the townspeople pretty much ran him out of town. It warmed Winters' heart to see that. His townspeople loved him.

As the economy started to tank, it became harder and harder to run the city and county. Businesses shut down in record numbers. A few years later, D2 — or the "Second Great Depression" — as some called it, really got rolling. Frederickson looked like a ghost town with all the boarded up buildings.

Tax money, Winters said to himself. That's what was wrong. Boarded up buildings didn't produce any tax money. At first, the "recession," as it was initially called, was a blessing to Winters.

That's right: a blessing. There was all that stimulus money to dole out — and Winters was the guy who everyone came to for all that big, fat federal money. He made sure the number of city and county employees didn't decrease during that time. He actually hired more government workers as a "local stimulus" project. It was all federal money, so who cared?

Then, the federal money ran out. So did the state money. Winters was faced with deciding what to do. Increase fees for everything? There was no one left to pay the fees. Winters had to start firing government workers, which was hard at first. So many of those people had helped him get where he was, but he was where he wanted to be so who cared? The townspeople, after all, were just little plastic figures playing a part in the train set Winters was running. It was actually much easier to fire them than he'd thought.

He had to fire about half the police and essentially empty the jail, which had a predictable effect. He needed to have a volunteer security force. He had plenty of volunteers; they were all the people Winters had helped over the years and their sons. (Winters didn't allow any Mexicans to volunteer for security. It was just understood that white people ran things.)

The volunteers were very eager to help, and maybe get a cut of what was going on. They later became the "Blue Ribbon Boys" due to the blue cloth strip they wore on their left arms to signify who they were.

As things were getting worse and worse with the economy, the state and Feds wanted to control everything. All that federal and state money came with strings attached. Winters constantly had to deal with all the officials in Olympia and DC; at least at first. But pretty soon, he noticed, Olympia, and especially DC, couldn't keep track of it all. There weren't enough bureaucrats to keep tabs on all the money flowing into even little Frederickson. Winters quickly realized he could essentially do what he wanted. He would just send in "everything's fine here" reports to Olympia and DC. They were reports that probably went unread.

When the "Crisis" hit on May Day, things got even better for Winters. There were plenty of government resources coming in during the "emergency." And the little townspeople needed Winters even more.

But, the best part about the Crisis was that this made Winters truly untouchable. No one from Olympia or DC would possibly have the time or resources to crack down on corruption like his. Even if they caught him, he'd just call a few of the many favors government officials owed him and he'd get a slap on the wrist. He decided to quit trying to hide what he was doing and figured that being out in the open about it reinforced that he was the boss. He was so powerful that he didn't even need to hide it.

Winters decided he would directly profit from the Mexicans instead of just indirectly. He had the police (what was left of the police) arrest the leader of the Mexican gang in town. He told the leader that the gangs had a new business partner: Commissioner Winters. They would get protection from the police in exchange for various cuts of different enterprises. The gang leader, Señor Hernandez, wondered what took Winters so long to make this deal. He was happy to have the government as his new business partner. It made everything so much easier.

The benefits to Señor Hernandez of his formal relationship with the police became clear when a rival Mexican gang tried to come in. The police dutifully arrested them, and the townspeople were so happy that Commissioner Winters was taking bold action to combat crime. Winters viewed it more as getting rid of a business competitor, but if the little townspeople wanted to think he was protecting them from crime, all the better. However, rival gangs kept coming. The Mexican refugees from the collapse down in Mexico continued to flood northward. Winters was getting dragged into gang wars and even family feuds that had started back in Mexico.

He proposed a deal with all the gangs. Protection for all of them; same price for all of them. They couldn't agree with each other and rejected his offer. They even started to kill his cops, which was the last straw.

Winters and Señor Hernandez's gang went after the other gangs. It got bloody. That's when Winters had to move from his house into the security of the courthouse. It didn't take long until a barbed wire fence went up all around it, which was where the term "outside the wire" came from. Winters was essentially under siege in his own courthouse. Heavily armed convoys of cops, Blue Ribbon Boys, and Señor Hernandez's men could move outside the wire, but that was about it.

After much in-fighting, the Mexican gangs finally came to an agreement: They would split up the Frederickson action. Gasoline, food, guns, drugs, and girls.

Girls. Winters really liked the young Mexican girls. He liked that he could do whatever he wanted to them. He got to be the boss. He got paid in "product" as often as he could. His wife had known this side of him for decades. She didn't care anymore. She stayed in a separate room somewhere in the basement of the courthouse. Winters never really liked her, anyway.

Soon after the Crisis started, there was a Mexican sector in town run totally by the gangs. Cops were not allowed in, except to collect money. Not "money" as in cash, but gas, food, ammo, gold and silver, medicine, FCards, and whatever else was valuable.

Winters was glad there was a truce—a very profitable one—for now, but he knew that the Mexicans' deal with each other could break down at any moment, which was what kept him awake at night. He never fully believed that he could keep control over the whole town like he had been doing so far. He knew this racket was too good to be true.

Another thing keeping him awake at night was the reports that his own Blue Ribbon Boys were going into business for themselves. He didn't like that. He let some of it happen; that's how he paid those guys, but he was starting to wonder if they wouldn't try to get rid of him and keep all the money for themselves.

Winters maintained the barbed wire around the courthouse even during the gang truce. By then, there were too many militia whacko "Patriots" out there. Winters assumed the Patriots were a gang, too. He was waiting for them to come to him and ask for a piece of the action.

Winters, after he heard about the armament at Pierce Point, assumed Pierce Point might be the first Patriot gang he needed to make a deal with. Before the Crisis, he didn't spend much time thinking about Pierce Point. They had always kind of been on their own, but now they were coming into town and using their FCards. That was money in Winters' pocket, and he got to tell Olympia how many more people he was helping with the "Recovery." He needed Pierce Point to be good little customers. He needed them to play ball.

And then, one night, someone faxed Winters a disturbing picture from Pierce Point.

# Chapter 186

## *Co-Opting Pierce Point*

### (July 9)

Fax machines, long forgotten as a communication device, were much more popular during the Collapse. The internet would go off and on. The phone lines still worked, most of the time. But old 1990s era phone-line faxes didn't require the internet. People were actually using them again.

Several weeks ago, Winters was given a fax that showed a picture of someone hung out at Pierce Point. He ignored it at first; he had a gang truce to broker. But now, in the middle of the night when he couldn't sleep, he started thinking about it. He found the fax on his desk. He got scared.

Winters was concerned with the picture of the hanging because that meant Pierce Point was running things themselves, and Winters didn't like that. Worse yet, it was in a newspaper called the *"Pierce Point Patriot."* Oh, great. Some redneck "Patriots" out there had their own little newspaper, Winters thought when he re-read the fax. This little newspaper of theirs showed a level of boldness — calling themselves a "Patriot" was daring the police (if any were around) to arrest them as a terrorists — that made Winters nervous.

Then Winters remembered that right after he got the fax a few weeks ago, Winters got a call from Olympia. They got the fax, too. They wanted to know what was going on out in Winter's county. They sounded pissed and said they thought some POI who did some right-wing podcast might be out there. Winters didn't need that.

Olympia had leverage over Winters and he didn't want to screw up his rackets. Olympia sent semis of food to him. They controlled the FCards. Winters needed that food. It was his biggest profit center, more than the Mexican gas or bootleg medical supplies. He needed that food so he could get a cut of it. Oh, and the townspeople needed the food, too. Winters didn't need them hungry and starting to notice how much food had been stockpiled in the courthouse.

Stapled on the back of the newspaper article was a new fax from a few days ago that Winters must have missed. It was Olympia telling him that they would be sending some FCorps investigators out to look into Pierce Point.

Winters knew what the FCorps asshole would say: "Take down Pierce Point. Arrest the teabaggers out there." He had his hands full with the Mexican gangs and the Blue Ribbon Boys and didn't need this. He didn't need Olympia to withhold the food.

But, if Winters sent his guys out to Pierce Point to haul in those hillbillies, his cops and Blue Ribbon Boys wouldn't be in Frederickson to protect Winters' investments. Winters was the most powerful man in Frederickson, but he didn't have the resources to go several miles out to Pierce Point and arrest some teabaggers. Winters was amazed that the stupid townspeople didn't realize how stretched thin the "authorities" were. Besides, Bennington told Winters a few weeks before that Pierce Point had some amazing defenses and a gate. They even had attack dogs. The last thing Winters wanted was to fight some whackos out there when, instead, those people could be loyal customers.

He thought of the perfect solution. Rich Gentry, who used to work for Winters as a Sheriff's deputy, was running Pierce Point. Rich had come in a few weeks earlier and signed up everyone at Pierce Point for FCards. Rich was a guy Winters could work with. He was a guy Winters could make a deal with.

Rich wouldn't be part of this Patriot nonsense, Winters thought. Rich had a good head on his shoulders. Winters stumbled — it was almost 4:00 a.m. — into the "Incident Command Center" in the courthouse, which was where they had all the radios.

"Get me Bennington," Winters said to the dispatcher, who was half asleep. It took about a minute for Bennington to come on. Winters had woken Bennington from a nap.

"What can I do for you, boss?" Bennington asked on the radio.

"Go out to Pierce Point and get me Rich Gentry," Winters said. "I need to talk to him. He's not under arrest or anything, I just need to talk to him." Winters paused. Should he tell Bennington what was going on? It was a secure radio and, besides, if Winters had been handed this fax, then everyone else in the courthouse had seen it. There was no way to keep this thing a secret.

"Pierce Point has some 'Patriot' thing going on," Winters continued. "They hung some dopers and have a newspaper called the 'Patriot.' Olympia wants to shut that down. Rich Gentry needs to understand that we can't have that militia stuff in this county."

Bennington realized that just talking to Rich wouldn't solve the

"Patriot problem" at Pierce Point. He had been out there and seen how organized and serious they were. Winters was a delusional politician holed up in a bunker who thought he could make deals and intimidate people, like this was the old days.

But, whatever. Taking Rich into town to see Winters wasn't a big deal, Bennington thought. Bennington was curious to go back to Pierce Point. He envied their independence and wished he could be out there instead of being Winters' errand boy.

Bennington looked at the clock. It was 4:01 a.m. He would get another couple hours of sleep and then go get Rich.

# Chapter 187

## *"What's for Breakfast?"*

### (July 9)

Rich Gentry slept in. Way in. By habit, he usually got up at 5:00 a.m., but this morning he woke up at 8:12 a.m. He slept in because he had been out almost all night with Ted and Sap showing them the Marion Farm.

Rich got up quietly—as he had for years—and got dressed for work without waking his wife, Amy. She was usually up by now, but had been working a lot on planning for the school in the fall and was sleeping in, too.

Amy was thirty six, the same age as Rich. She was a pretty country girl. They had been high school sweethearts. Before the Collapse, she had been a teacher.

Amy and Rich always wanted kids, but Amy couldn't have them. They talked about adoption for years, but in the years before the Collapse, one of the first things to be cut out of government budgets was adoption services. Even without the loss of government funding, the regulations and red tape for adoptions were completely out of hand. It seemed like for each kid adopted, there were two full-time government employees. Now that government had been forced out of the adoption business—and it was a business for government—the old kind of adoptions were possible again, which meant people informally took in orphans on their own, without all the government bureaucracy. It was pretty simple: a good family took in kids. People had been doing it for a few thousand years all over the world and it worked pretty well.

The pre-Collapse government's attitude toward adoptions had always amazed Rich. He couldn't understand why they put up barriers to doing something as great as adopting kids. Because the government made more money administering foster care, that's why.

But, not anymore. One of the only good things about the Collapse—and, at this point, the good things were far outweighed by the bad things—was that the government monopoly on, and discouragement of, adoption was over.

Amy had been eyeing the many kids that become orphans or

displaced from their families and told Rich that she wanted to adopt them. He was open to it, but he worked twelve- to sixteen-hour days and wasn't getting around to it. He told Amy to find some kids and they'd just take them in. Amy was thrilled. Rich was nervous about it because he'd never been a dad before. He hoped he'd do a good job. He knew the very long days would start to wind down as others were trained out there and life stabilized. That was already happening.

For the first time, Rich and Amy actually thought about having kids and a semi-normal life. This hope had unleashed a new spark in Rich and Amy's life. They were cuddling like teenagers and things had never been better in the bedroom.

But, there was none of that this morning. Rich had to get out to the Grange for the "breakfast briefings," as he called them. He got a report from Dan on the gate, the Chief on the beach patrol, and about a thousand other people, all of whom had a problem of some kind.

Rich and Amy lived about a mile from the Grange. His job required him to drive all over Pierce Point, so he had a personal vehicle. He was one of the few who always had the gas to drive around. Because all his driving was for Pierce Point business, people would just show up at his house with gas cans. As scarce as gas was, most people realized it was a good idea to have the coordinator of the community's security be able to drive around. This is not to say that everyone helped with gas. Of the five hundred or so houses at Pierce Point, maybe fifty were willing to give Rich a gallon or two of gas, but that was enough.

Rich got in his truck and turned on the radio. His favorite station, 107.1 Hot Country Hits, was back on the air. It had been static for the past few weeks, but now there was music back on. No DJs talking, just music. They must have a computer playing the songs. That was an improvement; both the fact that there was music again and that there were no obnoxious DJs. The authorities probably realized that people needed things like their favorite music on the radio to help them feel like things were "normal."

It was working. Rich was transported back in time a few years by a song that reminded him of the easy life, not too long ago. Of life before the Collapse. For a moment, he felt like he was back at the Sheriff's department driving into work.

That ended when he pulled into the Grange. Rich's old routine from a few years ago didn't include a parking lot full of people at the Grange. It had always been empty back then.

He got out and said good morning to everyone and went into

124

the Grange where Linda, the dispatcher, waved for him to come over. Dan was on the radio.

"Lt. Bennington is here and would like to talk to Rich," Dan said. That was scary.

"What does he want?" Rich asked.

"Says he needs to talk to you," Dan said. "You're not under arrest, or anything." Dan paused and then said, "Which is good, because my guards would shoot him in about half a second if he tried that. He's alone, so there's no way they're trying to pick you up by force."

Rich was scared. Why did Bennington want to talk to him? He doubted Bennington had good news. Well, Rich thought to himself, you're one of the leaders out here. Maybe *the* leader. With that comes the responsibility of answering for the community.

"I'll be right down," Rich said. He asked one of the Grange ladies to get him a breakfast to go. "Last meal," he chuckled to himself.

Rich took his breakfast to go—a paper towel with a ton of cornbread and a paper cup of "sweet milk," a milk and sugar concoction the Grange ladies invented, which was a valiant attempt at a milkshake without any ice cream—and got into his truck and headed toward the gate.

The nostalgic songs on the radio couldn't take his mind off of wondering why Bennington wanted to talk to him. He wondered if somehow they knew about Ted.

Rich pulled up to the gate and saw an unusual sight: a police car on the bridge. He got out and found the garbage can to throw out the paper towel and paper cup. Maybe they should save paper cups, he thought, but he didn't want the guards to think anything was wrong with Bennington's arrival, so he tried to act as normal as possible. And that meant throwing things away.

Dan came up to Rich and said, "Curious as hell what he wants." He looked around to make sure no one was within earshot. "You don't suppose he knows about the Ted project, do you?"

Rich shook his head. "Unlikely, but we'll see. Anything I need to know? Anything Bennington will ask me that I need to have a standardized answer for?"

Dan shook his head.

"OK, then," Rich said, "I have a guest to meet." Rich was acting calmly so the guards would think everything was OK.

He walked up to Bennington, who was sitting in his car, and motioned for him to get out and walk across the bridge. Dan motioned for the guards not to shoot. Dan gave a command to the dogs not to attack.

Bennington got out and came across the bridge slowly so he could look at everything and give a report to Winters on Pierce Point's defenses. He was trying hard not to have his jaw drop at how great the guard system was out there. There were at least two dozen well organized guards with plenty of weapons, including a fair number of ARs, AKs, mini-14s, and tactical shotguns. The dogs. Bennington's eyes were glued on the dogs. What an effective tool those were. The metal gate was impressive, too.

The Blue Ribbon Boys back in Frederickson didn't have any of that. All they had was some guys with hunting rifles who goofed off more than they guarded. Pierce Point was squared away. That's what happens, Bennington thought, when people are protecting their families and homes instead of protecting corrupt politicians and gangs. Motivation is everything.

"Hey, Rich, good morning," Bennington said.

"Mornin' John."

"You're not under arrest, or anything," Bennington said, putting his hands out to his sides away from his pistol.

"You're not dead, so I know I'm not under arrest," Rich said with a smile. Might as well have some fun with him, and convey a message of "don't mess with us."

Bennington laughed. "Hey, can we talk in the car?"

"Sure," Rich said, knowing that if Bennington tried to drive off with him, the snipers on the hill and Sniper Mike outside the gate would riddle the car with holes. Rich would die, but so would Bennington. Bennington knew this, too, and therefore wouldn't try to take Rich in.

But, just to be sure, Rich waited until Bennington was looking at him and then raised his hand and flashed the number four with his fingers, which was a pre-determined signal to Dan and the guards. Bennington assumed this was an elaborate signal of some kind that conveyed a tactical plan, like "Shoot the car if it leaves without me giving another hand gesture." That was the effect it was supposed to have, but in reality, the hand signal was meaningless. It was the fake signal they used to mislead people into thinking they had a very elaborate series of hand gestures worked out.

Rich and Bennington walked back to the police car. Bennington opened the passenger door for Rich as a gesture of respect. Rich nodded and got in.

"So, John," Rich said once they were both in the police car, "What brings you to Pierce Point?" Might as well get down to business.

"Commissioner Winters would like to talk to you," Bennington said.

That's what Rich was afraid of. He tried to act calmly. "About what?" "About this," Bennington said, handing Rich the fax with the picture of the hanging in the *Pierce Point Patriot*.

"Oh, that," Rich said nonchalantly, even though fear shot through him. He realized they had a spy in Pierce Point. An active spy who was trying to get them killed. He knew who it probably was and knew what needed to be done. He'd deal with that later.

"Yeah," Rich said with a shrug, "we tried calling 911, but no one answered." Rich looked at Bennington as if to say, "Duh." Rich pointed off in the general direction of the Richardson house and said, "We had a little felony murder and child rape thing we had to handle." Rich looked Bennington right in the eyes, "You understand."

"I sure do," Bennington said. "Frankie Richardson and what's her name, the article says. We knew them downtown, before all of this. Not surprised."

"So why does Winters care about this?" Rich said, looking at the word "Patriot" on the fax and knowing exactly what the answer was.

"This," Bennington said, pointing to that exact word. "'Patriot' is a word we don't like. Olympia got this fax, too, and is bitchin' to Winters to do something about Pierce Point."

Rich was scared. Really scared. Adrenaline-rushing scared. He was struggling to control his appearance and not convey how terrified he was.

His mind racing a mile a minute, Rich casually said, "The guy who does the paper is a big New England football fan." He looked at Bennington and forced a smile, "You know, the New England Patriots."

Bennington rolled his eyes. "That's all you got?"

Rich pretended to not understand what Bennington meant.

"Winters would like to meet with you," Bennington continued. "He said 'Rich has a good head on his shoulders.' He wants you to tell him that you're not into this 'Patriot' shit." Bennington looked Rich in the eyes and said, "He wants to make a deal with you so he can get Olympia off his ass."

What a relief. Probably.

"What kind of deal?" Rich asked.

"Pledge your loyalty, all that shit," Bennington said. Rich could tell that Bennington was not exactly a devoted government employee. Bennington knew how corrupt his boss was.

"No problem with that," Rich said, knowing he could lie to Winters, and Winters couldn't do anything about it. It was significant that Winters had sent Bennington alone. If Winters had the ability, he would have sent a force to bust through the gate and arrest the people responsible for two "murders" by hanging. Rich was getting solid evidence of how weak Winters really was.

"How about breakfast at the courthouse?" Bennington asked.

"How do I know you won't be taking me for a longer stay than just breakfast?" Rich asked.

"Fair question," Bennington said. "Well, it's pretty simple. If we piss you guys off, we'll be visited by your fifty Marines and the contractors you have." Rich thought Bennington actually believed that. Good.

"Not to mention," Bennington said motioning to the guards, "some of them."

Bennington shrugged, "All that violence just because we want to 'arrest' someone for hanging some druggie dirt bags?" Bennington shook his head, "Nah. Not a good deal for us. We don't really care about the hanging thing. It's just that Winters wants to know you're loyal        out        here        so        he        can        tell        Olympia."

Rich realized that Olympia thinking Pierce Point was "loyal" would be good for Pierce Point, so he was willing to risk getting arrested for that. Besides, Rich was fairly confident Winters was actually afraid of the "fifty Marines." Wow, that little story was paying off.

Rich knew that if he refused to go see Winters that Winters might try to attack Pierce Point, for his pride, if nothing else. Did Rich really want his community attacked just because Rich was scared for himself? No way, Rich thought. When this whole Collapse started, Rich had mentally considered himself dead. He just happened to be alive right now. He'd be dead soon, he kept telling himself. Might as well die with your boots on.

Rich pointed toward Frederickson and asked, "What's for breakfast?"

# Chapter 188

## *Deal Making from Behind Barbed Wire*

### (July 9)

Rich got out of the police car and flashed the number seven with hands, another meaningless hand gesture mean to imply deep tactical meaning. When he got over to Dan, he quietly said, "I'm going to see Commissioner Winters. Everything is cool. Winters got faxed the newspaper."

Dan mouthed the name of the person who must be the spy, and Rich nodded. "We'll need to talk to him."

"So, that's why Winters wants to see you?" Dan asked.

Rich rolled his eyes and said, "Yeah, he wants me to pledge Pierce Point's loyalty."

Dan laughed and said, "Kind of hilarious, given our conversation last night with the green team." Rich smiled and walked back to Bennington's police car.

Dan turned to the guards and gave them the signal not to shoot. This was a real hand gesture.

The ride in the police car to Frederickson was quiet. There was chatter on the radio. Rich missed that. He felt like he was back on the force as he rode in the Crown Vic and listened to the radio.

Rich was observing everything he could on the ride in. He noticed that there was only one other car on the road. No trucks. About half the houses and cabins on the way to town looked empty. There were abandoned vehicles on the side of the road. They had been looted. One was burned down to the frame.

They came up to the Blue Ribbon Boys and the checkpoint at the Frederickson city limits.

Rich said to Bennington, "I don't have my purple arm band with me but, let me guess, I don't need one when I'm with you."

Bennington nodded.

The Crown Victoria police car slowed down, but didn't stop at the check point. The guards just waved them through. Rich was amazed at what he saw. The Blue Ribbon Boys were a pathetic unit. They were goofing off. One was pretending to shoot another one with a real gun. They looked tired. Exhausted, actually. One was nodding off

129

in a lawn chair. Then Rich saw something amazing.

Some of them were passing a bottle around. On guard duty! In the morning! It was shocking and troubling.

The Blue Ribbon Boys looked like a gang, not a guard unit. They were the complete opposite of the Pierce Point guards Dan had whipped into shape. Rich could tell these guards were barely controlled by whoever claimed to command them. It was only a matter of time before they ceased to be a functioning guard unit and instead were a bunch of thugs camping out. Maybe there were already there.

Bennington didn't say anything to Rich as they passed through the checkpoint. Rich assumed Bennington, who was a decent guy, was disgusted with the Blue Ribbon Boys, but didn't want to admit that Commissioner Winters was not invincible. As they went into town, Rich saw a military Humvee escorting a semi- truck.

"Morning delivery to Martin's," Bennington said, referring to the town grocery store. "Good. They're late. They missed yesterday's delivery and we got a little nervous. So did the crowds outside the store."

So some food was getting into little places like Frederickson. But, sporadically, and under military escort. How long could that be sustained?

Rich was getting the impression that the Loyalists' hold on Frederickson was tenuous. The guards and police were too tired, scared, and stressed out to do much, except boss around a largely unarmed population.

The Blue Ribbon Boys and the lack of regular police in Frederickson reminded Rich of his one and only bar fight several years ago. Everyone had been drinking for hours and it was 2:00 a.m. They had tons of energy at the beginning of the fight. As they started getting hurt and tired out, their energy level went down. Way down. After a few minutes, everyone was exhausted and just sitting on the floor trying to get the energy up to keep fighting. But no one was. They just sat around looking at each other.

A handful of cops walked into the bar. They were outnumbered about five to one, but weren't afraid in the least. Those few cops managed in about one minute to take over that bar. How? Because they were fresh and knew what they were doing (and had guns and backup). That small number of fresh cops could have beat a group of tired, drunken idiots outnumbering them five to one.

Fresh and skilled fighters can beat a much larger force of tired amateurs, Rich thought. Then he thought of Ted and Sap and smiled.

Rich could now see that a small group of Special Forces-trained Pierce Point fighters could breeze through Frederickson.

Then Rich saw something that changed his mind about breezing through Frederickson as Bennington turned down Silver Street toward the courthouse. It was a fortress, barricaded with guards two blocks out and a machine gun nest one block out. There was barbed wire—two rows—around the courthouse itself. Pierce Point fighters couldn't take that place.

Rich looked at the courthouse fortress, which looked weird. There was the courthouse he'd seen a million times—but with barbed wire and guard stations. It looked like something out of a movie.

Ten years ago, when things were humming along in the economy and everyone was happy, it would have been absurd to think the courthouse would be a fortress. Five years ago, when things had started to really go downhill, it would have been unlikely—but not impossible—to think of the courthouse as a fortress. Two years ago, it seemed possible. But, even today, it still seemed hard to believe.

"I miss America," Rich thought. He'd seen that spray painted on a building as he was coming into town. "I miss America," he repeated to himself as he looked at the now-fortified courthouse.

Bennington drove right through the barricades and through the open gate. It seemed like he or people like him were the only ones to get into that place.

The guards at the courthouse and surrounding area were more disciplined. About half were in National Guard uniforms or FCorps helmets. They looked halfway professional. They looked almost as good as Pierce Point's guards, but with way better equipment, like belt-fed machine guns and good radios.

As they got closer to the courthouse, Rich noticed the parking lot was empty of the usual cars. Now the parking lot was full of military vehicles and two semis. There were two military fuel trailers, the smaller kind that could be towed by a Humvee. They held several hundred gallons apiece.

Bennington was pulling in toward them. "Do you mind if we gas up while we're here?" he asked Rich. "Commissioner Winters isn't expecting us for a few minutes, anyway."

"No problem," Rich said, glad that he was being given a tour of the Loyalists' facilities and supplies so he could report back to Ted and Sap.

Whoa. Rich realized what he had just thought. He was considering himself a Patriot on a reconnaissance mission. He had always been resistant to the idea of fighting the government, at least head on. He just wanted Pierce Point to be safe. He didn't want to fight the government, but now he was seeing this as a battle between freedom and the Loyalists who, except for the courthouse fortress, were weak. At least in Frederickson; but maybe everywhere else, too. Rich had wondered why Ted and Sap were risking their lives to take on the vastly superior military of the government. Maybe because they had seen things like what Rich was seeing: a weak government barely holding onto power.

It took a while to fuel up Bennington's Crown Vic. "Thirsty," Bennington said as he pumped the gas. So, Bennington was driving a lot. Good to know.

When the car was full of gas, Bennington put the nozzle back and motioned for Rich to get back in. They drove to another part of the parking lot and parked.

"Time for the meeting," Bennington said. He pointed to Rich's pistol. "Can't wear that in there," Bennington said pointing to the courthouse.

"Fair enough," Rich said and he took off his pistol belt. It felt weird not having that weight on his hips. He felt naked without his pistol but he had no choice.

"That'll be safe in the car," Bennington said. "The barricades, rows of barbed wire, armed guards, and," Bennington said pointing to the roof, "sharpshooters keep the riff-raff away."

Sharpshooters on the roof of the courthouse? Good to know, Rich thought. He wondered if Bennington was trying to give him all this information or was just being too chatty.

They got out and went into the back basement entrance to the courthouse. Rich had been there a million times because he used to be a Sheriff's deputy. But he couldn't believe what he saw.

The halls were full of cases of food and bottled water. There were generators and cans of gas. It didn't look like government-issue things. It looked like they had seized civilian items and were storing them there.

As they got up to the first floor, the stolen merchandise was no longer in the halls. The first floor offices were crowded. People were everywhere, working in cramped spaces. He recognized some of them as county workers. There were quite a few strangers. Some had National Guard uniforms and there were plenty of FCorps.

It took a surprising number of government employees there in the courthouse to run what little government was left, but then Rich thought about it. There was no private sector anymore (except the gangs and tiny businesses and people bartering). All the former grocery store employees, truck drivers, and the dozens of other people who were employed by the private sector in the past to stock up Martin's were no longer doing those jobs. Now it took dozens of government employees to get the food to Martin's. That's who was running around the cramped halls of the courthouse, which is why it took so many government employees to do so little governing.

Bennington took Rich up the stairs to the second floor, which Rich remembered was the top floor. There were two well-armed and professional looking guards at the entrance to this floor. It must be the VIP floor. Bennington walked right past the guards, who were looking at Rich carefully to see if he was armed. Out of courtesy, Rich lifted up his shirt and spun around to show them he wasn't armed.

They were headed for the county commissioner's offices. Bennington came up to the receptionist. A receptionist?

It seemed so weird to have a nice civilian woman—a very attractive one, by the way—sitting there like things were normal. She must be someone's girlfriend. Before the Collapse, when unemployment in the private sector was so high, cushy government jobs like this were highly sought after. Rich noticed that many of the old government workers who had been there forever were disappearing. Some got reassigned and some got laid off. But new employees—many of them beautiful women—replaced them. It was obvious what was going on. Everything was corrupt. Everything was unfair. Everything was a scam.

"Here to see Commissioner Winters," Bennington said to the receptionist. It was hard for Bennington and Rich not to stare at her. She was in her early thirties, gorgeous, and had nice clothes. Most people were wearing tee shirts and jeans nowadays; no one dressed up anymore. But she was wearing a nice dress and her hair was perfect. She had showered recently, too, which was pretty abnormal these days. She looked like people looked before the Collapse. It was quite a contrast to everyone else.

"He'll be right with you," she said. She picked up the phone and said, "Your guests are here."

A minute later, the phone rang and she got up and took them into Winters' office.

Rich saw Winters and was reminded about how he looked like a rat. A human rat. He had beady eyes and was slightly hunched over, like he sat a desk all day plotting and scheming. "Welcome, gentlemen," Winters said in that warm, charming, fake politician way.

Rich was struck by the old and the new in Winters' office. The old was that it was a basic government office with standard furniture. The new was that there were bottles of booze and boxes of cigars everywhere. There were antique shotguns, the ones that cost thousands of dollars. Winters' office looked like some high-end fencing operation full of stolen goods. It was.

"Have a seat, please," Winters said. He looked up at the clock. "Too early in the morning or I'd offer you a brandy. Oh, what the hell. Want a brandy?"

"No, sir," Bennington said.

"Me neither," Rich said.

"Well, you got me thinking about an eye-opener to get the day going, so I believe I will have one myself," Winters said.

The bottle of brandy he was pouring was now worth a month's groceries. Winters was pouring a glass like it was no big deal.

Drinking in the morning? Rich looked around and saw that most of the dozen or so bottles in the office were half gone. Winters must be drinking pretty heavily. That was more information that was good to know and then tell to Ted and Sap. He was under a lot of stress and the bottle and receptionist were probably how he dealt with it. Winters had not been known as a drunk or womanizer before the Collapse. Maybe all of this had brought it on.

Winters started the meeting with small talk. He asked Rich about his family, obviously not knowing that he and Amy didn't have kids. Rich answered politely. Winters told Rich how former Sheriff's deputies were doing, only mentioning about a third of them, the third who hadn't gone AWOL. Winters asked Rich how things were going during the Crisis and Rich answered that, after leaving the Sheriff's department, he had become a security consultant helping people with home security.

"You were an Oath Keeper back on the force," Winters said, suddenly getting very serious. "Isn't that right?"

"Yes, sir," Rich said. "But that was back then, when politics mattered. Who has time for that kind of thing now? Now I think about chopping enough wood for the winter. About making sure I get all the FCard food my wife tells me to." He said it very convincingly. He'd rehearsed it.

"Good," Winters said, trying to believe what Rich said. He desperately wanted to believe it.

Everyone around Winters said things like that all day long. The official line was that Oath Keepers membership had plummeted because people didn't care about politics anymore. The other official line was that Oath Keepers were militia whacko "terrorists" and had scared all the good people away from that organization. The truth was the exact opposite, but no one spoke the truth in the courthouse. It was a truth-free zone, where people just mouthed the same lines over and over again. The Recovery is working. The people appreciate all that government is doing for them. This will all be over soon. Things will get back to normal. We're Americans. We can get through this and democracy will be back.

If Winters had a clear head, he would have realized that Rich was an Oath Keeper, a Patriot, and a threat to Winters and all the corrupt thugs in the courthouse. It was very obvious. But Winters was distracted by paranoia and drunkenness. It happened slowly.

Winters had been scheming for years leading up to the Collapse about how to steer all that pork to his people. He broke many laws to do it, which made him progressively more paranoid. He thought everyone was out to get him. Someone would turn him in and try to take his power. He was saving the county. Anyone who got in his way was classed as some right-wing nut who was against progress. He wasn't sleeping much at all. He had terrible nightmares about…things he was doing to people. They would haunt him in his dreams. He was drinking all day long and never even knew what time it was. He would invite his receptionist into his sleeping quarters in the conference room, but could tell she hated it. Sometimes she would cry afterwards.

Winters looked for good news anywhere he could find it, even when it didn't make any sense. He would believe things were fine when, if he were thinking straight, he could have instantly seen they weren't. Now that he lived behind barbed wire, Winters had to have good news. He craved it. When people told him how great he was and how he was saving the county, he believed them. He became addicted to people kissing his ass and telling him things were fine, because at night, the nightmares came. He needed to spend all day thinking things were fine to make up for what the people in his dreams were telling him.

"Are you in charge out at Pierce Point?" Winters asked Rich. He wanted to make sure he was dealing with someone who could enforce whatever deal they came up with.

"Yes. I'm it," Rich said, lying. He knew that it was a community effort out there, he wasn't the only one running the show. Hell, they had a library committee; Rich wasn't a dictator.

135

"Good," Winters said. He leaned back in his chair and let it creak. He thought for a moment. He leaned over and got two cigars out of a box and motioned to Rich to take one.

"Don't mind if I do," Rich said. That cigar was worth about $1,000 in old dollars. Rich wanted to play the part Winters seemed to want him to play: Rich as the boss of Pierce Point, and this was two bosses making a deal over a cigar. Let him think that, Rich thought.

Winters lit his cigar first—to show who was in charge—followed by Rich's. They both puffed for a while to get them going.

"OK, here's the deal," Winters said, feeling that rush of power he loved so much. "I need to know that Pierce Point is loyal."

"Of course," Rich said quickly and with a shrug. "Why is that even a question?"

Winters handed Rich the fax of the *Pierce Point Patriot* with the picture of the hanging.

Oh shit, Rich thought. This looked really bad. All of a sudden, Rich didn't feel so safe and comfortable. He rushed to keep his body language and emotions in check so he didn't give away how terrified he was. He had been in stressful situations like this, like when he did undercover work, so he flipped into "no fear" mode.

"Yep," Rich said. "That's the paper someone is doing out there on some little tiny copy machine," he said as he rolled his eyes.

"Oh, and that's Frankie Richardson," Rich said. "Child rapist. Confessed." Rich looked right at Winters, to project a lack of fear. "You guys were busy, so we handled it." He shrugged like it was no big deal.

Winters sat back in his chair. It creaked again. He just stared at Rich, sizing him up. Winters was scanning Rich for body language that would indicate he was lying. He didn't see any.

"You 'handled it?'" Winters asked.

"Yes, sir," Rich said, nodding like he was seven years old and talking to his dad.

"Was it some mob thing?" Winters asked. He was fascinated that people were taking care of things like this. He had assumed everything was done through official channels—that is, through him—but was now realizing that he just controlled Frederickson, not the country side.

"No, sir," Rich said. "We had a trial with a jury and everything. We hung his accomplice and jailed two others. They were stealing things and would have been shot soon anyway breaking into a house." Rich shrugged again. He was amazing himself at how calm he was.

Winters was convinced. There was probably a lot of this kind of thing happening in the county. But there was something that bothered Winters much more than hanging people.

"What about this 'Patriot' thing?" Winters asked, with an obvious edge to his voice.

"That's the name that guy came up with for the paper," Rich said quickly, like it was no big deal. He had been anticipating this question and had an answer ready to go.

"We can't have that," Winters said, leaning toward Rich and exuding power.

"No, sir, we can't," Rich said quickly. "The name of the paper, now that I think about it, needs to be changed. I'll take care of it."

"Yes, you will," Winters said, again exuding power. The brandy was kicking in. Winters was in his element. He was smoking a cigar and ordering people around. It reminded him why he loved his job.

"I can count on you, can't I, Deputy Gentry?" Winters asked as he poured another glass of brandy. He wanted to use Rich's former title to remind him that he had recently been part of the "club" of government.

"Of course," Rich said. "Pierce Point just wants to make it through this and then help with the Recovery. Just like the rest of America. Recovery. That's what matters."

This was music to Winters' ears. He and the government people all around him constantly talked about the "Recovery." They promised it to the people. They explained that temporary things, like barbed wire around the courthouse, and seizing things like the brandy and cigars, was all to help the Recovery. The Recovery — well, the hope of the Recovery — was what gave Winters all his power. He loved that word.

"You're right, Deputy Gentry," Winters said. "May I call you Rich?" he asked, knowing the answer to that question. He did it just to be endearing.

"Yes, sir, you may," Rich said. He was sensing that Winters was a weak politician. A weak, drunk-ass politician. Playing little charm games like "May I call you Rich?" That was all Winters really had. Deal making from behind barbed wire.

But still. Why pick a fight, even with this weak drunk, when you didn't have to? Rich didn't want to bury one, or more, of his Pierce Point guards just to prove a point with this sad idiot.

"Rich, I like you," Winters said. Another politician's trick to

137

charm someone. "I'd like to help Pierce Point. Would you like me to do that?"

"Of course, sir," Rich said with a smile, like he was desperate for help. Rich was in full deception mode to convince Winters that Pierce Point needed things and could be bought off. That's what Winters wanted to believe so he might as well foster that delusion. And get some stuff.

"How you doin' on FCards?" Winters asked. "Your people getting fed?"

"We're doing OK, sir," Rich said. "Your people are issuing FCards and we send in a crew every day to make a grocery run. Save gas that way."

"Your crew is pretty well armed, I understand," Winters said.

Oh crap. The fifty Marines thing, Rich thought. Think fast. "Yes, I have some guys working for me at Pierce Point. Keeping order and all," Rich said with a wink. He wanted to imply to Winters that Rich ran a gang just like Winters did, but on a smaller scale.

"Marines?" Winters asked. He was still leaning back in his chair. He didn't want to lean forward and signal that he was concerned.

"Yes, sir," Rich replied. "Some were living out in Pierce Point with an old buddy of theirs. Good kids." Rich looked right at Winters and smiled, "They know how to follow orders," he said with another wink.

Whew, Winters thought. Pierce Point was taken care of. Rich was the boss out there and had some muscle—enough to keep order there, but not enough to be a threat. One more problem solved.

"Since I like you, Rich, and it's my job to make the Recovery even more of a success in this county," Winters said with a big smile, "I'm going to get you more FCards. I'll make sure that tomorrow's 'grocery run' as you call it, gets to the front of the line at Martin's. What kind of transportation do you have for the 'grocery runs'?"

"A pickup," Rich said.

"Want a school bus?" Winters asked. "A little one. It holds about six people with room to bring back groceries."

"That would be great, sir" Rich said, wondering what the catch was. "What do we owe you?" he asked, to find out what the catch was.

"Nothing. It's a Recovery grant," Winters said. He paused. "But I would ask you to buy fuel in town here. I have given an allotment of fuel to my Mexican friends who will accept FCards as payment."

"Thank you, sir," Rich said. So that was the catch.

What a douche he is, Rich thought. Giving Rich more FCards and a bus, just so they had to use the extra FCards to buy fuel for it. And Winters got to tell Olympia that he was making a "Recovery grant" and aiding rural residents with transportation to a feeding station. This was a trifecta for Winters: get bureaucratic credit for Recovery efforts, get more business for his gang gas station, and make Pierce Point dependent on him.

That was true, all except for that last part about dependence. What Winters didn't know was how self-reliant they were out at Pierce Point. Not totally self-sufficient by any means, especially not when winter would come, but they were far better off than most places.

"I'd like your people to know that they can thank me for the bus and the extra FCards," Winters said. "Could you do that for me, Rich?"

"Absolutely, sir," Rich said. "With pleasure," he said as he smiled.

Winters abruptly got out of his chair. The meeting was over. He had other things to do.

"Thanks for coming by this morning," Winters said as he stood up. "Bennington will make sure all the arrangements are made. I have a meeting in a few minutes."

"Thanks again, sir," Rich said with a big smile. "Consider Pierce Point to be loyal and one hundred percent committed to the Recovery." What a charade.

Winters just nodded.

Rich and Bennington got up and left.

Waiting in the lobby was an FCorps guy with one of those stupid helmets. The receptionist said something on the phone as Rich and Bennington walked out. Winters came out into the lobby. Winters looked at the FCorps guy, pointed to Rich, and said, "This is the Pierce Point guy. Everything's fine. You can talk to him if you want."

The helmet-head nodded. He wouldn't take a county commissioner's word for the fact that Pierce Point was loyal. There were terrorists everywhere. Maybe the teabaggers had infiltrated this county. Winters went back into his office. The receptionist told Rich, Bennington, and the FCorps guy they could go into the main conference room. That was where all the big meetings happened, like the weekly "community leader" meeting, which was the meeting with all the cops and the gang leaders.

They went into the conference room down the hall. Rich was sizing up the FCorps guy. He seemed semiprofessional. He was in his

139

late fifties or early sixties; retirement age. He had a pistol that looked like a police-issued Glock. He didn't seem like the fat cubicle-dwellers who usually were in those FCorps helmets. Rich got the sense that this FCorps guy was based in Olympia and worked at a higher level than most. He might even be a former cop.

"What's with this?" demanded the FCorps guy, as he put a copy of the fax in front of Rich.

"I talked to Commissioner Winters about that," Rich said. He repeated the story about the guy who did the newspaper on his little copy machine picking that name, and that Rich now realized the name of the paper was inappropriate. Rich said he would get the name of the paper changed.

"Fax each new edition to me," the FCorps guy said as he wrote out a fax number for Rich. He scribbled the fax number in distinctive cop handwriting, just like Rich's. This guy was definitely a cop, Rich thought.

"No problem," Rich said. He sensed there was something bigger at hand.

There was. "You know about any POIs out at Pierce Point?" the FCorps guy asked, referring to persons of interest.

"Nope," Rich said, in a home style cop-to-cop fashion. "Why? Are there any I need to go get?"

The FCorps guy wasn't stupid enough to tell Rich what they knew—or didn't know—about any POIs out there. They had reports that one of the Washington Association of Business guys had a cabin out there, but he had hundreds of leads to run down and never had the time to work up a case on just one. If he had the time to concentrate on one at a time, he could bring one in. One at a time, like he had done for the State Patrol's fugitive task force when he worked for them. But this was a bunch of scattered leads. He was told to go out from Olympia and make the people out in the rural areas feel like Olympia had a handle on the POIs. Scare 'em. That was about all he could do.

"I can't really give all the details we have on this WAB POI," the FCorps guy said. "You understand, Deputy Gentry." He threw in Rich's name to make him think that the FCorps knew everything about everybody. They kind of did, but they just didn't have the ability to go out and do anything about it.

"I have the POI list printed out from when the internet was working," Rich said, "and we keep track of who is living out at Pierce Point. I haven't found any POIs in my jurisdiction."

Rich decided to give the FCorps more reassurance that he was running a tight Loyalist ship out at Pierce Point. "Since I'm in charge out there, and I'm former law enforcement—once a cop, always a cop," he said with a wink, "I'm always trying to catch those bastards. I don't need troublemakers in my little community."

The FCorps guy just nodded. He wasn't really listening. In a few minutes, he had to go up the road a few towns to the north and do the same, "we have lots of details, but can't say" speech to a police chief up there who was suspected of being a para.

"I call the local authorities if I think I have one, right?" Rich asked the FCorps guy. "I mean, I will detain them, but I bet you want to question a POI. Aggressive 'questioning,' I'm guessing. So keep them alive, right?"

The FCorps guy nodded. He cared a lot more about the possible para police chief than he did about some stupid political POI or some stupid little newspaper name. Paras got people killed—people like FCorps guys. Newspapers just did stupid political games. Whatever.

Bennington didn't want to be left out of the conversation. He had sat through the whole Winters meeting silently. He was, after all, a police official, so all this talk about the local authorities apprehending POIs was his business.

"We have a great working relationship with Deputy Gentry," Bennington said. "We'll catch any POI out there." Bennington had absolutely no desire to lift a finger to catch anyone out there. He had enough problems in town and didn't need any more.

Bennington's "we'll catch them" speech was just another bureaucratic lie. He had to tell them all day long. Bennington just mouthed these things so often that he usually didn't even realize he was saying them. Everyone lied, all the time. It was just how it was.

The FCorps guy had heard enough. "We'll catch 'em' blah, blah, blah." He knew that most local cops still in uniform were more concerned about getting a cut of what the gangs were doing than about apprehending POIs. Bennington was not the person who concerned the FCorps guy. It was Deputy Gentry. A former cop, which usually meant a guy who resigned in disgust because he wasn't down with the program, who ran a small rural community. Classic profile for a guerrilla leader.

Oh well. The FCorps guy could check off this meeting on his daily list of appointments. Off to the next town.

"Report any suspicious activity to the proper authorities," the FCorps guy said like a robot. From memory. He waved to them and walked out of the conference room. The meeting was over.

"Let's get you back," Bennington said.

Rich nodded. He was surprisingly tired. The adrenaline from all the lying and terror had left him pooped.

Bennington stopped by the office of the person who doled out school buses. He explained the school bus thing and made arrangements for a Pierce Point representative to come to town tomorrow and pick up the bus.

Bennington didn't say much on the way back to Pierce Point. He was scanning the area for threats as they drove. They breezed through the Blue Ribbon Boys checkpoint. Rich noticed that it looked like a new shift had taken over. He looked at his watch to be able to report the time of the new shift. Good to know.

On the way back in near silence, he was thinking about who had faxed that newspaper article and caused all this trouble. Snelling. It had to be him, or his asshole sidekick Dick Abbott. Probably Snelling. Snelling had been so furious over the hangings. Rich needed to drop by Snelling's cabin and see if he had a fax machine.

When they got to the gate, Rich thanked Bennington for the ride. Rich looked at Bennington and said, "I don't view you as the enemy."

"Nor do I," Bennington said. Rich was getting the vibe that Bennington might be on the same side as him, but it was way too dangerous to ask. "You got a good little thing goin' on, Rich. Kinda wish I could be out here with you."

Rich needed to talk to Grant and Dan about the FCorps guy suspecting that a POI from WAB lived out at Pierce Point. He wanted to tell them about the condition of things in Frederickson and about the new FCards and the school bus that they'd pick up later. They also needed to talk to about changing the name of the paper, and about Snelling or whoever had faxed the newspaper.

Rich didn't say anything. Bennington was a good guy, but they didn't need law enforcement out there, so he stayed quiet at Bennington's apparent request to be invited out to Pierce Point.

"But I have things to do in town," Bennington said, to Rich's relief. He stared right at Rich and said ominously, "I have something very important to do there. I think you will appreciate it." When he said that, Bennington's demeanor went from being a casual to deadly serious.

"Good to know," Rich said. That's all he could think to say. He wondered what Bennington was talking about, but he had a pretty good idea, so he wouldn't ask for details.

Bennington and Rich then talked about the arrangements to pick up the bus and the FCards, and how to pay for the diesel from Winters' Mexican gas station. Rich got out of the car and waved at Bennington, who drove off slowly.

By this time, Dan had come to the gate. "So? What happened?" he asked Rich.

"We have a lot of work to do," Rich said to Dan.

# Chapter 189

## *Snitch*

### (July 9)

Rich pulled Dan off to the side so others couldn't hear. "You and I need to go talk to Grant," Rich said. "Don't radio for him to come down here. We need to keep it cool."

Dan looked concerned.

"Nothing urgent now, just a development we need to manage. Grant's probably up at the Grange. Hop in my rig and we'll go up there."

"Roger that," Dan said. He told Heidi, the comms chick, that he was going up to the Grange. He found Terry Maler, the second in command of the day shift of guards, and said, "Goin' to the Grange. You're in command for a while." Terry nodded.

Dan got in Rich's truck. In the meantime, Rich had checked the place in the volunteer fire station where the "Return to Grange" pile was. This was where people put things that needed to go back to the Grange. No one drove anywhere without seeing if something needed to be hauled somewhere. Everyone with gas and a vehicle was part of the informal parcel delivery service. Rich put the "Return to Grange" things in his truck and got in the cab.

As they drove by all the guards at Pierce Point, Rich marveled at how much better their guards were than the Blue Ribbon Boys he'd just seen in Frederickson. The Pierce Point guards seemed alert and somewhat glad to be there. They were taking the job seriously. They were organized. None of them were passing a bottle around, of course. There were about three times as many Pierce Point guards as the Blue Ribbon Boys, and that didn't count the sharpshooters in the woods on the hill, or Sniper Mike across the road. Rich had started the day thinking Pierce Point was vulnerable to the much bigger Frederickson. Now he thought the opposite.

"Well, some interesting stuff in town," Rich said as he began to give Dan the short version of what he saw. Dan was stunned at how weak the "legitimate authorities" were.

Rich and Dan pulled into the Grange and found Grant. "Need you down at the gate," Dan said to him. They didn't want anyone to overhear them, and they didn't want to waste gas driving back down to the gate, so they would just park the truck out of eyesight of the Grange and talk in the truck.

Grant grabbed his AR and kit thinking that he was going to the gate. They got in the truck and went a little ways to a little road where no one could see them.

Rich stopped the truck. Grant was wondering what was going on.

"Got some things to talk about," Rich said. He proceeded to tell Grant everything. Grant was worried about the POI thing. He had been assuming that the government was too overwhelmed to even keep track of him being out there. But they knew the WAB connection, too. That scared him.

"My name is on that damned list," Grant said. "Anyone here could get that list and find out my name. I use my real name out here. It's only a matter of time before Snelling tries to turn me in."

Rich explained how it seemed that the authorities didn't have the resources to track down all the leads they had and, besides, Pierce Point's guards could repel an assault by any force other than a professional military unit.

"Hey," Dan said, trying to be positive, "no one out here knows how you spell your last name. How about going with the Norwegian spelling of 'Matsen'? Maybe we say that your first name is something like Herman and you go by your middle name of Grant." These weren't bad ideas, but they also weren't enough to make Grant feel totally safe.

"Snelling," Rich said. "That's your problem."

All three men nodded. They were thinking the same thing, but they didn't want to say it.

Finally, Grant spoke up. "Is it treason to do what he's doing, if he's the one snitching on me?" Just saying that out loud answered the question.

Of course it wasn't "treason." Grant could not figure out a way to put Snelling in their makeshift jail. Besides, doing so would violate every constitutional principle Grant was supposedly all in favor of.

"Wait, guys," Rich said. "We don't know if Snelling is the one. Let's find that out first." They all nodded.

"I have an idea," Rich said.

# Chapter 190

## *"Lima Down"*

### (July 12)


Todd Snelling was enjoying lunch. Well, not "enjoying." He was having lunch. That was more correct. He missed all the normal foods he used to eat; all the organic and foreign foods. The high-end stuff, not the hillbilly food he had out at Pierce Point. Cornbread? Seriously? Might as well have a chicken fried steak at a truck stop. What he would have done for some fresh feta cheese and Belgian endive.

The internet was back up and he wanted to get online before it went off again. He was on the FCorps website getting updates. It looked like things were going well. The authorities were rounding up terrorists in big numbers. There were big raids in Denver and Boise. Not even redneck Idaho was a sanctuary for these teabaggers. Things were going well in Chicago. There were lots of stories about people there being thankful for all that the government was doing, like feeding people and protecting them. So much for those Neanderthals who thought all government was bad. Those limited-government types were so stupid. Everyone knew that there needed to be enough government to take care of all the hopeless people. That's what government does. Look at all the happy people on the internet who were so glad to be taken care of.

Snelling was startled by a knock at the door. No one ever came to his cabin, except Abbott, and that wasn't his knock. It was someone else. What could they want, he wondered as he walked to the door.

"Who is it?" he asked.

"Rich Gentry." It sounded like him.

"Coming," Snelling said. He unlocked the door and saw Rich. "What can I do for you?" Snelling asked, truly having no idea why Rich was there.

"I want to talk to you about Pierce Point."

The teabaggers were coming to their senses, Snelling thought. They finally realized that his way was the right way.

Snelling let Rich in.

"What about Pierce Point?" He said, not even waiting to make small talk. Snelling was so excited to be having this conversation.

"I think you have some good ideas, Todd," Rich said. "I don't think you're being listened to and I want to see if I can get a better dialogue going."

"Dialogue?" That was a magic word. It meant that this was going to be done like things were done in Seattle: With dialogue, not guns. Snelling could barely contain his glee that the world was not upside down. There would be dialogue even out in hillbillyville.

"I can't get a word in edgewise with that Grant Matson," Snelling said and rolled his eyes. "He's such a bully. Shutting me down all the time. I had pretty much given up. I wasn't even going to bother going to the meetings anymore."

"Oh, you should," Rich said. "Mind if I sit down?"

"Of course," Snelling said. He was going to enjoy this. Rich, the apparent teabagger, was coming with his hat in hand, ready to call a truce. Or maybe better. Maybe he was ready to let Snelling run things out there.

"Would you like something to drink?" Snelling asked.

"Water is fine," Rich said. As Snelling was bringing the water, Rich looked around the cabin. It was amazing, and must have cost a mint. Snelling even had some art. Weird art, but it was art. Foofy Seattle art. No one else had art at Pierce Point.

When Snelling came back, Rich pointed to a copy of *Architectural Digest* on the coffee table. "I always wanted to be an architect," Rich said. "What's it like being one?"

Snelling's eyes lit up. He talked for about fifteen minutes about being an architect and his work. He was so happy Rich asked him about it.

By now, Rich got up and was slowly walking and looking at all of the fancy art as Snelling was talking. He wandered from room to room looking at things and occasionally saying to Snelling, "Uh, huh. That sounds great."

Pretty soon, Rich had inspected the whole cabin, and went into Snellings' office.

Then he saw it. An old fax machine. It looked so odd – a 1990s fax machine there in the ultra-modern office. A copy of the newspaper with the picture of the hanging was next to the machine.

Suddenly Snelling appeared to get nervous.

"Let's go back to the living room," he said, realizing how defensive he looked.

147

Rich nodded and motioned for Snelling to lead the way.

"After you," Snelling said. "You are my guest." It was pretty obvious that Snelling didn't want Rich walking around the cabin unescorted.

"Thank you," Rich said. "You were saying that architect school was particularly grueling..."

Snelling started right back up where had left off. Something about how he loved to "express himself" in the buildings he designed, which was weird, Rich thought, because Snelling drew up the plans for a lot of post offices. There was not a lot of "expression" in those.

This was the oldest trick in the book, Rich kept thinking as Snelling continued to yammer about architecture. Get a suspect talking about themselves, walk around, and look at things. All in plain view. No warrant required. It worked like a charm.

Using this technique, Rich had now established that Snelling was the snitch.

Snelling's wife came up to the cabin, returning from some yoga on the beach.

"Well, I gotta go," Rich said. "I just wanted to encourage you to come to the next meeting and tell us your thoughts. I promise you that your opinion will be respected." Rich hated lying to a guy, but this guy was trying to get Grant killed, and probably Rich, too. All is fair in love and war.

"Oh, I will be there tonight," he said with a smile.

Rich thanked Snelling and his wife for the water and headed back to the Grange.

The five-minute ride back to the Grange was unsettling as Rich thought some terrible things. He was making a terrible decision. He couldn't believe he was actually thinking these thoughts.

When Rich arrived at the Grange, he motioned for Grant and Dan to get into the truck.

"It's Snelling," Rich said, once they were in the cab, away from the listening ears of other people. He started driving in the general direction of the gate. "I saw the fax machine and the newspaper by it. He got nervous and shooed me out of the room."

Grant had been quiet the whole time. He didn't know what to do. He knew Snelling was basically trying to kill him. Now Grant was calmly debating with himself whether he should give his OK to kill Snelling. Grant kept thinking about what kind of example that would set: Mr. Constitution urging a political killing. Treason required two witnesses and a jury trial under the Constitution. There was nothing in that document that allowed offing a guy because he had a fax machine.

Then again, as Ted and the others pointed out earlier, this was war. The rules were different. The Constitution contemplated war and some extreme measures. Besides, they were in a survival situation. Snelling could kill them as easily as untreated water, lack of food, or lack of shelter could. A person is perfectly justified to overcome those kinds of threats. They would treat the water, gather the food, and build the shelter. However, overcoming those threats didn't involve killing another human being.

Rich stopped the truck at the clearing near the Grange where they were doing all this discussing.

"Well?" Rich asked. They had all been waiting for someone to kick off the discussion. No one was too eager to start this conversation. It was still silent.

"Well?" Rich asked again. "What do we do about Snelling?"

"Something," Dan said. "We can't let him call the cops again. From what you described, Rich, we are stronger than the idiots in Frederickson, but...I don't want to bury one of the kids at my gate unless I have to."

More silence.

"I can see it both ways," Grant said, realizing how weak he was being. "Can we think about it more? Give it more time? This is a huge decision."

Rich said, "I guess, but we need to act soon. What if he finds out you're a POI? He was trying to get on the internet when I came over. He could find out and then fax that in, as well. A confirmed sighting of a POI. Think about that. You want to go to prison or get shot just to give Snelling another few hours on earth?"

Right then, Mark's truck with the Team went by. They saw Rich's truck and turned around to join them.

"What's up, guys?" Bobby asked. He was driving. Mark wasn't in the truck; he must have loaned it to the Team.

Rich, Grant, and Dan looked at each other. Might as well tell the Team. They were part of this, too. They had to be trusted. Rich explained Snelling's fax machine. Everyone was quiet. They all knew what decision they were making. It was one thing to get ready to kill people trying to crash your gate. But to murder someone? Over politics? Even someone who wanted to have you killed? This was hard.

Finally, Bobby said, "I wonder what Ted would think."

"Oh, he was pretty clear," Ryan said. "'Kill him' is what he said about Snelling."

"What about his wife?" Pow asked. "She hasn't done anything. And there's that Abbott jack off. What about him? How far does this go?"

More hard questions. This guerilla shit ain't easy, Grant thought.

"We should get back," Wes said. "Clean up before the Grange meeting." Everyone agreed, not so much about cleaning up for the meeting, but wanting to have more time to think about this huge decision. Grant got in Mark's truck and they went back.

Everyone was quiet on the ride to Over Road. These young gung-ho ass kickers were mature enough to realize the significance and severity of the decision they were making. There was no going back. They could justify forming an armed guard and even hanging child rapists. If the Collapse ended today, they could explain what they did and why, and probably not be charged with anything.

But the planned killing of a guy? That was not something that could be explained away if things went back to normal. Grant thought he had completely worked through the mental process of casting his lot with the Patriots when he agreed to join up with Ted. Now he was realizing that he hadn't fully committed. Killing Snelling would be a full commitment. There would be no going back.

When they got back to the cabins, everyone went off on their own. They weren't talking, just quietly cleaning their gear. Grant went to his cabin to see his kids. He heard a moped take off. It was Wes. Probably going to Kellie's. Is that all that guy thought about?

Grant was quiet around his kids. He cleaned up. He hadn't showered in three or four days. It felt amazingly good to be clean. He looked in the mirror. His beard was getting pretty full. His hair was getting long; he'd get a haircut. but the beard was staying. Shaving everyday seemed stupid, and wasteful.

Grant chatted with the kids and Eileen. He wasn't fully present for the conversation, though; his thoughts were elsewhere.

"Time to go to the Grange," Grant said to them. "I'll eat dinner there," he said to Eileen. "No offense to what you're eating here, but being there and talking to people is part of my job."

"No offense taken," Eileen said. "It means more food for the rest of us," she said with a smile.

Grant went out to round up the Team and pile into Mark's truck. Wes was coming back on the moped. He had a weird look on his face, as if he had aged ten years.

The Team quietly got into the truck without the usual "This

never gets old" thing; the mood was too serious for that.

Wes was the last to get into the truck. He had something in a towel. He looked around and opened up the towel to show the Team Scotty's silenced .22.

"Lima down," Wes said.

# Chapter 191

## *Pierce Point Truth*

### (July 12)

Everyone was shocked. This was so final. Wes had killed another human being. Snuck up on him and killed him. This wasn't self-defense.

No one talked much on the ride to the Grange. What little they said, they whispered to prevent Mark from hearing. Only the Team members would know about this. Grant wondered how Rich and Dan would react. Oh well. There was no way to undo this now, anyway.

Grant felt even closer to the Team than before, and that was saying something. They had gone all the way and there was no turning back. They had already killed together as a team before this when Pow shot that guy in the raid. They had hung those two child rapists, but this was different. It was planned. This wasn't reacting to a crime. It was committing one.

"Thanks, Wes," Grant finally said. He wanted everyone to know that he—the guy most troubled by this decision—was OK with Wes's actions. . "It had to be done."

"Had to," Ryan said.

"Yep," Pow said.

"He tried to turn us in," Bobby said. Scotty nodded.

"Whadd'ya do with the body?" Grant whispered.

Wes shrugged. "Just left him there." Wes paused. "Musta been a break in or something. Snelling had nice stuff. Someone probably wanted to steal it, and knew that he wasn't armed." Wes smiled at that last part. He had been counting on the fact that Snelling wasn't armed.

As the Grange appeared, Grant started thinking about how they would explain this to the crowd. Everyone would suspect Grant. He would have to lie to everyone and deny any involvement. Then someone would find out. Grant would be a liar and his credibility would be destroyed, although he hardly cared about his image. He was more concerned about the diminishment of his ability to get things done at Pierce Point.

When they got to the Grange, Grant motioned for Rich and Dan to come over. Grant found Chip, too, and the four of them went out to the parking lot, where Grant broke the news. They all just nodded. It was anti-climactic.

The Team ate dinner together as usual and tried to talk about meaningless things just so people didn't realize how quiet and serious they were.

The Team Chicks came over and had dinner with the guys, which lightened the mood considerably. Whispers of much sex later that night were exchanged. Wes was hugging Kellie so hard it looked like he might hurt her.

"What's wrong, honey?" she asked him.

"Tough day," Wes said. "That's all. Things are fine." Wes looked her up and down with a gleam in his eye and said, "What'cha wearin' tonight, darlin'?"

She whispered something to him and he smiled.

The meeting that night had all the usual reports. Things were going well; the community was humming along; things were tough but people were pulling together out of necessity. Rich listened to the reports and marveled at how much better off they were than the sheeple in Frederickson.

Grant kept waiting for Snelling's wife and Abbott to burst into the meeting and accuse him of the killing, but it didn't happen. The meeting broke up early and everyone went home.

The ride home was a lot more upbeat than the ride there because the guys were talking about the Team Chicks.

Grant had this overwhelming urge to go to Snelling's house. He realized this was stupid, but he wanted to go to the scene of the crime. He thought others might have a similar urge so he said to them, "Everyone just stay home tonight. We'll deal with the reaction to this tomorrow."

Scotty's ham radio crackled. It was the Chief. He said that a small boat carrying two people had left Pierce Point. The boat left from area right around Snelling's cabin, going at a high rate of speed and heading toward the inlet into the sound. The Chief tried to catch up with them but had no luck.

"There goes our problem," Grant said. "Good luck filing a police report. Take a damned number." He was relieved. Snelling's wife, and hopefully Abbott, had gotten the message and left.

Grant slept well that night. He had already gone through the mental process of wondering if the police would arrest him, like he had when he shot the looters back in Olympia. From Rich's description of the FCorps guy being too busy to care about a report of a POI at Pierce

Point, there was no way the cops would even try to come here. What cops?

Grant realized how much better Pierce Point would be without those Loyalist whiners. They were the only people getting in the way of making it a completely Patriot community. There were some of Snelling's friends still out there, but they probably wouldn't say much now that their leader was...no longer around.

After a restful sleep, Grant woke and got ready for work. He was anxious to find out how the news of the "break in" and sudden departure of Snelling's wife and Abbott would be received by the community.

The Team assembled in Mark's truck and went to the Grange. No one said, "This never gets old" or "beats the shit out of selling insurance." Not this morning.

The Team Chicks stayed behind. Gideon needed the night cabin to sleep in after his guard shift, so the girls who spent the night in the night cabin with their boyfriends went over to the yellow cabin with the other girls.

Wes was the first to speak on the ride to the Grange. "I've been thinking," he said. "I'm glad I did it. Son of a bitch was trying to get us killed. I'd do it again. I probably will have to."

This was a relief to everyone. If Wes was OK with what had transpired, then there was no reason they shouldn't be. And that part about probably having to do it again was important for them to hear. They needed to be mentally prepared for more death and knew this was the first killing of probably many.

Grant said, "You know, I've been thinking about Snelling as some kind of tragedy. It isn't a 'tragedy.' The only tragedy is that he was alive in the first place. People like him, those with power, who steal from everyone and then cry about being the victim. We're doin' what we have to do, gentlemen. Be proud that you're steppin' up. We don't have to enjoy this. But we have to do it."

Grant immediately thought of his Grandpa who didn't want to go to war, but had to. It was Grant's turn to do nasty things that needed to be done.

The guys nodded. Some smiled. They were stepping up and could be proud about that.

As they pulled into the Grange, they could tell that something was up. The place was abuzz.

"Did you hear? Todd Snelling is dead!" someone yelled.

"His wife and Abbott are gone!" someone else said.

"They were probably having an affair and Abbott shot him," Rich said. "That happened all the time when I was on the force." Good one, Rich. Good one.

"She left a note about the Team killing her husband," another person said.

"Ha!" Dan said. He pointed to the Team and said, "If they wanted someone dead, you'd all know about it. It would be very clear and messy."

Rich said, "Well, I'll go out and look at the scene, but a wife and another man fleeing? Pretty sure I've seen this before. The wife and Abbott are probably in each other's arms right now." Perfect.

The crowd discussed the apparent murder of Snelling by Abbott – or maybe the wife – and their apparent affair.

Grant made arrangements for Snelling to be buried. He talked to Pastor Pete about adding Snelling to the weekly memorial service. Grant felt a little dirty misleading a pastor into thinking he cared about Snelling, but this was war. This was one of the many things he was doing that he didn't want to.

The rest of the day, Grant worked as usual at the Grange. The Team went out and trained with the Crew at the Richardson House. Things were surprisingly normal. The routine was not disrupted.

At lunch, Lisa sat down next to Grant.

"Pretty shocking about Snelling," she said.

"Yeah. What have you heard?" Grant asked, which was not a good thing to ask. He worried that he sounded a little defensive.

"I mean his wife killing him and running off with another man," Lisa said. "Hey, that gives me an idea," she said with a smile, before biting into her lunch. They ate together, as if discussing Snelling's death was normal daily chitchat.

Later that day, Grant talked to Rich about renaming the newspaper. "Now that Snelling and his fax machine are no longer a problem, do we really need to change the name?"

"Yes," Rich said. "I told Winters I was in charge and that it would happen. I want those FCards and that bus, and I don't want to fight them if I can avoid it."

"OK," Grant said. "Changing the name might de-escalate the Patriot thing after Snelling's murder…at the hands of his wife," Grant said.

"What should we rename it?" Rich asked.

"How about the '*Pierce Point Truth*'?" Grant said. "Same content, different name. The 'Truth' is more universal than the 'Patriot,' anyway."

"Sure," Rich said. "Guess that makes the first and only edition of the 'Patriot' a collector's item."

# Chapter 192

## *Banging at the Door*

### (July 14)

"I've never, ever been happier," Kellie gushed to her mom. "He's so perfect. He's everything," she gushed.

Kellie's mom, Sheila, was so happy for her daughter. Sheila had been worried about Kellie who had seemed so depressed. There was no future for kids anymore. This Crisis, or Collapse, or whatever people called it, meant Kellie would never have it like Sheila did. No college, house, car, or spending money.

Kellie had a boyfriend in Pierce Point, that Ethan kid. Sheila wasn't impressed by him. He was a typical boy, and Kellie never appeared too interested in him. It seemed more like Kellie wanted to have a boyfriend so she'd have someone to go places with and do things.

Sheila understood why Kellie didn't seem to take boys too seriously. Kellie's dad was a drunk and had smacked them both around before he left. Sheila was dreading Kellie discovering boys and bringing home some loser, like her dad.

And then Wes came along. He was a great kid. Well, man. He was on the Team, which the Pierce Point residents took very seriously. He was respected. The Team members were brave young men who protected everyone. They were so polite and always helped people. Sheila remembered the first time she saw Wes. He was helping an older lady carry some heavy bags of rice. It didn't hurt that Wes was handsome and had that cute Southern drawl. He was perfect for Kellie.

The few times Kellie brought Wes over, Sheila had been very impressed by how much of a gentleman he was. "Yes, ma'am. No ma'am." Holding the door open. He was the kind of man Sheila wished she had met years ago instead of Kellie's dad.

What Kellie didn't tell her mom, because it was obvious and she didn't need to, was that sex with Wes was amazing.

"You know what he said, Mom?" Kellie was nearly yelling. "He said he wants to get a place with me! He has to get permission from the Team first because they are trying to stay together all the time to deploy or whatever. A place with me!"

Sheila had never seen her daughter so happy. It was like an announcement of an engagement.

Being Wes's girlfriend made Kellie a "Team Chick," which held an enormous social status. Those girls were fabulous. They had become her closest friends. Instead of sitting around worrying about all that was happening, they were taking life by the horns and actively doing what they wanted. Being a Team Chick was an adventure.

"I feel like I can help him by being there," Kellie said. "I can be there for him. I love that. I love it, Mom. I feel like it's what I'm supposed to do."

Sheila realized that her daughter was madly in love. Good. Wes was a great boy. A gentleman. A real catch.

"I'm so happy for you, honey," Sheila said as she gave Kellie a big mom hug, the kind of hug only a mom can give. They danced around the kitchen for a while.

"See!" Sheila said, crying with joy, "Not everything is horrible. Some things work out, Lil' Kel-Kel," which was what Sheila had called Kellie since she was a little girl.

Then someone knocked at the door. Assuming it was Wes, Kellie ran to the door. She stopped in her tracks and ran back toward her mom.

It was Ethan. He was furious.

"Let me in!" Ethan screamed. "I need to talk to you!" Kellie and Sheila were terrified. They froze.

Ethan kept pounding on the door. He sounded crazy and mad. Kellie and Sheila thought he would break the door down.

Sheila ran into her bedroom and got her .38. Kellie ran into the room behind her. She loaded it as quickly as possible. Her fingers felt weird and clumsy, like her hands were cold, but they weren't. It was the adrenaline. She couldn't make her hands move, in the one moment that she needed them to. Finally, she got the gun loaded. Sheila locked the bedroom door.

They knew Ethan could easily kick in that flimsy bedroom door and its tiny little lock. They had gone from one of the happiest moments they'd had recently to the scariest, in about five seconds.

The pounding stopped. Ethan yelled, "I know about you and him. I know all about it." He realized he was crying and felt humiliated. Would he turn that humiliation into action or run away like a wuss?

It was silent after the pounding stopped, and Kellie and Sheila waited in the bedroom for a minute or two. Kellie's tongue was all

158

tingly and she felt like she was floating a little bit. She felt stronger than ever. She knew she could run faster than ever, but she was terrified, as she sat there waiting for Ethan to break in and for her mom to shoot him, if she could. Maybe her mom would miss. Ethan probably had a gun because he was a guard. He probably had one of those big guns.

Kellie looked at her mom and whispered, "Are we gonna die?"

Sheila mouthed back, "No," and pointed the gun at the bedroom door.

Another minute or two passed. It was still silent. Maybe Ethan is pouring gasoline on the house, Sheila thought. Maybe he was getting in through the garage. Had she locked that door? Sheila couldn't remember. Kellie and Sheila were listening for any little creak or tiny sound. They jumped when the refrigerator went on and started humming.

Another minute or two went by; still nothing. If Ethan was breaking in or starting a fire, he sure was doing it quietly. Given how upset he was, and that he was crying, Kellie wondered how he could be so quiet out there. She expected to hear him sobbing, but she didn't.

Wes would protect them, Kellie thought. Ethan was like Kellie's dad; all angry and crazy and trying to hurt them. This wasn't the first time Kellie and her mom had been hiding in a locked bedroom, but this hadn't happened since Kellie's dad took off.

This time was different, though. Her mom had a gun. She had purchased it right as everything was going crazy before the Collapse and crime was so high. Kellie was glad her mom had that gun. It made things fair. If a big man was trying to come after you, that little gun made it fair.

Was this too good to be true? Sheila wondered. Maybe Ethan had left. She hadn't heard him for at least five minutes. If he were out there, he would have made some sound by then.

"I think he left, baby," Sheila said to Kellie.

"Maybe he is coming back with a gun," Kellie said, sobbing. She had been holding back the tears because she didn't want to make any noise, but hearing her mom talk, even at a whisper, released the stifled cry. So the tears came flying out. Kellie couldn't control her crying. "Maybe," Kellie said, "he is going to drive his truck through the house. Maybe..."

"Stop," Sheila said sharply. "You're making things up. You're scared. We need to get out of here. He's not here now. He would have made some noise. If we can hear the refrigerator, we could hear him. He's not here now, but might be coming back. We gotta go."

159

Kellie was terrified of opening the bedroom door; she was safe as long as it was closed. She looked up at it. He could be standing right outside the door and be waiting for them to open it. She was convinced that Ethan was standing outside that door and smiling, silently waiting for them to come out.

"No," Kellie whispered. "He's right outside the door. Waiting for us. Probably with a knife from the kitchen." Kellie thought about what it would feel like to be cut to pieces with a kitchen knife.

"You're not thinking straight," Sheila whispered. "He hasn't made any noise. We have to leave." Sheila slowly stood up and kept the gun pointed at the door. She needed to lead now. Kellie would follow.

Kellie cringed. "No. He's outside the door," she said out loud.

"Shhh," Sheila said. She was slowly walking toward the door. Kellie was cringing behind the bed.

Sheila put her left hand on the door knob and had her gun in her right hand. She slowly turned the knob.

Ping!

Kellie jumped and started screaming.

"It's just the lock on the door," Sheila said. That screaming had given away their position, so Sheila might as well talk at a normal volume. Besides, talking normally might reassure Kellie that Ethan was not in the house.

Sheila wanted to show Kellie that Ethan wasn't outside the door, so she confidently opened the door.

Nothing. No one.

"See," Sheila said. "Nothing." Sheila realized that saying that was the jinx in every horror movie. Once a person said that, an axe would come swinging through the air. Then Sheila felt stupid for thinking horror movies were a good predictor of what happened in real life.

She walked through the door, gripping the gun so tight that her hands were hurting. The sweat was making it slippery, but she had a firm grip. A very firm grip.

Sheila started walking slowly through the house, opening every door and slowly peeking in each room. She went around each corner, pointing the gun and exposing as little of herself as possible, like she had seen in the movies. She was amazed at how much she was moving like in the movies.

A rhythm was developing. Pointing the gun around a corner, moving a little bit, swerving around the room and swinging the gun around the whole room in case anything was in it. Looking behind herself and quickly moving to the next room. Doing the same thing, at the same pace, just like in the movies.

Finally, Sheila was in the living room, which was at the other end of the house. The front door that Ethan had been banging was still closed and locked.

Now Sheila had to check the garage. For some reason, she was extra scared and cautious opening the door from the house to the garage. She looked and it was locked. Thank God.

She started to open it slowly so that if he were in the garage, he'd have plenty of warning and would maybe make a noise, so she would know to start shooting through the door.

Finally, the doorknob was all the way to one side. It was time to actually open the door. Sheila pushed on it gently. The door creaked and she nearly jumped. That was the same creak that she had been meaning to fix, but today it was more scary than annoying.

She opened the door a little and looked into the dark garage. It was light out, but the garage didn't have any windows and the light wasn't on. She paused to listen for any little tiny noise.

Nothing.

Then she got brave. She had her gun in her right hand. She used her left hand to open the door and opened the door fully. She then used her left hand to flip on the light in the garage.

Nothing.

Maybe he was hiding behind the car. She slowly walked around pointing her gun at whatever was in front of her. She would stop and look behind her.

No one was in the garage. She was getting more confident. She started to walk at a normal pace and had lowered her gun so it was pointed down at the ground. Her hands were hurting, as squeezing that thing was painful.

Sheila stopped. This was what happened in the movies right before the axe, she thought again. She raised her gun back up and felt the pain in her right hand again. She resumed the rhythm of searching each nook and cranny for Ethan. She opened the door from the garage to the outside. It was locked. Thank God. She swore she would never leave a door unlocked again.

She looked outside. Nothing. Finally, she realized Ethan wasn't there. She felt a little silly taking so long to check each room, like she was overreacting. Then she realized it wasn't overreacting. It was smart.

She ran inside to get Kellie.

"We have to go now," she said to Kellie, who was still huddled in the bedroom. "He might come back."

That was all Kellie needed to hear to become motivated. She jumped up and started running to the garage to get into the car. She expected Ethan to jump out of a doorway and stab her as she ran down the hall.

Kellie was in the car. Alone. Where was her mom? Sheila came running to the car with keys in her hand. It had been so long since she'd driven — over two months — that she forgot where her keys were.

Sheila jumped in the car, hit the garage door button, and backed out. Fast. Too fast. She almost hit the garage door, which hadn't gone up yet. She hit the brakes and waited for the garage door to go up, which seemed to move in slow motion. Once she cleared it, she zoomed out. Fast. She forgot to close the garage door. Now he could get in and burn the place down, she thought as she sped down the road. But she didn't care. She had Kellie and they were safe in the car. They were getting the hell out of there.

"Keep your eyes out for him," Sheila said to Kellie, who had stopped crying by now.

"Wes. We need to go to Wes," Kellie said.

"Where is he?" Sheila asked.

Kellie thought. "He's at the Richardson house. Training or whatever."

Sheila knew where that was. She drove there like someone was chasing them.

Sheila and Kellie raced up to the Richardson house. The dog team started barking at them. The Crew looked around and wondered who they were. One of them raised a rifle at their car.

Kellie didn't care. She wanted to be with Wes. She got out of the car and started running toward the house.

"You'll get shot!" Sheila yelled from the car. She couldn't watch. Her daughter shot by mistake. Sheila shut her eyes.

Nothing. No shot. Sheila opened her eyes and saw Kellie hugging Wes and sobbing. Pretty soon, men started coming out to the car to see if Sheila was OK.

Sheila told the Team and Crew what had happened. The Team was getting their gear to go out and find Ethan. Sheila had the distinct feeling that the Team would kill Ethan if they found him. Good.

A truck came screaming down the road and bolted into the Richardson drive way. It was Ethan's truck. Sheila cringed as low as possible in her car seat. This was it. Ethan was about to die. And Kellie would have to see it.

The truck stopped and Ethan jumped out. He was out of his mind with anger; yelling and screaming. He started walking toward them. He must have seen Kellie and Wes hugging and went insane. He started running toward them.

Ethan didn't have a gun. There was no pistol in his holster. The Team and Crew realized that he was seemingly unarmed. They wouldn't shoot him unless he was a threat.

Ethan got a few yards from the front porch where Kellie and Wes were and he stopped. He had about ten rifles pointed at his head and was noticing it for the first time He put his hands up and just stood there.

Ethan looked around and sized up the situation. He was powerless. Weak. He was humiliated. He had guns pointed at him and his girlfriend was in the arms of another man. He was weak and pathetic. He could never show his face in Pierce Point again. Never. He had nothing left to lose.

# Chapter 193

## *Troop Discipline*

### (July 14)

"Shoot me!" Ethan yelled out. "Go ahead! Get it over with!" Then he started crying. Like a little baby. More humiliation. Ethan wanted to leave. He wanted to get in his truck and go, but he knew he'd be shot if he went back to it, so he just stood there. Humiliated.

Wes let Kellie go and started walking toward Ethan. Quickly. And gaining speed. In an instant, Wes was closing in on Ethan at a full run. He looked like a cougar pouncing on prey.

Wes tackled Ethan and started punching him wherever he could. Wes felt some of the punches land. A couple went into the ground and hurt his fists, but he kept going. He was an animal. Unstoppable.

After a few seconds, Wes felt arms pulling him up. He realized it was the Team and Crew pulling him off of Ethan.

When he got to his feet, he realized his hands hurt and he had blood on him. Ethan was standing, too and also had blood on him. Wes wondered if the blood on Ethan was his. He checked his face. No blood there. He saw blood coming out of Ethan's nose, however. Wes smiled. He must have landed at least one on Ethan's face. Hopefully he broke the bastard's nose.

"Want some more, bitch?" Wes yelled out to Ethan.

"Shut up," Rich said. "Both of you shut up."

"Fuck you!" Ethan yelled to Wes.

"Shut up," Ryan said as he pulled his pistol out and pointed it directly in Ethan's face. "Shut up," he repeated slowly.

"Cuff both of them," Rich said.

"What?" Wes yelled. Why him? He was the hero here. Ethan was the bad guy.

"Shut up and calm down," Rich said.

Bobby cuffed Ethan with the plastic cable zip ties they carried. No one on the Team would cuff Wes, a fellow member, so Rich cuffed him.

Kellie came running up and tried to hug Wes.

"Get her out of here," Rich said. He pointed to Kellie and

motioned for someone to take her into the house where she wouldn't spark another fight.

Rich was in cop mode. It was his job to restore the peace.

Rich went over to Sheila to find out what she knew. Sheila told Rich about how she thought Ethan might down their door.

"Get Dan up here," Rich said. He pointed to Ethan and said, "This is one of his guards." Someone ran off to a radio.

Grant went up to Rich and whispered, "What the hell are you doing?" He whispered because Rich was in charge and he didn't want to contradict him.

"Fighting isn't allowed," Rich said. "Troop discipline. We can't have our guys fighting, especially over a girl."

Grant couldn't believe it. Ethan was the bad guy. Wes was just defending Kellie. "Wes didn't do anything wrong," Grant said in a whisper.

"Yes, he did," Rich said. "He attacked an unarmed man." Rich looked at Grant as if to say, "Duh."

Grant wanted to help one of his guys. Then it hit him. "One of his guys." Grant was taking Wes's side because they were both on the Team. Wes had crossed the line by attacking an unarmed man. As understandable as it was, it still crossed the line.

"What are you going to do?" Grant asked Rich.

"Discipline both of them," Rich said. "A couple days in the jail."

"What?" Grant asked. That sounded preposterous. Jail? For Wes?

"Yep. To be an example," Rich said. Then he looked Grant in the eye and said, "An example that the Team doesn't get special breaks."

Grant bristled at this. The Team was doing more than anyone else there. They were risking their lives all the time, raiding houses when the guards just stood there and BS'ed. The Team guys were the only actual badass gun fighters in this whole place.

Then it hit him. It was exactly the kind of division that Pierce Point didn't need. Everyone with a gun was part of the community's security; the guards, the Team, the Crew, the beach patrol, the comms people. No divisions. No cliques.

Grant started to remember how much emphasis George Washington put on troop discipline. General Washington was almost fanatical about it. Fighting and drunkenness were a constant problem for the Continental Army during the Revolutionary War, as were divisions between the regular army and state militias. Fighting and drunkenness were dealt with by flogging. Stealing was a problem, too. Depending on the amount stolen, the death penalty was administered. Deserters were shot. In fact, the story goes, when one unit tried to desert, Gen. Washington ordered that unit to count off. Every tenth man from the deserting unit was lined up. Washington ordered the deserting unit to shoot their own members who were lined up. Desertions went way down after that.

Grant had always thought that Gen. Washington's discipline had been too harsh, but now he was beginning to understand why Washington had been so adamant about it. There was no way to fight a superior force with undisciplined troops. Look at how pathetic the Blue Ribbon Boys were, Grant thought. And a break down in order among the troops meant they could easily turn into a gang and terrorize the civilians, which was the very opposite of what they were trying to do out at Pierce Point. Maintaining order among the troops was more important than being precisely fair, he thought. Military discipline had to be fair enough to prevent a mutiny, but it didn't have to be one hundred percent fair. Precise fairness was the goal for the civilian courts. They didn't have the tough job the troops did, so civilians could afford to have precise fairness as the goal.

Dan arrived and was briefed. He was taking Ethan's side, then Kellie told them about how Ethan had come to the house and how they fled. Dan was no longer as staunch a defender of Ethan.

Rich came over to Grant and said, "This is a commander's call. Troop discipline is a military thing, not a court thing. Not a civilian court thing."

Grant nodded. Rich was right. Under the Constitution, the military got to discipline its own members outside of the civilian court system. Grant would not be the judge on this matter. Besides, he was biased in favor of Wes. Rich, who was not biased like Grant or Dan, could make an impartial decision.

Rich paused for a moment and then said to everyone assembled outside the Richardson house, "OK, fighting is not allowed. Neither is banging on someone's door and trying to do who knows what. I don't give a shit who did more fighting. Here's the message: Fighting and acting up is dealt with severely. And fairly. So both Ethan and Wes are in jail for three days. Starting now. This is a commander's call and I'm the commander. Period."

"What?" Wes said, looking at Grant for help. "Me? I'm going to jail?"

"Yep," Grant said sternly. "Military discipline is critical. And it's the commander's decision, not a civilian court thing. I support Rich's decision."

Kellie started crying. Ethan just stood there with a very strange look in his eye.

"What if I quit?" Ethan said. "And I leave here."

"You can't quit," Dan said. "You..." Dan thought about it. The guards had not pledged to serve for any period of time, and he knew he couldn't insist on the guards enlisting for several years. Dan had never thought about that. He just assumed the guards would serve as long as the community needed it.

"Well, I guess you can quit," Dan said. "But not Scot free. If you walk out of that gate, you can never come back. Never. If you try to come through that gate, you will be shot. And we keep all your stuff. That's the price you pay for us feeding you for so long."

Grant and Rich went up to Dan. Grant said quietly to Dan, "Dude, this guy knows all our defenses. You can't let him go into town."

"We can't keep him jail for a few years," Dan said. "We can't have him on guard duty if he's said he doesn't want to be there. Besides," Dan smiled, "I purposefully don't tell the guards much of what's going on just in case one of them ends up in the enemy's hands. Ethan doesn't know much more than a person observing us from a hidden position off the road for a day or two would know."

"What about the 'fifty Marines?'" Grant asked. "What if Ethan tells Winters they don't exist?"

Rich and Dan were silent for a moment.

"Ethan is a disgruntled guard," Rich said, "leaving Pierce Point over a woman. Not exactly the most trusted source of information, so I'd say Winters would strongly discount whatever Ethan says. But, yeah, Ethan will probably say that there aren't fifty Marines, though he can't say for sure that they don't exist. We've been hinting to everyone, including the guards, that some security people are secretly hiding out here, so the worst Ethan can say is that he hasn't personally seen fifty Marines."

Rich thought about it some more and then said to Dan and Grant, "Worst case: Ethan tells Winters that we have snipers on the hill. That keeps Winters out of here. I'm OK with that. And I'm not going to let Ethan stay here. Wes will kill him." Rich looked around to make sure no one could hear him. "It's not like Wes doesn't know how to do it," he said and then mouthed "Lima down."

167

"Besides," Dan said, "No one is going to leave Pierce Point willy nilly. They have food and security here. Only fuck ups like Ethan will go. Good riddance."

Rich, who was in command, got to make the call. He went over to Ethan and said, "So here's your choice: First option is three days jail and you go back to guard duty without any other incidents. Second option is you quit and walk out with nothing, never to return."

Ethan quickly said, "I'm outta here." He smiled. He hadn't done that in a long time. He was relieved. He never wanted to show his face there again. He'd take his chances outside the gate. It couldn't possibly be that bad out there.

Rich said, "OK. That solves that. We'll drive you back to your house where you will give us the keys to everything you have and then you leave."

"Great," Ethan said. "I'll be out of this little hick town." To Rich, who knew how bad it was back in Frederickson, leaving Pierce Point sounded insane. He realized that pride was a bigger motivator to a young hot heat like Ethan than safety and food.

Now it was Wes's turn to receive his punishment. Rich turned to Wes and said, "Surrender your weapons, Wes." The moment felt tense.

Wes realized that he had to obey. He thought it was crazy for him—the one who was protecting Kellie from a psycho—to go to jail while the bad guy just walked away. He looked at Grant and asked, "Really?

"Really," Grant said. "I fully support Rich's decision. He's in command. Period. The Team gets treated like anyone else." Grant really didn't fully support the decision because it was unfair, but he understood why it needed to be done, and he had to publicly support Rich. Grant also had to show everyone that the Team got no special treatment.

Wes, who was still handcuffed, motioned with his head to Bobby to take away his pistol. It felt weird to be disarming a handcuffed member of the Team, but Bobby did it. He handed Wes's Glock to Scotty. Wes motioned with his head at his AR, which was on the ground. Bobby picked it up, checked to make sure it was on safe, and handed it to Rich.

Bobby went up to Wes and pointed to his front pants pocket. "Sorry, dude," Bobby said and took out Wes's Zero Tolerance folding knife. "I'll take good care of this," he said, "for three short days, brother." That knife meant everything. Members of the Team always had their matching knives with them. Always.

Wes realized that all eyes were on him. Would he be a whiner or a man? "The sooner this starts, the sooner I get out," Wes said to Rich. "Who's taking me back there?"

Kellie started crying. She needed Wes right now. She needed him and now he was going to jail. This wasn't fair.

Rich made arrangements for someone to take Wes to the jail. As Wes walked by Rich, he pulled him aside and whispered, "Don't worry. You'll get the star treatment in jail. Comfy room. Good food. I just had to do this to show..."

"I know, I know," Wes whispered back, "the Team gets no breaks. I understand. One request: conjugal visits?" he said looking over at Kellie.

"We'll see," Rich said. "I just don't want you to get caught. It'll take away the 'no special treatment' thing I'm trying to do here."

Wes nodded and recognized that Rich was doing what he could. Wes decided to think of it as three days of rest, which he could use. They had been patrolling and training hard for weeks.

A truck came for Ethan. A few minutes later, one came for Wes. Kellie was crying while Sheila took her away in their car.

Things got quiet for the first time in a while. Finally Rich said, "OK, let's get back to work. Let's run through this raid one more time. In slow motion first, then full speed. Empty mags and empty chambers. Safeties on. Let's go, gentlemen."

Grant stood there and thought about the different things that motivate people. He was trying to motivate people to risk their lives and do some very nasty things with the promise of high-minded things, like freedom and liberty. That motivated a few people. But other people, like Ethan, were motivated to do life-changing things, such as leaving the safety of Pierce Point, by things like being scorned by a woman. Never underestimate wildcards like jealousies over women, Grant thought. Never think that this is some perfect chess game of political philosophies and predictable behaviors. Human beings are a crap shoot. Expect the unexpected.

# Chapter 194

## *Same Ole', Same Ole'*

### (July 17)

Wes did his three days in jail, no problem. He actually enjoyed the rest. The part he didn't like was no Kellie. Rich couldn't figure out a way to allow conjugal visits without getting caught. When Wes got out, he and Kellie spent about a day doing nothing but having the wildest and most passionate sex of their lives. Kellie was very glad to have him back and was so proud that he went to jail for her. She showed her appreciation in the bedroom. Wes went back to work with the Team. He had missed them and they had missed him.

Everything was back in a rhythm. There was actually a "same ole', same ole'" routine developing. Everyone had their specific jobs now and they were doing them, like the old days, except they were different than their pre-Collapse jobs.

Grant was spending most of his time at the Grange doing organizational things and a little bit of judging. He had a mental health commitment trial about once a week. He also informally resolved various civil disputes, most of which involved property line disagreements. One case involved who owned a generator. He tried not to spend time having a full trial for these civil disputes. He talked to each side and tried to get them to settle, which worked in every case. This was more than a way to save his time, and the jury's time; it was to come to a resolution of the dispute that both sides sort of agreed to instead of one side winning outright and the other side losing. Those things tend to simmer and lead to hard feelings for years. They didn't need that out at Pierce Point.

He and Drew were continuing to work on a very detailed roster of Patriots and Loyalists. Luckily, with Snelling and his people gone, there weren't too many "L"s left on the roster, but there were many "U"s: Undecideds.

About three quarters of Pierce Point remained Undecided. Maybe they were soft Patriots or Loyalists, but they weren't wearing their politics on their sleeves, which was pretty typical when two sides are competing for the support of the population and there is violence on both sides.

However, more and more people were openly identifying themselves as Patriots. But politics was a secondary — way secondary — thing for most people. They were focusing on gardens, FCard food, gas, medical issues, and all the other things it was going to take them to survive. Many people worked sixteen hours a day making sure they would survive. They were tired and didn't really care about philosophical discussions regarding the Constitution.

Fair enough, Grant thought. As long as they weren't Loyalists trying to get everyone killed, Grant was fine with Undecideds quietly doing their thing. In fact, Grant's vision for after the Collapse was to have the people who didn't care about politics go back to their lives of doing their own things. Grant's hope for a free society was that politics wouldn't matter because the government's powers would be constitutionally limited so it wouldn't make a difference who was in office. The ideal was that government wouldn't do much bad because it couldn't do much at all.

The hardest thing for Grant was hiding the Ted project from Lisa. Every time he was with her, he felt like such a liar. The longer he didn't tell her, the bigger the breach of trust would be. He struggled with this. He wanted a happy marriage, but he couldn't tell her. He was slowly realizing that his marriage would probably be over because of this stupid Collapse and the war that was coming. Grant could feel that he was thinking of himself more and more as a solider instead of a husband. He hated it. But he couldn't come up with a solution. "Play the hand you're dealt," he would always say to himself.

Lisa, on the other hand, was doing well. She was easing into the idea of being a doctor who got paid in cans of tuna. She was so glad she was out at Pierce Point instead of Olympia. She didn't know how to tell Grant that. He might get a big head and say "I told you so," which would ruin the whole good glow of the moment. So she never told him. He probably knew, she told herself.

Manda and Cole were doing great. Manda had emerged as quite a leader of the kids. They loved her. The group of kids she oversaw was growing.

Cole was doing amazingly well. All the busyness of suburban life—all those people talking all the time—had really worn him out. There was none of that in Pierce Point. His talking was getting better and better. It was amazing to see.

Drew and Eileen were getting used to their new lives. Drew was a huge help at the Grange. He was keeping everything running fairly by giving people credit for the donations they were making.

Eileen, who had grown up on a hard-scrabble farm in rural Eastern Washington, was right at home in the rather primitive conditions of post-Collapse America. She had gotten over her initial normalcy bias and was embracing life as it now was. She got to see her grandkids more than ever and loved it.

The Colsons, Morrells, Chip, Gideon, and the Team were doing fine. Everyone was easing into a "new normal" of their lives out there. Grant looked back at just the past almost three months and couldn't believe how far they'd come.

The rest of the people out at Pierce Point seemed to be adjusting to the new normal. It was amazing how quickly people had forgotten about many parts of their pre-Collapse lives of just a few months ago. Post-Collapse life was now how life was.

But not everyone was adjusting to the "new normal" as people called it. Some people dealt with the changes by complaining. They would whine that the mail didn't come that day; it hadn't come in three months. They would complain that nothing was on TV, or that the internet was down again that day. For these people, every little thing about their old lives that was no longer present was a topic to complain about. Most people were initially patient with the whines, but soon they started telling people to shut up.

For a few others, they were coping with the changes with some very odd behavior. One man brought old, pre-Collapse newspapers into the Grange and read them all day. Over and over again. He couldn't get enough of stories about how life used to be. A woman went from house to house asking people if they had old calendars from the year before. She would look at the old calendars all day and mark the past dates with little notes about what she had been doing back then, when things were normal.

Grant noticed that now, almost three months into the Collapse, something great was happening: boredom. After the initial shock of the Collapse started wearing off, people were getting a little bored. Good boredom, as in no one was trying to kill them today and they had the same meal again, but at least they'd had a meal.

Grant was amazed by the human spirit and resilience so many of them demonstrated after being faced with disorder and an unknown future. Human beings are amazing. In just a few short months most Pierce Point residents had gone from the chaos of the end of the world to a new same ole', same ole'.

# Chapter 195

## *Marion Farm Kicks Ass*

### (July 18)

Ted and Sap hadn't been out to Pierce Point for a week or two. They were getting things together at HQ and would check in periodically on the special radio they left with Scotty. One day, Scotty got the radio message that Ted and Sap would be coming out that night for a meeting and update. The Team kicked out their girlfriends and got down to business. Rich and Dan came out to the yellow cabin for the meeting.

The first thing Grant noticed about Ted and Sap was that their beards were even longer than before. That was true of most men, including Grant. Beards were the "new normal."

"Well, gentlemen," Ted said, "we'll be locating out at the Marion Farm soon."

"When do we go out there?" Ryan asked. Grant was dreading this. The day they went out to Marion Farm would be when he would have to tell Lisa what was going on.

"Oh, permanently?" Ted asked. "Not until right before we need to deploy. No, we'll have you guys coming out on day trips and occasional night training exercises in the meantime. We'll keep you at your day jobs here as much as possible. That's part of the deal with Rich and Dan: as low impact on the internal security of Pierce Point as possible."

"Besides," Sap said, "you guys are well trained. We don't need to show you how to shoot. We'll have you come in during the days and provide instruction. We'll teach you guys some basic military things, like how to move as a larger unit. That kind of thing. But it's all finishing-touch stuff for you guys."

"That's not because we're military bad asses," Grant said, "but because the level of training for an irregular unit is relatively low?" Grant didn't want the Team thinking they already knew everything so they wouldn't pay attention to the further training.

Ted shrugged and said, "Yeah. Kinda. You guys are very good, but there are still some things you need to know." Ted, too, wanted to keep up the Team's confidence, but gently let them know that there were still things they needed to learn.

"Before we get into the details of the training program," Ted said, "we have some intel to give you." Ted went on to describe how the Loyalists were crumbling. He gave updated examples of military units "sitting out" the war or joining the Patriots. Many cops were joining up with Patriot units or running pro-Patriot para operations. Montana had kicked out every federal official and sympathizer, and captured a huge military ammunition depot in the process. New Hampshire, surrounded by Lima Northeastern states like it was, was largely in Patriot hands. The Patriots had even managed to shoot up several key buildings in Chicago. A small team of former SEALs came in from Lake Michigan and swam up the Chicago River. The raid had no military significance, except that it caused the Limas to pour even more resources into defending Chicago, but it sure had a psychological effect.

Seattle was a functioning city, but it was teetering on the edge of lawlessness. There was so much money and so many people with government connections in the city that important people lived a luxurious life. What was left of the authorities—and the gangs cooperating with them—were maintaining order. But resentment was running high. Even the most strident Loyalists in Seattle were figuring out that this wasn't working well.

Olympia was the other Lima stronghold in the state. It was Seattle on a smaller scale: important people living pretty well, but resentment among the regular people was growing. They were maintaining order but only with increasingly extreme measures.

"Are people starving?" Chip asked. He had lots of friends still stuck in Olympia and wanted to know how they were doing.

"Surprisingly, no," Ted said. "People are hungry, and some are really hungry, but those semis keep rolling in with basic foods. They come in under heavy escort, but they're rolling. The giant corporate farms are churning out lots of food. Well, with slave labor pretty much. The Mexicans who were trapped up here or fled up here are working the farms. Pretty brutal conditions, but they're better off than going back home. Mexico is a giant killing field right now." It was silent.

Finally Ted said, "The Limas are sending prisoners to the farms to work. The conditions are bad, but it's not like a concentration camp or anything. Hell, some people are volunteering to work on the farms because they get fed and there are fewer security issues out there. It sounds kinda like how my Okie grandpa lived," Ted said, using the term referring to people from Oklahoma. "My grandpa and his parents lived as migrant farmers during the Depression. You know, Grapes of Wrath," he said referring to the John Steinbeck novel about people from Oklahoma who went to southern California during the 1930s to find work.

"The forces still loyal to the government are pathetic," Ted continued. "There are some loyal ground units—mostly Army and National Guard—run by ladder-climbing young officers who want to get promoted. There are tons of career opportunities for a young lieutenant when there are so many openings, like when the battalion commander is gone." He described how some military units were operating like gangs. "Not full-time," he added, "some of these units are soldiers for a few weeks and then, if an opportunity presents itself, they are a gang for a while, then they might go back to being soldiers. They're gangs of opportunity."

"Anyway," Ted continued with a smile, "it's pretty obvious the Limas are going to fully collapse. Soon. Very soon. It's our job to speed that process along, which brings me to my next bit of news." The room was spellbound.

"Marion Farm kicks ass," Ted said. Sap nodded. "We've been out there and fully assessed the place. It's perfect. Secluded. Beach access for supplies. Plenty of room. A farmhouse HQ, a couple of outbuildings and a big barn for sleeping a lot of men."

"How many?" Bobby asked.

"A hundred," Ted said. "That's with some pretty cozy bunking arrangements, but nothing a soldier can't handle." They let that sink in with the Team: a hundred-man unit. Wow. Much bigger than anything they'd thought of out there. A real military unit instead of what the Team had been: some civilians acting as semi-sophisticated law enforcement.

"We have orders from HQ to train up a hundred-man unit out here," Sap said. "They approved the plan and authorized us to have the supplies for it. This is going to happen. For real."

Sap let that set in.

"We'll slowly build up out there," Ted said. "A couple guys at a time. We'll bring them and supplies out here by boat. A couple guys, a couple sets of weapons, a couple weeks of food at a time. The new arrivals can settle in. We'll be making improvements to the farm at first. Mostly getting the sleeping quarters up and running. And the dining facility. And sanitation. That's a biggie."

"Who are the guys you're bringing out?" Rich asked. He wanted to make sure—even though he trusted Ted and Sap—that they weren't importing a gang.

"The first few boatloads are Patriot regulars," Ted said. "Guys from other units. Mostly Army. We've been assigned about a dozen 11 Bravos." That was the Army term for infantrymen.

"We have a couple Navy guys who know how to build up a facility," Ted said. "They're Seabee reservists actually," Ted said referring to the Navy's construction battalions or "Seabees." They were combat engineers and construction experts. Plus they knew how to pick up a rifle and use it.

"We have an Air Force electrician coming out. He was a RED HORSE," Sap said, referring to the Air Force acronym for a special team of airmen who went into a makeshift forward air base and got it up and running. And knew how to fight if the base was attacked.

Dan, the Air Force security forces veteran, gave a thumbs up. "Those RED HORSE dudes know their shit."

"What about comms?" Scotty asked, referring to communication.

"We got a Navy comms guy," Ted said. "Very squared away. We have some equipment coming for him, plus a surprise comms asset that will blow your mind." Ted and Sap smiled at each other.

"So a dozen infantrymen, maybe a half dozen Navy and Air Force guys," Grant said. "Who else?"

"We're not exactly sure," Ted admitted. "Most irregular units have the majority of their unit as volunteers. Raw civilians. Up to 90% of the unit is civilians. In a typical unit."

"Is this a typical unit?" Rich asked.

"Probably not," Ted said. "We are so close to all the large former military bases here. That means there are lots of guys like me and Sap near here. Our unit will probably get lots of former regular military. At least that's what I'm anglin' for."

This was very comforting to everyone. They were fine joining up with a unit of civilians, but if they were in a unit with lots of regular military, that would be much better. Way more effective and way safer.

"We'll take all the good civilians we can, though," Sap said.

"We're screening them at HQ," Ted said, referring to Boston Harbor. "We're finding out what skills they have, what military experience, if any, they have. We're checking out their fidelity to our cause, too."

"How?" Rich asked. He was a curious by nature and being a cop for several years taught him to ask questions in order to fully understand things.

"We try to see if they have anything obvious in their background, like former government employment," Ted said. "Non-military government employment, that is. But so many people worked for the government right before the Collapse that this is not a very selective criterion. We mostly rely on referrals from people we know are Patriots. We have a little test we do in some cases."

"What's the test?" Scotty asked.

"Well, it's classified but you guys are part of the club," Ted said with a smile.

Ted explained, "We give a revolver to someone we're not sure about. They don't know it, but they're dummy rounds in the cylinder. We tell them to shoot a captured Lima in the head. The 'Lima' is one of our guys pretending to plead for his life. If the recruit pulls the trigger, which makes a 'click' sound, then we know he or she is OK."

"This trick will get out soon and we'll have to move on to another one," Sap said. "But it's useful now. Besides, while we fully expect the Limas to try to infiltrate us, they have better things to do. I mean, they have a full-on war to fight with us—regular units versus regular units. They don't need to spend their time sending in guys to spend a year trying to infiltrate little guerilla bands like us. We have total control on all communication devices our people have, so it's not like an infiltrator could send out reports. Well, not without James Bond kind of equipment. And if the Limas have that stuff working properly, they won't be wasting it on going after 100 irregulars."

"These kinds of wars are messy," Ted said, who had spent over twenty years fighting guerilla wars like this one. "You just have to do what you can to screen for infiltrators. We spend a lot of time and energy watching them and making sure they aren't sending back reports." What Ted didn't tell them is that several regular military people, including him and Sap, would constantly be asking recruits the same questions to see if their stories were consistent. If an odd answer was given, the person who gave it would receive further scrutiny, maybe a formal interrogation. Maybe worse, if it turned out they were an infiltrator.

The guys on the Team were a little concerned that an infiltrator might make it into the unit and call in an airstrike on the Marion Farm. In peacetime, this would have been a horrifying thought and scared them away from doing whatever it was that would put them in that danger. But now, in wartime, this was just another risk they encountered in their new-normal daily life. They didn't exactly shrug off the risk, but it didn't stop them from doing what they had to do.

They just dealt with it. Besides, the Limas were having a hard enough time just keeping the semis rolling.

"I bet one of the reasons to isolate the trainees at the Marion Farm is to keep an eye on them," Pow said.

"Yep. Very much so," Sap said.

Grant was thinking about Al, the guy who oversaw the people coming into Pierce Point from the outside…so he asked a question.

# Chapter 196

## *Shanghai*

### (July 18)

"What about walk-ons?" Grant asked. "You know, people coming to the gate? Could you use any of them?"

"Sure," Ted said. "If they meet our criteria. Who would screen them?"

"There's a guy at the gate who does that," Grant said and explained who Al was. "I have established a relationship with him. I can talk to him about sending us potential military recruits."

"Whoa," Ted said. "Who is he and can we trust him? I mean, I don't want anyone to know what we're doing out here."

Grant was a little mad that Ted seemed to be assuming Grant would just blab to Al about what was going on at Marion Farm. "He won't truly know what's going on out here," Grant said. "He'll be told the 'rental team' cover story."

"Oh, OK," Ted said, "I guess that's OK."

Grant had another question. "What are you looking for in walk-on recruits? So I can tell Al what to be looking out for."

"Guys with nothing left to lose," Ted said. "Homeless, hungry, mean. Not psycho mean, but revenge mean. Preferably people who lost everything because of jackass politicians. Maybe they're looking for a way to get even." This kind of person had been the backbone of guerilla movements and revolutions for thousands of years.

Ted thought some more. "Single guys. We can't really take in their families. I mean, we can't have a daycare at a guerilla camp." Ted had actually seen that in some of the camps he'd operated throughout the world. "Well, maybe we could take in families, but they'd have to have the right skills. Some really good skills, like a guy whose wife is a nurse. I'd take that family."

"Do walk-ons need military experience?" Grant asked.

"Not really," Ted said. "However, it's a huge plus. If you get some AWOL FUSA guys, I'm interested. AWOL cops would be another good find. But I'm interested in people with engineering, construction, machining, and agricultural backgrounds. Of course medical is always welcomed. We need to have a mini town out at the

179

Marion farm for months before we deploy. We need people with..." Ted searched for the right term.

"Town-running skills," Grant said. It wasn't exactly a military term, but Grant wasn't exactly a military person.

"Yeah," Ted said, "'Town-running skills.' We're like Pierce Point: we need people who know how to keep a town running. We'll hand them a rifle before we deploy. We're an irregular unit, not Delta Force. But we need people with important camp skills or skills we'll need in the city we're occupying."

"People with town-running skills will be assigned to your civil affairs team, Grant, and they can go solve those problems in the city we take," Ted stated.

It sounded weird to Grant to hear Ted say "your civil affairs team," but totally normal at the same time. It was weird because now they were the civil affairs team, with no formal training whatsoever. But not weird because it just made sense and serving in the civil affairs role had basically been assumed ever since Ted and Sap arrived that first night on the beach.

"What about fidelity to the cause?" Grant asked. "'Cause that will be hard to assess with certainty as we're interviewing them at the gate."

"That's a tough one," Ted said. "You can't polygraph them at the gate." Ted paused. "Do the best you can on the fidelity issue. I suspect most people coming to the gate, wondering around with nothing, aren't exactly thinking about politics. They're like the homeless dudes the government paid to go out and protest and intimidate people at the beginning of the Collapse. Well, we can do the same. We can say to people 'Want to be fed and have a mission in life? Come with me.'" Ted felt bad using people who were in a bad situation, but war was a bad situation. Winning it was what counted.

Sap added, "We'll have some pretty good controls in place in the camp for making sure recruits aren't communicating with Limas or anyone else. Even if we get someone who is a Lima, we'll be able to handle him. So, take the risk at the gate and we'll correct it in camp if necessary."

"The walk-ons coming to the gate can't be told what we're doing out here, of course," Grant said. Everyone nodded. "We have the cover story of the 'rental team.' But that raises another problem."

"Shanghai," Ted said.

"Exactly," Grant said, amazed that Ted predicted what he was thinking. But, then again, Ted was a professional.

"Huh?" Scotty said. "Shanghai? As in the city in China?"

"Yep," Grant said. "You know, 'shanghai' is the term for when people get tricked or forced to join an army. They get 'shanghaied' and have to serve against their will. I think it came from a few hundred years ago when the British Navy would nab people and take them off to Shanghai and force them to serve."

"Oh, right," Scotty said. He'd heard the term before.

"We run into this all the time in indigenous guerilla units," Ted said. "We have volunteers come to us, but we can't tell them, at least at first, what we're doing and where we're doing it. So we take them into the unit without giving them full disclosure of what's going on. But, what if they don't want to be a soldier? We can't let them out of the camp and we can't spare the personnel to guard them at the camp while the unit is on the march. Plus, our guards watching them would be left behind in what might be enemy territory. And we can't have that."

Wow. This sucked, Grant thought. This war thing wasn't easy. It was full of problems. It wasn't like a video game, or like people just join up with the good guys and everything is fine. There are complications and moral questions. War was full of shitty situations.

"Thoughts?" Ted asked. He and Sap had a plan for this, and HQ had come up with some guidelines before they'd departed for Pierce Point, but Ted wanted to see what the Pierce Point guys came up with. It was quiet for a while.

Grant decided to pipe up. His rental team cover story went over so well that he was more confident in giving his suggestions.

"Well, these walk-ons are being told they have a job on the 'rental team,' right?" Grant said. "They know they'll be fighting and will be exposed to danger. They could be told that the rental team will not be hired out to government; just to citizens defending themselves."

Ted and Sap were smiling. They knew what Grant was about to say.

"Go ahead," Ted said.

"So," Grant said, "the walk-ons know that they'll be fighting — but not for the government." He sensed he was giving the right answer which made him speak even more confidently.

"This means," Grant continued, "the walk-ons know that what they're doing is totally illegal and the Limas could kill them on the spot. So, when they are told the rental team story, they basically know everything they need to know: They're fighters, not for the government, and they're breaking the law. They need to be cool with that."

Ted and Sap looked at each other and smiled.

"Exactly," Ted said. "The walk-ons, by being told they're a 'rental team,' basically know everything they need to know to volunteer for the Patriots; not fully everything, but enough that if they hesitate at being on an outlaw rental team, then they don't want to be in a Patriot irregular unit either."

Grant had one more pressing question.

"What do we do if one of the walk-ons finds out what we're doing out there and then doesn't want to be in the unit?" He asked. "We'd have to keep them guarded at the farm. That would suck. I mean, we can't shoot them, can we?" Grant was implying they could.

"No, we don't shoot them," Sap said, disappointed that Grant had come up with that.

"We've found that, once men come into camp, they don't regret it," Ted said. "They have a job and nowhere else to go. Camaraderie develops. We work hard on that. We foster camaraderie. I've seen reluctant men turn into a band of brothers. So, odds are we won't have this problem."

"But what if we do?" Grant asked. He knew that they needed a plan for every problem they could think of in advance, which wasn't even all the problems they'd actually face. But, at least they'd have a plan for the foreseeable problems and what to do with reluctant fighters was one of those problems.

"In the past," Sap said, "we've had a few personnel stay behind in the camp, if that's possible, and guard the people who refuse to go out with the unit and fight."

"What if it's not possible?" Grant asked.

"Well, in this particular situation, Pierce Point, that is," Ted said, "you have a jail, right?"

Grant nodded.

"We throw them in the Pierce Point jail," Sap said.

"What if they talk about how they just left a Patriot irregular camp run by Special Forces located out at Marion Farm?" Grant asked.

"We tell everyone that they're crazy," Ted said. "Hell, we'll lock them up in the mental ward you got out here." Ted thought some more and said, "And, if the unit is out of the camp and on the march, there's less damage they can do to us by talking. We're already out of the area."

Everyone nodded. That sounded like a decent solution; better than shooting them.

It was silent again. After a while, Grant came up with another question.

"What about women?"

"Depends," Ted said. "If they have skills, they're welcomed. I've seen some female soldiers in the IDF that would blow your mind." Ted was referring to the Israeli Defense Forces, which had many women soldiers.

Ted was being polite when he said how great it was to have women fighters, however. There was nothing wrong with women. They usually fought well when they had something important to fight for, like their families. They had the physical strength to do what an irregular unit did, which was carry a rifle, but not much else. An irregular unit wasn't a commando unit. They didn't need to carry an eighty pound pack for three days without sleep. Less is demanded of an irregular unit, which is why they could be full of civilians. They were secondary troops, and some women were perfectly fine secondary troops.

But, truth be told, Ted really would rather not have any women in camp. It wasn't that he didn't like women, or that they didn't have any skills, but they distracted men. Ted viewed women in camp like a river or minefield that needed to be crossed: something to be dealt with because it was just part of the landscape. Ted knew that men needed women and that men would fight the hardest for their women and children, but women just complicated everything.

Ted realized that the rest of the world might find that to be "sexist" but he didn't give a crap. All he cared about was successfully executing the mission he was given and bringing back every one of his fighters alive. Everything else was a distant second on his list of concerns. Very distant.

Ted knew quite a bit about the problems women caused in a camp. He knew, from spending years of his life in dozens of camps full of fighters in several countries all across the world, the effect women could have on a guerilla unit.

"Women can be in camp, but they must have a very clear and much-needed job," Ted said. "If they have town-running skills or medical skills, awesome. If our best engineer is a woman, she's the chief engineer."

"But," Ted said, putting his finger up for emphasis, "if women don't have a well-defined and needed job, they often turn into girlfriends and that causes all kinds of problems for discipline."

Everyone looked at Wes. He flipped them off.

Sap added, "To be honest, if you have a choice between letting in a pretty woman and a plain woman with the same skills, pick the plain one. There will be less fighting over her." The Team looked at him like he was crazy to not have the prettiest women possible around.

"Seriously," Sap said. "I know what I'm talking about." Ted nodded. They'd dealt with this before in Columbia when they were there "advising" that government on getting rid of the narco-terrorists.

"Speaking of women," Grant said, "our young fighters here" — he pointed to the Team — "have girlfriends. Let me guess, they can't bring them to the farm?"

"Correct," Ted said. "The only women at the farm are ones who are working there. Ones with skills we need or family members of men we need, and even they have jobs. No girlfriends."

Grant knew what his guys were thinking. Celibacy? Really? That might be a deal killer. They had signed up with the Patriots and devoted their lives to this dangerous cause. But no girlfriends? The deal might be off.

"I had assumed the Team would be in Pierce Point much of the time," Grant said. "I think you said earlier that the Team will train at the farm during the day and come home to Pierce Point at night most nights. Right?"

"Pretty much," Ted said, looking at Rich and Dan. "I'd like to see the Team spend about half their days at the farm and the other half on patrol in Pierce Point. Of course, the Team would be on call for Pierce Point even when they're at the farm. If something does go down in Pierce Point, you guys zoom over here to handle it."

Rich and Dan looked at Ted as if to say, "Damned right."

"There will be some night training, especially toward the end," Sap said. "For that, we'll need you guys spending the night out at the farm."

"Without girlfriends," Pow said.

"Affirmative," Ted said.

"How often will that be?" Bobby asked. He had fallen hard for his girlfriend, Sammie.

"Rarely for the next couple months," Sap said. "Then once a week, then every other night. Towards the end, when it's very close to deployment time, then every night." Sap shrugged. "It's the life of a soldier."

Ted quickly added, "And you are soldiers now."

That reminded the Team that they had taken an oath to something much more grand and important than getting laid. The

Team realized they were being a little whiny about the girls. They were soldiers now. This wasn't some big party at the yellow cabin. They were in a war and better get used to it.

"Understood," Pow said. He looked at all the guys and said, "Understood?"

"Understood," they all said. Ted noted that Pow was a leader. They followed his lead. He remembered Chip telling him that Pow was the tactical leader and Grant was the strategic leader. After seeing Pow and Grant in action that evening, Ted understood what Chip was talking about.

Grant decided to change the subject.

"How many walk-ons do you need?" He asked. "I mean, if you don't need many then we can be very picky about their skills. If you need a lot, we'll have lower standards."

Ted smiled. "An excellent question," he said. "The answer is that we can be picky at this point. We have a core of screened former military coming in the first wave. We will have some raw civilians that we've screened back at HQ coming after that. We have a few dozen already, so we have about half the hundred or so slots filled now. We'll fill the other fifty or so slots in a few weeks with a combination of more raw civilians that come to us from HQ and some of these walk-ons from here. So, be very picky now and we'll have a better idea of how many we need in a few weeks."

"Will you be using any other Pierce Point people?" Dan asked.

"Well, a few of your guards," Ted said looking at Rich and Dan, "but you guys get to limit the number of them. You guys talked to me last time I was out about which guards had skills, could be trusted, and could be spared. Only about eight, you told me. So about eight it will be."

Pow got ready to ask the question the Team had been waiting to hear.

# Chapter 197

## Special Squad

### (July 18)

"What, specifically, will we be doing?" Pow asked, referring to the Team.

"We have two uses for you," Ted said. He had been anticipating this question. "In the training phase, you will be trainers for the raw civilians. You will teach them basic firearms. My military guys will teach them the more intense stuff, like unit movements and explosives, although I suspect you guys will be able to teach this too."

Explosives? The Team looked at each other. This was pretty serious.

"When it's time to deploy," Ted said, "we plan on using you as a special squad."

Special squad? That got the Team's attention. Commandos? Blowing up bridges? Covert missions? Hostage rescue? The young guys on the Team had visions of glory swirling in their heads. Unrealistic visions.

"You guys know your shit," Ted said. He had rehearsed this part. He wanted to flatter the Team because he needed them to do a mission they would initially think was not a good use of their door-kicking and bad-guy-shooting skills.

Ted started the flattery, which was part legitimate praise and part salesmanship. "Hell, I trained you in the fundamentals, so I know you know your shit. And," Ted looked over to Chip, "I understand you've been perfecting these skills out here lately." Chip nodded, followed by Rich and Dan.

It worked. The Team was flattered. They would be a special squad in a Special Forces guerilla group. Their heads were spinning, even the head belonging to wise and mature Grant.

One of them wasn't flattered, however. "What kind of special squad?" Ryan asked. As a former Marine, Ryan knew "special squad" could be a good thing or a bad thing.

"Well, a SWAT team, basically," Ted said. The Team was pretty good, Ted thought, but not like the kind of urban-trained military units he had at his disposal when he was in the FUSA Army. The Team was no professional law enforcement SWAT team, but they would have to suffice. This was not to say they sucked; they were light years ahead of a bunch of raw civilians.

"Taking down small facilities," Ted continued, "especially in urban settings. You know, 'There's a bunch of Limas in that building. Go get them.' That kind of thing. You'll still need to know patrolling, communications, and larger unit movements like everyone else."

Ryan was nodding slowly. OK, he thought, that would be a good role for them, but he would make sure that "special squad" didn't mean "run through this minefield and see which ones blow up."

"I think of your specific role as an MP SWAT team," Sap said, referring to the acronym for a military police unit. "There are military aspects to MP law enforcement. It's a combination of a law enforcement mindset in a military setting. You guys have been operating as LEOs for a while now," meaning law enforcement officers, "So you have the LE mindset," he said.

This, too, was a little bit of flattery. Sap knew that the Team was not trained law enforcement; they were just some guys who had been doing it full time for a couple of months out of necessity. "We'll add the military skills and give you the overview of the military setting. You'll plop your LE skills into that," Sap said.

"Plus," Ted said, "You guys will also be a liaison with the locals here in Pierce Point. You know them. They trust you guys. That's important. And," Ted said pointing to Sap, "more importantly, we trust you."

The Team was a little disappointed. They were thrilled to be a special squad, but they had assumed the guerilla unit would be built up around them. That they would be the stars in a sea of untrained civilians. But, now there would be quite a few military people, including infantrymen who knew more than they did.

On the positive side, though, the Team realized that it was good that there would be experienced people around them, which increased their odds of making it through this alive. But, they had to admit, they kind of wanted to be the best trained people in the new unit. Oh well. The fact that there would be real military people in this unit meant that it would be more likely to get some good missions, with lots of bullets flying. That's what the young guys wanted.

Ted looked at Grant. "And, depending on the mission, the Team will be the core of a civil affairs operation that we'll be running out of this unit." Ted knew he needed to sell this mission to the younger guys on the Team who wanted to knock down doors and get in firefights. They were volunteers and could walk away at any moment. Ted couldn't order them to do things and then court martial them if they didn't. He had to sell, not order, which was the kind of diplomacy Special Forces employed when organizing teams of indigenous fighters.

The Team looked at each other. They were going from a special squad of MP SWAT to doing pansy-ass paper-pushing "civil affairs"? Ted could tell what they were thinking.

"By 'civil affairs,'" Ted said, "I mean Grant here will be spearheading some occupation matters for our little unit." Not only did Grant have a track-record of running Pierce Point smoothly, he was pre-positioned near the city his unit would be taking: Olympia. HQ marveled at their luck of having a guy with town-running skills who was already near the target city. Perfect. In fact, this unit was being built around this civil affairs capability.

Ted continued, "Civil affairs isn't paperwork, gentlemen. It's, you know, overseeing the things the civilian population of a city needs. Food. Finding remaining Limas. Seeing if enemy deserters can be trusted, or if they need to be detained. Putting up makeshift detention facilities. That kind of thing. Managing the civilians so the regular military can do their regular military thing." Ted was gauging the Team's reaction. He wanted them to be excited about the importance of their mission.

The Team just sat there staring at Ted.

"Well," Ted continued, trying to fire up the Team, "all this civil affairs shit happens in a very dangerous setting: a city we just barely took a few hours earlier. The situation is still fluid. It's not like all the bad guys show up in a city park and lay down their arms. There will be pockets of bad guys everywhere."

Ted scanned the Team to gauge their reactions and then kept going as they appeared to be warming up to the idea. "Pockets?" Ted continued. "Hell, there'll be buildings and whole neighborhoods that are still chock full of bad guys. They'll be desperate and they'll fight like hell, so our civil affairs people need protection. That calls for lots of urban fighting. Small-unit shit. It calls for us to be able to say, 'Go take down that building and then resume trying to feed these civilians.' You guys are already a cohesive and well-trained small unit. And Grant's part of it and he's the civil affairs guy. You guys should go into combat together. It's a no-brainer."

"Sounds cool," Bobby said. Others joined in.

Ryan was a little skeptical. He'd seen glorious assignments turn into shitty jobs before. He sat back and thought. He was the only one who wasn't nodding. He saw the wisdom in having the Team perform the MP SWAT/civil affairs role. It was a way cooler mission than most of the irregular units of indigenous fighters would get. But still, that "special squad" thing was concerning to him.

"MP SWAT is a very unusual role for a Special Forces guerilla unit," Ryan said. "Very unusual." Ted could tell Ryan was skeptical.

"You're the former Marine, right?" Ted asked Ryan. He nodded.

"You're right," Ted said to Ryan. "The usual mission of a Special Forces-led guerilla unit is to harass the enemy behind enemy lines, but guess what? There are no enemy 'lines' in this war. There is just Seattle and, to a lesser extent, Olympia where the old government has hunkered down."

Ted put his hands up for emphasis. "Civil affairs is very important in this war," he said. "Those 'enemy' people in occupied cities are not Iraqis, Afghans, Russians, or North Koreans, who, let's be honest, no one sheds a tear if they go hungry for a little while. No, the 'enemy' in the areas we're going into are Americans. We need to treat them as well as possible. They're our friends and, in some cases, our family. Some are Limas, but others aren't, and even the Limas are still Americans, so we need to do everything we can to help them. Getting their city back up and running and feeding them is what we need to do. They're Americans."

"So," Ted said to Ryan, "I see why you're saying it's unusual for us to be tasking you guys with this MP SWAT and civil affairs shit. It *is* unusual, but you guys are here near one of the objective cities. I personally know that you've got gun fighting experience, and a track record of running a town. It's a no-brainer."

"What about me?" Chip said. "I'm too old to do this shit."

Ted and Chip had been very close friends for years and Ted knew that Chip wanted to go into the city.

"It's Rich and Dan's call," Ted said, once again utilizing the diplomacy he'd been trained in. "I made a promise to them that the internal security of Pierce Point would not be weakened by having a guerilla unit out here. I know you run the day guards at the Grange, Chip, which I think needs to continue out here." Ted had already thought that Chip wasn't needed in the guerilla unit, except maybe as a trainer, and he wanted to show Rich and Dan that he wasn't taking too many guys away.

"You want to go?" Rich asked Chip, hoping the answer was

189

"no."

"No," Chip said. "I'm too old for that shit. I'll do it if I have to, but..."

"Say no more," Ted said. "You're needed here. That's important. Same with Rich and Dan," Ted said looking at them. "Of course you two are invited into the unit but, I gotta say, you're doing very important work here."

"We'll stay here," Dan said. He and Rich had already talked about it and instantly came to the conclusion that they had to stay in Pierce Point. Without Rich being the calm law enforcement leader of the community, Pierce Point could disintegrate. Without Dan and his amazing facility-defense skills, the gate could easily be breached.

The most Rich and Dan would agree to donate to the guerilla unit was the Team and a few of the good guards, but not all of them. Rich and Dan concluded that they were helping the effort tremendously by letting the Patriots train a guerilla unit at the Marion Farm. That was all they could do. They would do more if they could, but they couldn't risk everyone in Pierce Point just for this. Besides, after hearing about the plan to bring some military people into the unit, they realized the guerilla unit would do just fine without every last security force member at Pierce Point. Rich and Dan's first job was the survival of Pierce Point, and helping topple the remnants of the former government was a second priority.

"What can we do to help you?" Rich asked Ted.

"Well, not much right now other than what you're doing," Ted said. "We'll start bringing in boatloads of personnel and materials. I'm working well with the Chief and Paul on the beach landings." Ted paused and thought. "Can't think of anything right now."

Grant thought he knew the answer to his next question, but wanted to be clear with Ted on this important topic.

"The personnel you're bringing in are self-sufficient, right?" He asked. "We—Pierce Point—don't need to feed them, right?"

"Correct," Ted said. "We don't bring people out until we can sustain them. Everything. Food. Medical. Oh, that reminds me. We have a couple medics with us and they 'liberated' a ton of medical supplies from their former FUSA units. You guys need any?"

Ted always tried to get as much stuff as possible to the host community. It bought a lot of good will. Whether it was Afghanistan, Columbia, the Philippines, or Pierce Point, the principle was the same: take care of your local fighters' families and they'll do amazing things for you.

"You bet we can use them," Grant said, knowing that Lisa was very concerned that the initial batch of medical supplies they traded for in Frederickson was not enough. "Get them to me and I'll get them to our clinic," Grant said.

Ted smiled. He knew Grant would figure out a way to make sure the Patriots got political credit with the community for the medical supplies, thereby bolstering support from the host community. But Grant would do it in a way that didn't disclose the location of the guerilla unit out there. Perfect.

"Well," Ted said, "I guess that's it for us. You have any more questions?"

No one did.

"OK, we'll go to the Marion Farm now with some supplies," Ted said. "We've got a couple of guys down at the boat right now. They'll be staying at the farm and guarding things. I didn't bring them up because, well, you'll meet them soon enough."

Sap and Grant figured out the logistics of getting the future shipment of medical supplies to Lisa.

Rich looked at Ted and said, "I appreciate how you're going about this."

Ted nodded.

"I mean, you're not poaching all my guys," Rich said and then pointed at the Team, "just these shit bags." That got a laugh. "If you keep operating this way, I don't think we'll have any problems." Rich looked deadly serious.

"Message received," Ted said. "We appreciate the hospitality you're showing us and we'll put it to good use." He'd used that very line in several languages in several countries. And he sincerely meant it.

# Chapter 198

## *First Look at Marion Farm*

### (July 21)

The Team tried to lead a normal life after Ted and Sap left, but it was not easy. They did their day jobs while constantly thinking about their training at Marion Farm and then their eventual mission. They were excited about being in a guerilla unit. It was the thrill of a lifetime.

Grant was doing his day job of organizing and judging at the Grange and training with the Team one or two afternoons a week. He was hiding the Ted project from Lisa, which was really wearing on him. But, he had to keep it secret; not only were lives depending on him keeping quiet, but he knew that Ted would literally kill him if he talked. Grant knew that the longer he kept it from Lisa, the more betrayed she would feel. A couple of times, when he and Lisa were getting along extra well and he realized how great it would be to stay married to her forever, he thought about telling her. But he didn't. Every time he was tempted to tell her, he imagined what Ted's reaction would be.

Three days later, Scotty's special "Ted radio" crackled. Ted said they would be coming with a load of men and supplies and wanted to meet with the Team at the yellow cabin. The guys were very excited. They had been craving contact with Ted or Sap for days.

The Team Chicks were asked to go to their own places that night. Ted and Sap came up to the yellow cabin at 8:00 p.m. and told the Team to come with them and see Marion Farm. This time of year, it didn't get dark until about 9:00 p.m. The Team went to a bigger boat than the little one that Ted and Sap usually zipped around on. It was nice civilian boat, over thirty feet long, and several men were on it.

When the Team got on board, Ted said, "Gentlemen, I believe you know Stan and Carl."

There was Stan, the construction contractor from Capitol City Guns, and Carl the computer guy who used to hang out there, too. Everyone was thrilled to see their old gun store buddies.

"How've you ugly bastards been?" Stan asked. He had lost a lot of weight.

"I like the beards," Carl said, looking at the Team and stroking his own. "Never seen you guys unshaven." He, too, had lost a lot of weight.

They caught up on what had happened since May Day. Shortly after the Team evacuated the gun store, Stan and Carl, both strong Patriots, linked up with Ted. They helped Ted move his half of the gun store's guns and ammo from his Olympia-area home to Boston Harbor, which took about a month. They moved them in small quantities at night and would carry them around checkpoints, having to hike through back streets and, sometimes, the woods. They didn't tell anyone about the time when they had to kill two FCorps at a checkpoint. They had walked up to them with knives in their sleeves and did it the old fashioned, and silent, way.

After Stan and Carl helped Ted move all the weapons, they started helping around the Boston Harbor HQ of the Patriot forces. They were teamed up with two other guys, Tom and Travis. Tom was an Air Force load master at nearby McChord Air Force Base, where he helped arrange cargo on transport planes. Travis was a Navy guy from nearby Bangor submarine base. He was a machinist who worked on the subs. Tom and Travis, both Patriots, went AWOL and drifted around until they found a Patriot stronghold, like Boston Harbor.

Now, Tom and Travis were assigned, along with civilians Stan and Carl, to a "liberator" unit; as in, "liberate" government food and supplies from the Limas. They came up with a variety of ingenious schemes to do this. They made fake IDs and learned the forms that the Limas used to move their food around. They even drove a truck of food right out of a Lima warehouse one time. They got that one with a low-tech method: bribing the FCorps guard with two cartons of cigarettes.

"We brought out some snacks," Carl said and showed them the cases of food in the boat. "We're taking them out to the farm. We will be the supply officers for the guerilla unit."

"We'll be taking our 'liberator' operation on the road and start operating in your area," Travis said. "We'll need a briefing on where all the Lima storage facilities are."

Paul was steering the boat to the Marion Farm landing. The Team helped the visitors from Boston Harbor unload the boat. They then put the supplies onto two big landscaping carts that were stashed down at the landing. They were the big carts with the huge tires; the kind used to haul large plants around a landscaping site that worked great for moving supplies along the quarter mile road to the farm.

"This is the last load we'll do with the carts," Stan said. "We have a truck scheduled to be here tomorrow morning, which will make the unloads much easier."

They talked about how they would get the word to Dan that a truck with two guys would be coming to the gate. Grant would tell Al that these two were "rental team" guys, who, in turn, would nonchalantly tell everyone else that they were residents going to their cabin. No one would remember them and wonder why they weren't at Grange meetings. The majority of residents didn't go every night anymore because things were running relatively smoothly.

Grant had never seen the Marion Farm. When he came up on it, he was amazed. Even in the low light of dusk, he could see how perfect it was. It was huge and had a horse fence around it. The road from the beach was easily defensible. There was a little high spot facing the beach that was perfect for an observation post and a machine gun. There were two large outbuildings. Sap said they were empty but would be put to good use. The farmhouse was big. It could use a little cosmetic work on the outside, but it was solid. It was nice inside. It hadn't been lived in for a while, but someone had cleaned it up pretty well. The electricity and water were on. Thank God.

They went out to the huge barn. Like all barns its size, it had a hay loft. There wasn't any hay in it, just a large floor for sleeping dozens of men. Same with the bottom floor, which still had remnants of hay and general farm dirt in it. It would take a thorough cleaning to get it up to sanitary shape for human habitation, but the troops out there had lots of manpower and lots of time. Cleaning a barn and turning it into sleeping quarters was one of the unglamorous things soldiers did for the 99.9% of the time they weren't engaged in combat.

They met about a half dozen Patriot former regular military guys who were already there. The Air Force RED HORSE guy, Don, was in charge of getting the farm up and running. He was a thin, bald guy in his late thirties. He was everywhere and doing an amazing job. They didn't have any heavy equipment, like the truck that would be coming the next day. Most of the tools had been sold when the farm was abandoned. Don handed Ted a list of needed equipment and talked to him about the five hundred gallon underground diesel tank at the farm, which was empty. At least they had a tank they could fill and then use. It beat a bunch of gas cans stacked up.

Grant and the Team were going around and introducing themselves. The military guys had been briefed on the Team and what they would be doing, so they were warmly received.

The military guys were glad to be out at Pierce Point. They had been cooped up in Boston Harbor and were anxious to get out in the field and get the mission underway. This was a big adventure for them. Most of them had never been in combat, which was universally true of the Air Force and Navy guys out there. Some of the Army infantry guys had been in combat, but that was in Afghanistan and a little bit in Iraq toward the end of that war when things were pretty quiet.

But, even for the combat veterans, this mission was much more exciting. It wasn't fighting for Afghans or Iraqis. It was fighting for Americans. It was getting their country back. They seemed to be glad they had landed in a unit with other Patriots and were in a position to do some good things. It beat being a stranded "gray man" back in their own cities trying to sabotage the Limas.

Ted informed the Team that they wouldn't need to come out to the farm again for a while as he wanted to get everything up and running first. Ted had enough guys there already to guard the place.

"Hey, Grant, whatcha doin' tonight?" Ted asked.

"Not dating men, if that's where you're going with that," Grant said with a smile.

"Wanna come back with us to Boston Harbor?" Ted asked. "There are some people I'd like you to meet."

"Sure," Grant said. He had told Lisa that he might be working nights with the Team a lot in the future and not to count on him being home at any particular times. She understood…only because he hadn't told her the truth.

Grant reached into his pocket and felt to see if he had any of his caffeine pills. Yep. Good. He could stay awake tonight. He was glad he had squirreled away a few hundred caffeine pills before the Collapse. He knew he'd need them.

After some more introductions, it was time to head back. Stan, Carl, Tom, and Travis would stay at the farm. The Team went ahead toward the boat as a group; Ted, Sap, and Grant brought up the rear. They silently walked down the road back to the boat. The moon was out. It felt so odd to be walking down a road with some Special Forces guys and carrying an AR and full kit.

Grant felt like he was in a movie. Out at Pierce Point, he had been through lots of things that he never thought he would experience, but every once in a while something even more movie-like happened. Something that was unexpected, even by the new standards of "normal." Grant was just soaking it in. This was a memory he'd have for the rest of his life. Just let it soak in.

They got to the boat and met up with Paul, who was in his

element. He had lost a lot of weight and looked healthy for the first time since Grant had met him. He was smiling, which was also something new. He was doing something extremely important. He had gone from being the fat kid who played video games to the trusted guide covertly ferrying Special Forces to a secret base.

Grant was really happy for him. That's one good thing that's happened from this war, he thought. At least there was one good thing.

They drifted slowly in the boat as they pushed off from the landing. Once they got a hundred yards from shore, Paul radioed the Chief and sped up. They were back at the dock at Grant's cabin within a few minutes. The Team silently got off and went into the yellow cabin. Scotty radioed Gideon first so they didn't get shot.

It felt odd for Grant to stay on the boat. He always went with the Team and sensed things were different now. He felt slightly integrated with Boston Harbor, even though he had never been there. He wasn't just a guy on the Team or the judge anymore. He was now connected with the Boston Harbor HQ.

Was this what he was supposed to be doing? This was getting serious. He had gone way past a neighborhood defense group. He had gone past helping to make a community run smoothly. He was a rebel soldier now, and kind of a high-ranking one. He would have some big responsibilities in the civil affairs field. Is this what I'm supposed to be doing? He kept asking himself this question.

Yes, Grant thought, this is exactly what you're supposed to be doing. You've come this far. You have some very unique skills and assets. This was supposed to happen.

*Yes.*

# Chapter 199

## *"Yes, Sir. With Pride."*

### (July 21)

Hearing the outside thought verify that this was what Grant was supposed to do was exactly what he needed to hear. Grant was calm. It was that amazing peaceful calm that came when the outside thought told him he was on track and was doing what he was supposed to be doing.

As the boat quietly chugged along the shoreline of Pierce Point and out toward Boston Harbor, Grant looked up at the stars. There were millions of them; many, many more than he was used to seeing. Grant looked at all the millions of stars and thought, "I am just one of these little things. One of millions, but together they make up something bigger."

*Yes.*

The peace and calm was overwhelming. Grant knew he could do anything now. Well, not him alone. But, with help – from the most powerful thing in the universe.

Anything. Anything at all could be accomplished. Grant stopped worrying about Lisa's reaction to the Ted project. He stopped worrying about her leaving him. He stopped worrying about the Team getting killed or wounded. He stopped worrying about everything. He just sat back in the seat on the boat and looked up at the stars as they silently glided to Boston Harbor. It was another lifetime memory he was soaking in.

After a while, after the mild caffeine rush had kicked in, the radio crackled and Paul responded. They were getting near some lights. It must be Boston Harbor. Paul gave the right signals with his boat lights to the picket boats outlying Boston Harbor. As they got closer, Grant looked at the "fishing" boats. The boats had some very well armed men and big radio antennas. The men on the boat saluted them. Grant returned the salute without thinking. Then he realized what he had just done. Saluted. This was getting serious.

The boat slowed to a crawl as they entered the marina. Grant had been to Boston Harbor several times before. It was about ten miles from Olympia. He rented a boat out there and puttered around Boston

Harbor with Cole when he was little. Cole had loved it. Grant had great memories of this place.

As they pulled further into the marina, Grant was amazed at what a great place Boston Harbor was for a headquarters. The marina was easily defended and was on the remote southern tip of Puget Sound, which was the water superhighway for the entire Seattle metropolitan area. The little town of Boston Harbor looked like the American version of a Norwegian fishing village. It was full of nice buildings to house people. There was one really big and nice house right on the water with lots of guards around it and its lights on. That must be HQ.

Grant helped Ted and Sap tie up the boat as Paul put it perfectly into its slip. No one had said a word for the last twenty minutes they had been in the boat. It was a welcomed break. Grant talked and listened all day long. He needed quiet time, especially with the stars out, a big adventure ahead of him, and, most importantly, with the outside thought talking to him. It had been a spectacular night so far.

As Grant got off the boat he started to think for the first time about whether he would make a good impression on the brass. He laughed at himself. Who cares? He wasn't interviewing for a job. Hell, he'd be happy not to have the job of being a Patriot guerilla. He would be happy to stay in Pierce Point and do his Grange job and go out with the Team on occasional calls.

But, Grant knew he had a bigger job to do. He knew that HQ would have him do whatever it was that he was supposed to do. The outside thought had confirmed that he was on the right course. He was just there to see what the details of the course would be. He had never been more calm and confident.

And it showed. The way he walked. The way he carried his kit and AR. He looked like a professional. A quiet professional who had been doing this his whole life, which was hilarious. Only three months ago, he had just been a lawyer with a semi-normal white collar life. There was no way to tell that now by looking at him. He had totally transformed. Well, he hadn't transformed; he was the same guy he'd been. Instead, circumstances had brought out the Grant that was always there, but had never had a reason to come out.

Ted motioned for Grant to follow him. They came up to a guard at the marina gate, who knew Ted and Sap and waved them through. The guard stopped Grant, pointed to him, and asked Sap, "Is this the visitor you said you'd be bringing back?"

"Yep," Sap said. "Ketchup sandwich."

The guard nodded and said to Grant, "Welcome to Boston Harbor, Mr. Matson." Apparently "ketchup sandwich" was a code word. There were lots of those out there.

They walked across the dock to the little store at the marina. The lights were on and the shelves were entirely bare. This was the first store Grant had been in since he left Olympia. He was struck again by how odd the empty shelves looked. It made him realize how good they had it in Pierce Point.

Ted, Sap, and Grant walked to the road and up the hill to the big house with the lights on. There were guards everywhere. Radios were crackling as they headed toward HQ. The guards were very well armed. Most had impressive kit. These guys looked like military guys. Actually, they looked like private military contractors, but Grant knew that they were military, just without uniforms because the Free Washington State Guard didn't have its own uniforms yet. A few had their old FUSA fatigues—mostly Army, but a few of the different camo patterns of the Navy, Air Force, and Marine Corps—with "Free Wash. State Guard" sewn on the area where "U.S. Army" or other branch name had once been.

Most of the men looked like Grant. Many were younger than him, but he fit right in as far as clothing was concerned. Along with his AR, Grant had his black tactical vest with coyote brown pouches, gray t shirt, tan 5.11 pants, "hillbilly slippers" (Romeo boots), and his tan baseball cap. The cap had the Survival Podcast ant symbol on it. He thought about the ant symbol, which reflected the ant and grasshopper from the fable about how the hardworking ant prepped while the playful grasshopper didn't, and the ant made it through the winter but the grasshopper did not. The Survival Podcast ant hat was a statement to the world that "I am an ant."

As they came up to the porch, there were three guards and a stack of sand bags. Grant wondered if he would have to leave his rifle and pistol with the guards. Ted and Sap walked right past the guards, and no one asked Grant to remove his weapons, so he didn't.

They went into the front door and Grant started to remove his hat. He remembered from his extremely limited military training in Civil Air Patrol all those years ago, that you remove your "cover" (hat, helmet, or beret) when you enter a building.

Ted saw him taking his hat off and said, "Battlefield rules out here." While the little high school Civil Air Patrol cadets were never on a battlefield, Grant knew that "battlefield rules" meant that you could

199

keep your cover on indoors and you didn't salute. You kept your cover on because it was a waste of time taking it on and off. You didn't salute on the battlefield because that allowed enemy snipers to figure out who the officers were and shoot them first.

When they walked in the front door, there was a desk in the foyer, which looked weird in a home. It was a beautiful house with a giant open entry way and big staircase going up to the second floor. There were radios crackling and a lot of activity in the house. There were mostly men in there, but some women too. Everyone looked pretty serious, but not pissed off. They were busily doing their jobs. There was an energy in the place; a vibe like important work was being done there, and being done well.

After a minute or two, a soldier in her early thirties brought them into the office on the first floor. It was big for a home office, but small for a military commander's office. They walked in and everyone except the man behind the desk stood up when they entered the room.

The man behind the desk looked like a natural for a military commander. He was Lieutenant Colonel Jim Hammond. He was in his late forties and in great shape. He had about half his hair with a touch of gray on the temples.

Hammond was in Army fatigues. He had his "scare badges" sewn on: Special Forces tab, Ranger tab, airborne wings, combat infantry badge. He had a "Free Wash. State Guard" name tape instead of the former "U.S. Army" one. He had a military Beretta M9 pistol in a leather shoulder holster like some of the senior officers wore. The other men in the room were similarly in a uniform and had side arms, mostly on belt holsters and mostly military-issue M9s. They sat back down.

The commander looked up from his desk, smiled, and said, "Welcome Lt. Matson."

Lieutenant Matson?

There must be some mistake. Grant wasn't a lieutenant or in the military. Oh, wait. He was *kind of* in the military. He had signed up with Ted a few weeks ago back in the yellow cabin, but he didn't have any rank or anything. He was just a guy in an irregular unit for a while until he was no longer needed.

"Lieutenant?" Grant asked. "No, sir, I'm not a lieutenant. I'm just Grant Matson."

The commander laughed. "Well, that's what we're here to talk about tonight."

The commander stood up and extended his hand. "I'm Lt. Col. Jim Hammond. I'm the CO of the Free Washington Special Operations

Command." CO stood for "commanding officer." He pointed to Ted and said, "I worked with Master Sergeant Malloy. He's a damned fine soldier." Grant remembered Ted saying that his former Special Forces commander at Ft. Lewis had come over to the Patriots early on and was commanding Free Washington's special ops.

"Yes, sir," Grant said. Grant was standing at attention, another habit that came back to him from his Civil Air Patrol days.

"At ease, Lt. Matson," Hammond said with another smile. "We're just here to talk business." Hammond looked serious for a moment. "Should I call you 'lieutenant' or 'mister' Matson?"

Grant smiled. This was a business meeting, he could tell. He'd been in quite a few of those. It was time for him to get a little bit of the balance of power back.

"Depends on how the conversation goes," Grant said with a slight smile. "But 'lieutenant' works for now." That was Grant's not-so-subtle way of saying that he was probably agreeing to whatever was about to be asked of him. Probably, but he wanted to hear the details. His life was at stake.

Hammond smiled at Grant's remark that "'lieutenant' works for now." This Matson guy was not a pushover, Hammond thought. This guy had some moxie. Hammond opened up a paper file. Hammond looked at the file for a moment and flipped a few pages. Finally, he looked up at Grant and said, "Sgt. Malloy here tells me a lot of impressive things about you, Lt. Matson."

"Thank you, sir," Grant said. "I learned a lot from Ted, Sgt. Malloy, and I'm very lucky to know him. Especially in times like these."

"Yes, indeed," Hammond said. "Yes, indeed," he repeated.

Hammond looked at Grant, sizing him up. He had come to an initial impression about Grant from Ted's reports, but wanted to physically look at Grant and see if body language or anything else would change his opinion. Finally Hammond asked, "Has Sgt. Malloy told you about our plan for your services?"

Grant didn't know if Ted was supposed to have told him about the civil affairs role, but he thought it was best to tell the truth to his...commanding officer? That felt so weird.

"Yes, sir, very briefly," Grant said.

Hammond was watching to see if Grant's eyes darted over to Ted to see if Ted thought it was OK to answer the question. Grant's eyes did not dart. He looked Hammond right in the eye when he answered. Good, Hammond thought, he was truthful and confident.

Hammond could trust Grant to report to him truthfully and without hesitation.

"So what do you think about our civil affairs role for you and your Team?" Hammond asked.

"I think it's great, sir," Grant said, again looking Hammond straight in the eye. "For whatever reason, sir, I am the right person, at the right time, in the right place. I have some unique skills. But," Grant's body language relaxed and he got a little informal, "the weird thing is that I don't have any military training. I don't claim to be an expert, sir. Me and my guys can shoot a little, but we're amateurs."

"I know and that's what I like," Hammond said as he smiled. "You aren't playing Army. You're humble. You know your limits. But," Hammond was thumbing through the file, "you've got some organizational skills we could use. You can get a community up and running. We'll need that." Hammond kept looking at the file and nodding his head.

"You've done some amazing shit out at Pierce Point," Hammond said. "You're even keeping a list of Loyalists out there." Hammond looked up at Grant and said, "I understand that the Lima leader out there had an untimely death."

"Yes, sir," Grant said, once again looking Hammond right in the eye. One of the Team must have told Ted or Sap about Wes and the silenced .22.

"It was handled," Grant said sternly. "We had evidence; irrefutable evidence." Grant shrugged as if to say, "Just taking care of business."

Grant felt a little dishonest because he had been too weak to approve the killing; Wes had done it on his own, but Grant was willing to take credit for it now that everything worked out.

"What's your background?" Hammond asked Grant, knowing the basic answer, but wanting to hear it from Grant. Hammond had found that how people choose to answer such a question was very revealing; especially what they choose to talk about first. It was usually an indicator of their biggest priority in life. If they start by saying they have kids, then that means that they are their biggest priority. If they start off by saying which college they went to, that reveals something. If they shrug and say nothing, that says a lot, too.

Grant proceeded to tell Hammond about being a lawyer, suing the government, working for the State Auditor and resigning in disgust, prepping, coming out to Pierce Point, organizing Pierce Point, and then linking up with Ted and Sap. He never mentioned his family.

Grant didn't want to show weakness by saying, "My wife has no idea what I'm doing and would be mad at me if she found out." That wasn't exactly a bad-ass soldier thing to say.

Hammond was smiling again. In the absence of a real military-trained civil affairs guy, Hammond had a pretty good substitute here. And this Matson guy had known Ted from before the Collapse. Ted said he was solid. That was as good of a reference as one could have.

"What was your major in college?" Hammond asked. This was often a good way to find out a lot about people who had gone to college.

"American history, sir," Grant said.

"What period?" Hammond asked.

"Revolutionary War," Grant said.

Hammond leaned back and smiled. "Oh, Lt. Matson, when this whole thing is over, we need to talk over a glass of bourbon. I am a history buff. What part of the Revolutionary period interests you the most?"

"The differences between the Revolutionary War and the French Revolution," Grant said. "The differences in philosophy and political outcome. How we came out of it with a beautiful republic and the French ended up with a murderous dictatorship and two and a half centuries of statism."

Wow. That was the right answer, Hammond thought. The fact that Grant described the French Revolution as a murderous dictatorship was important. Hammond had been initially concerned that maybe Grant liked killing people. Maybe Grant enjoyed the thing with Snelling. Hammond didn't need any of that. He needed someone who did not want to repeat the French Revolution. Grant was perfect.

"Would you accept an officer's commission in the Free Washington State Guard, Mr. Matson?" Hammond asked, knowing the answer.

"Yes, sir. With pride," Grant said.

"You know the consequences of this?" Hammond asked very seriously. Because it was a life-or-death decision.

"Yes, sir. I am a traitor and will be executed if the Limas win," Grant said solemnly. He paused and then said, "Which means we have to win."

Hammond liked that spirit. "Will we?" he asked Grant.

"Yes, sir," Grant said with a nod. "Because we have the support of the population. The Limas don't. They might have soft support, but it's not deep or long term. The people will tolerate them as long as the semis are rolling. Take that away and there goes any support they have. We, sir, will do what the Limas can't: give people long-term hope. We will get things running with hard work, instead of stealing things and then handing them out to people."

Hammond was even more impressed. This Matson guy understood exactly what was going on. He just summarized everything Hammond thought about why the Patriots would win. It was uncanny; it was like Matson was in Hammond's brain.

Hammond decided to test Grant some more. "You say the 'support of the population,'" Hammond said. "Where did you get that?"

"George Washington and Mao, sir," Grant said. "An unusual pair. But they said basically the same thing: popular support is key. Logistics is key. The two are combined. Popular support is the key to logistics and logistics is the key to winning a war like this."

Hammond couldn't resist one more test question. "Do you think Mao really wrote 'On Guerilla War'?" Hammond asked, deeply probing Grant's knowledge of military theory.

"Oh, no, sir," Grant said. "It was all Sun Tzu and probably some Communist Party hacks. But it works. He got a lot right in that book, except the part about the government having the right to rule people's lives."

"Crap, Lieutenant," Hammond said, no longer able to contain his glee at how much Grant knew. "We need to have a drink when this thing is over. Wow." Hammond caught himself and realized that he shouldn't lavish praise on a subordinate, especially a brand new one who was basically a civilian, but what the hell.

Grant was flattered, but assumed he was being flattered just to get him to join, so he didn't let the compliments go to his head. He got down to business. He had a bunch of questions, but he didn't ask them out loud. Grant wanted to know if he would be in day-to-day command of the guerilla unit because he wasn't remotely qualified to do that; Ted was. How long was Grant's commitment? He assumed commissions could be resigned. He was an irregular commander and the irregulars were like the militia in the Revolutionary War: they could just leave if they wanted. Would he get paid? Not that he wanted the money, but it was a natural question to ask. Would he have to keep his commission a secret? He assumed so. Would he have to wear a uniform? He hoped not. He was about to ask Hammond these questions.

Hammond's anticipated Grant's questions and said, "I imagine you have a few questions about the details of your commission, Lieutenant. Sgt. Malloy will answer those questions later, because you and I have a meeting to go to in a few minutes."

"Yes, sir," Grant said. "Thank you for commissioning me."

Grant paused, "Permission to speak with candor, sir?" Grant had learned that in Civil Air Patrol.

"Granted," Hammond said.

"I'm supposed to do this, sir, and so are you," Grant said. "You sense it too, don't you Colonel?"

"Yes," Hammond said, stunned that Grant could pick up on what he was feeling. "I most certainly do." This was spooky, Hammond thought. They were on the same wavelength of "we're supposed to do this."

Hammond concentrated on getting ahold of himself. He was trying not to show any emotion. Hammond closed the file and said, "We have a meeting to get to."

"Yes, sir," Grant said. He remembered from Civil Air Patrol that he should not turn his back on a superior officer until he was dismissed, so he waited to be dismissed.

Hammond, seeing that Grant was waiting to be dismissed, said, "Oh, you're coming to the meeting with us, Lieutenant."

# Chapter 200

## *The 17th Irregulars*

### (July 21)

Everyone got their things together and waited for Lt. Col. Hammond to stand. He did, and dismissed them by saying, "To the hall, gentlemen." He looked at two female soldiers and said, "And ladies, of course." Everyone started walking out.

Ted said quietly to Grant, "Nice job, Grant. Hammond likes you."

"Where are we going?" Grant asked. He was all business tonight. He didn't want to start patting himself on the back when there was important work to do. He had the quite boat ride back that night to think about how well things went.

"The community hall, a block away. It's where we have big meetings," Ted said.

"What's the meeting about?" Grant said. It was 1:30 a.m.

"You'll see, Lieutenant," Ted said with a smile.

"Lieutenant" sounded so weird. The idea of him commanding a military unit seemed so crazy. "You're in day-to-day command of the unit," Grant said softly to Ted. "You know that, right?"

"Roger that, Lieutenant," Ted said. "We'll talk about it later, but don't worry. You don't have to be some battlefield commander."

"Thank God," Grant said. As confident and calm as Grant had been the whole night, he had been terrified of being responsible for knowing how to command a combat unit. But, that's what Ted and Sap were for.

The hall was not visible from the marina so Grant hadn't noticed it when he first got off the boat. But, hidden away, was a big community center. It looked modern, probably built with stimulus money from a few years ago. Might as well get something out of that money, Grant thought. How ironic: using a hall built with stimulus money to plan how to topple the government that built it.

The closer they got to the hall, the bigger the crowd became. Most were military people, but there were lots of civilian-looking people like Grant. Some of them looked like true civilians, in pure civilian clothes, not the tactical clothes Grant had on. There were many contractor-looking guys, but they were probably SF, like Ted and Sap.

The crowd settled into the community hall. It seated about a hundred and was almost full. A soldier was sitting at a desk, checking names at the entrance. It was Grant's turn.

"Grant Matson," he said. Ted mouthed to the solider, "He's with me."

The soldier looked on the list. "Yes, sir, here's your name. Welcome."

"Welcome to what?" Grant asked Ted.

"You'll see, Lieutenant," Ted said. "You'll see." It continued to seem so odd for Ted to be calling Grant "Lieutenant." It was also odd that Ted could instantly go from calling Grant by his first name to "Lieutenant" without even thinking.

Everyone sat down. Most people didn't seem to know each other. People were upbeat but fairly businesslike. There were others in the room that appeared like Grant, unsure of what the meeting was about.

Grant was surprised to see a large group of Arab men in a corner. They were dressed in American clothes. They kept to themselves and talked in a language Grant couldn't understand. What were they doing there? Grant wasn't a racist or anything, but weren't there Muslim terrorists out there blowing things up? Had the Patriots joined some anti-Loyalist alliance with the Muslim terrorists? That was not what Grant signed up for.

"Who are those guys?" Grant whispered to Ted.

"They're cool. You'll see," Ted whispered back. Grant was completely mystified why the Arabs were there.

After about one minute, most people stood up abruptly. Grant looked around, saw them standing, and did the same. He didn't know why they were standing until he saw Lt. Col. Hammond walking in.

Hammond went up to the podium and said, "Please be seated." Everyone sat. The room was silent.

"I am Lt. Col. Hammond, commander of the Free Washington State Guard's Special Operations Command. I'm in charge of things like our irregular units, which are led by Special Forces personnel. This meeting is about the irregular units."

Hammond continued, "At the outset, let me say that irregular units are essential to our strategy for victory. These aren't bands of poorly trained, poorly equipped 'bubbas.' There are some of those and we'll use them effectively, but not as irregular units. No, the kind of irregular units we're talking about tonight are trained and led by FUSA

Special Forces personnel with whom I formerly served at Ft. Lewis. Our SF Irregulars will be, for the most part, tying down the Limas in their rear areas. Attacking strategic assets in Lima territories. Eliminating Lima officials. Stealing supplies from the gangs and getting them to our units and the people. Causing maximum chaos for the Limas, and thereby requiring them to siphon off their regular units to deal with our little, elusive, irregular units. This means they'll have fewer regular units to deal with our regular units, which gives our regular units an advantage. And that is what our irregular unit strategy is all about: giving our regular units an advantage."

Hammond looked at the audience and smiled, "This strategy of using SF-trained irregulars as a force multiplier to tie down lots of enemy regular units has worked in every part of the world it's been tried." He knew because he'd done it.

"Many of you came from long distances," Hammond said. His voice was loud enough to be heard in the hall without a microphone but he wasn't yelling. His voice projected strength and competent leadership.

"You came through dangerous territory to get here," Hammond said, "so I'll be as brief as possible and get you back on the road or water, or in one case, air, so you can travel back in the dark."

"The purpose of this meeting tonight is to get all the irregular units together, get some basic briefing, let you meet each other, and get your quadra," Hammond said.

Quadra? What was that? Grant wondered.

"This will probably be the first and last time we're in the same room for the whole war," Hammond said. Then he smiled and said, "Don't worry, we'll have a nice party when we win. One hell of a blowout." Most people smiled at that.

Hammond turned to a subordinate and said, "Captain, have them count off."

The captain said, "I need a representative of each irregular unit to come up to the podium and form a line from left" he pointed, "to right."

Grant looked at Ted who said, "You're the representative, Lt. Matson." Ted motioned for Grant to get up and go to the podium.

Grant reluctantly did so. As he was standing up and looking clueless, he realized that he still thought of Ted as being in command of the unit.

That needed to change, at least for things like this meeting. Grant needed to accept that he was the officer for the unit, but that Ted was the day-to-day and battlefield commander. Grant needed to start working on his command presence. He was being properly humble by acknowledging that Ted was the real commander, but he needed to have the rest of the world know that he was the lieutenant. It was understood that a lieutenant, while technically in command, wouldn't know everything; the highest ranking sergeant would. In the two seconds it took him to finish standing, Grant became confident about his new role. He strode up to the podium with command presence.

Grant walked up the front of the room and stood next to some others. There were about two dozen, including two women. Nearly half were in military uniforms, two others were apparent civilians in tactical clothes like him, and the remaining half or so were civilians in purely civilian clothes.

Grant looked into the audience and saw Ted and Sap and similar FUSA military-looking guys. Most of the audience seemed to be Special Forces trainers, like Ted and Sap, with some regular military walk-on guys sprinkled in. The audience was smiling, like they knew the people at the podium were about to get an award or something.

Once all the representatives of the various units formed into a line at the front of the room facing the audience, the captain said to the first person, "Count off." The first person said, "One." The second said, "Two" and so on. By the time it got to Grant, he said, "Seventeen." The counting ended at twenty three.

Hammond looked at the men and women in the line at the podium and smiled. "Welcome to the Special Operations Command, ladies and gentlemen."

The audience clapped. They seemed to know what was going on.

Hammond said, "The number you have is your unit number." He let that sink in. "So you, Lt. Shaddock" he said pointing at the person who said "one" "are the First Irregulars. You, Lt. Potach," Hammond said pointing at the person who said "two," "are the Second Irregulars."

Grant had called out "seventeen" so he must be...the 17th Irregulars. Grant thought about it. He was the commander of the 17th Irregulars. Wow. This was for real. Commander of the 17th Irregulars. He let that sink in.

Grant looked out at the audience. Everyone was smiling and clapping. Now he understood why. This was a big moment. These would be the unit numbers described in the history books...if the Patriots won and got to write the history books. If they didn't, then these unit numbers would be used in indictments and military tribunals for treason. That was a dark thought. Grant felt, when he first told Ted and Sap at the yellow cabin "I'm in," that he had committed to the cause. Now he really felt like he'd committed, in a very no-going-back way.

Grant looked side to side and saw his fellow commanders. They started shaking hands and grinning. This was something to be proud of.

Hammond let the commanders shake hands and exchange pleasantries, but needed to keep this meeting moving. They had to be out of there soon to get back home by dawn.

Hammond looked into the audience and said, "Now I have something to tell you that none of you saw coming."

# Chapter 201

## *Quadra*

### (July 21)

"Ashur, could you come up here?" Hammond said to the Arabs in the back of the room. One of the Arabs, the oldest one of the group, came up to the podium. He looked like an elder and was dressed in American clothes, but he looked like he should be dressed like a Saudi prince.

"Everyone," Hammond said, "I'd like you to welcome Ashur and his family." Hammond pointed to the back of the room and said to the Arabs, "Please stand up gentlemen." They did. The audience started applauding. The new lieutenants at the podium had no idea why, so they politely clapped, too.

"Ashur and his family are very special people and will help us a lot," Hammond said. "A whole lot." He looked at the group of Arab men and smiled. He was obviously very happy they were there, like it was a triumph that they were in this room.

Hammond continued, "I can't provide the details, but suffice it to say Ashur and his family speak a very, very rare language. No one else in this state other than his extended family speak it. One of his family members will be assigned to each of the irregular units as a code talker."

Grant remembered that phrase from World War II. Code talkers were Navajo Indians in front line combat units in the Pacific who spoke Navajo on radios. The Japanese had no idea what language it was and thought it was an extremely complex code. This allowed the code talkers to talk on regular, non-encrypted radios and did not require time-consuming conversions of the messages back into non-encrypted text. It was brilliant.

Hammond went on, "Ashur and his family are taking extreme risks by helping us this way. Let me be candid. There are some Muslim terrorists out there. Ashur, please explain to everyone why we can trust you."

Ashur said in a thick Arabic accent, "First of all, we are Christians, not Muslim. My people have been Christians for about two thousand years. The Muslim terrorists want to kill Christians like us

211

and already have destroyed several of our cities and villages back home."

Ashur continued, "We came to America several years ago when things were going badly in..."

Hammond held his hand up, "Sorry, Ashur, please don't describe the country or the language. We'll keep that a secret. Sorry to interrupt you, sir," Hammond said. It was apparent that Hammond genuinely respected Ashur.

"Things were going badly in my home country," Ashur said, "and we came to the 'land of the free.' But guess what? It wasn't free. It was when we got here, but it changed. Now America is like my home country. Bribes, corruption, no freedom. The authorities in Seattle targeted my business because I had a cross up in my store that was 'offending' to people."

Ashur continued, "People were robbing my store — pointing guns at my sons — all the time and the police wouldn't do anything about it. Then my son was jailed after shooting a robber. The police knew my son was innocent, but no one cared and he went to jail. The police wanted bribes to let him out. I decided that we needed to leave Seattle. The authorities made me give up the store to them, along with all of our inventory, in order to leave. One of my sons knew one of your 'Oath Keepers' and here we are."

Ashur got a very angry look on his face and he started talking louder. "We know what oppression is. We lived in it back in our home country. I promised my father when I left there that his family would live somewhere free. My family has taken a...the closest English word is 'vow.' This vow is a very serious promise in my culture. To dishonor this vow would bring shame to my family. Our vow is to fight for the Patriots to bring back freedom. I am risking my family's lives to help you to get our freedom back."

The room was silent. Grant was moved to hear someone who had come from a corrupt third-world country and eventually found the same thing in America.

Hammond said, "Ashur's family, the women and children, are staying with Patriot families. Ashur's vow is that if he or his men dishonor the Patriots or are spies that we have permission to kill his family." Exchanging voluntary hostages as a way to seal an alliance was common in Ashur's culture.

That stunned the audience.

"And you will do it," Ashur said to Hammond.

"We try not to kill women and children, sir," Hammond said to Ashur. "But if your men get my people killed...I cannot promise that I can protect your family from my men." Hammond was serious.

Hammond knew that he needed to convince the unit commanders that these Arabs were trustworthy. The Patriot's ability to kill the code talkers' families was pretty reassuring in a grisly and sickening way, but it was reassuring nonetheless. Hammond wanted to give the irregular commanders another reason to trust the Arabs.

"Ashur's family has already run some missions with us," Hammond said. "They have performed outstandingly. They are brave and competent."

Ashur's chest puffed out in pride. He was so proud of his family and their bravery. He was fulfilling his vow to his father. That meant everything.

"So," Hammond said, "I have no trouble whatsoever trusting one of Ashur's family members with the lives of each and every one of my soldiers."

Grant was convinced. Besides, by having the Arabs at Boston Harbor who could tell the Limas about the place, Hammond was trusting his own life to the Arabs.

But, there was a bigger lesson here than just whether a particular family could be trusted, Grant thought. This is what happens when a government mistreats people. It causes them to fight for the other side. Ashur and his family were perfect examples of it.

Grant remembered George Washington's and Mao's writings on popular support. They were right. Now, because the government mistreated Ashur's family, each irregular unit had an unbreakable code. They could quickly talk on the radio while the Limas would have to spend time and resources with encryption. Having code talkers was a huge advantage. That was a high price the Limas were paying for treating Ashur's family so poorly.

This was happening all over the country, Grant thought. People were standing up to the government because of how it had treated them. Grant was now more convinced than ever that his side was going to win. For exactly the reasons Ashur was working for the Patriots.

The captain said to Ashur, "Could your men count off, sir?"

Ashur nodded and said something in his language. One by one, the men counted off in their language. They stood up as they did. The Arab men ranged in age from late teens to about forty. Grant was trying to count with them (in English) to see which one was "seventeen" and would be joining his unit. He couldn't keep up. They counted so fast.

Ashur said to the captain, "Counted off."

The captain said, "Please have each man join his new unit." Ashur said something in his language. The Arab men started to walk up to the commander of their new unit.

A twenty-something college-looking kid came up to Grant. Grant expected the man to speak broken English.

"Hi, I'm Jim," the Arab man said in perfect English. Grant was stunned.

"Oh. Jim, glad to meet you," Grant said, extending his hand and wondering if the Arab knew about shaking hands. Grant thought maybe they did that hug and fake kiss thing like they did in the Middle East.

Jim shook Grant's hand like he'd been doing it his whole life. Because, duh, Jim had been doing this his whole life. Jim had grown up in America, spoke perfect English, and was an American in every way. It was just that he spoke a very rare—and valuable—language at home. Grant felt stupid.

"My real name is Khnanya Al-Halbi, but I go by 'Jim' for obvious reasons," Jim said.

"I'm Grant Matson," Grant said. "I go by 'Grant'," he said with a laugh.

Jim laughed, too. That was a good sign.

"So, is it Grant or Lieutenant Matson?" Jim asked.

"Grant," he said. This kid was pretty sharp. "Except when we're around other members of the unit. Then, unfortunately it's 'Lieutenant Matson.'" Jim nodded.

By now, all the code talkers had been introduced to their new units. The captain got everyone's attention.

"Sorry, ladies and gentlemen," the captain said, "we need to move this meeting along. Your code talker will be going back with you to your units so you can get to know each other at that time."

"Thank you, Captain," Hammond said. "Yes, we need to move it along." Hammond looked at his notes.

"Oh, one thing," Hammond said. "We obviously can't refer to these gentlemen as 'code talkers.' That would tip off the Limas—although good luck figuring out what language it is, let alone finding anyone around here to speak it. We have every single male speaker of this language who is known to exist in Washington State, but we don't want them to now we're using code talkers. The units in various states

214

are similarly using code talkers of languages from all over the world."

"So," Hammond said, raising his right finger for emphasis, "we will call our code talkers a 'Quadra.' Think of 'Quad' as in Latin for 'four' with a 'rah' added at the end. 'Quad-rah'. Say it with me, 'Quah-rah'."

The room said "Quadra."

Ashur grinned. He was very proud. "That is our word for 'honor,'" Ashur said. He could feel his father smiling from far away.

Grant always made up nicknames for people. It was a way to bond with them. He whispered to Jim, "Dude, your new nickname is 'Jim Q'."

Jim smiled. He was fine with that.

Grant realized a minute later that he, a lieutenant, probably shouldn't refer to his troops as "dude." He was learning, though. Old habits are hard to break.

Hammond motioned to the captain, and then the captain said, "Please be seated." The new lieutenants and their Quadras sat down back in the chairs for the audience.

Grant went out of his way to signal Jim Q. to sit down with him instead of sitting with his family. He wanted to emphasize to Jim Q. that the 17th was his new home.

Hammond noticed that Grant and a few other new lieutenants sat with their Quadras. That was a sign of leadership and fostering unit morale. Hammond was even more impressed with Grant than in their meeting a few minutes ago.

Hammond collected his thoughts. What he was about to say next was important. It could have a big impact on how things turned out.

# Chapter 202

## *"Take it back! Take it back!"*

### (July 22)

"Why are you doing this?" Hammond asked the audience. Everyone was silent.

"Why?" He let that question sink in for a few seconds.

"Why not just sit back and let the government take care of you?" he asked without any sarcasm. It was a sincere question.

"Seriously," he said. "Each of you is smarter than average. You all have very valuable skills. Quite a few of you are military and could be in command of some hollowed-out FUSA unit and livin' large on some base where you have plenty of everything you want. People calling you 'sir' or 'ma'am' all day long and kissing your ass," he said.

"Why are you here, starting the mission that you're starting?" Hammond asked. "I want every one of you to think about that question. Why are you here?"

It was silent.

"What did you come up with?" Hammond asked the audience. "I bet I know."

Hammond started to get animated. He had been like a very controlled CEO running a meeting up until this point. Now it was time to get fired up.

"You're doing this to make things right," Hammond said emphatically. "You're doing this to protect the innocent. To save your families from what's ahead, if these bastards keep screwing things up."

Hammond looked into the audience. He seemed to make eye contact with every single person in the room. "You know you're supposed to do this. You know it. You are supposed to do this. Consider me standing here saying this to be your official sign. You are supposed to do this."

Grant wondered if his statement to Hammond a few minutes earlier about how they were both supposed to do this had made its way into Hammond's speech.

"You have skills," Hammond said. "Every single one of you," he said holding up a file. "Each and every one of you has some skill that got our attention. We looked into each one of you. We chose

216

you…you," he said looking at the whole audience. It felt like Hammond was speaking to each person personally. Grant certainly felt like Hammond was speaking directly to him.

"But, us choosing you is only half of it," Hammond said. "The other half is that you chose us. You agreed to do this. Again, I ask: why?"

Hammond looked at Ashur. "You want to restore the 'land of the free.' You want to avenge an injustice to your family that never should have happened."

Hammond looked at one of the new lieutenants in the front row. "Or, like Tadman here, those bastards killed your family. Trying to get you. But they settled for your family."

"They are animals wasting our oxygen!" Hammond yelled out of the blue. For the first time, he was showing his real emotions.

"Animals," Hammond thundered. "Animals that need to be put down. Animals that need to no longer hurt us. Animals that need to be dealt with, so they're just a memory. So you can tell your kids and grandkids about how, way back when, there were some animals that hurt people, but you and a group of very decent people made the animals go away. Now they're gone and everyone can live their lives. In peace."

"Peace," Hammond said nodding his head. "Peace is what a soldier wants. Trust me, with what I've seen and done, and what many of you have seen and done, too, no one wants peace more than us."

"You know what I want?" Hammond asked in a very conversational, not military commander, tone. "I want to retire. I want to get an RV and travel around with my wife and kids. I barely know my kids." Saying that hurt Hammond. He had sacrificed a lot to do all those deployments.

"And my lovely wife," Hammond said. "Who I really haven't seen for several years. Who I wonder sometimes if she really still is my wife. I mean, is someone your wife when you've seen them two weeks in two years? I want my wife back. I want to get her and the kids in that RV and go sit under the stars talking about nothing in particular. I want that." Hammond was bearing his soul.

"But guess what?" Hammond said, back in his military commander tone. "Life ain't sunshine and lollipops. I am supposed to be here, doing this. I know I am supposed to be doing this—just like each of you know you're supposed to be doing this. Each of you has made similar sacrifices, and," he said looking at Tadman, "some of you have made bigger ones. Much bigger than the RV."

Hammond let that sink in. Tadman looked eerily forward without any emotion.

"So," Hammond said, "I asked why you're doing this and you probably said to yourself that you're supposed to do this. That's a good enough reason, but...," he paused for effect. "I have one more reason for you."

"Because we'll win!" Hammond yelled.

"Ladies and gentlemen," Hammond said emphatically, "we're all brave, but this isn't some suicide club. Remember: I want some RV time. I got somethin' to live for."

Hammond motioned to the whole crowd, "Most of us will be back together for a hell of a party when we beat these bastards. They're running on fumes. You know it. You've seen it. They're running out of other people's money to steal and hand out to their buddies. The people are figuring this out. Their military units are a joke. Hollowed out paper tigers, manned by the paper-pusher boot lickers who want to boss people around and still think they're getting some fat military retirement. The real warriors got out and joined up with us. We have the real warriors. We have you."

"Name one thing they're doing right that will lead to long-term success for them?" Hammond asked the crowd. "Name one. Is it treating the population fairly and getting their support? Ask Lt. Tadman about that. Ask Ashur that."

Hammond started walking from the podium to the first row as if he were quizzing each one of them. "Are they feeding the people?" he asked the first person, who shook his head.

"Well, kind of," Hammond said to the next person. "But not for long. Those FCards—which are easily counterfeited by us, I might add—are drawn on seized bank accounts. Those accounts are running dry, friends. The foreign countries those funds are going to are about to cut us off. Besides, they want their investments back. You know, the trillions of dollars we borrowed from them to pay for all the pre-Collapse crap we voted for ourselves. The Chinese are just softening the blow of a total collapse. They want their collateral, which is what America is to them, to stay as intact as possible, so it will be more valuable when they repo it."

Hammond went back up to the podium and shook his head, "Ain't gonna happen." He looked out at the audience again and said, "Repo America? Are you kidding me? They ain't gettin' in boats and comin' here. So what does that mean? It means the FCards will start to go dry soon, just like the EBT cards went dry."

"No more FCards," Hammond said. "Soon. About six months, tops, according to our intel analysts. And, believe me, we have some highly placed sources on that."

"What happens then?" Hammond asked the audience. "You know. You know exactly what happens then. You've seen what happens when the shelves go bare. You saw it on May Day, but this time there won't be any FCards and commandeered semis to roll in and save the day."

Hammond put up his hands for emphasis and said, "You think the May Day riots were bad? You ain't seen nothin' yet. You know, we've had semi-functioning government services up until now. And, to be very honest, this is not how the collapse scenario was expected to play out."

"Everyone," Hammond said, pointing to himself, "including me, assumed the 'Mad Max' scenario of total anarchy and chaos. Like in the book 'Patriots.' Well, it was a slower descent than we thought. A car wreck in slow motion, not at full speed, but a car wreck just the same. It took a matter of months, not days, but the ultimate result is the same. When the FCards dry up, everything that resembles order goes away." Hammond snapped his fingers for emphasis. The snapping was loud enough for everyone in the whole hall to hear it.

"The utilities, which are still on, to my surprise, can't stay on when there's nothing to feed the utility workers," Hammond continued. "What's going to happen when the electricity goes off for good? How will people react when there is no water coming out of the faucet?"

Once again, Hammond let all of this sink in. "So, no food and no utilities. How many people are in this country? Three hundred million, right? Most of them will die. Two hundred million dead, and then some. I'll say that again: 200 million dead. Rotting corpses will be everywhere. I've seen it elsewhere in the world. I'm going to see it here, too."

The audience was horrified.

Hammond paused and raised his hand with his index finger pointed up, and said, "Unless."

"Unless," Hammond repeated. "Unless they're stopped. Unless we push them aside and start getting this place back on its feet. You see, we know how to get people fed, how to let them grow their own food and trade. Without gangs and the government stealing from them. Unleash the private sector, actual free enterprise, not what we have now, and people will feed themselves, like they've done for

219

thousands of years in places much less hospitable to growing food than here. This country has the best agricultural land and other natural resources in the history of mankind. We fed ourselves—and a big chunk of the rest of the world—up until just a few years ago. Are you telling me we can't do that again? What the hell else are they going to do back in Iowa? Grow daisies?"

"Yeah," Hammond said, nodding, "it'll be a rough winter and lots of people will die. The Limas have done so much damage to this country that we can't wave a magic wand and make things instantly right. But you know that. The fact that you're here in this room means that you know that there is no magic wand. You would have waved that first before you committed yourself to joining a rebel army."

"So," Hammond said, "that's reason number two why you're doing this: you know that at least 200 million people will die unless the Limas are stopped. And, because you're a decent human being, you can't sit back and watch that. Little kids dying of starvation. Can you just watch that and not do something? I've seen little kids starve to death in other places. There is no way to sit there and not do something. No possible way. And, if 200 million out of 300 million will die, what makes you think you'll be one of the minority who makes it? What makes you think your family will, too? If there is a two-thirds odds of you dying, add in a wife and the odds of you two making it go down further. Throw in a kid and you're even lower. The sheer odds of you and your family making it are, what, ten percent? You gonna bet on that?"

Hammond scribbled something on the file in front of him. It seemed like too serious of a moment to scribble something. Then he pointed to the captain, "Quick, Morris, pick a number between one and ten."

"Two, sir," Captain Morris said.

Hammond held up the file folder, which had a big "eight" written on it.

"Your family is dead," Hammond said. "You didn't make it into the ten percent club."

Hammond looked back at the audience and said, "Only a fool will bet on making it by just sitting back and letting other people take care of them and their family. The Limas have such a brilliant track record of taking care of people, don't they? Anyone with any sense will take care of themselves and the ones they love."

"Well," Hammond said, throwing his hands up, "how you gonna do that? By voting? Elections have been cancelled, and electing the lesser of two evils is what got us where we're at right now. Elections will not save you. It's too late for that. If you thought elections would work anymore, you'd be in a room tonight for a new political party. You're not. You're in a room tonight for a rebel army."

"Nope," Hammond said, "you're not going to look to elections to save us. You're going to drive off the animals attacking you. You're going to push and then—bam!—the tipsy government that is barely holding on will fall over and shatter into a million pieces. You'll be amazed at how tipsy it was. You'll look back and say, 'It looked so solid, but fell so easily.' And you'll be right."

"So we already have three good reasons why you're doing this," Hammond said, putting up three fingers. "One," he said holding up one finger, "You know you're supposed to be doing this.

"Two," Hammond said, holding up two fingers, "we're going to win. The Limas are weak."

"Third," he said, holding up three fingers, "you can't sit back and watch most of your country starve to death, including—odds are—your own family."

"Oh, but there's more," Hammond said, holding up a fourth finger. "How about this? Your place in history. Now, it's hard for people to think about how they'll be viewed in the future. Fair enough. So look back at how you view people in the past. You see, every couple generations or so, Americans have to do big and nasty things, but then the country, and sometimes the whole world, thanks them. I'll give you an example. My granddaddy was in World War II. He was a war hero, actually. The rest of his life he was respected and honored. Before him, were my ancestors who fought in the Civil War or, as I'm now coming to realize, the War Between the States. There was heroism on both sides of that one. One of them saved a family from a fire started by enemy troops. Then there's the Revolutionary War, which is the best example of what's happening now."

"If just a handful of men and women," Hammond said, "had decided to take it easy during in the Revolutionary War, there never would have been an America. How many people can say they did something that made life immeasurably better for millions of people for hundreds of years? That's no exaggeration. Think about that, people."

Hammond let that sink in. "Well, congratulations," he said loudly. "That's you. That's you," he said pointing to the audience, "and you and you and you."

"So," he continued, "to summarize—for you to remember

when you're cold, hungry, scared, and wondering if we'll really win — here are the four reasons why we're doing this. One, you're supposed to do this. Two, we're going to win. Three, you and probably over 200 million Americans are dead if we don't do this. And, four, you will be part of history. Four damned good reasons to do this. Now let's get to work."

The room burst into applause. People started standing and clapping. Hammond stood at the podium with extreme pride and confidence. He smiled. He was proud to be leading these people and it showed.

Hammond screamed, "Take it back! Take this country back!"

Chants of "Take it back!" started. Pretty soon, the whole room was screaming "Take it back! Take it back!"

It was intoxicating. Grant, and everyone in that room, felt invincible, which was good, because they'd need that for what was coming.

# Chapter 203

## *"The Unit"?*

### (July 22)

After the chanting died down, Hammond said, "It's time to go back to your AOs," referring to areas of operation. Hammond couldn't resist. "Go and...take it back!" This started a new round of chanting. The place was bursting with enthusiasm. Grant had never seen anything like it.

The chanting died down for a second time. Hammond motioned to the captain that it was time for people to leave, and the captain said, "Each unit will form up and be dismissed." Grant wasn't sure what that meant, but, being number seventeen, he'd see at least sixteen examples of what he was supposed to do before it was his turn.

The captain yelled out, "1st Irregulars!" and the new lieutenant, his Quadra, and two Special Forces-looking guys from the audience stood up. The captain and Hammond started clapping. So did the audience. The 1st Irregulars went up to the podium. The captain said something to the new lieutenant and led his unit out of the meeting hall to thunderous applause. Hammond was at the exit and talked to each man as they left. He knew the names and backgrounds of each lieutenant, most of the Quadras, and all of the SF guys. Hammond literally stayed up at night memorizing details about his people. He made every single person feel important and that he was personally counting on them. Because he was.

This happened fifteen more times and then it was the 17th's turn. "17th Irregulars!" the captain yelled. Grant gave the thumbs up, motioned for Jim Q. to stand with him, and then motioned for Ted and Sap to come up front and get some applause. They did.

There they were: the four of them, as a unit. It was a brand new feeling. But, it was a completely comfortable feeling, too. Grant, having seen sixteen previous examples of what to do, crisply led his men through the hall to cheers. As he approached the exit, there was Hammond extending his hand for a handshake.

"Really glad you're with us, Grant," Hammond said sincerely, using a rare reference to a first name.

"Me too, sir," Grant said, without standing at attention. Grant wanted to communicate that he, too, was temporarily breaking with military protocol to show his sincerity.

"We have some big plans for the 17th," Hammond said. He looked at Ted and Sap, both of whom nodded. "Let's just say you guys are pre-positioned in the right place."

Grant had suspected all along that the 17th's target was nearby Olympia. Now he knew it.

"We're supposed to be here," Grant said. Hammond smiled. He had been thinking the same thing. "Supposed to be, sir," Grant repeated. He had never met anyone like Hammond who was on the same outside-thought wavelength.

"You take good care of Ted and Sap, Lieutenant," Hammond said. "They were in my old unit and I think the world of both of them. They're good men; Oath Keepers and superb warriors. Plus, Ted knew you from peacetime. Perfect, just perfect. And I understand you have some hardware in your basement that might help equip quite a few of your unit." He was smiling.

Wow. Hammond knew details about every unit. "Yes, sir," Grant said. "Well, they actually belong to…"

"Chip," Hammond said. Man, this guy knew everything. Impressive. "I understand they split up the inventory of Capitol City Guns," Hammond said, "and that Chip's already donated them. Thank him for me. Ted will be bringing out a similar number, and then some." Hammond was getting a little hoarse from all the yelling and talking. His hoarseness just emphasized that he was giving this his all.

"Yes, sir," was all Grant could manage to say. He was still stunned at all the detail Hammond had mastered. Hammond was this up-to-speed on each of the twenty-three irregular units. It was one thing to say that was his job, but it was more than just a job for Hammond—he was making sure his guys came out of everything OK and that the Patriots won.

When Grant and Hammond were done talking, Grant stepped aside so Hammond could talk to Jim Q. Hammond said Jim Q.'s real name, "Khnanya," pronouncing it exactly like Jim Q. had, and then said something in some foreign language. Hammond spoke the code talker language? At least a little. Wow.

Then Grant realized that Special Forces soldiers had to learn lots of languages to operate in the foreign areas where they worked. Hammond was fluent in Spanish, Russian, Pashto, and French. He spoke a little of six other languages, some of which had no written alphabet. Hammond majored in linguistics at West Point.

After Hammond said something in the code talker's language, Jim Q. smiled, puffed out his chest and said, "Yes, sir. Very much, sir. Thank you, sir." Jim Q. had never heard someone outside his family ever speak his language. It was surreal to see someone else saying these words.

Next in line for greetings from Hammond were Ted and Sap. "You guys take care of my young lieutenant and Khnanya here," Hammond said.

"Yes, sir," Ted said.

"Will do, sir," Sap said.

"Sap, how is your mom doing back in Wisconsin?" Hammond asked.

Sap looked down at the floor. "Dunno, sir. Can't get in touch with her, but she needed some pretty serious medications and…well, you know."

Hammond looked like his own mom had died. "Sorry to hear that, son. Anything I can do?"

"For my mom? No, sir," Sap said. "We can win this war and not have things like my mom's situation come up again."

"Indeed," Hammond said with a nod to Sap. "You're a good man, Brandon. Go out and make me proud with the 17th."

"Yes, sir," Sap said. He tried to smile, but couldn't now that he had been reminded about his mom, though it was his dad he worried about. His mom and dad had been inseparable since high school.

"I sense great things from the 17th," Hammond said with yet another smile. "Go out there and take back our country, gentlemen." He shook each man's hand, looked them straight in the eye, and said, with absolute sincerity, "Take it back."

Grant had become ultra-confident about winning the war on the boat ride in when, looking at the stars, the outside thought told him they would win. He assumed the details of how they'd win would be chaotic. They were taking on the largest and, supposedly strongest, military on earth. But now he knew how they'd win: They would be led by people like Jim Hammond.

Hammond had been placed in Washington State with some amazing skills, Grant realized, and following Hammond would lead to victory. In that moment, Grant was even more confident than when he was looking up at the stars. Not only did he know with absolute certainty that they would win, he now felt like he knew how and why.

Except it hadn't happened yet. They still had lots of hurdles. Probably awful, awful hurdles. This wouldn't be a cakewalk, but they would win.

The 18th was right behind them and Hammond was greeting them and similarly showing a mastery of every detail of them and their mission.

Grant, Jim Q., Ted, and Sap walked out of the hall.

Ted and Sap had heard some pep talks before, but this was the best they'd ever heard by far. Here they were, experienced combat Special Forces veterans, and they were pumped up like little kids.

As they were leaving, a Navy petty officer with a clipboard and "Free Wash. State Guard" on the name tag of his fatigues, said to them, "The 17th, I presume?"

Grant nodded. It took him a second to realize that he was in charge. He would answer questions like that. This was quite a change from a half hour ago when the question was whether he was "Mr." Matson or "Lt." Matson.

"Your craft is waiting over at slip twenty-two, down this way," the petty officer said, and pointed to a corner of the marina. "Good night, gentlemen and good luck." The petty officer looked at Jim Q. and said, "I'd say 'good luck' in your language, but I don't even know what language it is. Better that we don't, but good luck." The petty officer tipped his head instead of saluting. Battlefield rules on saluting were in place. Boston Harbor, as beautiful and joyous as that place was that night, was technically a battlefield.

"Thank you," Jim Q. said. He was told not to use words from his language unless absolutely necessary. Saying "Basima," his word for "thank you," with the petty officer would be polite, but if the petty officer were a spy, the Loyalists would know what language the code talkers were using.

Jim Q. wanted to be polite, so he said to the petty officer, "I would say 'thank you' in my language, but..."

The petty officer put his hand up and said, "Understood. OPSEC, sir," which was the military acronym for "operational security." That term basically meant, "Don't be a dumbass and give out little details that allow people to find you and kill you."

Grant and the rest of the 17th walked down the marina toward the boat for the ride home. They weren't talking. They moved as quietly as possible at all times. It wasn't natural for Grant to walk around with friends and not talk. He'd been talking with friends instead of walking silently for over forty years during peace time. But now, even though Boston Harbor was as secure as possible, it just seemed stupid and unprofessional to blab. It was like hunting.

Everyone's quiet until they're in camp.

Grant was starting to like the silence that came with his new military duties. All day long at his Grange day job people yammered to him or he had to talk to people. Sometimes, at the end of the day he couldn't stand it if one more person talked to him; he was overloaded. The only quiet he ever got was when he was in the woods or on the water with his unit.

"His unit"? Did he just think that? It was still sinking into Grant that he was the commanding officer of the 17th Irregulars of the Free Washington State Guard. He had foreseen all the big things that had eventually happened — the Collapse, surviving out at the cabin, the Team — but he had not foreseen this lieutenant thing. He looked up at the stars and said to himself, "Awaiting further instructions."

There was Paul ready to take them back. He was happy to see them.

Paul realized that they had one additional passenger. He pointed at Jim Q. and asked Ted, "Is he cool?"

"Yep. Jim Q., meet Paul," Ted said. "Paul is our boat guy. He lives out at Pierce Point. Paul, Jim Q. is our radio guy." Ted knew not to tell a single person who didn't need to know that they had a code talker.

Paul extended his hand. "Radio guy, huh? Cool. Nice to meet you Jim Q."

Paul pointed to a duffle bag in the boat and said to Jim Q., "A Navy guy came by and said this belongs to one of you. Is it yours?"

Jim Q. looked at the duffle bag and asked for a flashlight. Ted, Sap, Grant, and Paul each had one. Along with carrying a pistol everywhere, another new habit Grant acquired was having a flashlight, notepad and pen, and a folding knife on him at all times.

"Mine is green light," Paul said, referring to his flashlight. "Saves your night vision." Paul handed it to Jim Q., who looked at the duffle bag with the green light and said, "Yep, this is mine. Thanks."

Grant looked at his watch. It was 2:15 a.m. "Time to boogie," he said to Paul. Grant's caffeine pill was wearing off a little. He was emotionally exhausted. So much had happened that night.

Paul got on the radio, said something, and got an answer back. "We're on hold for a little while. Each boat leaves with some time interval. No bunching us up. Easier for the bad guys to take more of us out if we're bunched up."

That reminded Grant that this war wasn't going to be a cakewalk. He grabbed a pair of binoculars and started to scan around.

It couldn't hurt to have as many eyes as possible looking for threats.

Through the binos, Grant could see a boat that had made it out of the harbor. It turned its running lights off and kept going, veering right, which was the route up the Puget Sound toward Seattle. Paul's boat would be going left.

After a while of straining to look through the binos, Grant could tell his eyes were becoming unfocused. He decided he needed to work on his command presence. Not to be bossy, just to be a lieutenant.

He handed the binos to Sap and said, "Sergeant, my old eyes are too tired to keep looking through these. Why don't you take over?"

"Yes, sir," Sap said.

Ted, realizing that Grant was working on his command presence, turned to Paul and said, "Grant here is now Lt. Matson."

"What?" Paul asked. "Lieutenant?"

"Yep," Ted said to Paul. "He is now your commanding officer. He is the CO of the 17th Irregulars. That's your unit now."

"What's the 17th Irregulars?" Paul asked after a brief pause. Ted told him about the unit and a little bit of what had happened in Hammond's office and then the meeting hall.

"Cool," Paul said. He stood up straight and his chest puffed out a bit. He was proud to be part of this. He kept thinking how far he'd come. Now he was a soldier. Or a sailor. Or whatever he was.

Although Grant was tired, and tired of talking in particular, he couldn't resist the opportunity. He said to Paul, "The boat guys were very important in the Revolutionary War. Did I ever tell you about how George Washington got a little navy together and used them to do some pretty amazing things?" That resulted in a ten-minute talk. Paul was very interested. He was realizing how important his job was.

A minute after Grant was done talking about George Washington's navy, the radio crackled. Paul answered with a call sign Grant didn't recognize. Paul said, "We're cleared to go. We'll be going fast at first, then we'll slow down and go in circles for a while. We'll come close to another boat, which also won't have its lights on, then we'll cruise out at a weird angle, and then straighten out. It's part of a thing to make it hard for an observer on the shore to keep track of the boats. Like three-card Monte, where they move their hands around to keep you from seeing which one is the money card. Anyone on shore watching us will think we're just smugglers doing a drop or something. That's the idea."

Grant was realizing that all this zooming around the water, coming close to other boats with their lights off, and then taking off at

228

weird angles, all in the dark, was pretty dangerous. Given how weak the Limas would probably be in straight-on combat, Grant bet that many of the military deaths in this war would be from accidents. Most people thought the only way to die in the military was to dramatically take a bullet to the chest while shooting at the enemy. Not true. Those kinds of deaths were actually pretty rare. Accidents and friendly fire were much more common, and just as deadly.

"Untie me," Paul said. Grant and Sap jumped off the boat, untied it, and jumped back on.

One more crackle of the radio and Paul moved the boat slowly out of the slip in the marina. When they had cleared the end of the marina, Paul said, "Find a seat and hang on." He started to take off at a steady and moderate rate of speed. Pretty soon, after his wake was lessened, but not completely eliminated, he punched it. Everyone was pushed back in their seats. This boat had some horsepower. Whoever they got it from had a hell of a boat.

They sped to the middle of the inlet. It was scary as hell speeding through the water in the pitch dark, but Paul did it like it was no big deal. He was scared, but not showing it. He had a job to do and was damned glad to be doing it.

From the reflection of the moon on the water, Grant could faintly see another boat without its lights on. Paul saw it, too. He slowed to a stop and drifted. The radio crackled again and Paul put the boat in a steep left turn and sped up. They went in two circles. Grant could faintly see the other boat doing the same. The radio crackled again and Paul straightened out and headed straight toward shore. Grant knew that Paul was doing this on purpose and was skilled at it, but he was still terrified. The faint outline of shore was getting close. Really close. Grant was just about to say something when Paul turned hard left and started going through the inlet about a hundred yards off shore. "Tide is in pretty high or we couldn't do this," he said.

"Plus, at this distance from shore, it's harder for people there to shoot us," Ted said.

As they went down the inlet and got farther from the lights of Boston Harbor, the moonlight made it easier to see things without the man-made lights diluting the moonlight.

The inlet was empty. There were almost no lights on the cabins along shore. Grant wondered why. Duh, because it's the middle of the night. People are asleep. And people along shore didn't keep the night lights on because that would just tell pirates that there was a cabin there. In fact, Grant had heard at the Grange that some of the people in

Pierce Point right on the water would put blankets over their waterside windows to prevent any light from showing through.

Grant thought about the modern day pirates out there. They were gangs in boats. Grant hadn't heard of any confirmed pirates in Peterson Inlet off of Pierce Point. The beach patrol made sure of that. Pierce Point probably had the only organized beach patrol with good radios in the area and the pirates knew they could have a much easier time elsewhere. Why not take the easy stuff first? Then move onto the harder targets. Grant knew that Pierce Point was vulnerable from attack by sea, but, on the other hand, Pierce Point could also easily transport things by sea, like the 17th. Sea access was a double-edged sword.

In the quiet of no one talking and the hum of the engines and water, Grant fell asleep. He woke up, embarrassed that the old dude was napping. He looked around and saw they were almost at the Marion Farm landing.

"You were only out a couple of minutes, Lieutenant," Ted said, giving the answer to the question he anticipated Grant would ask.

# Chapter 204

## *A Good Gang*

### (July 22)

Hearing Ted call him "Lieutenant" forced Grant to quickly think about what he needed to do after they landed at the farm. He realized he had to walk Jim Q. into the camp and explain what a Quadra was. And that Grant was their CO. Actually, Grant realized as he was waking up, this introduction of his rank and Jim Q. was pretty important. First impressions were everything. Grant started to get mentally ready for another important meeting. It was almost 3:00 a.m. and it was time to go to work.

They slowed down to a drift. Grant was impatient. He wanted to go ashore and get this meeting over with and then go to bed. He realized this wasn't going to happen. Tonight was a work night. He could sleep in tomorrow. Or, technically, today since it was after midnight. Way after midnight.

Grant took the opportunity of the silent drift to prepare for his speech. He got some thoughts in order and decided on the political approach to take. He would confidently tell the men that he was their CO, but not be a dick about it. As a civilian, and, worse yet, a lawyer, people might assume he would be a dick on a power trip. Grant knew how to handle this.

"Hey, Ted," Grant said, "I need you to introduce me as the new lieutenant. You know, Lt. Col. Hammond commissioned this guy, that kind of thing." Ted nodded.

"I'm just a UCG," Grant said, using the Team's self-deprecating term for untrained civilian goofball, "so I need some credibility. You're Special Forces and a master sergeant. You introducing me gives it some credibility."

Ted nodded. He had been thinking the same thing.

Grant continued, "I'll introduce Jim Q. and tell people about how I'll be running things." Grant smiled and said to Ted, "Which is to say, how you are running things. I'm in charge but you're the day-to-day guy. Any recommendations on my approach, Sergeant?" Grant was practicing his style of command, which would consist of gathering lots of input from the people who actually knew what the hell they were doing, while he remained in command.

Soldiers needed to know their CO is in command. Even if he doesn't know everything, they need to know there is a CO. Showing some humility by asking for a master sergeant's "recommendations" was the perfect middle-ground approach.

"Sounds good, Lieutenant," Ted said. "I have to get in the habit of calling you 'Lieutenant'."

"Oh, I know, 'Sergeant,'" Grant said, "I'm doing the same, Ted. We'll make this work, Sgt. Malloy."

"Yes, sir," Ted said to Grant, still practicing. "It's good you're taking your commission seriously, but not too seriously. Of course, military protocol is vastly relaxed in an irregular unit. But these guys need to see, at least at this early stage when they're setting their views on what kind of unit this is, that there's a CO who is taking the job seriously...and that there's a sergeant around who knows what the hell he's doing," Ted said with a smile.

"Roger that, Sergeant," Grant said, "Roger that." Grant smiled. He and Ted would do a great job at this. Together. Like Grant and Rich would do the civilian side well. Together. There are no Lone Rangers or ego trips out here, Grant thought. That will get you killed.

Finally, it was time to land. The boat softly bumped up on the shore. They jumped out one by one. Grant's hillbilly slippers were waterproof up to about the ankle. The water was about that deep, but he jumped in and the water went over his ankle and into his socks. Oh well, it was pretty warm out.

Ted and Sap helped Jim Q. with his duffle bag. He put it over his shoulders and started walking. Sap took point. Everyone had their rifle in hand, except for Jim Q. who hadn't been assigned one yet. For all they knew, Marion Farm had been overrun and was now manned with Limas who were waiting to ambush them along the road. It was unlikely, but possible. Sap keyed the mic three times on the radio hanging from the left shoulder of his kit. A second later, there were four mic keys in response. Sap gave the thumbs up. The Patriots at Marion Farm were expecting them. Grant took up the rear, AR in hand and walking backwards half the time to watch for anyone behind them who shouldn't be there.

The quiet. Once again, Grant loved the quiet of moving through the woods. He heard the wind gently swaying the evergreens. It was so peaceful. Then Grant would turn around, sweep the rear looking through the red dot and circle of his EO Tech sight on his AR, watching and listening for anything trying to kill him and his guys. It was armed serenity, despite the whole people-might-be-trying-to-kill-you thing.

After a few minutes, Sap halted them and keyed his mic twice. One keying of the mic was the answer. Sap kept moving forward.

By now, they could see the guard station on the little hill at the entrance from the beach to the farm. As they got closer, one of the two guards said, "Welcome, gentlemen. How 'bout them Packers?"

Sap quickly said, "Offensive line could use some work" and kept walking. Grant realized that this was a code for testing friendlies. The mic key code could be compromised pretty easily, but references to Sap's Wisconsin upbringing would be a much harder code to break.

They were now in the lights of the outbuildings and farmhouse. Grant was stunned at how large, and perfect, the place was. He was tired and it was dark, so he wasn't fully taking in all the sights of the facility.

Grant did notice that there was a lot of activity at the farm for the middle of the night. Then again, people in this business probably worked a lot at night, like Grant was tonight.

They got to the farmhouse and went in the front door. Don, the Air Force RED HORSE guy, was in command in Ted's absence. Ted said to Don, "Get everyone together, we have an announcement and," he said pointing to Jim Q., "an introduction." Don rounded everyone up. In the meantime, Grant and the others who had been in Boston Harbor had something to eat; cornbread from that night's dinner, to be exact. Don brought everyone into the kitchen where Grant and the others were eating. There were about ten of them, including civilians Stan and Carl, Tom in his Air Force fatigues, and Travis in his Navy fatigues. There were a couple more Air Force and Navy guys helping Don put the facility together. The rest were a couple of infantrymen, all in their fatigues with the "U.S. Army" name tape taken off. This core group was a good sample of what the full unit would be: civilians, support troops from the Air Force and Navy, and infantrymen.

"All here, boss, except the guards." Don said to Ted. Ted nodded.

"Well, ladies and gentlemen, I have an announcement," Ted said. "I would like to introduce you to Lt. Grant Matson, the commanding officer of our unit, the 17th Irregulars of the Free Washington State Guard." Ted started applauding and the rest of the group quickly followed.

When the applause died down, Don said, "So we're the 17th Irregulars, huh?" He thought about it and said, "Cool. What's our mission?" Ted explained the mission—the short version—to Don and the others. They would train a mixture of FUSA military and civilians to be guerillas and to occupy an objective after the regular Patriot forces had taken it. Ted didn't go into the details about Grant and the Team doing their civil affairs mission. They didn't need to know all the details just yet.

Grant was embarrassed to admit that no one asked about him. The attention was on the unit and what it would be doing. That made sense when he thought about it, but Grant expected to be grilled by the troops on whether he had any military experience and whether he could be a battlefield commander. Instead, the troops just seemed to accept that he was the lieutenant and go on with their jobs.

Ted realized that Grant needed a little attention with the big announcement about him being in command. "And the guy you knew as Grant," Ted said, "was commissioned by Lt. Col. Hammond of the Special Operations Command as our lieutenant." Everyone applauded.

"Lt. Matson," Ted said, "do you care to say something to your troops?" This was Grant's chance to describe his philosophy of command and set the tone for the unit. This was a chance he would only get once, and he knew he had to make it good.

"Thanks, Sgt. Malloy," Grant said. "Here's the deal folks. I was a civilian my whole life. I will rely heavily on Sgt. Malloy here. I am not pretending to be something I'm not. Never have. I found that life goes much more smoothly when you're not trying to be something you're not. So, while I know quite a bit about tactical things and I know how to organize people pretty damned well, I have no military background to speak of, so I compensate for that by listening to Ted, or," Grant caught himself, "as I now call him, Sgt. Malloy."

Grant looked at each person in the kitchen for a moment and said, "But I am in command. I am responsible for each of you. I am working with HQ on some stuff that I am pretty good at," he said, keeping the civil affairs thing vague. "Bottom line: Special Operations Command put me in charge. So I am. Gladly. This is how I have been called on to serve in taking this country back. It's what I'm supposed to do, and I'm damned glad to be doing it."

"Battlefield rules out here, obviously," Grant said, trying to show his troops that he had some military knowledge. "No saluting, no attention when I walk in, none of that stuff. I would have you call me Grant like you have been, but I need to show the people who aren't out here yet that I'm the CO, so I'll ask you to call me 'Lieutenant' around the others. But when this core group is alone, I'm fine with Grant. All I want to do is win and bring each and every one of you back home to wherever home is for you. The rest of it—titles, saluting, that kind of ego shit—I could do without."

"Here is one thing I insist on in this unit," Grant said in his command voice. "Every single person is a warrior. Every single one. No matter what your job here, you are a warrior first and a dishwasher, or whatever, second. This isn't like the military units some of you came from where things were so specialized that you only worked on one particular piece of equipment for four years and someone else took care of the 'gun part' of the mission. Not here. You will all be trained as fighters and you will get some rifle time. It might be guard duty, or it might be infantry duty, or it might be some high-speed commando shit in a raid, but you will all be rifle-toting fighters. If anyone isn't OK with that, you'll need to go. So, is everyone OK with that?"

A thunderous, "Yes, sir!" broke out in unison. Grant smiled. That's the spirit he wanted to see. "Another thing," he said, "that will be new to you military people is that, when the unit is up to full strength, it will have lots of civilians. I need the military people and civilians to work together seamlessly. This is a military unit, albeit it an irregular one. You military guys will know more than the civilians and will need to train them. But, we're all Americans, we're all Patriots, and we're all risking our lives to make things right again. I want each of you military guys to take a civilian or two under your wing. Can you do that for me?"

Another thunderous, "Yes, sir!" The conversation was going better than Grant had expected.

"Another thing," Grant continued. "Let your chain of command know if you need things or have suggestions on how to make this work better." Grant wanted to get all the good ideas he could out of these people. "Hey, let's be honest: We're making this up as we go. None of us have ever been in an irregular unit. The U.S. hasn't had irregular units for over two hundred years, but ask the British, and I'm sure they'll say that irregulars can mess you up." That got some cheers. Grant wanted to make the connection with the troops that the 17th was like the militias during the Revolutionary War. He hoped for the same outcome as in that war.

Grant continued, "We're out here at a farm. None of you have ever set up a base at a farm. None of you have ever operated without the full logistical support of the United States military. Sergeants Malloy and Sappenfield have set up indigenous units, but with local tribes in far off places, so that's a little different for them too, but the idea is just the same. This means we'll look to them on a lot of matters, but I want each of you to tell us what's working, what's not working, and what would work better."

"I mentioned chain of command," Grant said, "so I better add that we'll come up with squad leaders in a while." Grant hadn't talked to Ted about squad leaders, but just assumed that would be done. "When we have a couple squads worth of people out here, we'll do that. I'm not rigid on many things, but the chain of command is important, especially because I won't be out here full time. Unfortunately, I have to be back in Pierce Point during the days most of the time. I have a cover to maintain and some work back there that directly benefits the unit." Grant was being vague and painting a slightly rosier picture than reality, but was referring to recruiting Pierce Point guards and walk-ons from the gate. Plus, Grant had to make sure Pierce Point ran smoothly. It wouldn't do the 17th any good if all the residents in the vicinity of the Marion Farm were starving and killing each other. "It sucks that I'm not here 24/7. But," Grant said pointing to the crowd in the kitchen, "we're in good hands. You guys can handle anything." They were nodding. "Sgt. Malloy will solve most of the problems," Grant continued, "but he can get a hold of me whenever, so I'm always available by radio." Sap told Grant he would give him one of the secure military radios they used to communicate with Scotty earlier and would show him how to use it. Grant would have the military radio with him at all times, and Scotty would keep the radio he had and would be back up for contacting Grant.

"Oh," Grant said, because he almost forgot this important part, "I want some traditions out here. We're a new unit starting from scratch. We can have our own traditions. Something like, I dunno, dinner on Sunday where we all sit down and relax with a big meal. Something like that. This is a family. Families have traditions. Traditions will be part of the great memories you have from being in this unit. Let's have some traditions and stories to tell our grandkids."

Ted smiled. He liked the idea of a Sunday dinner tradition. That was how things used to be. Once upon a time, America took time out and relaxed, without cell phones and computers, and without working second jobs to pay their taxes. People talked to each other.

"Any questions?" Grant asked.

There weren't any.

"OK," Grant said, "now to introduce the newest member of the unit, Jim Q." Grant pointed at him, and he waved to the group.

"He's our Quadra," Grant said, "which is HQ's term for these very unique radio crypto guys." Crypto was short for "cryptographer," which meant a code expert. Grant didn't want to give out the details of the code talkers just yet. "Jim Q., why don't you tell everyone about yourself?"

Jim Q. smiled. He wasn't nervous about meeting a bunch of strangers. "I'm Jim and since I'm a Quadra, I'm going by Jim Q. I know a very, very unique code that I can use on the radio to talk to HQ and other irregular units. I can also use this code to write notes for HQ and read their notes that come in. They're written in a code that the Limas absolutely cannot break. They've never seen or heard anything like this before."

The soldiers were very impressed that HQ had cryptos out here, and felt special, like HQ cared by sending them a code guy. They were reassured that their communications would be encoded.

"I'm Arab, but Christian," Jim Q. said, addressing what he knew most of the guys were likely thinking. "I'm not some terrorist." He'd been explaining this since he was a kid. After September 11th, people got nervous at just the sight of him. He understood. He got nervous at the sight of young Arab men, too. "In fact, the terrorists love to kill Christians like me, and often do, especially in the country my family came from."

"An Arab working the codes?" Grant said. "You're probably wondering if we've lost our minds. Fair enough. But there are things you don't know about that give me absolute trust in Jim Q. and the other Quadras. Here's one: all of the Quadras' families are in Patriot 'safekeeping.' One little incident and they'll never see their families. And this 'safekeeping' was their idea."

Grant looked at each soldier and said, "Here's the bottom line: Jim Q. is our code guy, HQ extensively vetted him and all the others like him, and I trust him with my life and yours. Anyone have a problem with Jim Q.?"

It was silent and a few heads were shaking. "That's what I thought," Grant said, sounding a bit like a dick, but he needed to make this point in his command voice. He couldn't have people distrusting any member of the unit, especially not the very crucial code guy. It was more important for everyone to trust Jim Q. than for Grant to not be a slight dick for a few seconds.

Anderson, one of the Army infantrymen out there, who was black, said, "Don't worry, Jim Q. I'll keep these cracker-asses away from you." He laughed, letting everyone know he was kidding. Anderson had a great sense of humor and wanted to show everyone that the unit was cool with Jim Q. Grant appreciated the humor. It was a great way to put people at ease.

Ted said, also jokingly, "What Corporal Anderson means is that we have a diverse workplace and all are welcomed."

Jim Q., not missing a beat, said, "A diverse workplace? That's fine. Just keep the cracker-asses away from me." Everyone laughed. Humor was a social lubricant. It made otherwise sticky situations flow smoothly.

"One more thing, Lieutenant," Anderson said. He was on a roll and wanted to get another laugh. He made the number one with his thumb. Then he folded in his next two fingers, so just his right ring finger and pinkie were out. Then he held up all five fingers on his left hand.

"See," he said looking at his thumb. "That's a one." Then he looked at the remaining two fingers, and the five on the other hand, and said, "That's a seven."

He looked up and smiled, "The 1-7, y'all. The 1-7."

"That's our gang sign," Grant said. Some people were stunned. A Patriot guerilla unit with a "gang sign"?

"That's right: our gang sign," Grant said. "We're a gang here at the 17th. A good gang."

Everyone was smiling and nodding while flashing each other the "1-7" sign.

Grant sat back and watched his unit bond. They were a good gang, indeed.

# Chapter 205

## *This can't go on much longer*

### (July 24)

Steve Briggs got up at 4:30 a.m. as usual. He didn't even need an alarm clock anymore. He went to bed early because there was nothing else to do in the evening. No TV. Well, there was TV on the air, but it was all propaganda and truly mindless sitcoms and reality shows, with all the "commercials" being "public service announcements" from the government containing more propaganda. Steve couldn't watch TV anymore. Even when he would lose himself in some classic sitcom from the past, he would be jolted back to reality by the obnoxious propaganda ads that interrupted the show. That wasn't relaxing.

"Same ole', same ole'," Steve said to himself as he got dressed for work. "Work" was solving problems all day in Forks.

They still hadn't seen any semis roll into town. It was a hundred miles to the closest town and no one was surprised that the authorities hadn't made little, isolated Forks a high priority.

People in Forks were living on fish and game, mostly elk and deer. It seemed like everyone had a garden by now. Most people were sharing and trading food.

Most people. There were still some loners who didn't. They tried to live off of their own food, and some of them stole from others. The town's deputized civilian police force kept that down to a minimum. Actually, the fact that almost everyone in town was armed kept it to a minimum. There had been over two dozen burglars shot by homeowners since the Collapse, out of a town of about three thousand.

But things had become "normal" in Forks. It was a new normal, granted, but Steve was worried about what was coming. Winter. Summer was easy living, but that wouldn't be true in a few short months.

Things were different, but somewhat the same, two hundred miles away in Olympia. Back in the Cedars subdivision, Ron Spencer was a "gray man," a saboteur against the government who kept to himself. He stayed under the radar. He didn't even tell his wife he was doing it. Ron's contribution to the cause was to spray paint graffiti messages at night. His favorite was "I miss America."

His "job" – the thing that put food on the table – was operating an underground taxi service running on barter, driving people around to important things. Ron had some silver he'd squirreled away before the Collapse which he used to buy gas from the "gang gas" station. He would then drive people who had no gas and, in return, would get food and other things.

And, in all this driving around, Ron would observe things that might be helpful to the Patriots. He learned when the shift changes were for the pathetic FCorps guards at the police station. Ron had made contact with Matt Collins who was a Patriot and would pass along things to him, like the shift change and other tidbits. Ron laughed at the pre-Collapse Homeland Security slogan of "See something. Say something." He was doing that alright, but not for the side Homeland Security had been talking about.

Ron's other "job" was volunteering as an FCorps accountant because he had been a CPA before the Collapse. His FCorps accounting job was a joke because the FCorps was corrupt as hell and didn't exactly keep good records of its corruption. Ron didn't care. In fact, he used the volunteer job to get his family a decent FCard allowance, although food shipments were pretty unpredictable to the "regular" stores that the little people like him could shop at. The politically connected people got to go to special stores that were always well stocked.

Ron supplemented the FCard food and the taxi service barter items with the small amount of food his family had stored. They were Mormon, after all. People assumed they had lots of stored food, but they didn't. They had some, though. Far more than most, especially in "commieville," as Ron called ultra-liberal—and thoroughly dependent—Olympia.

In his travels around Olympia and the surrounding areas, Ron could clearly see how this was going to end. The government was becoming more corrupt and desperate. The socialist economy was definitely not working. Ron could tell that the government was running on fumes. They had some money left in everyone's retirement accounts that the government was using to buy food, much of it from overseas, and some diesel to get the food out to the stores. But this wouldn't last long. More and more people were saying little things to him that let him know that they were turning from Undecideds to Patriots. They weren't about to go out and join some Patriot guerilla band, but they were not lifting a finger to help the "legitimate authorities," as the Loyalists preferred to be called. It seemed as though everyone was waiting for some event. Some huge, dramatic event that would be their chance to go out and finish off the Loyalists. Ron knew it was coming. He knew it, and he felt it. He just didn't know when.

Just sixty miles north in the Loyalist stronghold of Seattle, Ed Oleo was another "gray man." The former real estate broker who had been the target of a vicious and corrupt state regulator was now getting by with his little side business of small home repairs. Ed was, to all outward appearances, a Loyalist. He had the "We Support the Recovery!" yard sign in his front yard like everyone else. He didn't talk about how much he hated the government. Not even to his wife. Ed would go over to his Russian neighbor, Dimitry's, house and ask him to tell stories about how the gray men resisted the Soviets back in the day. Ed would take the wisdom from Dimitry's experiences and think about how to apply it to undermine the American government.

Ed was doing a minor gray man mission. He was figuring out who the serious Loyalists were—the "true believers" as the Patriots called the hardcore Loyalists. The true believers were the ones who were actively helping the government. The true believers were not the majority of people in his neighborhood who were just mouthing the government slogans to keep their FCards. There was a huge difference.

Ed would go around to houses in his subdivision and a few of the surrounding ones and ask if people needed home repairs. Most didn't. Well, probably needed some repairs but they didn't have anything to trade for a luxury like fixing something. Ed used these visits to get to know people. He had nothing else to do all day so he figured he would chat with people and gather intelligence.

Pretty soon, Ed had a good list of the true believers in the area. He drew a map of the subdivisions and put an X on the homes of the true believers. He numbered each one and had a corresponding note with information on that household. He tried to make sure he knew which people in a household were guilty and who were innocent bystanders. He couldn't always get to this level of detail, but he tried.

Ed noticed that the Loyalists' hold on power was slipping. Once in a while, the semis wouldn't make it to the local grocery store, and this began happening more frequently. Crime was getting worse. More and more people were openly complaining about how scarce everything was. Some were even talking openly about how the gangs were gaining even more control.

Ed thought to himself, "This can't go on forever." Just like Ron, Ed knew something was coming. He didn't know when, but he knew he had that old shotgun in his basement and he would do his part when the time was right. He knew who in his neighborhood had it coming.

Back in Frederickson, John Bennington also knew who had it coming. His boss, Commissioner Winters, did. Bennington was growing increasingly disgusted with what was going on in his rural county. Before the Collapse, Winters had always been a politician, and that was bad enough. But now Winters was a dictator. Corrupt, power hungry, spiteful, petty and sadistic.

There was one thing in particular Winters did that Bennington couldn't stand. Winters hurt women and girls. It started with Winters' receptionist, Julie Mathers.

Julie was the gorgeous receptionist Bennington saw when he took Rich Gentry to see Winters. Bennington got to know her.

"Can I talk to you?" She asked one day, as she started to cry.

"Yeah, sure," he said. Most men are incapable of ignoring a crying woman. It was hard wired into them.

"I needed a job," she said, sobbing. She described how she needed a job before the Collapse and Winters gave her a very cushy county one. But there was a price.

"He makes me..." She couldn't finish the sentence. But, Bennington knew exactly what it was.

"I hate doing it," she said, trying to quiet down her crying in case anyone heard her.

"One time he said that if I didn't do it," she whispered, "then I'd have to 'live outside the wire,'" referring to living outside the barbed wire-fortified courthouse.

Bennington knew that if she was outside the wire, she'd be dead in ten minutes. So many people outside the wire hated Winters and resented anyone with a big fat government job. Winters knew she couldn't leave. She was in a prison and he was in total control of her.

Bennington figured that Winters never enjoyed sex much without having control over the person. Now that he had absolute control over her, it made sex exactly what he'd been looking for his whole life. Power and control.

Winters did more than just sleep with Julie. He humiliated her. He took pictures of her and showed them to his political buddies. He made her do things in the pictures. Bennington had been shown one by a fellow cop at the courthouse. It was terrible.

The worst part was that the men at the courthouse who saw the pictures would then see Julie every day at work and she knew they had seen the pictures. She had to sit there, knowing what all the men were thinking.

This was intentional. Winters made it known in the courthouse that anyone who saw the pictures of "his pet" could comment on them to Julie. Underlings were told that Winters viewed it as a sign of loyalty to him—and a way to get favors with him—to ask Julie to do the things they saw in the pictures and then laugh at her. She had to sit there and take it. They all knew they couldn't touch her, but they could say anything they wanted to her. Making Julie cry got someone big points with Winters. He felt warm inside when Julie cried.

Winters didn't stop with Julie. He had a thing for Mexican girls. Young ones; sometimes, very young ones. He would get them from the gangs as a prize. He wrecked about one life per day and loved it. He was out of control.

Bennington had a little girl of his own. She was living with her mother in the Seattle area after the divorce. He could see Winters coming after his daughter if Winters got a chance.

Bennington knew what he needed to do.

# Chapter 206

## *Greetings from the Think Farm*

### (July 25)

Life at the Prosser Farm had become routine. The farm was producing lots and lots of food; plenty for the Prossers and their guest families.

At first, Jeff Prosser was concerned that people in his area would figure out who the guest families were and rat them out. However, people taking in families became so common during the Collapse that no one thought much about it. The local families, all relatives of the Prossers, could keep a secret. The Prosser relatives were all Patriots, anyway. They had suffered through the insane environmental dictates of the government and had a very healthy dislike of the Loyalists.

The kids of the guest families were getting used to farm life and even enjoying it. The wives of the guest families were adapting in varying degrees, as well. But all were grateful to be there, away from the police who wanted to take their husbands to jail and the mobs of Loyalist protestors who wanted to drag them into the street and beat them to death. The men at the farm were adjusting to farm life, too. Once a week, one of them would leave for guard duty at Delphi Road for a full week.

The WAB guys—Tom, Brian, and Ben—continued to put out their Rebel Radio CDs highlighting the political situation and encouraging people to rise up. Dennis, one of Jeff's cousins, would take the CDs into Olympia and get them to Adrienne who would make copies of the CDs and get them out to Patriots. Then the Patriots who would listen to them, make copies, and pass them along to trusted friends. It was an amazingly good distribution system.

Tom, Brian, and Ben had no idea if anyone was listening to the CDs, but Dennis would come back from Olympia and tell them which graffiti messages were spray painted in town. They were stunned when they realized the phrases they used on the Rebel Radio CDs were popping up on walls and overpasses in Olympia. Adrienne told Dennis that the phrases were being spotted in Seattle and elsewhere. For the first time, the WAB guys thought that people were listening and,

244

surprisingly, their little podcast was having an impact. That made them work harder at making Rebel Radio even better.

Jeff was glad he had that five hundred gallon underground tank of diesel at the farm. It fueled his tractor and a few of the trucks that transported the guards from the other farms out to the guard station at Delphi Road, which was the only way in and out of the area. The diesel used to transport guards, and the one man per week for guard duty, was the "tax" the Prossers and their guests paid for their security. A very good deal, Jeff thought. Considering how badly other farm communities had it.

Jeff looked out at his fields and mentally counted all the food they'd be able to harvest. There should be more than enough for themselves and some extra to barter with. But winter was coming. Would they have enough? Would his kids go hungry? What would it be like to see his children die from starvation? Would his guests have enough to eat? Would they get weak from malnutrition and come down with the flu or some other illness that wouldn't' be a big deal in peacetime but could be deadly when bodies had been weakened? He tried not to think about it, but he couldn't get the thought out of his mind.

The most interesting thing to happen out at the Prosser Farm happened at the Delphi Road guard station one bright and beautiful sunny morning.

Ben was doing his week of guard duty when a young woman came walking up to the gate. She was short and had curly brown hair. She had her hands up and looked very nervous.

The alert went up and the guards were ready to shoot her or repel an attack from another direction if she were a decoy. Things were tense. Ben aimed his shotgun with rifled slugs at her. He had never pointed a gun at a person before and it was a very odd feeling for him.

She stopped when she got about fifty yards from the gate and just stood there trying to get up the courage for what she was about to do. She was shaking.

"Is there a 'Ben' here?" she yelled.

Everyone looked at Ben.

"Ben who?" the guard commander yelled at her.

"I can't really say," she yelled back.

"We can't help you unless you can tell us who 'Ben' is," the guard commander yelled.

She started crying. Ben thought he recognized that cry. He motioned for one of the guards to give him some binoculars. Ben looked at the girl.

"Oh my God!" Ben yelled. "Carly! Come here, Carly!" Ben motioned for the guards to let her in.

"You know her?" the guard commander asked Ben.

"Yes, and she's fine," Ben said. "Let her in."

Carly was a former WAB intern. She worked there when she was in college before she had to drop out because of the economy. She was a great kid. A conservative. A fighter. She was a true believer that the government was corrupt and destructive, especially to small businesses. Her dad owned a little logging company and had been run out of business by the taxes and regulations.

Carly, at the ripe old age of twenty-one, had been a key political strategist for WAB. She had this way of breaking complicated political and public policy issues down into simple terms that regular people could understand. Before the Collapse she would have had a magnificent career as a political strategist. Now she was officially unemployed.

The guard commander yelled to the girl that she could come to the gate but to keep her hands up. She'd never had guns pointed at her. It was scary. She stopped crying when she realized that they were letting her in.

As she got closer, Ben came running up to her. She had lost a lot of weight so Ben didn't recognize her at first. She looked terrified.

"Carly!" Ben said, thrilled that she hadn't been captured. "What you doin' here, girl?" They hugged. Ben could feel a gun in her belt.

"I've come with a message for you," Carly squealed with delight. She was extremely excited. She didn't think this crazy mission would work.

"How did you know where I was?" Ben asked. Now that their location was compromised, he was scared the WAB people at the Prosser Farm would have to move. Fast.

"I was there when you guys were at the office talking about buggin' out to Jeff's farm," she whispered. "I was outside the door. I could hear through it."

"But how did you know where the farm was?" Ben whispered to her. He didn't want the other guards to know who he was or that Carly was from WAB.

"Oh, I came out once for an office barbeque," she whispered back. "Remember? That one two summers ago? Your boy ate that hot dog off the ground. Remember?"

"Does anyone else know we're out here?" Ben said, right as he realized he just gave away to her that Tom and Brian were also out there.

"No, of course not," Carly said, a little offended. "Why would I do that? I know what they want to do to you."

And my family, Ben thought. "OK, so no one knows?"

Carly shook her head with pride. "Yep, I told our guys that I could get a letter to you and left it at that. I asked to be dropped off at the Black Lake exit," which was one exit away on Highway 101 and about three miles from Delphi Road.

Ben nodded. He wasn't entirely sure he could believe that no one else knew where they were hiding, but he had to trust Carly.

"A message?" Ben asked. "And who are your 'guys?'" By now he had walked with her over to a place where no one could hear them so he was talking at a normal level.

She nodded with glee. Ben started to realize how dangerous it was for her to come out there with a message. Walking around the countryside full of murderers, rapists, and robbers just to deliver a message. It must be pretty important.

"From who?" Ben asked.

Carly put her finger up to her lips as if to say "Shhh." Ben's curiosity was increasing rapidly. What was all this about? Was she going to pull that pistol and try to kill him? Why would Carly do that?

Carly looked around to make sure no one was around. Then she looked Ben in the eyes, smiled, and whispered, "The Patriots want you to be the next governor."

Governor? Ben's blood went cold. What? That was crazy. Did she just say that? He squinted and looked at her. He couldn't understand what she just said.

"What are you talking about?" Ben finally got out. If this was some joke, it wasn't funny sending a nice girl out into a combat zone just to do some gag.

Carly was brimming. "Yes, Ben, isn't this great!" she said in a loud whisper. "You. The Governor. Super cool, huh?" Her youthful enthusiasm was such a contrast to something so grown up and serious, like being the governor.

"OK, I have no idea what you're talking about," Ben finally said. Maybe she was high. But that didn't make sense.

"We want to have an interim government in place for when we win," she said with a huge grin.

"Who's 'we'?" Ben asked.

"The Patriots, silly," Carly said with a "no duh" look on her face.

"Who are the Patriots?" Ben asked. He knew that Patriots were the good guys, but he didn't know who was speaking for them.

"You know, us," she said with that same "no duh" look.

"Just a bunch of people in a room saying 'We're the Patriots' or some organized group?" Ben asked. "Who, specifically?"

"The Free Washington Interim Government," Carly said. "That's who we are. We're the political arm of the Patriots. The Free Washington State Guard does the military stuff. The Interim Government—the people who sent me—are the civilian commanders in charge of them. We're the government—not the one in charge now. The one that will be when we win."

"Is this some group of people claiming to be the interim government or are they for real?" Ben asked.

"We're for real," she said. "John Trappford was our leader."

Trappford was the conservative state legislator from Eastern Washington who was the leader of the good guys before the Collapse.

"He put the Interim Government together before they got him a month ago," she said. She looked sad. "They killed him."

This was starting to seem plausible to Ben. If Trappford put this group together, they were the real deal. And Carly was solid. She was a true friend. There was no way she was making this up. She started naming conservative legislators and others they both knew from their days at WAB who were part of the Interim Government.

"How are you involved with this?" Ben asked.

Carly explained that when the Collapse started she was at her parents' house in rural Lewis County. Without any plan, she got in her little car and went up to Olympia. She knew that's where she needed to be. Trappford was taking in conservatives from all over who were coming to Olympia for the big showdown. They stayed at his house in Olympia where he lived during the legislative session and they became a revolutionary cadre. They stayed up all night talking about how they would run things once the Loyalists were thrown out. They built up a network of political sympathizers and, as the Collapse got worse and the union thugs were out looking for them, they helped Patriots get to safe places. Finally, after Trappford went back to his Eastern Washington home and was assassinated, they went fully underground.

They were mostly public policy people from think tanks and lived on a farm outside of Olympia, dubbed the "Think Farm" which was a play on the term "think tank." The group didn't have any contact with the outside world, except for the messengers who came and went. It was at this little farm where they planned out the Interim Government. They picked the temporary legislators and governor for after the military victory. They also planned the constitutional convention to rewrite the state constitution that they would hold once they had control. They would then hold an election to ratify the new constitution and elect the legislators, governor, and the handful of the other officials.

"Totally libertarian," Carly said. "We're not going to repeat the mistakes of the past. We'll have real controls in place to prevent the government from growing like it did," she said excitedly. She started going over the details of the new government.

Ben stopped her. "Hey, Carly, we can talk about that later," he said. "I need to know that this group is legit before I go any further."

Carly smiled and reached for her belt. Ben stepped back and instinctively drew his shotgun at her.

She jumped back and threw her hands up. "A letter," she said. "I have a letter."

The guards had been watching Ben and Carly from a distance. When they saw Ben reach for his shotgun, they shouldered their rifles. When he found out she had a letter, Ben motioned to the guards that they could lower their weapons. Ben still had his shotgun halfway ready, but not pointed at her.

"The letter is in my jeans," Carly said with her hands up. "Sorry, but I couldn't get caught with it."

"OK, you can get it," Ben said. He was a little uncomfortable when Carly, who was now a very attractive young woman after all the weight loss, unzipped her jeans right in front of him. He started to turn his head out of respect for her privacy, but he realized she could still shoot him so he decided to keep his eyes on her. Above her jeans.

She pulled out an envelope and handed it to him. It had some kind of logo on it that said "Free Washington Interim Government." If these guys were goofballs, at least they had a decent logo, Ben thought. It sure looked official. Ben just looked at the envelope again and couldn't really believe this was happening.

"Go ahead and open it, silly," she said with a flirtatious smile. She always had a crush on Ben. Now she was on a dangerous mission to recruit him as the next governor. She was so excited. She knew Ben was married, but she could still have her harmless little crush.

Ben hesitated to open it. He had a feeling that, once he opened it, things would never be the same for him if what Carly was saying was true.

Ben was happy to be hiding out on the Prosser Farm with his family. He was done with politics. Just look at what politics had done: armed guards, food shortages, and all the rest. He wanted to spend the rest of his life growing some food and pulling his week of guard duty every month. That was fine with him. He wanted nothing to do with this Interim Government or whatever it was.

His curiosity got the best of him, though, and he opened the envelope and removed the letter. It was on fancy Interim Government letterhead that matched the envelope and had been printed on a printer instead of handwritten.

"Dear Ben:" the letter began. It was dated June 1. It went on to describe how the Interim Government had come together and dropped lots of names that Ben knew, like John Trappford. It mentioned Carly and many other conservatives Ben knew from back in Olympia. There were messages from them saying things that only they would know.

The letter said, "Russ Finehoff is working with us. He said that his dog, Sprucey, finally quit barking at the neighbor cat." It was a reference to Ben's friend Russ who worked for one of the few good legislators. Russ had Ben over for a BBQ one time and his dog, whose name Ben had forgotten, spent the entire party barking at a cat.

They couldn't be making up these details, Ben thought. This letter was legit. Or the government had tortured a lot of people and gotten little tidbits like Russ's dog out of them. But the government was so inept and had their hands full right now that it was highly unlikely they went to all that trouble just to write a fake letter to Ben.

The letter transitioned from friendly shout outs to serious business. It described how weak the Loyalists were, how many military units were defecting, how the Patriots were forming guerilla bands all over the state, and how the population was turning against the so-called "legitimate authorities."

"Why you, Ben?" the letter asked. "A fair question," it said. "We know you and trust you. You are a Patriot. And you have thousands of followers from Rebel Radio."

That really caught Ben off guard. Other than Dennis' observations around town of their slogans going up as graffiti, he had no idea that people were taking Rebel Radio seriously.

The letter went on to describe how, after the military victory, the Patriots would set up an interim government. They would appoint temporary legislators, a governor, and judges. They would hold an election—at least in the territories they controlled—to ratify the temporary officials. They would then work on a constitutional convention to draft a new state constitution—with real checks on power. The letter went on to proudly state that they would adopt a "high five" constitutional provision. This was the provision Ben and the others had always talked about that would limit the state spending to a maximum of five percent of the state's gross domestic product, hence the label "high five." These were all things Ben and others had talked about many times over beers before the Collapse. Things they said they would love to do if they ever could.

"Well, now we can," the letter said. "It's our time to fix things, Ben. We need you. We need you for governor. We've talked about it and talked about it, and no one can come up with a better person to be the Interim Governor. This will be the most important thing you ever do. People will remember it for generations. We need you."

Ben was stunned. The letter was so personal, with all those references to people he knew so well, and seemed to be written by someone who knew him well. He got to the end of the letter and saw who signed it.

"John Trappford." He must have written this a few days before he was killed. Ben looked at the handwritten note below the signature.

"PS: You're dead anyway, Ben. They're looking for you. They'll find you eventually—if they stay in power. You might as well help us prevent that from happening. John."

How could Ben say no to John Trappford? And Carly, who had risked her life to get this letter to him. And, Ben admitted to himself, that postscript about being dead if the Loyalists stayed in power was a motivating factor, too.

"This is the chance we've been waiting for," Carly said when she saw Ben was done reading the letter. "This is what we've always talked about. It's time to do it."

Ben knew she was right. He knew he wanted to do it. He'd have to talk to Laura, his wife. They had always talked about him running for office if the state ever got its crap together and was actually open to someone like him. As the Collapse started, they knew that getting elected was even less likely. Both Ben and Laura thought about the possibility of the Patriots winning by force and then utilizing the services of Ben and the other WAB people. But they never really thought through the whole part about people trying to catch them and kill them. It added a whole new seriousness to what used to be just a daydream.

"I've got to talk to my family about this," Ben said.

"Of course," Carly said. The people at the Think Farm had told her that Ben would probably say this.

"How do I get back to you guys?" Ben asked.

"There's no real good way to do that," Carly said. The people at the Think Farm had no radios because they could only use very, very high-tech encrypted ones. The Loyalist might not be putting too much effort into rounding up garden-variety POIs, but they would spare nothing to take out the Think Farm. The Patriots didn't yet have any ultra-encrypted radios for them. They relied on messengers, which was less than ideal.

"I will come back in a few days," she said. She was not excited about making the trip out again with all the dangers, but a return trip would be much safer and easier. Besides, she told herself, she would be coming back with some friends; well-armed friends.

# Chapter 207

## *Life in the Loyal Areas*

### (July 26)

Life was going really well in Seattle for Professor Carol Matson. Well, going as well as could be expected given all the terrorists and teabaggers trying to prevent the government from helping people. Carol still had her job – thank God – at the University of Washington teaching Freedom Corps volunteers Spanish, which was her specialty.

Kind of. She was a world-renowned scholar of the literature of the Simon Bolivar era. But, in these times, there wasn't a use for that now, so she taught beginning Spanish.

Actually, she was tasked with keeping an eye on the FCorps volunteers. "Patriot" spies had infiltrated the FCorps and Carol was helping the legitimate authorities figure out who they were. In fact, teaching beginning Spanish was only a small part of what she did. Getting to know the FCorps volunteers, and finding out all she could about them, was her real job.

Her FCard had a good balance put on it each month. She could get her beloved lattes at the University book store. With coffee beans being so scarce, only faculty like her and important officials could get lattes there. She was very glad to get special treatment like that. She felt a little guilty about this, being a progressive and all, but she had to admit she'd do just about anything for that daily latte.

Carol continued to worry about her Patriot right-wing whacko brother, Grant, who was on the POI list. She was worried the authorities would hold her brother's insanity against her. So far they hadn't.

This should all be over soon, Carol thought as she sipped her daily latte at 9:15 a.m. Time for that latte and the caffeine rush that would get her through the day. The news said that the military and police were rounding up many teabaggers and stopping dozens of attacks on a daily basis. She saw teabaggers confessing on TV every night. They admitted doing horrible things, but were sorry now. One time, she thought she noticed the same teabagger confessing twice, only with a different name. There was a rumor that the confessions were fake, but that was just right-wing propaganda.

The initial shock of Crisis was over for Carol. The first few weeks were horrifying. The empty shelves, the crime, the terrorist attacks, but things were now in a "new normal" phase.

Carol felt like she was part of something new and very big. The right people were running things now and the legitimate authorities had nationalized almost everything. Progressives like her were in charge. They were getting so much done with all these new emergency powers to overthrow the capitalist power structure. She hated to admit it, but she was a little glad about the Crisis. It was a way to get some things done that couldn't be done with the knuckle dragger macho men in control of everything.

It had been such an adventurous spring and early summer, and things would be heading toward autumn in a few months. This would all be over soon. Probably by the winter break. Or, as the teabaggers called it, "Christmas."

Carol finished her latte and went to work. She was so lucky to be in Seattle.

Jeanie Thompson also felt lucky to be where she was: Camp Murray, the Washington State command center at Ft. Lewis. It was extremely secure. A thousand troops guarded her and the people she worked with, who consisted of the Governor, the command staff of the Washington National Guard, the state police, several federal agents, and miscellaneous state officials. Her boss was one of those state officials. Jeanie felt extremely secure there. She could hear the faint sound of gunfire "outside the wire" in the surrounding area. There was more and more gunfire at night, and now there was even some during the day, though it sounded far away.

While she was glad to be "inside the wire" of Camp Murray, the downside was that her career was basically over. Jeanie was a public relations genius. She had been so close to being the communications director for the next governor. Back then, she had been in all the important top secret briefings and had been spinning stories to the media. She was in heaven.

Then Jeanie was abruptly yanked off those cool duties. Her friend from the past, Grant Matson, was a POI and the police found out. Damned Facebook. They took her out of the top secret briefings and relegated her to doing stupid "happy smiley" tours for VIPs, who were very important people, like city council members from medium sized suburban towns or water district commissioners from who knows where. Or the employee of the year for the Department of General Administration. Wow. Real celebrities.

"I'm not out there," Jeanie would say to herself as she looked out past the barbed wire to the chaos and God-knows-what going on outside the wire. Even though she was no longer getting the top secret briefings, she knew that things weren't going well. The Recovery was stalling. They had dodged a bullet early on. After a few weeks of total disarray, the government finally got food rolling into the stores and contained the riots. The relative calm of most people being fed had been going on for several weeks now. It was much better than the "crisis of the hour" mode they had been in at the beginning.

Despite this, Jeanie could tell that things were not going well. There were some all-night sessions in the briefing room with lots of yelling. She still got to eat in the DFAC, the dining facility, with all the others and people in the DFAC looked pissed all the time. They were tired—so tired their brains weren't working, like they were on drugs—and they were worried. Deathly afraid. Terrified of how out of control the situation was. She even saw some of them crying as they ate. No one came over and comforted them. They just cried alone. People tried to ignore that it was happening.

Lately, people were withdrawing into themselves, no longer chatting or hanging out. It was almost like people were afraid to be seen with other people or were afraid they were being plotted against. Every few days, the police would arrest someone at Camp Murray for espionage. Apparently, the Patriots—she caught herself; the "teabaggers"—had spies right there in Camp Murray. Right there, where the Governor was! Jeanie heard that entire military units were getting arrested. They were not following orders to engage in combat. She couldn't figure out if the units were actively supporting the teabaggers or just sitting out the fight. They had hastily built a military prison at nearby Ft. Lewis. It was a giant outdoor tent city with massive rows of barbed wire and, she had heard, even landmines. But, she also heard, sometimes whole units would just be let out under some kind of deal. It was all very weird and chaotic.

Jeanie didn't want to go to one of those prisons, so she was very careful to follow all the rules. She constantly worried about the fact that one of her friends – ex friends – was a POI.

It was lunch, but Jeanie wasn't hungry. She was too worried and distracted to eat. She just sat there in the DFAC watching people. They would just silently eat some food and then shuffle off like zombies back to work. Jeanie noticed that people were eating less. The stress was doing that. She also noticed that occasionally, a person would not show up for a few days in the DFAC, and then she would later find out that they were in the base hospital suffering from some stress-related condition. Sometimes they came back, and sometimes they didn't. She was starting to wonder if the "hospital" really meant prison.

The longer she was at Camp Murray, the more she was beginning to believe that everything was a lie, and she had been one of the chief salespersons of the lies. At first, she believed everything she was telling the TV news, radio, newspapers, and internet sites. Then she started to question it a little. She'd only talk about the good news, because at that point, there was still some good news to tell. Slowly, though, the good news became more and more scarce.

A few weeks into the Crisis, she would have to make up the good news a little, then a little more until she was full-on lying about everything. "The Governor asked me to tell you how much she appreciates your work at the (fill in the blank of some stupid little government agency). Things are going well. Excellent, actually. The Recovery is taking off. We'll have things back to normal in a few months. The Crisis has been an unprecedented event for the United States, but we've always bounced back from adversity before. We're Americans." Blah, blah, blah. She could recite that crap in her sleep. Sometimes she actually did.

Jeanie knew things were going badly when they had a meeting with all the staff to go over the evacuation plan. The National Guard colonel who gave the briefing said an evacuation plan was just a formality. They didn't really expect to evacuate. But just in case.

Jeanine quickly noticed that there were definite tiers of people who would get out first, like the Governor and her immediate staff, of course. They would go by convoy to Ft. Lewis and then by helicopter to Seattle. No one told her that; she pieced it all together.

Next out would be the other officials, police, and federal agents. They would take a massive motorcade up Interstate 5 to Seattle. Then, after them, the last to go would be the expendable people, like her. No one told her that; she just knew it. They would get to ride up to Seattle in school buses and were assured they'd have an armed escort, but that was probably a lie like everything else.

Jeanie looked at her organic fajita wrap and fruit cup. One thing was going well: the food remained top notch. They had the best of everything at Camp Murray. She looked out the window in the DFAC toward the surrounding area outside the wire. "I'm so glad I'm not out there," she said out loud to herself. It was no longer weird for the exhausted and depressed people in that DFAC to mumble to themselves.

Jason, the sharp young staffer from the Governor's Office, was also glad he wasn't outside the wire. He knew much more about how bad things were. In fact, he knew more than anyone else at Camp Murray. Sometimes his assistant would hand him a note containing a coded phrase that told him he needed to get on the ultra-secure phone or internet connection at Camp Murray. From the secure phone and internet, he would get information and report back to Washington D.C. on what was really happening in Washington State. The federal government, for whom Jason secretly worked, didn't trust state officials anymore. The Feds only trusted their own people like Jason to give them the straight facts.

Jason didn't know where to start on his list of worries. He figured starting with the ways millions of people could die would work, as he sat in the DFAC eating lunch alone two tables over from Jeanie. The federal government had lost control of dozens of their nuclear weapons. Whole submarines were missing, but they couldn't launch without a code from the President – at least that was the theory, but in all the chaos of the Collapse, who really knew?. The Russians and Chinese were not reassured. They said they would launch against the U.S. if a "stray" missile came toward them. They were serious. With some of the nukes in the hands of the teabaggers, and others for sale on the black market, who knew what could happen?

No one was answering at a few of the land-based missile silos left in the U.S. arsenal. One of the Legitimate units tried to investigate a silo in North Dakota and got cut to pieces by the personnel defending it. The silo was either a teabagger unit or they decided to freelance although they couldn't launch without the codes. They did, however, have a nuclear device, and it was rumored that they could be detonated manually, without the codes. Maybe it was for sale. No one knew.

Aircrews had "lost" some of their nuclear bombs and air-launched nuclear missiles. They didn't have the codes to launch them, but they physically had the weapons and, once again, there was the rumor that they could be manually detonated if someone knew what they were doing. And some of the people who had defected to the teabaggers knew how to detonate them. That was the rumor, anyway.

The scariest nuclear rumor Jason knew of involved the teabagger national military commander, Gen. Warrilow. Jason only got bits and pieces of this from his briefings, but what little he knew was alarming. Gen. Warrilow had informed Washington, D.C. that he had several operable nuclear devices and asked if they needed a test detonation to confirm this. He asked them to pick the location. Of course, they wouldn't, so he picked a spot off the East Coast where the winds would take the radiation out to sea toward Europe. The Patriots sent the latitude and longitude in the Atlantic to the Feds and an hour later, a satellite picked up a bright ball of fire and steam.

This changed things. At first, the Feds were convinced that Warrilow would use the nukes on a northern city or somewhere in California, which was the heart of the area still loyal to the federal government. They were getting ready to surrender.

Then a Loyalist spy in Warrilow's camp distributed a communication that Warrilow was not prepared to use a nuke on American soil. The feds tested this by daring Warrilow to detonate one in the U.S. He declined, so they knew that he wouldn't use the nukes — at least not yet. It was a stalemate. A nuclear stalemate on American soil. Great. But at least it was a stalemate.

Even if a domestic nuclear war were off the table, Jason still worried about other things. Food production was not what it needed to be. They were distributing stored food now and basically living off warehoused quantities of food. They couldn't get the fuel and fertilizer to the agricultural areas fast enough to grow the next crop. And even if they did, they couldn't process it fast enough into flour, corn meal, etc. And even if they could process it, they couldn't distribute it quickly enough. Even if they could distribute it, much of it would be stolen by corrupt officials. The list of "even if" problems went on and on.

Thank God, Jason thought, that some people were growing their own food. Another relief from the supply problem was that the federal government quit delivering food to the Southern and mountain west states that "opted out" of the United States. As everyone seemed to know by now, the Feds also quit trying to get much, if any, food to the disloyal parts of the loyal states, like the rural parts of Washington State. Besides, Jason thought, the rednecks in the South and other disloyal areas were good at hunting, fishing, and gardening, right? They better be. It wouldn't take care of all their food needs, but would lessen the blow of not having federal semis rolling in. The last thing the Feds needed was massive starvation, even in the teabagger areas.

Things were better in the loyal areas, but not perfect. The people in the cities were in for a very lean winter. They were doing well now, but that would be over soon, just in time for winter.

The Feds had no plan. Well, no plan for fixing things. They had a plan for themselves: they would hunker down and defend themselves. Officials, and the people they did business with, would get enough food and would build up defenses to keep the regular people out. The regular people were on their own. Jason chuckled at the teabaggers: They didn't want the government and now they got their wishes. They would be on their own this winter. We'll see what's left of the country after that, he thought. That was the federal "plan." They would feed themselves during the winter and see what's left of the country in the spring. This wasn't going well long-term.

Jason was working on the Washington State portion of this plan. They would evacuate the key personnel to Seattle from Camp Murray, which was on the very southern end of the Seattle metro area and dangerously close to some teabagger rural areas. They would keep Camp Murray and the surrounding Ft. Lewis in the hands of the Legitimates. They had a massive military facility at Ft. Lewis that was the only place they could house various equipment and personnel; they couldn't move those assets. They also had a massive prison at Ft. Lewis and couldn't just let all those teabaggers and criminals go. Besides, the Legitimate military brass insisted on having a big base to defend. They didn't want everyone else to evacuate to Seattle – and leave them alone to fight off the Patriots. The military would try to literally hold down the fort. They insisted on having a giant "last stand" military base and that was Ft. Lewis.

As a second priority, the Legitimates would try to build up the defenses for Olympia, the state capitol and a key stronghold. But, try as they might, they all knew they probably couldn't keep Interstate 5 open all the way from Seattle down to Olympia, which would be the first city they would abandon when the teabaggers started the attack everyone was waiting for.

# Chapter 208

## *"Battle Stations!"*

### (July 27)

Up in a remote inlet of the Puget Sound, the waterway surrounding the Seattle metropolitan area, Joe Tantori's radio crackled very early in the morning. He was in bed, just waking up. Crap. Would he ever get a full night's sleep?

"Visitor coming straight at us," the voice of the dispatcher said. "Armed vessel. High rate of speed." The dispatcher was trying to be calm, but it was obvious he was nervous.

"Battle stations!" Joe yelled into his radio. He jumped out of bed, got some pants on, and told his wife to get the kids and go into the safe room. His wife was already out of the bedroom and heading for the kids' room, just like they'd practiced over and over.

A second later, a siren went off in Joe's compound. People were scrambling around, grabbing rifles and donning gear to go out onto the patrol boats. This was the first time they'd had a real "battle stations" call. They'd practiced it, but it was pretty much chaos now that it was for real.

We might die today, Joe thought. Things had been going so well that it was inevitable that something bad would happen. Joe and his guys had been guarding the new bank in town and making a mint. They got a share of the safe deposit fees and were paid in gold, silver, ammo, food, and other valuables. Morale was sky high. Joe's Marines, military contractors, and ex-law enforcement guys had just about the best jobs in the whole county.

But Joe—an Oath Keeper and Patriot—had decided to take the huge risk of being a privateer, making him a person who basically stole Loyalist and pirate goods on the water and gave a portion to the Patriots. Like in the Revolutionary War.

This obviously made the Loyalists and pirates very mad. And the amount he kept wasn't much, making it not worth the risk, if business was all he cared about.

But Joe wasn't a businessman. He was a Patriot who made an honest profit. Well, "honest" in the sense of stealing from people who stole it from others. The Loyalists and the pirates were the same in Joe's mind. One might steal from taxpayers via the law, but the other one stole it the old fashioned way.

"Military vessel!" the dispatcher said. "Heavy machine guns fore and aft!"

Oh crap, Joe thought. Probably the Loyalist Navy. Probably the first vessel in a wave of attacks. They were hitting at dawn, which made sense.

"Second vessel," said the dispatcher. "Civilian vessel with machine guns," he said calmly. The dispatcher was calming his voice down so he didn't worry the men, but his voice was the only part of him that wasn't terrified.

"Flag?" Joe yelled into the radio. The Loyalists would have the old flag on their ship. Probably.

"Cannot verify," said the dispatcher a few seconds later. "No verified flag."

By now, Joe was out of the house and in the parade grounds as they called the big common area in the middle of all the buildings. People were running around all over. The Marines seemed fairly calm. This was another drill, right? They'd done this a million times back at Indian Island Naval Magazine and the Bangor sub base where they formerly guarded huge weapon stockpiles before they went AWOL and joined Joe's company. Joe's military contractors and ex-law enforcement men seemed less calm. They hadn't done drills like this nearly as many times.

"Friendly! Friendly! Friendly!" the dispatcher yelled. He was joyous and relieved. He realized how emotional he was getting and calmed it down. "We have confirmation of friendlies," he said very calmly.

"Code blue," Joe yelled. "Do not fire, though. Do not fire unless fired upon!"

"Roger that. Code blue," the dispatcher said. "Code blue" meant a vessel or vehicle that appears to be friendly, but still should be treated as hostile by aiming weapons at it. Don't fire, though, unless fired upon.

The siren blaring through Joe's compound changed from a series of three short blasts signifying "battle stations" to two long blasts, which meant "code blue." Hearing this change, the troops were relaxing a bit, but they were still ready to destroy whatever was coming into the dock. The Marines were checking the skies for helicopters. If the Limas were coming, it would be a coordinated air/sea and possibly, a land attack.

"Flag confirmed. Gadsden. Friendly flag," the dispatcher said, now fully in control of his emotions. The vessel had the yellow "Don't Tread on Me" flag, which was a very welcomed sign.

"Code blue," Joe repeated into the radio, making sure everyone knew this was still a code blue, not a picnic. "The Limas could be flying a Gadsden. Code blue. Copy?"

"Copy," the dispatcher said.

"Copy," the voices of several squad leaders reported.

The siren remained at two long blasts. There was no letting up just because of the color of the flag.

A few tense seconds passed.

"Radio confirmation," the dispatcher said. "Confirmation of a friendly. Code used. Finally."

"Sirens to code yellow," Joe said. "Yellow" as in Gadsden yellow, the color of the Patriot flag. A few seconds later, the sirens went to four short blasts. Everyone was relaxing.

The first boat pulled into the dock. It wasn't a military vessel as the dispatcher had first reported. Joe knew, first reports—especially when people are scared—are seldom entirely accurate.

The second vessel, which was a thirty-foot civilian cabin cruiser and likely a transport, came in second. Both boats were seemingly harmless civilian-looking ones that would blend in with the other boats on the water, which would come in handy when FUSA naval forces or pirates came near. The only disadvantage to the civilian boats was that that thin fiberglass in the hull wouldn't stop a .22 bullet, let alone what was just about to fly from Joe's compound if those vessels hadn't properly identified themselves.

Joe had about ten men behind sand bags with rifles and one M240 light machine gun pointed toward the approaching vessels. He walked up to the first boat in a sign of confidence, wanting to show his guys that he was fearless. He was reasonably certain he wasn't going to die that day. Guess I'll find out, he thought.

"Lieutenant Commander Dibble sends his regards," yelled out a sailor in FUSA Navy fatigues as he approached Joe. When he got closer, Joe could see the "U.S. Navy" tag was off the fatigues and had been replaced with one saying, "Free Wash. State Guard."

He didn't look like Dibble, the Patriot naval officer who had landed there before and given Joe his "letter of marque" which was a letter from the commander of the Free Washington State Guard allowing Joe to operate as a privateer. The sailor was a younger guy, in his early thirties. When he finally came into the light and Joe could see him, the sailor was tan, suggesting he'd been out on the water a lot that summer.

So far, so good, Joe thought. He smiled and relaxed. He cinched his AR tight against his chest. He wasn't going to need it right away. Out of habit, he checked to make sure it was on safe.

"May I ask why you didn't radio ahead and let us know not to shoot you?" Joe asked. "You were a few seconds away from being blown out of the water." He was serious. He was just about to order his men to annihilate the boats. Joe wasn't pissed, but he was concerned. He didn't want an incident like this to happen again. Next time, things might go poorly. Dying was bad enough, but dying from friendly fire was even worse. Not only are people dead, but those who kill them feel guilty for the rest of their lives. Besides the human toll, friendly fire destroys morale.

"We had the wrong frequency, sir," the sailor said. "We called in one number off from what was on our cheat sheet," he said. "We realized it and called in on the right one right before..."

"We shot you full of holes," Joe said. Mistakes like this one accounted for more deaths than brave fights against the enemy. Details mattered in this business. Those details often mattered the most in the times when people were sleep deprived and scared to death, which was when people screwed up details the most.

Joe had already made his point about the radio frequency and didn't want to be a dick, so he smiled and extended his hand for a shake. "I'm Joe Tantori. And you are?"

"Petty Officer Yearwood, sir," the sailor said. "T. G. Yearwood of the Free Washington Navy." Yearwood pointed to three others on board. "This is my crew." The three tipped their helmets and nodded. No saluting on the battle field. Besides, Joe was a civilian. There was no need to salute him. Maybe, Yearwood thought, Joe had been commissioned as an officer in that letter of marque, but oh well. Not a lot of formality out here. Just getting a job done.

"I have some goodies for you, Petty Officer, but I need a little more identification," Joe said. "I would hate to give away Patriot supplies to a thief, no offense."

"None taken, sir," Yearwood said. "I can do one better than identification. You are encouraged to contact Lt. Cmdr. Dibble on the frequency you have already been given." Dibble had given Joe a piece of paper along with his letter of marque that had a special radio frequency on it and a code word. "Once you contact him," Yearwood told Joe, "I will give you a code phrase, you will give it back to him, and he will verify that I am authorized to pick up the cargo."

Joe nodded. "'Preciate it, Petty Officer." Joe keyed the radio on his tactical vest and said, "Jeff. Bring me the letter of marque."

A second later, a voice said, "Roger that."

"Go ahead and relax, gentlemen," Joe said to Yearwood. "You guys need some food, water, a potty break?"

"Yes, sir," Yearwood said. He arranged for the transport vessel to dock so they could load up and avail themselves of the facilities. Joe arranged for the kitchen to start cooking up some breakfast for the sailors.

By this time, Jeff arrived with a piece of paper and a larger radio. Joe looked at the paper and saw the frequency, which Joe entered in the larger radio and looked at the first code word. It was "John Barry," a Revolutionary War naval hero who almost no one knew of. Joe called that frequency and asked for "John Barry."

A voice, which didn't belong to Dibble, came on and said, "John Barry here. And who might this be?"

"Water buffalo," Joe said, reading the second code word. Water buffalo? Why did he get a lame code name like that?

"Right on schedule," the voice on the radio said. "Get the code word from your visitors and let me know what it is."

Yearwood said, "Cheetah."

Joe repeated "Cheetah" into the radio.

"OK, good to go, sir," the voice said. "Your visitors are authorized to make a pick-up. Thank you for your support, sir."

"Roger that," Joe said. Joe got the inventory sheet of the booty and had a detail of Marines help the sailors load it. Lots of ammunition, medical supplies, cash, some gold and silver, some jewelry, and lots of miscellaneous things of value. There had been several bottles of booze, including some high-dollar brands, but Joe kept those for his boys.

He got a signed copy of the inventory to show what he donated and made sure the sailors rotated into the kitchen and got some chow.

"Home-cooked breakfast," Yearwood said to Joe as he came back from the kitchen toward the boat. "Haven't had that in a while. It was good, sir. Really good. Thanks." There is something about a good meal that makes life so much better. Especially when you didn't expect one.

"My pleasure, man," Joe said, dispensing of military formality, since he wasn't an officer. Or, maybe he was; Yearwood kept calling him "sir," which could be because he was an officer or because Yearwood said "sir" out of habit. Joe made a mental note to look at his letter of marque later to see if he had been commissioned as an officer. Regardless of what it said, though, it didn't matter to him. He wasn't going to start acting all military. He was a Patriot just doing what he could for the cause. And getting reimbursed for it.

"You need to fuel up?" Joe asked Yearwood.

"That would be great, sir," Yearwood replied. He was just about to ask Joe for some fuel, but Joe beat him to it. Yearwood had enough to make it back to base, but with only a very tight margin for error. If they had to chase a vessel — or if they got chased — they would run out.

Joe told a Marine to have both of the vessels topped off. Both ran on diesel, which was good because Joe had a few hundred gallons of diesel in his underground tank. He started off with five hundred gallons and kept replenishing the tank with the diesel he got from the bank work. The fuel he was giving the two boats was a significant contribution, almost as valuable as the booty he was providing. Joe — ever the business man — thought about the portion of the booty he was keeping and realized the fuel he was using on patrols and giving to Yearwood was actually worth slightly more than what he was keeping from this deal. No biggie. The booty was just a way to finance the maritime patrols. If Joe was in this to make money, he would be a pirate.

Joe noticed that one of the sailors was talking to Marty, who was the gunnery sergeant in charge of the Marines. He walked over and listened. The sailor was briefing Marty on the most recent intelligence they had. Marty was with a corporal who had a nautical chart of the area, which they were marking with a pencil.

When he saw Joe, Marty said, "I'd rather be us than them. The Limas are in bad shape in Puget Sound. We pretty much own the water. Lots of little pirate craft. No way to interdict all of them. The Limas have massive protection for their big naval convoys."

Marty smiled and said, "Get this. The Limas have full anti-sub protections going."

That didn't mean a lot to Joe at first.

"They are worried about Patriot subs sinking them!" Marty said. "That means we have regular units on our side making their lives miserable. Outstanding. Outstanding!"

Joe stood there and took it all in. Patriot naval forces making contact with him at this compound to haul away letter-of-marque booty. Lima forces bogged down trying to protect against Patriot submarines. Patriots having nearly free use of the water. This was going much better than Joe had thought it would. Much better.

"How many men you got?" Joe asked Yearwood.

"Seven," Yearwood said. "Eight if you count me."

Joe opened up a bag he had. He counted out eight cigars. "After you get done fueling, enjoy these on the ride back, gentlemen. I appreciate what you're doing."

Yearwood smiled. A home-cooked breakfast and a cigar. That's when Yearwood knew they would win this war.

# Chapter 209

## *Simplified... But More Complicated*

### (July 28)

Grant was doing less and less of his "day job." He had people in place who were taking care of just about everything. He was constantly amazed at how Pierce Point had come together for mutual aid. A prime example of this was Sandy McPherson's battery bank, where people were donating their unused batteries, which had become incredibly valuable now that the stores no longer had them There were still problems—mostly greed, selfishness, and jealousy due to scarce resources—but, overall, Pierce Point was humming along. They continued to hear about how things were going in Frederickson and elsewhere. They were very lucky to be where they were.

People were getting accustomed to death. The most common source of death was the lack of medications and simple medical conditions, especially infections, which had been no big deal during peacetime. There were some suicides, too. Pastor Pete's Sunday services were growing, as were the funeral services afterwards.

But for every horrible thing that happened, there seemed to be one good thing. People were sharing. People were finding out that, after a few months of not having any peacetime luxuries, they weren't the weak and dependent sheeple they thought. They could actually take care of themselves. People were discovering themselves and their strengths.

The "new normal" everyone was talking about had definitely settled in. The guards guarded. The farmers farmed. The Grange kitchen ladies cooked for a growing number of people who contributed to the community with their labor or donations. The FCard crew made their daily runs to town and returned with enough food to make a difference. The clinic treated people. The librarian collected and checked out books—and politely reminded people when their books were overdue. The adults and kids socialized at Saturday night events. People seemed to be living their lives almost like they had for centuries all over the world, just without all the comforts—or craziness—of pre-Collapse America. It was the acoustic version of life.

On the other hand, life got much more complicated after the

Collapse. It was simplified in some ways, like no more running back and forth to soccer practice, but it was more complicated in other ways, like hiding the fact that you're the commanding officer of the 17th Irregulars. Simplified, but more complicated.

The secrets and the lying were really bothering Grant. Lying and keeping secrets was all he did anymore. He had so many secrets, cover stories, and lies going that he couldn't keep track of them. Around Pierce Point, he started a new policy with people, including his family: not saying much. The less he said, like about why so many strangers had been seen out by the Marion Farm, the lower the chances that he'd contradict himself and tip someone off that he was lying. He'd still chat with Pierce Point people and his family about mindless things, but he tried not to talk about anything important. It was killing him. He hated to be deceptive, especially with Lisa.

A few times, when he would abruptly change the subject, she would ask him what was wrong. "Nothing," he'd snap. It was unfair to her, but lives literally depended on it.

Lisa wondered if everything that Grant had on his mind, like helping to run Pierce Point and maybe even the looters he'd killed back in Olympia, was starting to get to him. She was worried that her husband was changing right before her eyes from a good man into a grouchy killer. She was afraid he was changing forever. She looked for signs that "old Grant" was back. She would seize any little shred of good news, like when he wasn't grouchy. She was worried about him and about them. She could feel their marriage slipping away.

So could Grant. He hated it when he snapped. He would try to make up for it. He would explain to her over and over again, "It's not you, honey. It's all this crap I have on my mind. It's not fair to you. Sorry." Then something would happen, like when they thought a FUSA reconnaissance helicopter was snooping around, and he'd be back to snapping. He couldn't help it. And he hated that.

Grant had mentally written off his marriage twice before. The first time was when Lisa had initially refused to come out to the cabin. The second time was when Grant had signed up with the Patriots. At that time, he figured his marriage was one of the prices he would have to pay when he had to bug out and fight this war. "Lives, fortunes, and sacred honor," he recalled from the Revolutionary War. The only question was whether he would also pay even more by going to jail, getting wounded, or dying. Or maybe all three.

Even if Grant didn't get captured, wounded, or killed, his marriage was a cost that would almost certainly be paid, especially if things continued like they were going. He went back and forth in his mind—sometimes for hours a day—about whether there was a way to get through this without damaging his marriage. Yes, there was. By quitting the Patriots and not putting his very special skills to good use.

But, try as he might, Grant could not get past the absolutely undeniable conclusion that he was there for a reason. People were counting on him. He had a job to do. A really important one. One he didn't want to do, but he had been placed there, at this time, and with these people to do. He had no choice. If his only concern was never making Lisa mad, he wouldn't have prepped and he would have stayed in Olympia. And, he would very likely be in jail or dead now. So not making her mad could not be the sole thing he had to consider.

As Grant did less and less of his Pierce Point day job, he filled up that time by doing more and more for the unit. He went out to Marion Farm as often as he could, which was at least every other day. He had Sunday dinner out there. That tradition was really taking off. Pretty soon he was going out to Marion Farm every day. Then he started staying overnight there a few times a week. He told Lisa that he had to work with the Team. She was actually glad to have "grouchy Grant" out of the house.

The Team was integrating very nicely with the rest of the unit. Just like when they rolled into Pierce Point for the first time, they were not acting like they were experts. This was even more appropriate because they were now among regular military personnel, some of whom were accomplished infantrymen. The Team, with some initial guidance from Grant, approached their role within the unit by thinking of themselves as specialists. They specialized in the SWAT stuff. They had a very specific job. They didn't try to be infantrymen. Or medics, or RED HORSE, or electricians, or communications guys, or cooks. They learned all they could from everyone else. They were always the first to set down their rifles and help unload supplies. They made sure and took their turn on KP, which was the military acronym for helping in the kitchen with washing dishes and other unglamorous tasks.

While they were integrating with the 17th, the Team still did their own thing and remained a tight group. They trained together at the Richardson House in Pierce Point. They did their day jobs out at Pierce Point, away from the 17th out at Marion Farm. They only spent about ten percent of their time at the Marion Farm with the 17th, so they were the same close-knit band of brothers the other ninety percent of the time. Training, working, and living together.

The Team Chicks were getting more and more used to the

Team being gone much of the time, especially overnight on their "training" which was at the secret place they couldn't tell the girls about. While the Team still wanted to spend every second they could with the Team Chicks, especially in the privacy of one of the cabins, they had been together for several weeks now and things had cooled down a bit with the girls. Things were still smokin' hot, just not white hot, which made it a little easier to be away.

Sure enough, people were starting to wonder what was up out at the Marion Farm. The 17th was doing a great job of remaining hidden. They took secrecy seriously. They only came in from the beach landing at night, had hidden guards around the perimeter to keep others out, limited guests to very trusted people like Grant and the Team, and kept the noise down.

But still. It was hard to have a few dozen people in on a big secret and not have them talk, which was especially true when the only form of entertainment was the rumor mill. Luckily, most people discounted the rumors they heard because most gossip had proven to be notoriously unreliable. But it became almost a sport for people to sit around and say, "You know what I heard?" and then slightly exaggerate a story that had been slightly exaggerated when they heard it. These slight exaggerations added up over a short period of time into big exaggerations until the rumor became unbelievable and most wouldn't believe it, though a few always would.

Some people in Pierce Point knew that something was going on in the area around the Marion Farm. The cover story about the "rental team" was proving a good one because people took the story and then tried to analyze it. How many fighters were on the rental team? Were they from around here? Were they ex-military or law enforcement? How much rent was Pierce Point getting? But they were confining their rumors to talking about the details of a "rental team" instead of a new topic, like whether there was a Patriot irregular unit out at the Marion Farm. A rental team was much, much less of a threat to the authorities.

One of the topics of conversation between Grant and Ted in Grant's frequent trips to the Marion Farm was exactly what the Pierce Point rumor mill was saying about the "rental team." It seemed that most people in Pierce Point thought a rental team was out there, but they realized they needed to keep it secret for the safety of the rental team—and to make sure Pierce Point got the rent. That was the beauty of the rental team cover story: people had a personal incentive to keep the secret.

Ted told Grant that the unit was now up to thirty-seven

fighters. They were mostly ex-military recruited and screened by HQ at Boston Harbor. They came out in boatloads of two or three, along with supplies. Paul was ferrying them in every night. Sometimes, a couple of runs a night. The Chief would make the runs, too.

One night, Grant was out at Marion Farm and had just met the latest boatload of fighters, which he always did when new fighters joined the group. On this specific night, the first boatload had three new fighters; two were former Army. One was an MP, or military policeman, and the other was an air defense technician. Grant and Ted were glad to have the MP; he would help the Team on their unique mission.

"Air defense, huh?" Grant said to the former technician when she came into the farmhouse kitchen, which was becoming the "office" to meet the new Commanding Officer.

"Yes, sir," the very attractive twenty-something woman said as she stood at attention in the kitchen. Better get a big stick to keep the men away from her, Grant thought. Ted had a system set up for the females to have separate quarters and facilities. There was a strict no-fraternization order. In an ideal world, the distractions between men and women would be dealt with by completely separate facilities, but this was not an ideal situation. Grant and Ted needed every fighter they could get, especially those with skills. This woman could shoot and march and build up the facilities at the farm, which was really all that Grant and Ted cared about.

"What was your unit?" Grant asked.

"The 5-5 of the 31st Air Defense Artillery Battalion at Ft. Lewis," she said. Her name tag said "Sherryton."

"You were a technician, Corporal Sherryton?" Grant asked. He had her file in his hands. Her first name was Anne and she held the rank of a Specialist 4 in the FUSA Army, but was made a corporal in the 17th Irregulars.

"Yes, sir," she answered. "I kept the computers running." What she didn't say, because it wasn't the most best point to make, is that she joined the Army to pay for college, which was very common before the Collapse. The military was another way for people to qualify for entitlements. This was not universally true, but was often the case, especially among the support personnel such as the technicians who kept the high-tech military running.

"Why are you here, Corporal?" Grant asked in an inquisitive, not demeaning, tone. He knew that she had passed the screening at HQ, but was interested in each of his soldiers.

"This can't go on any longer, sir," Sherryton answered. "I want my country back. It's that simple, sir."

She paused. Should she tell him and all the people in that kitchen the truth? Tell them the awful things that had happened? Oh, what the hell. He asked a question and she had an answer. She looked at Grant and felt like she could trust him. Besides, she had nothing to lose. Everything had been taken from her. This guerilla unit out in the sticks was her home now, and probably her final home. It was the last stop on a train ride through misery like she never thought she'd see. This was it –the end of the line. Might as well get it all out now. It would feel good to tell people why she was doing this, and to get it off her chest, which was easier said than done. Telling the story would probably make her cry, and that was not a good thing for a soldier to do, especially in front of other soldiers, and definitely when first meeting the new commanding officer. Not to mention that crying was ten times worse because she was a female soldier and being emotional could be used against her to say she wasn't "combat ready."

She was trying not to get emotional. She quickly got the quiver in her lip under control, which she had been doing a lot of lately. Turn the crying into anger, she told herself. She listened to herself and took a few seconds before she turned the crying into anger. Then more anger. Then more. Now she was ready to tell the world why she was out there.

"The gangs, sir," she said at attention, tough as nails. "They got my family back in Chicago while I was training in Oklahoma; my mother, my father and...my poor little sister. That's all I'll say."

Sherryton straightened up even more than when she was at attention, looked Grant straight in the eye, and said, "Payback, sir." She squinted her eyes, her voice got icy and scary, and she repeated, "Payback." The room was silent and the tone of her voice was frightening. She wanted to kill people. A lovely and charming young lady wanted to kill people.

Perfect, unfortunately. That was exactly what Grant was looking for. A motivated fighter with nothing to lose. She'd already lost everything back in Chicago. Forget that there was no air defense computer system for her to fix. She had what it took out here.

"Welcome to the 17th Irregulars, Corporal Sherryton," Grant said as he extended his hand for a handshake and smiled.

Then Grant turned his smile into a fearless stare, looked her right in the eye, gritted his teeth, and said, "We'll give you a chance for payback." He quickly turned back into a compassionate person. He felt horrible for this innocent young lady. "My condolences about your family."

She nodded and mouthed "Thank you," and looked down at the floor.

Grant sensed the guilt she felt. So many people had been away from home when terrible things happened to their families.

He said, "You couldn't have stopped them. But," Grant pointed all around the kitchen to all the people there, "We can. And will. I can't wait until we unleash on them." Sherryton halfway smiled. It was the closest thing to a smile she could muster.

Grant got his composure back and said to her, "Report to Sgt. Sappenfield here and he'll get you squared away with your quarters."

Grant paused and wondered if he should say the next thing that came to his mind. Oh, what the hell. She had opened up with him. He took her hand in a handshake and looked her right in the eye.

"Welcome, Anne." Grant wanted to add that personal touch, even though it wasn't military protocol, so she would feel like this was her new home. He needed one hundred percent out of every fighter. Connecting with each one of them on a personal level—a level much deeper than just military protocol—was essential. Who gave a crap about military protocol? Grant wasn't even a "real" officer, anyway.

It was past midnight and Grant wanted to get home for a little sleep. "What you got for me, Sergeant?" Grant asked Ted, requesting his briefing on what was going on when Grant was off in Pierce Point doing his day job. The two men left the crowded kitchen and walked into the downstairs bedroom of the farmhouse, which was where they could talk behind a closed door.

When they got into the bedroom and closed the door, Ted said, "Things are going pretty well." He went over the new arrivals. There were some skilled people, but mostly ones like Anne people who had the general soldiering skills necessary and were physically fit, emotionally sound, and could shoot a rifle, but, more importantly, who wanted to take their country back. The civilians had no military training, of course, but had reasons to be there. They were people who had been in the crosshairs of the government. One was even a POI, like Grant.

"We're at about one-third strength now," Ted said. "We have some more work to do to get this farm ready to house about one hundred personnel. But we're slowly building it up as the new arrivals come. We put them to work on the facilities. We're getting them slowly integrated. That's the advantage of getting them a few at a time. We

273

can see what skills they have, if they are leaders, that kind of thing."

"How we doin' on supplies?" Grant asked. That was always at the forefront of his mind.

"Decent. So far," Ted said. "Food is largely taken care of. We have basic FCard foods like pancake mix, cornbread mix, and oatmeal. We're getting a garden going, some chickens for eggs, and Paul and the Chief are getting us fresh fish most nights. Oh, and Anderson shot a deer last night. He was pretty proud of his city-boy self becoming a hunter."

"We only have a minimal amount of medical supplies," Ted continued. "HQ is getting us more. Soon, or so they say." Ted thought they would come, but he had spent his whole life being told that supplies were just about to arrive. This was different, however. Unlike his FUSA Army days when there were unlimited supplies and it was just a bureaucratic battle to get them, now supplies were actually scarce.

"Weapons?" Grant asked.

"Got a decent supply," Ted said, with a smile. "We basically have the inventory of the gun store." Ted and Chip had split the inventory up when they evacuated Chip's gun store after the Olympia riots started. Ted took about half and got them to HQ in Boston Harbor, where they were earmarked for the 17th and distributed in dribs and drabs. Chip had the other half and they were in Grant's basement. Or, had been. Chip had moved them out about a week ago over the span of two nights.

"How many is that?" Grant asked.

"I have seventy-one ARs. Almost all with iron sights, but a few with optics, mostly red-dot sights. About 250 magazines. About 15,000 rounds of 5.56. About a dozen AKs, decent supply of mags and ammo. A handful of tactical shotguns and butt loads of 12 gauge ammo, mostly bird shot. Assorted side arms. Different calibers and magazines, but lots of 9mm Glocks and Berettas. Some Sigs and XDs. Some in .40, and some 1911s."

"Any heavy stuff?" Grant asked.

"Two M240s machine guns," Ted said. "One is at the beach landing entrance you saw. The other one is being unpacked and cleaned up right now. We have a little ammo for the 240s, but I'd like more."

"Explosives?" Grant asked.

"Not much," Ted said. "We have a handful of grenades, but that's it. Some training grenades, which will be more important now than live ones. I'm harping on Boston Harbor for more grenades and some grenade launchers, but they're a bit overwhelmed now."

"I bet we'll get more of the good stuff as regular units come over to our side," Grant said, half predicting it and half just being hopeful.

"Probably. I never count on that, though," Ted said.

"Comms," Grant said. "Can't forget comms." He was trying to be the wise commanding officer, even if he wasn't.

"We have a decent assortment of handheld radios and a couple secure ones for talking to Boston Harbor," Ted said. "Jim Q. is all over that. Man, that code talker shit is awesome."

"So he's workin' out?" Grant asked.

"Yep. Very well," Ted said. "He stays in the background, but is social. He lets everyone know he's not a Muslim, which is prudent, unfortunately. He talks to them about modern American culture: movies, music, sports. He speaks perfect English; no different than you or me. The troops can tell real quickly that he's been living in America his whole life. And he's mastered the comms plan. He knows it all, except how to fix radios, but that's really not to be expected from a civilian."

"What's next out here?" Grant asked, wanting to wrap it up. It was late and he was tired.

"We keep getting more personnel and supplies in a couple boatloads at a time just like we're doing," Ted said. "Then it's training time."

"When do you want the Team here full time? Grant asked.

"Not until we've got the cadre," Ted said, referring to the term for the troops in a Special Forces guerilla unit, "basically trained. Then we'll fold in the Team. We'll have them get integrated with the cadre. Then we'll practice moving and communicating as a whole unit."

Ted looked at Grant and said, "Then it's go time. Probably in a couple of months." Grant could tell that Ted knew something that Grant didn't. He could also tell that when the time was right, Ted would tell him. It would be uncool now to ask for the details. Grant knew that in a real military unit, with a real commander, he would be in on all the details. But this was different. Grant was away from the unit most of the time and could be captured in Pierce Point if the Limas got in there or had a sympathizer. Grant was actually glad he didn't know the specific details.

Grant nodded to Ted. A couple of months? Wow. This was

serious and only kept getting more serious. First, the riots. Then the bug out, the hangings, joining up with the Patriots, Snelling getting whacked, building up the troops at the farm, and now "go time" in a couple of months.

It all just naturally progressed. At any given time, it would have seemed that combat was unlikely. But one event slowly and naturally flowed into the next, and then the next. It was going to happen. What would have seemed like a crazy concept only a year ago was now becoming a reality.

Combat in a couple of months? Grant was glad to get it over with. He wanted to either die or win. One way or another, he just wanted to get this thing over with. He was scared and excited at the same time.

Ted could tell that Grant—a civilian who had never been in combat—was scared and excited. The new guys always were. New officers were especially scared and excited because they wanted to see if they had what it took. New officers wanted to see if their units had been trained and led well enough to make it through those few minutes of hell that were coming.

"We'll be fine, Grant," Ted said in a soft and reassuring voice. "We're not going out until we're ready. I have that assurance from HQ. I insisted on it. Besides, Hammond knows this. He's an SF guy. He's been in indigenous units that weren't ready. He knows that it's my call when we're ready." Grant wasn't offended at all that it wasn't his call; he was relieved. Ted was the professional here.

Grant relaxed. All the "coincidences" started flashing through his mind that put him in this place at this time. Then he thought about the message from the outside thought on the starlight boat ride to Boston Harbor that everything would be fine. Grant looked at Ted and put his hand on his shoulder.

"I have every confidence in you, HQ, and these guys out here," Grant said with a smile. Grant was truly happy. He knew things would work out. He just knew it. And it made him joyous.

"And, I gotta admit, I have confidence in me," Grant said to Ted. "Between you and me, Ted," Grant said with a big smile, "we'll do this job right."

Ted smiled, too. He was glad his untrained civilian lieutenant had some self-confidence—and the good sense to trust a twenty-five-year Special Forces veteran like him. It was the perfect combination of what was needed in an untested lieutenant.

Ted put his hand on Grant's shoulder, too. "Yes, sir, we'll do this job right," he said. Then he grinned and added, "Hell yes, Grant. Hell yes."

# Chapter 210

## *Handing Away the Keys*

### (August 1)

"Dad, what's going on at the Marion Farm?" Manda asked Grant one morning. The two of them were having a late breakfast in their cabin after everyone else had left.

"What are you talking about?" Grant asked, not very convincingly. He couldn't lie to his kids. Well, not easily. He'd been lying to his whole family for weeks about what was going on out at the farm.

Manda put her fork down and looked straight at Grant. "C'mon, Dad," Manda said. "You know what's going on out there. The 'rental team.' You're training a second team and going to rent it out to another town." She rolled her eyes like Grant was stupid.

Wow. The rumor had taken off pretty well. Good.

"Oh, OK," Grant said, acting like he was letting her in on a big secret. "Maybe there is a rental team. But you cannot—I mean strictly *cannot*—tell anyone about it, or that I just confirmed it. Understand? People's lives are at stake. This is serious, Amanda." He used Manda's full name for effect.

She smiled. She loved being on the inside of things. "Does the rental team need people?" she asked.

Grant put his hand up and raised his voice so loud he was almost yelling. "No way! Absolutely not. You are *not* joining the rental team. Don't even think about it." That was the most absurd thing he'd heard in quite some time, especially from a smart girl like her with good judgment.

At first, Manda was startled by her dad's loud reaction. Then she realized he was talking about her. She laughed and said, "Not me, Daddy. Jordan."

That was Manda's boyfriend. They were getting pretty serious, although Grant consciously tried not to know all the details. He was afraid he'd shoot the young man. And out at Pierce Point…Grant could actually get away with it.

"He will turn seventeen next week," Manda said. "He is just doing dumb stuff now at the Grange." Grant knew that Jordan was waiting for a spot on the gate guard. They had enough people and, at seventeen, they had more experienced people. Judgment was a critical factor for a gate guard; shooting too early could start a war. So Jordan was in a holding pattern to be a gate guard. He was working hard at the Grange by performing miscellaneous labor.

"He's a hunter and knows all about guns," Manda said. "He wants to do something cooler than the Grange work. He wants to be on the rental team." Jordan and Manda had talked for a week about how Manda would ask her dad to get Jordan a slot on the rental team.

Manda looked at Grant with her "please, Daddy" eyes, which had always worked on him. Not this time.

"Let me get this straight," Grant said, which was a clear signal to Manda that the answer would be no. Anytime Grant wanted to demolish someone's argument, he started with "let me get this straight," reframed what they were saying, and then blew it away. "You want your boyfriend to join a very dangerous and sorta mercenary team of outlaw fighters to shoot it out with gangs and professional military and police?"

It sounded like a bad idea when it was put that way, but Manda nodded anyway. Jordan wanted on the rental team and Manda said she'd help him get on. She wasn't afraid of Jordan getting hurt because she assumed her dad would have a fabulous team so they'd win every fight. She was sixteen and that seemed rational to her.

"Why?" Grant sarcastically asked. "So you can get him killed and hook up with your other boyfriend on the side?" He was kidding, but it was the only explanation that made any sense.

Manda rolled her eyes. "No, of course not. He wants to be a soldier and I want him to do what he wants to do." Manda was clearly the opposite of her mother when it came to encouraging men to do dangerous things.

It was pretty obvious that Manda was using her dad to get her boyfriend a cool job. It was a common occurrence in cultures around the world since time began. Pierce Point was no exception.

"Hell no," Grant said. "The rental team is very, very dangerous work. I'm sure Jordan is well qualified," which was a polite white lie Grant was telling, "but I'm not putting a teenager in danger, especially one my daughter cares a lot about."

Manda started getting mad and frustrated. Her dad didn't understand what a great idea this was. Jordan would be on the rental team and would then be considered an adult and then they could get married. It was perfect. It made sense to them in their teenage minds.

Perfect sense.

Grant realized that he had to be gentle. He didn't want to alienate her and have her run off with this Jordan kid. That's the last thing anyone needed.

"You have the kernel of a good idea here, dear," Grant said as if he was deeply thinking about the proposal. "Jordan is nearly seventeen and if you say he has good firearm skills, then I believe you. You know what you're talking about, because you have firearm skills." Grant thought he'd lighten up the discussion. "Show me your G 27, honey."

Manda pulled the compact Glock out of the cargo pocket of her shorts. She did a press check to show that a round was in the chamber. She kept the gun in a safe direction and her finger off the trigger the whole time. She looked like a pro.

"See," Grant said, "you know guns and so you know if Jordan has skills." This was all Grant could think of that was positive and complimentary while he was struggling to think of something more substantive to say.

"And Jordan seems like a great young man," Grant said. He didn't really know Jordan too well. He'd met him several times. Jordan always looked Grant in the eye, shook his hand, and called him "sir." These were all great signs. Grant had been meaning to sit down and get to know the kid, but he always had work to do. Now that Manda and Jordan were getting serious, Grant would have to make time to get to know his...future son-in-law? At sixteen? Oh, no.

Before the Collapse, Grant had always thought of Manda getting married at about thirty, after getting her post-graduate degree and starting her important career, whatever that might be. Now things were back like they were fifty or one hundred years ago with people thinking of getting married younger and not waiting to start careers...because there were no more "careers."

When Manda heard Grant say that Jordan "seemed like a great young man," she perked up and smiled. That was the approval she'd been waiting for.

Grant could tell how important that approval was. This was a good sign. It meant she valued his opinion about Jordan. Now Grant had to use this advantage to make sure nothing bad happened to his little girl.

"You know," Grant said, "I think I could get Jordan a cooler job. A gate guard." He could ask Dan to create a "junior varsity" spot for Jordan on the gate guard. "That involves guns. He could prove himself at the gate and then try out for the rental team after a while."

After all this was over and there was no more danger, Grant thought to himself.

Manda thought about it. It wasn't what she and Jordan had been talking about. But it made a lot of sense. Her dad was understanding that Jordan was a man and could do a job involving guns. Being a gate guard—Jordan would probably be the youngest one—meant that he would have a real job out there. It probably wouldn't be the job that allowed them to get married, but it would be a real job.

All of a sudden, Manda realized how crazy the whole rental team and quickly getting married thing was. She had gotten caught up in it. A gate guard job would be OK.

"That makes sense, Daddy," Manda said. "I'll talk to Jordan and see what he thinks." She knew he'd be disappointed, but would eventually see the wisdom of it.

"I have a better idea," Grant said, realizing the opportunity he had. "You and I will talk to Jordan about it. Maybe the three of us can go shooting. Then I can give him a tour of the gate and introduce him to Dan. Maybe Jordan would like to watch the Team train today?" Grant was using his power to hook this Jordan kid into Grant's world. He wanted Jordan to see that cool things happen via Grant, not around his back. Besides, this was the perfect setting for getting to know the young man.

Manda jumped up and yelled, "Yes! Today?"

"Today," Grant said. "I've been meaning to spend more time with you and Cole. Today is Manda's day. And Jordan's."

Manda was brimming with pride. Her dad was listening to her. And he wanted to involve Jordan in some of the cool things he did. Jordan would be thrilled. She was so relieved her dad seemed to approve of Jordan.

Cole had heard the conversation from upstairs in the loft. He could basically understand what they were talking about. He knew that dad and his sister were going to spend the day with Jordan. He was sad that his sister wouldn't be with him that day. That was the routine. He came down the stairs.

"Sister, you won't be playing with me today?" he asked.

Manda felt guilty. She loved taking care of all her kids, as she called them, but she so wanted to have this day with her dad and Jordan.

"Sorry, little brother," Manda said to Cole, "Sister and Dad have some things to do today. Marissa will be playing with you guys today." Marissa was a fifteen year-old who hung out with the kids. She was the second in charge of the kids, taking her lead from Manda. The kids called Manda and Marissa "M&M." They thought that was the funniest thing.

"Only one 'M'?" Cole said with a smile.

Whoa! Cole just made a joke. A play on words. That was supposed to be impossible for autistic kids.

"Yes!" Manda said, clapping at the joke Cole had just made. "Just Marissa for today, but Sister will be back at dinner time to help you and Grandma make dinner."

Grant, too, was thrilled about the joke. This was a big improvement for him. He had been doing so well out here. Grant realized that the long school days and crazy pre-Collapse schedules were hard on Cole. But out here, he just played with younger kids and could relate to them because they could speak at his level.

Cole was smiling because he made a joke. He was proud of himself. He knew he had a hard time talking or understanding people talk, but he knew he wasn't dumb. It was just the talking part that was so hard.

"OK, Sissy, just Marissa today. One 'M.'" He was saying the joke again to get more attention. It worked the first time.

Manda and Grant clapped again and laughed.

Grant realized he needed to know a little more about Jordan Sparks and his family. He hated to use his power for his own purposes, but, hey, this was his daughter. "I need to run to the Grange real quick, but I'll be back in a half hour." Grant already had his pistol belt on; he always had that. He put on his kit and got his AR; the things he never traveled without. He was still a member of the Team and never knew when he'd be called out to go to a gun fight.

"OK," Manda said, "See you then."

Grant made a quick pit stop in the bathroom. He looked at himself in the mirror. The beard. His beard was getting full now. He just stared. He looked so different. He'd lost a few pounds and was tan. He looked like a military contractor with that beard and full kit—but he was standing in the bathroom of his cabin. Contractors were only in Afghanistan, not Pierce Point. Grant stared at the military contractor in the mirror of his cabin. It was so unbelievable and totally believable at the same time.

He snapped out of it and left the cabin. He grabbed one of the mopeds—donated, he remembered, by the Sparks family—and zoomed to the Grange. He knew that since Drew wasn't at the cabin he was up at the Grange. He needed to talk to Drew.

When he got there, Grant dispensed with the chatting he usually did. He was in a hurry. He went over to Drew and pulled him aside. "Sparks family. What do you know about them?"

Drew got out his map, verified the address, and then went to his index cards. "Good donors. Those mopeds we use all the time. A bunch of other stuff. Their oldest son, Jeremy, is a guard. Their younger son, Jordan, works here at the Grange. The dad is an ex-construction contractor. He helps with fix-it projects for people around here and gets paid in barter. He seems like a good guy. The mom is a former teacher. She is working for the school that they're hoping to start up."

"Politics?" Grant whispered. He was checking the political purity of his daughter's boyfriend's family. Not because he was close-minded, but because, in post-Collapse America, politics could get you killed.

"I have them down as 'U/LP,'" Drew said. That meant Undecided but Leaning Patriot.

Grant smiled. U/LP was good enough.

Drew asked, "Is this because Manda is dating Jordan?"

"Yep," Grant said. Manda was Drew's granddaughter so he was part of this. "I'm meeting Jordan today, going to spend some time with him, and meeting his parents. I just want to make sure this is a family I can be OK about."

"Anything going on with Manda and Jordan I need to know about?" Drew said. "I mean, I lost a daughter to a wild-eyed hillbilly," Drew said with a smile. "I know how awful it can be for a girl to fall for a young man from a bad family."

Grant smiled and thanked Drew. He jumped back onto the moped and headed home. It was another magnificent summer day. The weather had been unusually spectacular this year.

When Grant rolled onto Over Road, John was pulling guard duty at the guard shack with his lever action 30-30. He hadn't been there when Grant left, but he was there now. Day guard duty had become pretty slack lately. There just weren't the threats there were before, when Pierce Point wasn't as unified and secure. Besides, Gideon was sleeping in the night cabin. If anything major happened and woke him up, he would be there to help. So now John, Mary Anne, and Mark did daytime guard duty when they wanted a break from whatever else they were doing. There were periods during the day when no one was on guard. Grant wished that wasn't the case, but he couldn't justify pulling a guard from elsewhere just to guard his road.

In the past, the major reason, besides his family, to guard his road was all the ARs in the basement. Now those were at the Marion Farm so that reason for a full-time guard had gone away.

John waved at Grant as he rode past. Manda was waiting for him.

"I texted Jordan and he's ready to go," she excitedly said once Grant got to the cabin.

"His parents are home, too, if you want to meet them," Manda said with a huge smile indicating how she wanted Grant to meet them.

"Great," Grant said as he wondered how they would get there. Mark was gone; probably out hunting, fishing, or digging clams. How to get there and then to the Dayton place to go shooting?

My car, Grant thought. He hadn't driven it since he came out to the cabin. His car—the "Tacura" as he jokingly called his "tactical Acura"—was parked up the hill in Mark's empty lot by his house overlooking Grant's cabin where they parked all the extra vehicles. He had been meaning to periodically turn over the engine to keep it in good condition. That way, he could drive it again when the gas supplies came back, assuming they ever would.

Grant got the key to the basement and told Manda to stay in the cabin while he went in there. He had become so accustomed to secretly entering the basement alone without any witnesses.

When Grant opened the door to the unfinished basement and turned on the light, he realized that all of Chip's goodies were gone. They were safe and accounted for at Marion Farm. Chip was the only one besides Grant who knew where the basement key was hidden.

Now, just Grant's stuff was in there. He went to the old glass-door gun display case Ed Oleo had given him when Ed's dad passed away. The gun display case was where Grant kept his "butter knife" guns. That was a term Grant got from the novel *Patriots*. It described miscellaneous guns—usually old hunting guns—distributed to use on enemy forces. They were second-tier guns about as lethal as a "butter knife" compared to military weapons. The people with the butter knife guns would use them on the enemy and then take the enemy's good guns. The shooter would pass the butter knife gun on to the next person to repeat the process.

Grant's "butter knife" guns in the glass-door display case were basically guns that he could live without if they got stolen. He had a .17HMR, which he called his "crow gun," an inexpensive, but very accurate Savage 110 in .223, and a Remington 1153 in 20 gauge that Ed gave Grant when Ed's dad died.

The display case also had Grant's prized Ruger 10/22 in .22LR. It was the first gun he ever bought, back in the day at a gun show for $100. He had a Hogue rubber stock on it and a BSA rimfire scope. He could hit anything with that gun. It was very accurate, and pure fun. And cheap to shoot because .22LR was much more plentiful than larger calibers.

He got the 10/22 out of the case. Looking at it took him back to the "good old days" when guns were just for fun, not something his life depended on. He got the sense that things just might be back to normal someday. Maybe he could just shoot that 10/22 for fun again. Someday.

Grant went and got a brick of 500 rounds of .22 ammo from his two plastic tubs of .22 he had amassed before the Collapse. He still had about fifty bricks of .22. That was good; .22 ammo was like money now, traded like currency. A gallon of gas cost about a hundred rounds of .22.

.22 ammo had numerous uses. Because it was worth less than other ammunition, it could be used as "change" in barter. It was great for hunting small game, like squirrels, because it didn't damage the meat. Another crucial use for .22 was training. Instead of shooting expensive combat ammo like 5.56, new recruits could train with .22. Grant had an AR in .22, a fantastic Smith and Wesson M&P 15-22 that operated exactly like an AR, but it used inexpensive .22. Before the Collapse, Grant would shoot a thousand rounds a month of .22 in his M&P 15-22. Those skills transferred perfectly over to his AR-15 in 5.56. Grant had given his M&P 15-22 to Ted for realistic, yet cheap, training for the unit.

But today, shooting .22 was purely for fun. Plinking. Socializing. And that was a very good use of a few hundred rounds. Grant locked the gun case back up, took the 10/22 and the brick of .22, turned off the light, and locked the basement back up.

He walked up to the deck where Manda was standing. "Let's go," Grant said, handing her the 10/22 and the brick of ammo.

As they came up to John, Grant said, "She and I are going out shooting today with Jordan. Just for fun."

"You're not going to have an 'accident' out there and just leave his body in the woods, are you?" John asked with a smile. "Maybe he has misbehaved with Manda."

Manda smiled, but she was getting tired of all these jokes about people killing her boyfriend. All the guys, especially the old ones, seemed to think it was so funny. And the fact that her dad had actually killed people made it even less funny.

Manda started walking. It was about a half mile to Jordan's house. She knew the path well.

As they walked down Over Road toward Jordan's, Grant suddenly veered off the road and up the hill to Mark's.

"Where are we going?" Manda asked.

"You'll see," Grant said. "We're making today special."

They walked up to Mark's empty lot with all the parked cars. Grant got out the Acura keys and said, "We're taking the 'Tacura' just like old times."

Manda smiled. Riding in that car would take her back in time to just a few months ago, before everything was so crazy.

Grant unlocked the door to the Acura, just like he'd done a million times before. The sound of the door unlocking, the feel of the key. It took him back. He needed this. He needed some normalcy. He'd been valiantly fighting normalcy bias for so long and realized he needed a little "normal" himself. Feeling the 10/22, going shooting for fun with Manda, driving the Tacura. He and Manda had smiles on their faces. It felt like the good old days.

Grant opened the door to the Acura and put the 10/22 in the back seat, out of habit. He got in the driver's seat which felt exactly like it did months ago when he came out to the cabin on that horrible night when he left Olympia.

The smell. The car smelled just like it used to. He was back in time. He just breathed in that smell. Manda was doing the same.

Grant put the key in the ignition and looked to see how much gas was in the tank; about a half tank. He turned the key and the Tacura started right up. Grant remembered that he needed to put some Stabil in the tank to prevent gasoline from breaking down over time. Any gas that wouldn't be used for a few months needed to have Stabil added to it.

As the car started, the radio came on and it was playing music from the last radio station he had been listening to. The United States of America had collapsed, but there was still a classic rock station. Some things never change.

He turned off the radio and let the car idle a minute. He and Manda just sat in the car enjoying it, not saying a word, just listening to the sounds of the car and smelling its smells.

Grant put it in gear and slowly took off. It was weird to be driving the Tacura again. He almost felt like they could drive that car back to Olympia and everything would be normal again.

They drove the short distance to Jordan's house and got out. Jordan's parents were standing outside, happy to meet Grant and Manda. Jordan's parents also recognized the "meet the potential future in-laws" nature of this visit.

Grant liked Jordan's parents. Salt of the earth. Hardworking. Nice. They chatted for about ten minutes. Grant got to know them and vice versa. Grant was convinced the Sparks were "good people."

Jordan and Manda were standing next to each other and couldn't wait to be away from their parents. Finally the adults were done talking. It was time to go shooting. Manda moved the 10/22 from the back seat so she and Jordan could sit close together. Grant remembered those days when sitting together was a big deal.

They drove out to the Dayton place where people went shooting. Almost no one did this anymore because ammunition was quite literally money. Once in a while, people sighted in their rifles there, but usually with only a handful of shots.

They spent the next hour shooting and talking. It was very casual. Jordan was as casual as a boy can be when he's with his girlfriend's dad—and her dad is a killer, has a gun, is a judge, can kill people and get away with it, and everyone is in a secluded wooded area.

Grant watched how Jordan handled the rifle. Very professionally. He always kept the muzzle in a safe direction. He kept his finger off the trigger until he was on target. He put the safety on in between shooting sessions. Jordan brought his own hearing protection, too. He stood up straight and called Grant "sir." Jordan loaded Manda's magazines for her. A nice touch. Except that Grant used to load her magazines. Oh well. It had to happen sometime.

After a while, Grant asked Jordan, "So what are you doing at the Grange?" Jordan told him that he was doing miscellaneous jobs like moving heavy things, and cutting firewood.

"You want to try out for the gate guards?" Grant asked, knowing the answer.

"Yes, sir!" Jordan said. "Absolutely."

"OK," Grant said, "I think I can arrange that." Jordan and Manda were beaming.

In that moment, Grant had an overwhelming sense that he had some things to tidy up before he went off to war. He felt like he had to make some arrangements now in case he didn't come back. He knew what he needed to get in order before he left.

"There's talk, Jordan, about a 'rental team,'" Grant said. "You

287

heard about that?"

"Yes, sir," Jordan said. Good to see that he was honest. Grant halfway expected him to play dumb.

"The rental team is not for you, Jordan," Grant said. He looked Jordan right in the eye and said, "Trust me. The rental team is not something you want to do."

Jordan stared at Grant, not knowing what to say.

Grant continued, "Promise me, Jordan—and promise Manda, too, right here and now, that you will stay on the gate guards and not join anything else."

Jordan was bewildered, but would have agreed to anything Grant said that day. "Yes, sir," Jordan said.

"Promise us," Grant said politely. "Please promise us."

"Sure," Jordan said. He looked Grant right in the eye and said, "I promise, Mr. Matson."

Grant breathed a sigh of relief and smiled. Grant had now done what he could to make sure Manda had Jordan around in case Grant didn't come back.

Jordan and Manda couldn't figure out why this promise meant so much to Grant, but they trusted that he knew something they didn't.

"In a few months," Grant said to Jordan as he put his hand on Jordan's shoulder, "you'll thank me for this. So will Manda." And, Grant didn't say, Manda's mom will, too.

Jordan nodded. Grant could tell that all this seriousness was creeping out Jordan and Manda. It was time to have fun again, Grant thought.

"How fast can you put ten rounds into that tin can?" Grant asked Jordan as he handed him the 10/22.

In a few seconds they had the answer; pretty damned fast.

"Nice shootin'," Grant said to Jordan. This was high praise, and Jordan knew it.

They went back to the Sparks' house and Grant made sure to tell Jordan's dad what a good job Jordan did. Grant pulled Jordan's parents aside and asked them if it would be OK if Jordan became a gate guard. They were fine with it. They were happy, in fact, to have the youngest gate guard come from their family. They were impressed with how Dan ran the guards and looked after them.

"Hey, Manda, you remember how to drive, right?" Grant asked.

"Yeah," Manda said. "Kinda." She had taken driver's education class and had her learner's permit just when the Collapse hit.

"I can drive, sir," Jordan said. He'd had his license for a while before the Collapse.

Grant realized what an opportunity he had. "OK, Jordan, could you drive me to the gate and then drive Manda home?" Trusting Jordan with his daughter and his car. That was a bonding experience.

"You bet," Jordan said. He felt like a man today. Grant handed Jordan the keys. Grant could feel the symbolism in that.

# Chapter 211

## *Immigrations Report*

### (August 1)

Jordan drove Grant and Manda to the gate. To give Jordan the full measure of respect, Grant volunteered to ride in the backseat and let Manda sit up front with Jordan where they felt like grownups.

Jordan wasn't a perfect driver, but he did OK. It was the first time he'd driven in months. The guards didn't recognize the Tacura and a few of them slowly shouldered their weapons, but didn't aim at the car, as they drove up. Jordan felt like a million dollars driving a car, with his girlfriend at his side and Judge Matson sitting in the back seat.

Jordan slowly brought the car to a halt and then put his hands out the window to show the guards that he was unarmed. That was a good idea so Manda did the same. Grant was impressed that Jordan thought of this. That showed some judgment.

"I'll take care of this," Grant said as he got out of the car. All the guards recognized him and lowered their weapons.

"How's it goin', gentlemen?" Grant asked them. "Hey, is Dan around?"

Someone ran to get Dan. While they were waiting, Jordan and Manda got out of the car. Jordan knew a few of the guards and was talking with them. They knew his older brother, Jeremy, who was a guard, but working the night shift. Jordan was introducing them to Manda.

Dan came up and said, "Hey, Grant, nice to see you. What's going on?"

Grant pulled Dan over by the car so no one else could hear.

"Dan, I need to ask you a favor," he said in a hushed tone.

"Sure," Dan said. "What can I do for you?"

"My daughter's serious boyfriend," Grant said pointing toward them, "Jordan Sparks—Jeremy Sparks' younger brother—said he wants to join the 'rental team.'"

Dan rolled his eyes. Young men and their dreams of military glory, he thought. He'd seen it too many times.

"Well," Grant continued, "I'm not too keen on that, so I needed to make him a deal to make sure they didn't elope or some other crazy shit."

Dan nodded. His kids were grown up but he remembered worrying about crazy eloping, too.

"So I told him I would ask you to give him a try out for the gate guards," Grant said.

"How old is he?" Dan asked.

"Seventeen in a couple of days," Grant answered.

Dan slowly nodded. "Does he know guns?"

"Yep," Grant said. "I went out shooting with him today; .22s. He did fine. He's been hunting since he was little."

"Judgment?" Dan asked. "Does he seem mature?" The last thing they needed was another Ethan out there.

"Yep," Grant said. "I trust him with my daughter."

"That tells me everything I need to know," Dan said. He furrowed his brow and said, "You know, he's a little younger than I'd like so I'm giving him preferential treatment by letting him try out."

"Understood and appreciated," Grant said. "You can create a junior varsity for him if you want. Your call."

"OK," Dan said. "Young Mister Sparks gets a try out. No guarantees, though, that he makes the guard, even if it's the JV squad."

"Also understood," Grant said. "Thanks, man," he said as he shook Dan's hand.

"No problem," Dan said. They walked back over to where everyone else was. Dan was talking to Jordan and making arrangements with him for a try out. Jordan and Manda were thrilled.

Grant saw Al and went over to him, as he had been meaning to talk to him for some time. He wanted to see if any walk-ons were coming by, which he should have done earlier, but he was so tied up with things at Marion Farm.

"Hey, Al, how's it going'?" Grant asked. They shook hands.

"Pretty good," Al said. "What brings you here?"

"Needed to talk to Dan about a try out for a young man," Grant said. "So, how are things going with immigrations?"

"Good," Al said with pride. He knew he had been doing a great job at the hard, and often unrecognized, task of screening people wanting to come in. He was glad that people like Grant recognized the importance of the job.

"How many new people recently?" Grant asked Al.

"Four," Al said. He looked at this clipboard. "A family of four. The dad is an Army medic who's AWOL. The mom is a mom with two little kids, who are adorable. They're Mormon, so a Mormon family

291

here took them in."

"How did they get out here?" Grant asked. If they were Mormon, they presumably had lots of contacts who would take them in. This made Grant curious why they chose Pierce Point.

"They're from Utah, believe it or not," Al said with a smile. "He was at Ft. Lewis and said things were too hairy there for him and his family so they left. They came out to some Mormon family in Frederickson, but that family was gone from their home. Just vanished. He said things were getting pretty rough in town, especially for Mormons. People in town were saying that the Mormons had food stored up, so the medic and his family left and were heading here to meet up with the Mintons here, when their car broke down."

"An Army medic, huh?" Grant said, trying to hide his obvious joy at this find. "When did they get here?"

"About two days ago," Al said. Grant realized he should have been on top of this. He was slacking. He needed to step up his game. There was a war going on. Important things were happening, and at a quickening pace. Grant needed to treat his Pierce Point job more seriously. He wouldn't let that happen again.

"Where are they now?" Grant asked. Al told him where the Mintons lived.

"I left a note for you up at the Grange," Al said. Grant hadn't had time to read it. That made him wonder how many other important Pierce Point matters had been slipping through the cracks.

Al lowered his voice and said, "This medic guy, Nick Folsom, would be great for the rental team. A no-brainer."

"Al, I have been too busy to tend to this properly," Grant said. "But that's going to change. When you get a perfect," Grant looked around to make sure no one was listening, "rental team candidate, have Dan get me on the radio. I need to come down here and meet them. I can take care of the hand-off to the rental team, personally."

Al nodded. "We spend most of our time turning people away; probably a hundred so far. They don't have skills. We spend a lot of time interviewing them. We try to detect BS stories, like this one guy who claimed he was a machinist. We got a guy here who is a real machinist and could tell in five seconds that this other guy was making it up. One other guy claimed he was a dentist. He didn't know what a 'molar' was when I asked him."

Al looked out at the gate and said, "The hardest part is the kids. Families will come here with little kids. We have to turn them away. We feed them and give them water to take with them. We treated one little girl's dislocated arm and then we sent them on their way."

"Are people showing up hungry?" Grant asked.

"Kind of," Al said. "Not starving. Hungry, maybe in the sense that they haven't eaten in a day or two, but that's pretty rare. They're traveling, so it's harder to eat on the road. There are no restaurants anymore. There is a soup kitchen at a church in Frederickson. So if you're in town for a while, you can eat. But not on the road so much. Most of the people we're seeing have food in their vehicles."

"So they're coming by vehicle, not on foot," Grant asked.

"Yep," Al said. "There have been a couple people just walking down the road. One was a hippie chick—bad idea to be a female alone out here, but it's her life. The other was a deranged homeless guy. Everyone else comes in cars. They stop at the gate to see if we have gas to sell, which we don't. Surprisingly, lots of them stop to use the bathroom. We don't want to go through all the hassles of bringing them in the gate if we don't have to, so we hand them toilet paper and show them the bushes. They thank us profusely for the toilet paper." Another thing modern Americans took for granted before the Collapse.

Al thought some more. "A few people, like the Folsoms, have their vehicles break down and walk up. We try to help them fix their vehicles, but only if we can. We're not diverting a group of our guards to go walk a few miles down the road with some wrenches to find out that a computer in their engine is shot."

"How many broken down vehicles are you seeing?" Grant asked.

"A handful," Al said. "There is almost no traffic on the road anymore. A couple vehicles an hour. Nothing like it used to be before all of this."

"You keep up on any epidemics, right?" Grant asked. "I mean if there's some disease going around, you're ready to screen people coming in for that?"

Al nodded. "I'm no doctor, but we have a plan for that. There's always a medical person here at the fire station. We have a little quarantine area and are working on having a bigger quarantine area inside the gate for more people. We'll be using a couple of parked RVs for that. They're the perfect for quarantines."

"Good," Grant said. Disease was a big concern, and would especially be so when winter arrived. Grant didn't want to think about how bad it would be then. He knew that disease killed more people than bullets in conditions like the Collapse.

Grant shook Al's hand. He had a medic to go recruit.

# Chapter 212

## *Your Country – the Real One – Needs Your Help*

### (August 1)

Grant went over to Jordan and Manda, who were chatting with the younger guards. "Time to go, guys," Grant said. He threw Jordan the keys and Jordan grinned. All his friends thought that was very cool.

Grant opened the front passenger door for Manda. "Thank you, Daddy," she said. He was treating her like royalty today. She deserved it. And Grant may not have much more time with her. At a minimum, he'd be very busy. At worst…he wouldn't be around at all. He wanted to get as much good times in with her as possible.

Grant got in the back seat and told Jordan they had to go visit someone on the way back. Grant told Jordan how to get to the Minton house where the Folsoms were staying. Al had thoughtfully drawn Grant a map, which he gave to Jordan to see if he could read a map. It was another test that Jordan passed.

The family that the Folsoms were staying with had a nice house. A dog was barking and a middle-aged man came out with a shotgun. Grant didn't recognize him, but the man recognized Grant.

"Judge Matson, what can we do for you?" the man asked as he lowered the shotgun.

"Could I talk to Nick Folsom?" Grant asked.

"Sure," the man said. A minute later, a young guy in his early twenties came out. He had black hair and was average looking in every way.

"I'm Nick Folsom," he said. "What can I do for you?"

The middle-aged man also came out and said, "We have some lunch for you if you'd like." Perfect, Grant thought. It was always easier to get to know someone over a meal, and Grant needed to get to know Nick quickly and make some key decisions about him. Besides, Grant was hungry.

"Sure," Grant said. "Mind if my daughter and her boyfriend join us?"

"No problem," the man said. He extended his hand, "I'm Jay Minton."

"Nice to meet you, Jay," Grant said. "I'm Grant Matson."

"Oh, we know," Jay said. "We've been to some of the Grange meetings." Grant felt like a mini-celebrity. His first thought was that any credibility he had from his Grange work could be used to recruit Nick into the unit out at Marion Farm.

The families assembled for lunch, which consisted of sandwiches on homemade bread. They were really good. The Folsom babies, ages one and two, had just gone to sleep. Nick's wife, Rita, looked tired. She looked young to be a mom. Then again, Nick looked young to be a dad.

They made small talk. The Mintons had been in Pierce Point for about five years. They had moved here from Colorado. Jay's job as a store manager took him to this area. He used to work in Olympia at the mall, but his store closed about a year ago. They had been living a simple life since then. They had enough to eat and did OK, but it was definitely a much less extravagant life than before the Collapse. They were getting by in a different way than they were used to, but getting by. Grant didn't ask, but he suspected the Mintons were living on the one year worth of food Mormons were supposed to store up.

In the course of the small talk, Grant had a favorable impression of Nick. He was a young guy who joined the military to get some college money. He went into the combat medic field because he wanted to go medical school, but the Collapse ended that. That gave Nick a personal motive to get things back to normal, Grant thought. Nick's dreams had been destroyed.

Grant wanted to know two things about Nick. First, his politics. Given that he was Mormon and in the military, the odds were pretty good that he wasn't a socialist. Second, would Rita let him go off to war? That was a biggie. Grant could relate to that.

"So, what do you guys think about this whole situation, if you don't mind me asking," Grant inquired after a while. He didn't have all day to beat around the bush about politics.

"Totally predictable," Jay said about the current situation. He described all the insane regulations and taxes imposed on his store before the Collapse. He described how the police wouldn't do a thing about the ever-increasing shoplifting. Then it became violent crime in the parking lot of the mall. Pretty soon, it became too dangerous for his employees to go to work.

"I realized about a year ago that this was absolutely inevitable," Jay said. "So we..." Jay paused. He didn't want to say how prepared they were and how much food they had.

"...did some commonsense things," Jay said. "Glad we did."

"What do you think will happen next?" Grant asked. Jay was silent. He didn't want to say it. Neither did Nick.

Fair enough, Grant thought. He walked into their house and was asking them if they were waiting for a revolution. He recognized that he needed to respect their privacy a little more.

"Well," Grant said, "I think there is going to be armed trouble." That got their attention. They were thinking the same thing. Grant knew there were two directions to take the "armed trouble" talk. So he chose the safe route.

"You know, gangs," Grant said. "That's why we have a pretty amazing gate guard and a beach patrol. And our internal SWAT team, which I'm fortunate enough to be a nominal member of. I'm the old guy they let hang out with them." That got a few smiles. Grant was warming them up to the topic of "armed trouble." The topic of gangs was always the way to ease into the topic of fighting the government. If people accepted that fighting was necessary because of the gangs, the next logical step was fighting the biggest gang of all: the government.

"Nick, what did you see at Ft. Lewis?" Grant asked. He was cutting to the chase. Normally, he would have taken a few visits to get to this topic. But he didn't have time. He didn't want Nick to get too settled into the Minton house. And he needed a military medic out at Marion Farm right then.

Nick was trying to avoid this topic, but the judge had asked a question, so he answered. "Lots of bad stuff," Nick said, darting his eyes to Rita.

"I'm so glad we're out of there," Rita said. "It was horrible. The base was like a prison. And people thought we were hoarding food. I felt like they were going to turn on us."

Good. Rita was not exactly suffering from normalcy bias.

"So you left?" Grant asked to get them to tell the story. They gave Grant the short version. Things were bad at Nick's unit. Soldiers were taking off. They were trying to get back to their families all over the U.S. Crime was out of control and they were needed back home. Pretty soon, half the unit was gone. The commanding officer left, too. The first sergeant was holding things together until the Southern and mountain West states were talking about "opting out" of the union. Then the remaining soldiers knew something bad was coming. Most took off. That's when Nick realized it was time to go.

Nick and Rita got in their car and headed to a family in Frederickson suggested by someone at their church. The trip took four days with many roadblocks and hassles to get gas. They spent all the money they had on gas. They ran out of money and got hungry, but had plenty of food for the babies

When they got to Frederickson, the family they were supposed to stay with had already left. They weren't sure why. They went to their backup plan, which was to meet the Mintons in Pierce Point. Their GPS unit wasn't working so they couldn't find Pierce Point. Their car broke down and they thought they were doomed.

"I'll never forget when we told that Al guy that we were looking for the Mintons," Rita said, "and he goes, 'Oh, yeah, they live here.' I will never forget that."

"It's almost like you're supposed to be here," Grant said, shameless appealing to their faith. Grant needed a medic and he truly believed that it was a miracle that the Folsoms got out to Pierce Point.

"Yes," Nick said, slowly nodding his head. "Yes, sir, it is."

Grant felt like this was the moment to make The Ask. "Nick, could I talk to you for a moment?" Nick looked surprised. Rita nodded and Nick got up from the table. They went into the living room.

"Nick," Grant said in a soft voice, "I need your help. We need your help. Your country—the real one—needs your help." Grant had decided to not even use the "rental team" story. He didn't want to deceive Nick. Either the real Patriot story would motivate Nick or he wasn't right for this job.

Nick realized what was coming. "Yes, sir," he said, waiting to hear more.

"Nick, do you want to fix this place so you can go to medical school?" Grant asked. He was using Nick's dreams to motivate him. It was for a good cause.

"Yes, sir," Nick said. He looked toward the room where his son and daughter were asleep. "I want to fix this country for them."

"You know how to do that, don't you?" Grant asked Nick. Grant knew that Nick had been thinking about joining the Patriots. That was probably a hot topic of discussion at his unit as it was disintegrating.

Nick nodded. He didn't want to say it out loud. He didn't want to admit that joining the Patriots is what it would take.

"Have you heard of Oath Keepers?" Grant asked. He started to explain what that was.

"I'm in, sir. I'm in," Nick blurted out. "I know why you're here and what you're asking of me. I will do it. My wife and I have already talked about it. She and I believe this is what God sent me to do. She is

OK with me not being around for a while. We have the Mintons to help us with the babies." Nick straightened his posture, looked Grant in the eye, and said, "I'm in."

That was easier than Grant expected. He was stunned.

Grant started to think of what Nick would need. "You can have some days off during training and come back here to be with your family, but you can't tell them what you're doing or where we're at. Understand?" Grant said that last part with a slight grit in his teeth. He wanted Nick to appreciate—with body language, not just words—how important secrecy was.

"Yes, sir," Nick said. "Absolutely. Last thing I want is for the Limas to find us."

Limas? Grant smiled that Nick was using the lingo.

"How soon can you start?" Grant asked.

"Now," Nick said. "This is meant to be and I'm going to give it my all."

"OK," Grant said. He paused to think. He hadn't planned on this happening so quickly. "I'll take you to our base. You'll go blindfolded until we check you out further. No offense."

"None taken, sir," Nick said. "I'd do the same." Then Nick looked puzzled.

"What kind of unit is it?" Nick asked. "I mean, I owe my wife the assurance that I'm not joining up with five guys with shotguns." Nick realized that he might be offending Grant because the unit might actually be five guys with shotguns.

Grant smiled. "Let's just say that we have plenty of your former colleagues from Ft. Lewis." Grant grinned and said. "Plenty."

"Roger that," Nick said. He was getting back in the swing of the military.

"Let's go finish lunch and then you can tell your wife," Grant said. "I'll be back an hour later to take you out there. Bring all your stuff. You'll be living in a covered building. We have water and electricity. It's not roughing it, but it's not luxury."

Nick nodded. He was starting to realize the enormity of what he just agreed to do.

Grant put his hand on Nick's shoulder. "We're going to get our country back. I'll be calling you 'Doctor' someday."

Nick forced a smile. It was the kind of smile when you're having a bad day and someone makes you laugh. Nick was forcing a smile because, while he appreciated the positive thought about being a doctor, he knew how dangerous this would be. He knew he'd be away from his babies and wife for months or maybe years. Or maybe forever. But he knew he had to do it.

Nick's daughter started crying. Nick instinctively started to go toward her.

"That's why you're doing this," Grant said as he pointed toward the room with the crying baby.

"Yep," Nick said. "I'll have a great story to tell them when they're older."

Nick walked out of the living room and said to Rita, "Got it, honey. Eat your lunch."

# Chapter 213

## *Just Like Normal*

### (August 1)

Grant went back and finished lunch like nothing happened. So did Nick, after he took care of the baby. A real man, Grant thought. Taking care of the baby like that. Letting his wife rest a little.

Manda and Jordan were catching up Jay Minton and his wife, Grace, on what it was like being a teen out at Pierce Point. The social scene and how their pre-Collapse lives had been changed. For the better in some aspects, worse in others.

Lunch was over and it was time to go.

"Thank you so much for your hospitality," Grant said. Grant wanted Nick to break the news of his pending departure to Rita himself so Grant didn't say, "Be back in an hour." Grant, Manda, and Jordan left and, by habit, Grant went toward the driver's seat. Then he remembered someone else was driving.

"You can drive, Jordan," Grant said. Jordan smiled and held his hands out for the keys to be thrown to him. Which Grant did. They drove back to the Sparks' house and dropped him off. Jordan gave Manda a goodbye kiss in front of Grant. Good for him. He's not a wimp, Grant thought.

Grant drove back to the cabin. John waved them through at the guard shack. He was surprised to see Grant driving the Tacura.

"Just turning the engine over every couple of months," Grant said. Actually, he would shortly be using the Tacura to go to Marion Farm, but John didn't know about Marion Farm. Yet another person Grant wasn't being honest with.

It was getting hard to keep track of who knew which story and who didn't. Especially when some people, like John, knew some of the true things, but not others. Grant knew he would slip up soon.

Grant dropped off Manda. "Her" kids were already there. They were glad to see her. So was Cole. She resumed her role as the CEO of the babysitters.

Grant had a little time to kill before he had to be back at the Minton's to get Nick. He wanted to give Nick a sufficient amount of time to say goodbye to Rita, at least for a while until he could visit her and the kids again.

Grant couldn't stand to waste time; he had to do something productive at all times. He went to the shed at his cabin and looked at all of the plastic tubs of food, stacked almost to the ceiling. He had the inventory list out, with the contents of each numbered tub. This way, they didn't need to move a bunch of heavy tubs to find the ones with some oatmeal if oatmeal was what they were looking for. And the inventory had the expiration dates for the various items so they could eat the soonest expiring ones first.

Grant looked at the inventory list. The date of the list caught his eye, which was almost two years ago, and remembered how crazy it seemed to most people back then to buy up and store food. There was lots of food in the stores. Why go to all this trouble? This is why Grant did this in secret. So he wouldn't get "caught" by Lisa and have to answer these questions. So his wife wouldn't think he was crazy.

But she enjoyed oatmeal for breakfast now. Many others didn't have any breakfast. Grant had long ago gotten over the "I told you so" feeling. He didn't look at all the food in that shed as an "I told you so." He looked at it as a "Thank God I can take care of my family."

Besides, there was no upside to saying "I told you so." Grant knew how Lisa worked: She couldn't admit being wrong. Once she realized she was wrong, she would just be nice to Grant and act like she had never been wrong.

That's what she was doing now. In fact, she was adapting incredibly well—better than he thought—to her new life as a doctor living out in the sticks and getting paid in cans of tuna. Grant had underestimated her. He was glad to have been wrong.

Grant looked at the date again. He swelled up with pride that he had done all this prepping. "Pride" maybe wasn't the best word. "Thankful" and "at peace" was more like it. He might pat himself on the back for something wise he did that was less important. If, for example, he would have bought a snow shovel in the summer and it snowed a lot that winter and the stores were out of snow shovels. That was pat-on-the-back material. But having food for his family when few others could count on feeding their kids—that was way too important for a pat on the back. That was just pure thankfulness and peace.\Grant looked at the inventory list. He saw all the can openers from the Dollar Store. He got about a dozen and had given most of them away. People were so thankful to have a can opener. Many didn't have them because they always ate drive-through or microwave food. For a one-dollar can opener, Grant had made some lifelong friends who would now literally die for him. Not a bad deal. All it took was the self-confidence to buy a bunch of can openers when times were good and not worry that the cashier thought you were crazy. Once you get over that, saving your family's life gets much easier. Not a bad deal at all.

Grant looked at his watch. He had slowly gotten used to wearing one. In peacetime, he never did. He was around a clock all the time. His cell phone, his car clock, his computer screen. Not anymore. And now that he was doing things that sometimes involved armed men being at the same place at the precisely the same time to counter other armed men, being on time was critical.

Half an hour had gone by. Grant had a stop to make at the Grange so it was time to leave and then go get Nick and take him to the farm. He wasn't looking forward to tearing Nick away from Rita. He wasn't looking forward to that at all. Grant got back in the Tacura and took off. John waved him by.

On the way to the Grange, Grant noticed that there were no other cars. Lots and lots of bikes, though. Most people, especially those with kids, had bikes but rarely used them in peacetime. That had changed. Now it was the primary mode of transportation in Pierce Point. And, Grant suspected, elsewhere in America.

Grant pulled into the Grange to the strange looks of everyone who saw a new car they hadn't seen before. They were surprised when Grant got out of it. They'd never seen him drive it.

Grant went in and found Drew. "I need a meal card for Rita Folsom and her two kids," Grant said. He whispered, "Make up something that she's donating. Trust me." Drew nodded and a few minutes later came back with an official Pierce Point card for Rita "and two infant children." Grant thanked him and left.

Grant pulled into the Minton house and rang the doorbell. He could hear a woman crying. Jay Minton answered the door and, without saying a word, waved Grant into the living room. Jay's wife, Grace, was crying. Rita wasn't. Rita just kept hugging Nick. She gave him each baby to hold one last time. For a while, at least. He would be back to visit. Grant was amazed at how understanding Rita was. Amazed.

Grant felt like he was the mean sheriff taking someone away from their family to go to prison. He was trying to avoid eye contact with Rita, but she wasn't avoiding him.

"I understand," Rita said to Grant. "I understand," she repeated.

She paused and got teary. "Take good care of him, OK?" She didn't want to cry because she knew that would make this even harder on Nick. She needed him to have a positive attitude and go do his job safely. And come home. She knew that crying or telling him he couldn't go wouldn't work and would just make things worse. Besides, back at Ft. Lewis and on the trip out to Pierce Point, they had talked about the fact that Nick would probably join up with the Patriots if an opportunity came up. They had prayed about it. They both knew it was what Nick was supposed to do. That made it easier. But it was still hard. Really hard.

Grant handed Rita the meal card and said, "It's the least we can do for you, Rita." She had never seen a Pierce Point meal card so he explained what it meant.

"I got you a temporary card because, in a little while, Nick will be back and your contribution to the community will officially end. Then you're off the gravy train, ma'am," Grant said, hoping she would laugh. She did. It was a tension-breaking laugh.

Grant felt awkward watching the final goodbye hug. "I'll be in the car," he said. Jay motioned for Grace to come with him into the kitchen. It was just Nick, Rita, and the two babies in the living room.

Grant went out to the car. He expected to be there a few minutes. Instead, Nick came out after a few seconds. Apparently they didn't like long goodbyes.

Nick got into the car and was all business. He wasn't going to let this affect him. Sure, Grant thought, maybe not now, but tonight Nick will be a mess. Grant knew. He'd been there. Except when he had to leave his family, it was against their wishes and he thought they didn't want him back.

Grant handed Nick a tiger-stripe camouflage handkerchief. "Sorry, dude, OPSEC," Grant said, using the acronym for "operational security" that an Army guy like Nick would know. Nick nodded and put the handkerchief over his eyes.

Grant had never driven a car with a blindfolded passenger. It was a very weird experience. Grant felt like he was in a movie or something.

Grant drove to the farm. He had never been there from the road; he'd always come by water. He knew from a map how to get there and wondered what kind of guard they had at the road entrance.

Duh. Better call ahead so he didn't get shot.

Grant pulled over and grabbed the handheld ham radio in the pouch on his kit. He kept it on the Team frequency, but they didn't talk much on it. About all Grant did with the radio, other than using it a handful of times to talk to the Team or to dispatch at the Grange, was to check the battery each night and occasionally charge it.

Just because he didn't use it often didn't mean it wasn't important. Having ham radios, which had lots of frequencies and much longer ranges than CBs, was critical. Today was a perfect example of how that little radio could save his life. Friendly fire sucks, as Ted used to say.

"Green 1, Giraffe 7, over," Grant said. "Green 1" was obviously Ted. Sap, who was from Wisconsin, got "Cheese 2."

But "Giraffe 7"? Grant never understood why he got the lame call sign of an animal with an absurdly long neck. And "7"? Was he the seventh most badass out of...seven? Oh well. Grant cared more about not getting shot by the Marion Farm guards than about what his call sign was.

A few seconds later—remarkably fast considering that Ted was probably in the middle of something—Grant heard Ted's voice. "Giraffe 7, Green 1, copy."

"Tacura with two friendlies at the front door," Grant said. Ted would remember the reference to the "Tacura" from when Grant went out shooting with Ted in that car and they mocked him for having a car instead of a truck.

"Roger that, Giraffe 7," Ted said. "Flash us when you get up near the gate."

"Roger that, Green 1," Grant said. "Giraffe 7 out."

"Green 1 out," Ted said. Nick was impressed. He couldn't see anything because he was blindfolded. These guys weren't hillbillies. Radios. And call signs. Nick's amazement at the sophistication of the unit was just starting.

Grant drove slowly and turned off down the dirt road to the farm. He looked first to make sure no one saw him. The dirt road was long. He went very slowly and came up to the gate where he slowed down to a stop. He flashed his head lights.

"You can take your blindfold off now, Nick," Grant said. They were already on the dirt road so Nick would have no idea what roads it took to get there. Besides, if Grant showed up to the gate with a blindfolded passenger, the guards would assume the blindfolded man was a prisoner and might shoot him if he made a sudden move.

Nick took off his blindfold and Grant rolled down his window. Grant put both hands out the window to show the guard, or guards, that he was not going to ram the gate. It was hard to do with his hands

304

off the steering wheel. Nick, seeing Grant put both hands out the window, did the same.

A minute later, a bearded man in military fatigues opened the gate. Grant had the unmistakable feeling that one or more rifles were aimed at his head and the Tacura's engine block.

The man in fatigues, who was partway behind a stump to remain out of sight and for cover in case Grant or someone else started shooting, waved Grant in through the now-open gate. Grant drove slowly. He got past the swinging metal gate, a typical farm style one and a second man in fatigues popped out from behind a big tree and gave him a signal to stop. He, too, was bearded, which looked weird with the military fatigues.

The first man, who was now behind Grant's car, closed the gate. The second man still had his hand up telling Grant to remain stopped.

Once the gate was closed, the first man came up behind the car on the driver's side. He said in a stern voice, "Out of the car." Grant could recognize the first man, and now the second man, as soldiers he had met at the farm. He forgot their names.

The two soldiers were being very serious and professional which Grant appreciated. This was serious business. Goofing around—especially at a gate—got people killed.

Grant's AR was laying barrel-down in the passenger's foot area with the stock near the gear shift. Grant could grab it by the stock if he needed to get it. He wanted to check and see if it was on safe, but didn't because he realized he'd need to handle it to do so. And he didn't want to reach down for a rifle and handle it now. Oh well, he told himself, he didn't need to check his rifle. It was always on safe when it should be. He laughed to himself about the irony of making a safety check and getting shot as a result.

Grant said to the first soldier, "I'll come out the driver's side. The passenger will await directions."

The first man said "OK" and the second man, who had his rifle shouldered and pointed at the engine block, nodded. Grant noticed that the second man had an M1A in .308. That could stop a car better than an AR in 5.56.

Grant got out slowly. He was not afraid, but he was cautious. He wanted to make sure something didn't drop from his kit and then he instinctively lunged to catch it. No sudden movements. He thought how embarrassing it would be to die because your pen fell out of your pocket and you went to catch it and got shot by your own guys.

Embarrassing. Hardly a hero's death.

Grant got out and kept his hands to his side. They weren't raised up like in the movies, just out to his side. Grant stood there. He didn't want to turn directly toward either of the men.

"OK, now the passenger gets out," the first soldier said. Nick got out and did the same thing Grant did with his hands to the side and stood in the same direction with his sides to each of the men.

"OK, sir, please open the trunk," the first soldier said. Grant very slowly turned and motioned for whether it was OK to get his keys out. The first soldier nodded. Grant slowly got his keys out and showed them to the soldiers. Grant hit the trunk release. He very slowly turned back around with his key in his right hand and his left hand to the side. He stood facing the same direction he had been.

"Moving," the first soldier said.

"Move," the second man said. That meant that the second man was now covering both of them. The first man looked in the trunk. He saw Nick's two sports bags of clothes and a military back pack. Grant's "get home bag" was in there, too, where he'd kept it since before the Collapse. As the name implied, that was a bag of things Grant would need to get home if he was in his car and a disaster happened.

The first soldier realized that searching all these things for a bomb would take a lot of time. He also knew that with the driver being his commanding officer the odds of this being a terrorist were pretty slim. The first soldier looked in the back seat. Nothing. He came up and looked in the front seat.

"M4 in the passenger side," the first soldier said to the second. "Secure." That meant that it was in a secure place.

The first soldier thought a moment. "Tell you what, Lieutenant," he said to Grant, "It'll take a while to search all of this gear back here and the underside of the car for explosives. It's only a few hundred yards to the farmhouse. How about if you keep the car here and we do a quick search of any gear you will be bringing there?"

"Makes sense to me," Grant said. "Just so you guys know, I'm bringing Nick here to the farm. He's your new medic. Nick, you need those two bags and your backpack, right?"

"Yes, sir," Nick said. He hadn't known Grant was a lieutenant, but one of the guards just referred to Grant that way. Nick had been calling Grant "sir" because the Mintons told him that Grant was the judge. Now Nick was seeing that Grant was also a lieutenant in this Patriot unit.

"I'll get the bags and the backpack out," the first soldier said. "I assume the ruck goes with the medic, right?" He motioned for the backpack.

"Yes," Nick said.

"The civilian backpack is my get home bag and can stay," Grant said.

The first soldier got the two bags and the ruck out. He gave them a quick search, looking for a really big bomb. He opened the ruck and saw it was full of medical supplies. His eyes lit up. Lt. Matson had brought an awesome guest.

"All clear," the first soldier said. "Go ahead and go down the road gentlemen."

"Can I get my rifle?" Grant asked. He couldn't stand to leave his gun unattended. Not like he thought these guys would steal it. He just couldn't stand to leave his AR behind.

"Of course, sir," the first soldier said. They were searching for a car bomb, not something less lethal like a rifle.

Grant looked at the second man and said, "Nick here will get my rifle and hand it to me." The second soldier nodded. Everything was done overtly in such situations. The smallest little thing needed to be announced and acknowledged. No surprises.

Nick slowly got the rifle from the passenger side, checked that it was on safe — it was, of course — and, with the muzzle pointed down and with his finger off the trigger, walked around and handed it to Grant who checked that it was on safe and slowly slung it over his shoulder.

"Nice job, gentlemen," Grant said to the two soldiers. "I appreciate a secure gate."

"It's our job, sir," the second soldier said. "You're our first stop so far so we were making sure we had our procedure down. Looks like we do."

"Yep," Grant said. Grant looked at the first soldier, who by now had come up to Grant. Grant said to him, "Would you like the keys?" That way they could move the Tacura if someone else came in.

"Yes, sir," the first soldier said. Grant got out his keys.

Grant took one of Nick's bags and Nick got the second one and his ruck. The second soldier said something into his radio. "They're expecting you at the house," he said to Grant and Nick.

"Thanks, guys," Grant said, instantly realizing that he needed to work on being the lieutenant and being more formal. "As you were, gentlemen," Grant said to the guards. He and Nick started to walk the few hundred yards to the farm. Nick's eyes became huge as he started to see the Patriot's facilities.

# Chapter 214

## *Pretty Squared Away*

### (August 1)

Nick was stunned at how perfect this place was. It was huge. A big barn, outbuildings, and a farmhouse. There were soldiers and armed civilians everywhere. Fatigues mostly from the Army, but some from the Navy, and Air Force. Nick even thought that he saw one man in Marine fatigues. Most of the men had beards, which looked weird with the military uniforms. The civilians were decently equipped. Most of them had ARs slung over their shoulders and others had pistol belts. A handful of the civilians had kit and looked like contractors.

"Wow. You guys are pretty squared away. You're a real unit out here," Nick said. "We kept hearing at Ft. Lewis that guerilla units were forming up with mostly civilians but plenty of AWOL military people in them. The brass were very afraid of these units. I thought maybe it was propaganda that the Patriots had all these irregular units. Guess it's true."

Grant nodded. This was further validation that Hammond and the whole Boston Harbor operation was for real and not some small group of goofballs masquerading as a "Special Operations Command." The irregular units were serious business. And now Grant was getting confirmation that the Limas knew it.

Grant saw something out of the corner of his eye. He recognized that the Team was there; those were the contractor-looking guys Nick had seen.

Grant yelled toward the Team, "Hey, homos, what are you doing here?" Not exactly military protocol from a commanding officer, but Grant wasn't exactly a military officer. He had been calling the Team "homos" for a couple of years. Old habits die hard.

The Team turned at the familiar voice and came over. Grant gave each one of the Team a "bro hug." They talked for a while. Grant introduced Nick and showed off Nick's backpack with medical supplies.

"A combat medic? Nice," Pow said. "Very nice."

By this time, Ted and Sap had come up to them. Grant introduced them to Nick who couldn't believe how many soldiers were there and how military they seemed to be, albeit with some civilians and non-regulation facial hair like beards. But still. This was not a hillbilly unit. It was a military unit dispensing with some military protocol, but still deadly serious.

"What was your unit?" Ted asked Nick.

"2nd Battalion, 23rd Infantry Regiment, 4th Stryker Brigade, 2nd Infantry Division, at JBLM," Nick said. Translated, that meant that Nick was assigned to the 4th Strykers—which were like armored personnel carriers—at Joint Base Lewis McChord, the giant military base between Olympia and Tacoma that included Ft. Lewis.

"Stryker, huh?" Ted asked. The Stryker units saw plenty of combat in Iraq and Afghanistan. Their medics were good. They had to be, unfortunately.

Ted wanted to test this new guy to make sure he was a real medic. "Who was your CO?" Ted asked Nick.

"Col. Pete Lowe," Nick said without hesitation. The name sounded vaguely familiar to Ted, although he didn't know all of the COs at Ft. Lewis now that he had been out of the Army. The COs changed pretty often.

"What was your MOS?" Ted asked. "MOS" was the acronym for military occupational specialty. Each job in the military had an MOS.

"68 Whiskey, sir," Nick said instantly, using the phonetic alphabet term "whiskey" for the letter W. Ted knew that 68W was the correct MOS for a combat medic.

"Sergeant, not 'sir,'" Ted said. "I work for a living." Ted did not have any rank insignia on—almost no one did—so Nick assumed he was an officer and called him "sir."

Ted continued the questioning to see if this supposed medic was legit. "Where'd you go to medic school?"

"Ft. Sam Houston, Sergeant," Nick said instantly, again. Ted knew that was the correct answer.

"You got your CMB?" Ted asked, referring to the combat medic badge, a designation showing that a person had been a medic in a unit engaged in combat.

"No, Sergeant," Nick said. "Went from Ft. Sam straight to Ft. Lewis. No deployment overseas."

"Why did you leave your unit?" Ted asked.

"Things are bad, Sergeant," Nick said, shaking his head. "There is no discipline at all. As in, none. Everyone is taking off. Well, took off. I was one of the last to go. Shoulda gone sooner, but I was following orders."

"Why do you want to join a rebel unit?" Ted asked. He knew that this new medic had come straight from Pierce Point and therefore had not gone through vetting from HQ. So it was up to Ted to screen this guy. Grant must have already done some screening or he wouldn't have brought him out here.

"I've seen what's happening," Nick said, still standing at attention. "It's out of control, Sergeant. I want things back the way they were. I have a wife and two babies. They aren't growing up like this. Not if I can help it."

"Sgt. Malloy," Grant said, "Nick here has an incentive to not screw us." Grant didn't want to be a dick, but he wanted Nick and the others standing around listening to know that Grant took this job very seriously and was willing to do horrible things in order to win this war.

Nick nodded, knowing exactly what Grant meant. "My wife and kids," Nick said, "are here in Pierce Point and Lt. Matson knows where they are. You guys control everyone coming and going. My family isn't going anywhere. They are in your hands."

"We don't kill women and children," Grant said, "but we would keep them in 'protective custody' if Nick...well, didn't work out."

Grant put his arm on Nick's shoulder for a little dramatic flair and said, "But that won't be necessary. I've talked to Nick a fair amount. He volunteered for this unit before he even knew what we did."

Nick nodded. Then he asked, "So what do you guys do?" Grant and Ted filled Nick in on the 17th Irregulars. They didn't mention the ultimate mission, of course. That would come later.

Nick was smiling. "Cool. Looks like I'll get my CMB now." Grant and Ted didn't say anything. They both wanted to say "Hopefully there won't be any combat" but they knew that wasn't true.

"Report to Sgt. Sappenfield here and he'll get you squared away...what was your last name?" Ted asked.

"Folsom," Nick said.

"Well, Private Folsom, welcome to the 17th," Ted said. "We're very glad to have you."

"Glad to be here," Folsom said. He walked off with Sap. Grant filled Ted in on Nick's background.

"Does he know where this place is?" Ted asked.

"Blindfolded him on the way in," Grant said, with a smile, proud of his foresight. "Not only does it prevent him from seeing how to get here, but it reinforced with Nick from the get-go how important OPSEC is."

Ted smiled. This lawyer Grant wasn't as much of a...lawyer as Ted had feared. Grant was not exactly a soldier, but he wasn't a typical dickhead lawyer either.

Grant told Ted that he had promised Nick that he could see his family on occasion.

"I'd rather keep all the guys here 24/7 for OPSEC," Ted said, "but I understand why you would let Folsom go home periodically. Normally, if I let one guy go out of camp, I'd need to do that for everyone. But," Ted said pointing to everyone, "no one here has any family nearby to go see. If that starts to change, if people in the unit have people out in Pierce Point, we'll need to revisit this."

"Good point," Grant said, embarrassed that he hadn't thought of that. Wait. Of course he hadn't thought of that. He hadn't been a Green Beret for twenty-five years. That's why Ted was there.

Grant spent the rest of the day checking on how things were progressing with the facilities at Marion Farm. He met a few more new arrivals. He chatted with each man or woman out there. He wanted to get to know them and let them know their CO a little better. He was constantly motivating and encouraging them. Not over-the-top, rah-rah motivation, just the subtle and laid back motivation he had been doing his whole life. Several hours went by.

"Joining us for dinner, Lieutenant?" Sap asked.

"Nah," Grant said. "Love to, but the Grange has no idea where I am." Grant had his radio on the Grange frequency so he would know if they really needed him. But what he really meant was that his family had no idea where he was. He didn't want them to worry. Besides, he really wanted to eat dinner with them. He hadn't had dinner with them in several days, but he couldn't tell his troops that he needed to go home for dinner with his wife and kids.

"Understood," Sap said. "I'll let the guards know you're coming back and they'll have your car turned around for you."

Grant thanked Sap, walked to the gate at the farm, got his car, and drove home. Just like normal. Driving his car home to have dinner with his family. After spending the day with his guerilla unit. Just like normal.

# Chapter 215

## *Raid on Pierce Point*

### (August 2)

"We got a target near Frederickson," Joe Brown, the military intelligence officer, said to Tom Kirkland. They were in the briefing room of the Tactical Operations Center, or TOC, at Camp Murray. "An insurgent base at a farm out there."

Another one? Tom wondered. They'd been seeing them pop up all over the state. Well, they were seeing what appeared to be insurgent camps, but it was hard to tell from the satellites. They could see the outlines of camps, possible camps. But it usually took human intelligence – a person on the ground – to verify a location.

Satellite intelligence was one of the only things that still worked. Well, sort of worked. The satellite technicians were primarily located at various agencies in DC. They were still going to work. DC was solidly in Loyalist hands. Much like the Loyalists focused their resources on Seattle and Olympia in Washington State, they did so on an even more massive scale to protect their capital of Washington, DC.

Even though the satellites could see anything, there was several million square miles of the United States to look at. They needed something to point them at a particular little chunk.

"Some former insurgent named," Brown said looking at his notes, "Ethan Meecham escaped from their compound. He told the local authorities in Frederickson about a 'rental team' the insurgents had out there at a place called," he looked at his notes again, "Pierce Point."

Tom looked up. That name sounded familiar. Tom was suddenly very concerned.

"So we asked DC to point the bird," Brown said, referring to the satellite, "at this little patch of ground and, bam, we saw some interesting things. Then a Navy ship in the Puget Sound that actually had its radar working for a change saw some strange comings and goings of small watercraft in the area. The rare thing is that the Navy actually called it in, and, even rarer, our DC people actually put two and two together."

"Nice work," Tom said and high-fived Brown. This was a much

more definite target than most of the "missions" that took off from Camp Murray, most of which only happened on paper but, so far, had never actually involved a raid.

Tom leaned back in his comfortable chair at the TOC. "This is a first," he said to Brown. "We see possible camps all the time, but to piece it all together like this hasn't happened so far." What he didn't say was that they almost never had HUMINT, or human intelligence, because few people seemed to want to risk their lives to infiltrate Patriot groups.

"I'll put a package together," Tom said, meaning that he would assemble the landing team. "I got a special one for this Pierce Point place." Brown smiled.

If they had the normal military resources, Tom would have had several Blackhawk helicopters full of men going in after several Apache helicopter gunships had blown the hell out of the target. But they only had one Blackhawk operational today. They could do quite a bit of damage with that, though. The Blackhawk had plenty of firepower and could destroy a building or two.

Tom got to work. They had to act quickly, not because they thought the camp would pick up and move, but because there were numerous leaks at Camp Murray. They had to hit Pierce Point before the teabagger spies found out they were coming.

"Get me Lt. Mendez," Tom said to the sergeant at the TOC. Mendez was the co-pilot of one of the helicopter crews. A few minutes later Mendez came in.

"Yeah, Tom," Mendez said, dispensing with military protocol for an officer like him to address a sergeant like Tom. But the two had been friends for a long time when Mendez flew Tom and the rest of the First Group of Special Forces on various training missions at Ft. Lewis. Special operations personnel often called each other first names; it was a privilege accorded to the very best.

"Paco," Tom said to Mendez, using Mendez's nickname, "I got a little job for you." Tom smiled. So did Mendez. They went outside and talked for a while.

A few minutes later, Tom had his preliminary plan ready to go. He found Brown and told him, "None of the contractors is right for this job. We have just the guys near Olympia. The air crew will pick them up there and then go out to Pierce Point." Brown nodded. Whatever, he thought.

Tom was getting very excited. More excited than he'd been in quite a while. This mission was big. Very big. It had to go right.

Tom heard that sound again. The sound of a helicopter warming up and getting ready to go out. Tom wished he could join them. Not really, but kind of.

Tom went out to the helicopter and met the pilot, Captain Nedderman. Mendez and Nedderman rarely flew together, but Tom had picked out Nedderman for the mission. Nedderman was a "true believer" Loyalist. He always volunteered for missions to go shoot up teabaggers. He'd be perfect for this job, Tom thought with a slight smile.

This time there were no mechanical malfunctions. The helicopter lifted off and headed to Olympia to pick up the contractors.


- End Book Six -

Made in the USA
San Bernardino, CA
13 January 2015